Picture This

ALSO BY JACQUELINE SHEEHAN

Lost & Found

Now & Then

The Comet's Tale

Picture This

Jacqueline Sheehan

HARPER LUXE

An Imprint of HarperCollinsPublishers

HarperCollins books may be purchased for educational, business, or sales promotional use. For information please write: Special Markets Department, HarperCollins Publishers, 10 East 53rd Street, New York, NY 10022.

FIRST HARPERLUXE EDITION

HarperLuxe™ is a trademark of HarperCollins Publishers

Library of Congress Cataloging-in-Publication Data is available upon request.

ISBN: 978-0-06-210712-1

12 13 14 ID/RRD 10 9 8 7 6 5 4 3 2 1

To the sibs: Frances, Harry, Mary Ellen, and Martha

You will not find the unexpected unless you expect it, for it is hard to find, and difficult.

—HERACLITUS (500 BC)

Chapter 1

Natalie

Natalie had seen more therapists in her life than she could remember. She couldn't remember a time without them. Therapists come with the territory in foster care, along with caseworkers and a slew of people who control where you live, where you go to school, and when and if you get medical care. And here's what they're good for: getting a kid a new foster family when the kid has been stuck with whack jobs, that's what.

When she was five, she didn't know to tell the therapist lady about eating only at school. Her foster family told her those were the rules, and she believed them. Here's what Natalie figured at five: if you were a floater like her, and you didn't belong anywhere, you ate at school and no place else. There were always rules in life, and when you were a little kid, that's what you learned all day long: the rules. If you were a bio kid, if you were born from the parents in the house, you ate dinner upstairs with the parents, instead of sitting huddled in the basement on a cot praying that the next day would come faster so that the churning hunger in your belly could be quenched by school food. Natalie wasn't the only foster kid in the basement; a little boy who was even smaller than she was slept in the next cot. Sometimes they could smell the food from upstairs, and they knew it had to be the most delicious food on the planet. Her favorite aroma was meatloaf, dense and rich. The foster mother made a meatloaf that smelled so good, Natalie wanted to cry. When the food smells came running down the basement stairs, the little boy would stick his hand down his pants and hold on to his penis. Natalie didn't know how that helped him, but she understood that you take whatever helps, and at least he had something, which was more than she had.

She must have said something to a teacher or to somebody. Maybe it was the boy, because the next thing you know, a car shows up for her and the other basement dweller and the caseworker is looking at where they sleep and they are out of that house before you can say "protective services." Natalie was delivered to another home, and she never saw the little boy again. With the next family, she learned that in some houses all the kids eat at home and nobody sleeps in the basement. Very interesting. She also learned that therapists were good for something. They could broker a deal, and she needed them.

Between then and now, she had seen every kind of therapist. She was officially done with the foster care system now that she was eighteen, but in her time she had seen enough therapists to earn a P-h-fucking-D. Natalie made a study of therapists, watching what made them respond, what made them cool down to the temperature of frozen fish, and what made them sit up and help. Because they were so busy trying to change her, they didn't know she was studying them. She was sure of it.

Natalie got sprung out of the foster care system when she was seventeen, legally and all. One therapist helped her do it. Her name was Vivien, and she said it looked like Natalie needed to graduate from foster care. Vivien didn't see how it was helping Natalie to go from foster home to group home, back to another foster home. Vivien said that Natalie didn't attach well. What a genius that Vivien was. Attaching to a family was directly linked to trouble. So with a little help from Vivien, she dropped out of high school, enrolled in a GED class, and got a job at Subway because she liked their food better than the other fast-food places'. That's where she met Franklin. Not Frank, and God help you if you called him Frankie. Franklin, like the president.

Franklin did not use crack, which elevated him to the top rung of her choices. Marijuana, yes, if he was in the mood, and a little X here and there, but no crack. And he was awesome on the computer. Franklin broke through firewalls just for fun. He had graduated from high school and went to college for a year.

"The professors were too slow, babe. It was like being in a special ed class," he said.

One night lying on his mattress, she said, "Can you find people? I mean, suppose I was trying to find someone and had hardly any information, just a name from long ago. Could you find them? I'm looking for my real father." She had on his baseball cap and nothing else.

"You've got to be kidding me," Franklin said. "You just watch me, watch and learn."

Which is exactly what Natalie did. She studied what Franklin did. It would take time to learn everything that he knew, but she didn't need to know everything. Sometimes you get lucky or all the stars turn in the perfect direction, and it only happens once every thousand years. And sometimes you're like Natalie and you know how to find a good man like Franklin, good enough to get the job done.

Chapter 2

Peaks Island, Maine

"Is this Roxanne Pellegrino?"

Rocky's landline had rung, which almost never happened. Isaiah, her boss, had insisted that she get a cell phone for her job. And who ever called asking for Roxanne? Nobody, except for solicitors from non-profits and political campaigns. Cooper, her black Lab, regarded a ringing phone as only one notch down from a knock on the door. He roused from his morning nap at Rocky's feet to heightened attention.

"Yes. Who's calling?"

Rocky was waiting for a carpenter scheduled to replace some rattling windows in her rental cottage, but a carpenter was less likely to call, more likely to show up.

"You don't know me. . . ." The voice was young, a girl with her voice stuck in her throat, never hitting the full registers, staying high and timid. An unlikely carpenter.

"Are you calling about the windows?"

"Windows? No. I got your number—"

"If this is for a fund drive or donation, I want you to take me off your call list," said Rocky. It wasn't that Rocky disliked donating to libraries or animal rescue organizations, and she considered explaining that to the caller, but she didn't like being called. She didn't like the membrane of this fragile, tiny house being punctured by the outer world.

"I'm not selling anything. I've been looking for my father, my biological father. If everything that I learned is true, then Robert Tilbe is my father. Is he there? I'd just like to talk with him."

The floor fell away from under Rocky's feet and left her dangling in midair with a thudding pain in her chest. The barrel-chested black Lab stood up, ears alert, sensing alarm. It had been well over a year, a year and two months, since her husband, Bob, died. After his death, she had methodically informed Social Security, the banks, the credit card companies, the retirement accounts, the entire world that had documented Bob's life with accounts and file folders. There had been unending layers of Bob's identity: alumni associations, reminders from the licensing board for his veterinarian's license, even the Red Cross still wanted him to donate blood.

But it had been months since she'd had to say to anyone, "I'm sorry. You didn't know. He died. Yes, suddenly. Thank you. We're all sorry." That's what she had to say to old friends who emerged from his past, people she hadn't known. Every time she had to announce his death again, the words sliced through her and she was pulled back to the months after his death when she had fallen into a bottomless pit of grief. No one had called looking for a father, until now.

"Who are you?"

"Natalie. Could you leave him a message? Tell him I don't want anything from him. It's not like that. I just want to talk to him. If he's not there, can I leave my number?"

Rocky took a breath and her feet connected with the floor again. "My husband died over a year ago."

Even as she said it, she knew this would never be enough. The girl had opened a rusty can, and closing it would be impossible.

The girl chugged out a few sounds, hard consonants mostly, unconnected to words, the brittle beginnings of sentences, started and abandoned. The clatter of sounds struck Rocky in the chest. A note, a familiar note among the rest. It was a thread of Bob, a way that he had moved his lips, the way he could make the harshest words sound like a brush of velvet, a way of moving his tongue.

"Where are you? Where are you calling from?"

"Worcester, Mass. Do you know where that is?"

Rocky recognized the adolescent naïveté, the girl thinking that Worcester was an obscure location to someone in Maine, as if it were on the opposite side of the globe.

"Yes, I do know where it is. I'm from Massachusetts. I'm not sure how I can help you. You must have him confused with someone else. My husband never mentioned anything about a child. We told each other everything." The bile of sorrow rose up her throat.

"Are you just saying he's dead to get rid of me? Please, he can't be dead. I promise I don't want anything, not money, and I won't make any trouble for you. Maybe he didn't know. I mean, that happens with men. But I just turned eighteen, so I'm an adult now, and I have some of my records, my birth records, and his name is on one of them."

Rocky saw a tsunami rising up, reverberating from the shifting of Bob's tectonic plates. Before a killer wave strikes, the ocean draws out, sucking water, fish, seaweed, all life, including oxygen, along with it.

Rocky's tender hold on the new life she had built on Peaks Island, the one where she didn't think of Bob every second, was sucked under, and she struggled to find a foothold.

"What do you want?" she asked. She slid down onto the floor, her back pressed against the fridge. Cooper came to her side, pressing into her, and put his head on her shoulder, an uncharacteristic move even for this highly expressive dog.

"I want to know who I am, where I come from. Medical stuff too. You know, did he have diabetes or something that I need to know about. Um, how did he die? I should know that."

The certainty of meeting with the girl had solidified before Rocky had exhaled. She had to put a face on the voice. If there was any chance that a part of Bob existed, surely she could tell right away by looking at the girl. If Bob was the father, there would be a hint of him in her eyes, bone structure, the big smile; surely Rocky could sense his DNA. The desire to see the girl was suddenly overwhelming, but a small voice in her head, barely audible above the roar of possibility, urged her to step back.

Using every bit of strength she had, she said, "Give me your number. I promise to call you back. I'm in the middle of something right now."

Hill had started as her archery teacher, prodding her competitive spirit back to life in the dark months of autumn after Bob's death. Rocky had dipped and dodged Hill's steady advance since late winter, and now, by the last week of June, she felt like the full surge of the Maine rivers, bursting with snowmelt from a heavy winter, pounding with new life. They both knew it, and the sweet anticipation was almost too much for her. Before Hill had left for his annual camping trip with his friends, he had said, "I don't have to go to man camp this year. I've gone camping with these guys plenty of times. We drink beer, sit around the fire, stay up too late, eat way too much bacon for breakfast, and only as a sidebar do we actually do any archery. I'd rather be with you." They had been at his house, one week before the school year ended. Hill had a smaller pile of homework to grade than usual. They sat across from each other at his kitchen table, and he had put both of her hands in his, stretching across the table. His crooked smile was imperfect and glorious, and his voice slid along Rocky's lean torso. Without thinking, she extended her toes out and touched his shinbone through his pants, her toes sliding up and down.

"I don't want to be the cause of canceling man camp. I'll be here when you get back," she said. She still found it hard to believe that love, if this was love, was not a finite entity. She had loved her husband ferociously and had never considered that another new love would ever have been possible. Yet here it was, pulsing in their hands, both of them vibrating with anticipation.

"I won't be able to call you. We go up near the border of Canada, and there's no cell phone reception. You won't hear from me for two weeks." He had stroked her hand, tugging softly on her fingers, one by one.

He was an impossibly strange combination of archer, high school English teacher, and hunter. Rocky's dormant battery of desire revved up every time he came within ten feet.

"We'll have all summer to figure this out," she said, with considerable willpower. Here was a man who did not push; she knew that he wanted more than anything to ask her if she had decided to stay on Peaks, if she had decided about her job back in Massachusetts, and yet he did not. She had stood up to leave, and he walked with her to her car, his arm draped over her shoulder. "I'm not leaving without this," he had said. He held her face in his hands and kissed her long enough that Rocky felt the last of the distance between them dissipating. She made a sound like a moan/squeak. This was a relationship on the precipice, a launching pad ready to go.

Hill was not due back for another week, and he was exactly whom she wanted to be with at this moment. A phone call from a possible daughter of her dead husband's was beyond sharing with even Isaiah, her boss and friend, at the moment. He would be rational and deliberate. Her friend Tess lived across the island, and without hesitating, she headed out the door with Cooper, jogging the two miles to Tess's house, praying that she was home.

Just as Rocky and the dog arrived at Tess's driveway, she spotted her friend opening the trunk of her black Saab. Tess was nearly seventy and had proven to be a solid friend, with the side benefits of being a physical therapist. "I need to talk with you. Please tell me you're not headed to Portland," said Rocky.

"No, I was just over on the back shore collecting seaweed for the garden beds. The seaweed can wait, and I could use an extra pair of hands to spread it on the garden beds later. Come on in."

Rocky noticed the large garbage can in the trunk with strips of seaweed poking out. Cooper's tail twirled in appreciation of Tess. He pushed his body along the sides of her legs and wound around her.

"Don't tell me there's something wrong with Cooper. I don't think I could stand that, and neither could you," said Tess as they walked up to her deck. Her faded prayer flags, strung from two trees, snapped in the breeze. She stepped inside her house and returned with two glasses of water and a bowl for the dog.

"It's not Cooper. Someone just called me, a girl, who said she was looking for her biological father. She was looking for Bob. My Bob. She thinks Bob is her father," said Rocky. She heard the waver in her voice and felt her recently established balance tipping precariously. "Her name is Natalie. She said that she has evidence that Bob was her father. The only thing harder than saying this out loud was hearing it on the phone," said Rocky. She sank into a chair.

"Good Lord, you must be turned upside down. Tell me exactly what the girl said," said Tess, sinking into a cross-legged position on a cushion. "What did you tell her? How can you possibly know if this is true? Did Bob ever tell you this, or that there was even a chance of a child?"

"No. No to everything. I told her that I'd call her back," said Rocky. She described the phone conversation, line for line. Tess made her repeat it all twice.

"In the rush of this, we should not forget that Natalie didn't show up when Bob was alive. It is worth noting that she had a lot of years to look for her biological father. Why now?"

"Because she was a kid and probably she didn't have access to all her records until now. Because she was probably trying to survive," said Rocky. Why did she say "survive"? Rocky didn't know anything about this girl. She didn't know what she was expecting from Tess, but it wasn't immediate doubt. Rocky pulled closer to the as yet unknown girl.

"Don't bite my head off. I'm just saying, here's something to remember. I'm not sure what it means either. Promise me, in the rush of things, that you'll remember the odd coincidence of death and emergence," said Tess.

A cloud blew past, and a sudden ray of sunlight caught Rocky. In the single-minded need to talk with Tess, she had forgotten her baseball cap and sunglasses.

"I heard something in her voice, a catch, the way Bob's voice broke when he heard that a college friend had been killed in a motorcycle crash, this very guarded place that only showed up once every few years, and each time I heard it I wanted to weep. How could this girl have sounded the same?" Rocky wriggled on the plastic version of an Adirondack chair and pulled her knees up, hugging them as if the temperature had dropped.

Tess tilted her head in response to a sound in the dense brush. "Pileated woodpecker. We don't get those very often."

"Tess! I don't care about the damned woodpecker, pileated or not. Someone just told me that Bob had a child."

"I know, dear. If I were you, I'd grab at anything that smacked of my dead husband. Given what you've told me, you had the kind of marriage that doesn't come around that often. You miss him unbearably, and you think that you heard a strand of him in a stranger's voice. What are you going to do?" Tess wore a straw hat with a rawhide tie under her chin. She had tucked her considerable white hair under the hat, exposing her slender neck.

"I feel like my brain is sizzled. I'm trying to sit on my hands so I don't call her back this instant. That's why I came here, so you could slow me down and help me think."

"There you go again, imagining that I'm wiser just because I'm older. I can tell every time this happens. I hate to disillusion you, but age doesn't make you more brilliant. It's being willing to step into the unknown that will keep you from premature aging."

Cooper lay between them on his belly, flicking his deep brown eyes from one woman to the other. Rocky let her hand fall to his favorite spot at the base of his spine, and she rubbed with familiarity.

"I want whatever you've got. Help," said Rocky.

"If you need someone else to say it, then I will. Wait twenty-four hours before you call her back. Can you do that?" said Tess, adjusting the string on her hat.

Rocky sighed. "I can try. But I can't stop thinking about her voice."

"Let me give you something else to think about," said Tess. "Distractions are highly underrated. Isaiah said he's fielded a complaint about you this week. Something about insulting a guy in the post office."

"I didn't insult him. I just described, as the animal control warden, what I'd have to do to his car if he didn't stop leaving his dog inside with the windows rolled up. That's not an insult, it was descriptive information. People don't understand how quickly cars heat up."

"I believe that's what Isaiah told him, except more diplomatically."

Rocky said, "How do you stand it? This was a perfectly good island until the population tripled with tourists. The island is four miles around. How many people can we fit on it before it topples over into the ocean?" Rocky sat up and reached for the water and downed the remainder in two gulps.

"I've lived here for fifteen years, so I've built up a certain immunity to the summer people. Not immunity, they're not like smallpox. But their reason for being here is different. Just like yours is different. This is your first summer, so it will be your worst, the same way teachers have to endure their first year of teaching. Teachers catch every cold and flu that blows through their classroom during the first year, until they build up a resistance. But you get used to it. There's a flow to life here." Tess slipped off her sandals and dropped them on the deck. "You do realize that you are a newcomer and that we all had to adjust to you. Some very wonderful people first came here as a tourist. Like me."

Rocky had not come to Peaks as a tourist, more like a refugee, but Tess was right: she had felt a level of acceptance that was slow and qualified, but acceptance nonetheless. Rocky tapped her foot and frowned. She had been sufficiently chastised, and it had worked its magic. Her brain was now only filled to 95 percent capacity with the strange girl who had called her.

Tess said, "Let's keep moving. Walking helps to soothe the anxious beast in us." They walked around her house to her backyard, skirting her piles of rocks, stacked in gravity-defying cairns. The desire to arrange the rocks, smoothed by ocean and sand, tempted nearly everyone.

"The back side of my house looks like an archery range," said Tess. Rocky used her friend's backyard for archery practice. A plastic-coated paper target had been tacked securely to a triple pile of hay bales on the far right side of Tess's yard.

"I should post a sign that says, DANGER. YOU HAVE ENTERED A WEAPONS AREA. I used to live in fear that you'd overshoot the target and nail one of my neighbors. Fortunately, your accuracy has improved," said Tess.

Archery was one of the things that had saved Rocky—the repetition, the rekindling of the desire to challenge herself, to dare to learn something so incredibly hard that her shoulders screamed in the first few weeks. She had found an archery teacher, Hill Johnson, and he had prodded her competitive spirit, which had gone dormant after Bob's death. She had been humbled by the deceptive simplicity of the action: you pulled back on a bow and released an arrow. Starting on a child's bow, she had imagined that her swimmer's shoulders would help her, but her improvements had been microscopic; gradually, however, she had moved up. Now she relished the way she had to still her breath, drop her energy to the soles of her feet, and ease her body into the rhythm of slow, exacting power, projecting her vision to a point on the target, then the release.

Archery practice was the one time when Cooper was banished from her side. When she had first found him, he had been abandoned and left with a nearly fatal injury by an archer. Tess had agreed with Hill: neither of them could bear the thought of Cooper seeing her with a bow in her hands.

"There is a predictability, a cycle to the year, and summer on the island has its own color. In my world, summer is orange and purple, unless you add in the horrible loud music played at the dock on Saturday night, and then you've got to factor in the strips of red. Maroon, really. This is what my life used to be like, before my gorgeous synesthesia evaporated," said Tess.

The phone call had obliterated everything from Rocky's mind, even the loss that plagued Tess. In late winter, Tess had experienced a medical convergence of appendicitis and bowel obstruction. The emergency surgery had saved her life, but her lifelong condition of synesthesia abandoned her in the aftermath.

"I can't imagine what it must be like to lose your wonderful multisensory world," said Rocky. "But remember? Len said that anesthesia does weird stuff to people." Len was Tess's ex-husband, a retired surgeon. "It's a poison, and it ran laps in your bloodstream for five hours while you were in surgery. The docs told you that surgery on your intestines should not change a neurological condition, that your synesthesia could return at any time." Nothing that Rocky said sounded as consoling as she wanted it to. She hoped that her friend's Buddhist approach to life might offer a buffer to sadness.

"You have no idea how rich my multisensory world was. This is like seeing the world through a black veil and constantly wearing thick leather gloves. It's not your fault. There's no way for you to know. You're right. I should try not to catastrophize," said Tess, unconvincingly.

Cooper chewed a piece of wood, securing the stick with one large black paw. He trimmed the stick to his satisfaction and delivered it to Rocky.

"You want me to throw this, big guy?"

Cooper kept his eye on the stick and slowly backed up, bumping into a low stone wall that serpentined through the yard.

She heaved the stick as far into the surrounding woods as possible. It bounced off a tree trunk, and Cooper was there before it even hit the ground. The faded prayer flags suddenly fluttered to a burst of sea breeze.

"Dealing with tourists takes a special kind of finesse with the human condition that you may not currently possess, despite being a psychologist," said Tess. "If you want to deal with animals, you have to learn how to deal with humans again. May I remind you that you have lived here since last October, and some of these tourists have been coming back every summer for fifty years? They could show you amazing things about Peaks and about continuity." Tess stretched her arms over her head, and her slender body moved like beach grass. "You look like a storm is hovering over your head, and I suppose it is. Stray children don't show up every day."

"I guess we're done talking about my job and tourists, aren't we?" said Tess.

"Yes. Did the distraction help?"

"A little," lied Rocky. Natalie's voice had already hummed into the marrow of her bones.

She did not remember exactly when Bob had first looked at her, dreamy-eyed from sleep, night crust in the corners of his eyes, and said, "I can see a baby of ours." It was during the year before he died, in the innocent months when Rocky never contemplated life without him, when they woke entangled, talking of children. The idea had pumped low and insistent in her belly. "I can see a baby too," she had whispered, and she had pulled his hand to cup the soft pouch below her belly button, where a baby would grow if there was one, which there had not been. If Bob hadn't died, she would be thirty-nine years old, a baby in her arms, and Bob would be an unbearably proud, strutting father at the ripe age of forty-three. Instead, he was dead. He got to be forty-two forever. She was a thirty-nine-year-old widow. And someone out there in the world believed she was Bob's daughter.

Chapter 3

Rocky held out for three hours before calling Isaiah to say that she had to talk to him and that she'd meet him at his office in the Public Works Building. She had walked the circumference of the island and ducked into a narrow path called Snake Alley. She moved a lilac branch out of the way and trotted along the dirt path, with Cooper twenty feet ahead of her. Alleys were really footpaths, and if you lived on Peaks all your life, you knew how to avoid downtown altogether by staying on them. There were no signs for paths like Snake Alley; you either grew up knowing about them, a knowledge passed down through generations like a secret language, or someone had to take pity on you and tell you. Isaiah had only recently told Rocky about Snake Alley.

"It's called Snake Alley because it winds around like a snake, not because it's loaded with snakes. You've lived here the better part of a year and no one has seen fit to tell you about Snake Alley? That's a shame," Isaiah had said.

Rocky dropped off her monthly report to Isaiah's office. He took it and said, "I'll read this later. Let's see if they have coffee left at the dock." They walked along the sidewalk to the Island Café with Cooper leading the way, his thick tail ticking like a metronome. It was late afternoon, and the tiny eatery was set to close in thirty minutes.

The café hung personal coffee mugs for regular customers on hooks above the counter. When Isaiah walked in, Francine, the owner, immediately reached up and grabbed his cup and handed it to him. She never made a mistake about who had which cup. Isaiah's cup said MUTUAL LIFE. Rocky went to the far end of the counter, picked up a paper cup, and filled it with Ethiopian dark.

"Was it just an oversight or have you guys been hazing me? I still haven't rated my own coffee mug at the café."

Francine put a cinnamon roll on a plate and handed it to Isaiah. "The thing is that you have to be a resident to rate a coffee mug, and you made it clear to us that you'll be gone by the end of the summer. This is how we keep our hearts from being broken. You wouldn't want us to get overly attached, would you?"

Rocky's stomach clenched. The idea of leaving Peaks was suddenly front and center, gnawing at her each day. She had promised her boss on the mainland that she'd be returning for fall semester, and now the idea filled her with dread. Each September the new college students arrived with their ill-fitting clothes, wearing too much makeup and perfume, terrified of making social mistakes and thus guaranteed to make tons of mistakes, waiting for their parents to drive away so that they could start drinking and hooking up. She found them genuinely interesting because grappling with mistakes (having sex with the wrong people, ending up in the hospital with alcohol poisoning, getting bounced out of the residence hall for possession of a joint) was the stuff of becoming really human. Rocky called them neo-adults, and she adored them. How could she not go back?

Rocky and Isaiah were among the last customers. Cooper was allowed in the café, and he had wedged himself under the table. Two carpenters walked in. One wore work boots with socks rolled down over the tops. His shorts ended below his knees. His calves were pumped to a thirty-year-old ripeness, fresh from climbing ladders all day. Rocky imagined Bob's calf muscles when he was twenty-four, tangled up in someone else's bed.

Isaiah tipped his head to the two men. He knew everyone who lived on the island year-round and made a heroic attempt to get to know tourists who stayed on the island more than a week or two. Isaiah's face stretched into a smile that produced a series of facial folds emanating out from his lips. His dark skin was suddenly etched in even darker lines, highlighting the smile. He and his wife, Charlotte, were the only black family on the island. His hair—and he still had a full head of it—was leaning heavily in the direction of white.

"There's something I need to ask you about. I got a phone call from a girl who said she's looking for her biological father. She was looking for Bob."

Isaiah was mid-swallow when he sputtered out a brown spray and his cup hit the table so hard that an explosion of coffee erupted, landing on his forearm. The coffee was a few shades lighter than his skin, and Rocky took one second to admire the aesthetic impression while Isaiah wiped down the table and himself.

"You were leaving this as a secondary agenda item to your report? Tell me what she said."

Rocky told him almost all of the little bit that the girl had offered on the phone. She left out the part about the sound of Natalie's voice, the way it had settled in her. As Isaiah listened, his brow folded into the accordion frown that she had grown to love.

"It's too convenient," said Isaiah. "Now that your husband is dead, this girl shows up. How old did she say she was?"

"She said she had just turned eighteen. If it's true, Bob would have been twenty-four. That was four years before I met him. I've been working the math all day."

"Do you know anything about his girlfriends before you?"

Rocky shrugged her shoulders. "I never actually quizzed him on all his previous girlfriends. I mean, I did in a global kind of way. He had a couple of girlfriends in college. But if he'd had a child, that would have been the kind of thing he would have told me."

"Most young men don't worry too much about the consequences of sex. It's when we get older, and I've seen it happen, that one day you get a phone call, or a letter, or a fully formed human being, allegedly sprung from your own loins, shows up and turns out to have been living thirty minutes from your backyard, put up for adoption by the woman you had sex with once. Very likely, both of you woke up the next day trying to act casual, but you had turned shy again and wanted to button up your pants and had nothing to say."

"That's the longest sentence I've ever heard you say," said Rocky.

"Men have very little to say about a lot of things. This is one of the things that I have a lot to say about."

"Do you mean this happened to you? Did you get the phone call from a fully formed human being sprung from your loins?"

"No. But I could have. I was not a careful young man."

With his head on Rocky's feet, the dog, having successfully pinned her in place, heaved to his side, stuck his legs out straight, and created a four-foot perimeter around her. Having done so, he went back to a semi-sleep state.

"I know what you're saying, and I've thought the same thing. I understand that it's possible Bob didn't know. A lot of things are possible. Someone might have given this kid the wrong information too."

"And it's possible that it's not true. How did you leave it when she called you?"

"I told her that I'd call her back," said Rocky.

Isaiah put his elbows on the table. He rubbed his forefinger with his thumb. "I know you. This is not an injured dog. I want you to proceed with caution."

"Oh, I will," said Rocky, remembering the sound of the girl's voice, the way something had pulled her out of the sky like a shotgun, the familiar catch in the throat that sounded so like Bob. And if there was anyone out there who could bring a bit of Bob back to her, then Rocky had to take a chance. "I promise, I'll wait until tomorrow before I call her back." She looked down at Cooper, avoiding Isaiah's gaze.

"I want to ask you something else," Rocky said. "I was out running this morning, down the spine of the island, near the dump, and I saw the most amazing thing out by the old Costello house. Wisteria has gone wild out there. Big gobs of purple wisteria are hanging from all the trees, as high as thirty feet up. I couldn't believe how beautiful it was. I've never seen anything like it." Rocky had felt like she'd been struck in the chest by the wisteria, as if she'd found the heart of the island. It was like she had stumbled on a personal message, and since the phone call from the girl she was looking for anything that made sense. The sound of the girl's voice had left a seed in her chest that had already carved out a space there.

"That's a sight, isn't it? I'll have to tell Charlotte that the wisteria bloomed late after all. It must be the climate change. The lilacs went early this year by two weeks."

"But why is there wisteria gone wild out there?" she asked.

"There used to be an old farmhouse out there, but it burned down to the ground over sixty years ago. If you want, I could show you the foundation. The only living thing that survived was the wisteria. And since there's been no development on that property, it's been undisturbed. It must be the perfect conditions for wisteria. The property is smack up against the Costello house."

"Is the Costello place still for sale?" she asked.

"It's been for sale for three years. Half the houses on the island are for sale. Why?"

"Just wondering."

Isaiah tapped his fingers along his full lips. "And you're suddenly pondering real estate here? If I had to put your two topics of child and house together, I'd be flabbergasted at your impulsivity."

Why was she suddenly looking at a house? Rocky was getting pressure from all sides about when she was going to return to her job in Massachusetts. A perfectly good job awaited her, a job that she had loved, along with her house and her former life. Cooper would chew sticks endlessly in the dense forests behind her house near the Berkshires.

Ray had called five times with long messages, bursting her message machine with his insistence that she come back to the university. Her brother, Caleb, wanted to know when she was moving back. Melissa, her teenage neighbor on Peaks Island and Cooper's chief fan, had asked her, "Will Cooper be going with you when you leave?" even though they had been over this point many times before.

Rocky pulled out her chair, and Cooper scuttled to attention, his black claws finally gaining traction on the rug.

"If I was acting impulsively, I wouldn't be asking for advice from the smartest man I know," she said with what she hoped was a convincing smile. Francine flipped the OPEN sign to CLOSED as Rocky, Isaiah, and Cooper left the café. She kept to the alleys and dirt roads on the walk home.

The second Rocky walked into the little rental cottage, she walked directly to her phone and dialed Natalie's number. There was no answer and no message machine.

Chapter 4

Natalie

N atalie had been afraid of the dark when she lived with her third foster family, or was it the fourth? She was only seven years old, and although she had tried to hold on to her sense of time—in the same desperate way she had tried to hold on to everything, including her favorite baby blanket—she could never be entirely sure of her actual age when she reached into her memory. The early years in foster care were fluid. The third family did not beat her, and they fed her, and no one in the house told her to take down her pants to hurt her; along with the second family, the third was a vast improvement over the first. But they would not let her keep a light in the bedroom, not even the tiniest night-light. She was not allowed to keep her bedroom door open so that a welcome wave of light might wash into the room. She could have slept if even the slimmest blade of light had pierced the room.

Mr. Burkhardt, the dad, said big girls didn't need to have night-lights or hallway lights. He was of the opinion that total darkness provided the essential ingredient for the best sleep.

"Why would you need lights to go to sleep?" he asked. But he wasn't asking, and Natalie finally understood that his question was meant as an absolute rule after she offered every reason under the sun for a night-light. The darkness was solid and wet and unforgiving. There were no streetlights outside the Burkhardts' house, and Natalie pulled the covers around her face as much as she could without smothering herself.

Creatures of the night waited for her to move or show fear; they thrived on it. Even at age seven, she understood this. Monsters wanted to see her fear. She lay stiff and unmoving, frozen in place, praying to live until daybreak. When enough of the dense night had dissipated to convince her that the dawn was emerging, sometime around 5:00 A.M., she could afford to move and soften her body. Then she slept, only to be startled awake two hours later by Mrs. Burkhardt.

"Time for school. Get up, Miss Sleepyhead."

Did other children live with this same danger each night, living one breath away from the monsters that threatened to rip them to pieces? Mr. and Mrs. Burkhardt had each other, and Natalie knew they fell asleep to the blue light of the small television set in their bedroom. She longed to sleep on their floor, to slip along the baseboards so that she could be in the light with them. She craved it the way she had craved food in the other family. If she could only have the smallest bit of light, she'd be safe and she could sleep.

Natalie found pillow-padded nooks and crannies in the classroom where she could sleep for precious moments until the teacher came looking for her. There was a tunnel in the play structure where she could curl into a ball and fall asleep to the safe hum of fluorescent lights and the voice of her teacher and the other children. At the Burkhardts', she began to hide in the house long before bedtime; sometimes she turned into a flat piece of paper and slid under the couch. Other times she hid behind the big chairs in the living room, tucking her head into her knees. She only vaguely recalled the screaming and spitting when the Burkhardts found her and had to carry her to her bedroom.

The trick with darkness was to become the boss, to own it, to have control over it. Now, at age eighteen, Natalie loved the absoluteness of the darkness, the density of it, the way it dared her to lay open her secrets. When she moved to her own apartment in Worcester after the emancipation, she did not turn on her lights for the first week. The first night left her huddled in a corner, her cell phone gripped tight, a flashlight in her pocket pressed to her belly. She dared the creatures of the night to show their ugly faces, and when they did not, she uncurled her spine. As long as she made the rules, darkness was unable to slide its damp tongue along her neck. This place was hers, and she could choose whether to turn on the lights or not. She steeled herself to join in with the terrors of the night. She showered in the dark, walked the perimeter of the small apartment in the dark. This place was hers; it lacked the monsters of other places. She had checked every closet, under the bed, every shelf, and she had rubbed her hand along every crevice. This was a place where she could live in the dark because she chose to.

Chapter 5

Rocky had owned one house, and that had been with Bob. She had been thirty-one when they bought their house, and she had wondered if she was old enough or smart enough to buy a house. All along, however, Bob had said, "It's only wood and mortar." Together they had purchased the house in the foothills of the Berkshire Mountains.

They had a friend from Boulder, Colorado, who had visited them, and he asked, "Aren't the Berkshires really foothills themselves?" And it was true: compared to the Rockies, with their sharp peaks and ridges, the Berkshires were rubbed down like half-eaten muffins, dotted with thousands of acres of white birches.

Rocky was now a newly minted thirty-nine, and she was looking at the house on Peaks Island, the one that had sat vacant and uncared for. If she bought it, she would have to figure out everything on her own.

"It's just mortar and wood," she said unconvincingly to her brother. She held the cell phone uncomfortably close to her ear as she sat parked in the beat-up yellow truck in front of the Costello place. On the second story, the house had three gabled windows that stared back at her, their dark green shutters like mascara on three eyes. A widow's walk perched on the top of the house, a tiny room ringed by a deck. A wide porch faced the road. She had called the agent who handled the property the night before, after making two more calls to the number that Natalie gave her.

"Let's see if I've got the whole picture," said Caleb. "Unless you can do therapy long distance, and I so hope you can't, this means you're quitting your job at the college. Have you told them yet? Have you told Mom yet?"

"Negative," said Rocky. "You know I always talk to you first."

Aside from college and graduate school, Rocky and Caleb had never lived more than twenty miles apart. Until Rocky moved nearly four hours away after Bob died. Summer was Caleb's busy time painting houses; she had reached him on the job, two stories up on an old colonial in Leeds. In the winter months, Caleb made sculptures of musicians: euphoric, sax-playing women and spine-tingling men, arms held high with a fiddle. Rocky had sold five of them through a gallery in Portland over the winter, with a list of people who were willing to wait. She chose not to tell him about Natalie. Not yet.

"**Full disclosure** means that I have to tell you of the dire circumstances related to this house before I sell it," said the Realtor. He was a young man with a sober demeanor who had introduced himself as a first-generation Puerto Rican from Brooklyn. His body was compact and muscled. He drove an old Ford Bronco.

"Does that mean your family has been in the States for one generation?"

"My parents were born in PR, and I was born here. Like I said, first generation."

Rocky already knew all about the dire circumstances of the house. This was where an old fisherman had killed himself after the debilitating illness and death of his wife. His wife had been dead and buried for two weeks when Mr. Costello had cleaned the house, carefully covered the stacked firewood with a blue tarp, and nailed a warning note to his front door that admonished the visitor to call the Portland police and not to enter until the police got there. Then he covered his head with the side bag from his lawn mower and shot himself. His attempt at tidiness was not entirely successful: the cleanup crew was forced to wash down the living room walls with bleach. Who would want a house that was soaked in pain, remembrance, and unbearable tragedy? Which was precisely what Caleb would ask later when she called him back.

"Why do you want to buy a crap house that's got mouse shit for insulation when you have a good solid house back here? And that is just plain gross about the lawn mower bag."

Why did she want this house? There were over fifty houses for sale on Peaks. But a house where grief took a stranglehold on a widower more than three years ago? Somehow that seemed within the realm of good judgment; she understood the landscape.

When Carlos the Realtor showed her the house, he said, "I assume you'll be tearing down the old house and building new. It's a valuable lot, almost big enough for three parcels if you apply for a variance." He stood in the entryway and made sure that he touched nothing. His thick black eyelashes grazed his glasses as he spoke.

Rocky leaned her spine against the molding of the kitchen door. "This house has good bones." She had heard people say that before but never imagined that she'd be the one saying it.

"Nothing's going to happen without an inspection. Can't get a mortgage without one," he said.

"What happens if I don't want a mortgage?"

"What do you mean?"

"I mean I'd like to buy the house outright. Cash."

"Is there something you don't like about the mortgage system?"

"I want to move quickly, before I change my mind. Forget the inspection," said Rocky. "I have money from my husband's life insurance. This would take a massive bite out of it. . . ."

Carlos shifted his weight. He put his clipboard on the kitchen counter.

"This is important. You're not buying a pair of shoes here. I personally will not let you buy this place without an inspection. I don't care if you have all the cash in your back pocket right now. You need to know if the roof is ready to cave in, if the place has termites." Carlos paused and seemed to reconsider his approach. "I don't know what your husband did or how he died, but you should respect his memory by doing this right. He meant for you to have life insurance money to take care of you, not for you to throw it away. I'm scheduling an inspection, and you need to chill about this."

It had been twenty-four hours since the girl had called her, and Rocky was well on her way to buying a house.

Carlos was able to make things happen quickly. The heirs of the property were thrilled with Rocky's offer and never haggled over one cent. Carlos brought in an inspector in record time. By the next day, Rocky and Carlos were in Portland, waiting for the real estate attorney to arrive so they could sign, initial, and date the final ream of documents. As they waited, Carlos filled Rocky in on his rise in the world of real estate.

He told her that he'd grown up in a single-parent household in Brooklyn. His mother smoked crack and most of the time left the kids alone to raise themselves. "I was in Juvie Hall by the time I was twelve. All the other boys liked it there because it was the best they had ever had. That's what turned on the light for me: I knew I didn't want jail to be the best place I'd ever live. From that moment on, I made choices. Did I want to smoke crack with my mother and be like her? No. So I didn't smoke crack. That first choice helped so much that I kept making other choices. Did I want to have a job other than selling drugs? Yes, since I wanted a life expectancy beyond age twenty-three. So I finished high school. Did I want my younger brothers and sisters to live in foster care? No. So I got a job and took care of them. My youngest brother goes to college now. He's in his third year, studying criminal justice. Did I want my kids to have a father who walked out on them? No. So I had to learn to be a father, which is a lot harder than selling houses and anything else I've ever gone through."

Rocky had gradually accepted that life on the island was more personal than her life had been in the Berkshires of western Massachusetts. There was something butt-naked about the way people did business here. Once again, she was conducting a business transaction thinking that it might be an in-and-out sort of event. Now, after she'd heard about the decline and rise of Carlos's lineage in heart-rending detail, Carlos had given her his stamp of approval on her housing choice.

"Nobody wants to buy real estate with bad history," he said. "I didn't go to college, but I can tell you that the history that happened in this house is gone and you're getting an island house for $50,000 less than the going rate. In my old neighborhood we called that. . . ." He paused, censoring his memories. "We called that a very good deal. Congratulations." He nodded with approval.

After signing all the final documents and acquiring the keys, she hopped the first ferry back to the island and took care of business in her little cottage. Isaiah had rented it to her the previous October, almost apologetically. It had two small bedrooms, a kitchen with hard-worn linoleum, and one room that served as living room and dining room and looked out to the ocean over the top of a quarter-mile stand of dense bittersweet. Peterson the cat appeared on the deck, responding to the sound of Rocky's crunching footsteps on the driveway. The calico had a daytime life amid the bittersweet that had a lot to do with rodent annihilation. Cooper greeted Rocky's entrance with his full-throttle, body-twisting euphoria, as if he was amazed at her return. She fed both animals and made sure that Peterson was inside for the night.

"Cooper, I need your stamp of approval on the new house. We're sleeping over." The dog lifted his head from his post-dinner grooming and cocked one eyebrow.

This was one reason why she should go back to the university: she was seeking validation from a black Lab. But she wanted to see what it felt like in the new house with Cooper by her side, and she was a bit spooked about spending the first night alone in the house. She was considerably braver with a ninety-pound dog on her side of the equation.

They stood in front of her new front door, and she said to the house, "Show me your worst and loudest. Let's get everything out on the table." It had been forty-eight hours since Natalie called.

Rocky unlocked the side door to the kitchen and began her private inspection. The sink had gone yellow with singular determination. Piles of mouse droppings dotted the kitchen drawers. Cooper's black claws clicking on the linoleum announced his movement around the kitchen. He lowered his head and sniffed, following ancient scents of children, family pets, and the final months of illness and death.

No one had lived in the house for three years except right after Mr. Costello's death, when his horrified cousins had spent just a week emptying the house of personal possessions. Catastrophes of such proportions formed a solid, epic fable for the islanders. Speculations about what makes a man take his own life flew around the Island Café for months, according to Isaiah. Did he do it out of love? Madness? Profound depression? Every man gripping his coffee cup wondered aloud if he would do the same thing. The Costellos had been married for forty-seven years. Had there been no kind friend, brother, or bighearted niece to hold tight to Mr. Costello until the worst of his grief began to ease? Rocky had tasted the desire to end her life in her addled thinking during the months after Bob's death. What was it that pulled her so securely to a safe harbor? Finding the big black dog for one thing.

Three years is a deadly time of loneliness for a house. Just like cats, houses shouldn't be left untended for longer than three days; three years is devastating.

A house has its own mental health requirements, the primary requirement being occupancy. Carbon dioxide must be exhaled into the drywall, skin detritus needs to flutter about the crevices like snow, and houses even welcome bits of flicked earwax in reserved spots along the far corners. Left alone too long, a house forgets how to breathe and grows anxious as the water sits too long in the toilets tanks. An old woman had been gripped by disease here and died in the arms of her husband. And he had been unable to conceive of life without her. Love had exhaled and never inhaled again here. Nearly all of the consciousness that remained in the floorboards, cupboards, and windowsills was gone when Rocky arrived and said, "I'll buy it."

She wanted to resuscitate the house. She opened the kitchen windows. A breeze brought in the thick scent of wisteria from the adjacent property.

Rocky and Cooper spent the first night with only a leaky air mattress that she dragged in and inflated with her bike pump. The living room, with its gaping fireplace, seemed the most central location to camp and get to know the house. She dove into her sleeping bag as soon as it was dark. Cooper lowered his bulk to the side of the mattress. Rocky scrunched her way closer to him and let one hand fall onto his warm back. She wanted to see and hear everything the house had to say. When the weight of darkness took hold without the benefit of ambient light from any human source, she was grateful that Cooper was by her side.

Rocky didn't know what to expect, but something had repelled others from the house, some continued taint of suicide from Mr. Costello that would be loud and ominous. What she wasn't expecting was how the house would voice itself.

Was a house like a child or a dog, reverberating to emotions around them, unable to put the waves of sadness into words? Rocky unzipped the sleeping bag, determined to take the pulse of the house even though her heart pounded and she felt small in the belly of the house. She wasn't like Tess: she didn't smell colors or see time passing in shapes. But if this house had come to her, if it had walked into her therapy office, she would have said, "Tell me why you're here." Which was what she said to the house now.

"Tell me . . . ," she started. Before she could finish, she was sure she heard the house sigh, the kind of sigh that a child makes after a long crying spell has ended. Then she sat for hours, as witness to the sad house, letting it expel the shudders of crying so that it could move on to begin its new life. She would later think that the sound had to be the wind or the house settling, that she had perhaps dreamed about the muffled noise.

And she did fall asleep several times, waking to listen again. She wanted her 4:00 A.M. brain to experience the house, the time when thinking goes spiral and catastrophic before morning light restores reason.

She woke once and saw moonlight reflected in Cooper's eyes as he sat by her mattress. The wall with the open windows looked oddly wet, gleaming as water does, as if a steady sheet of water flowed along the wall from ceiling to floor. In her half-slumber, this phenomenon seemed understandable, even a sign of rebirth. Such is the way of 4:00 A.M. thinking. In the morning, she only half-remembered the water, but when she did, she touched the wall in many places and all that she felt were the brittle flakes of wallpaper.

Chapter 6

The House

The house had been waiting, stuck in time at the moment of unimaginable despair, staring in vacant hunger. There had been deaths before; the ebb and flow of people had washed through the old house like tides, but grown children or new people had always followed. First came the young lovers, bleary with the fright of buying a house, not knowing that the house had selected them, called to them as they drove by, heads hanging out of car windows, or walking by, pausing as the house issued a call to them if they were a suitable fit. As the house pulled them into the heart of the kitchen, blowing future dreams into their palms that stroked windowsills and banisters, the couple would talk and murmur. *We could put the nursery here. . . . I could look out the window when I cook. . . . Do you think this hot water heater will last? . . . Oh, how the windows rattle; we'll freeze.* On and on they would talk, inhaling the memories of others, the people who had lived in the house before them, through babies, love, dogs and cats, clamorous sounds, coughing in the night, birthday parties, doors slammed in anger, the muffled murmurs of sex that followed.

If these visitors were not right for the house (and so many were not), there were ways to send them away—a precipitous drop in temperature, a door creaking shut as they examined the darkest corner of the basement or a closet.

The last inhabitants had ended with calamity after a long and good life. The crack of the shotgun had jarred the house to the foundations, a final assault after the prolonged agonies of illness. No one had been drawn to the house for years, and without people, the house had grown soft and overrun by encroaching rodents, colonies of ladybugs, and the persistent battering of wind, rain, snow, and sun. The demise of an abandoned house is marked by a sagging roof, door frames tilting from lack of touch so that doors can no longer close, the floors on the verge of buckling. Not that all this was happening in the old Costello house, but it was coming. The house longed for the press of bare feet on the floor, the good scrub of vinegar and water on the windows, and the pelting sound of human voices bouncing off the walls and ceilings.

A good house, a truly good house, can hold multiple generations, stacking up layers of families like cordwood. This house had waited so long and had all but accepted its demise, ready to let go of hope, when the woman and dog had slowed their walking outside the property. She had been drawn by the scent of the wisteria down the road, lapping at her in drunken waves of fuchsia and purple. She had picked an armload of flowers, and then she came back and stood directly in front of the house, her feet spread wide, her head tilted as if she heard the halting heartbeat, the dog at her side. The house took a chance and let loose with a vibration of light and sound, squeezing the cellulose in the beams, letting the iron in the nails add to the subtle symphony. The dog led her in closer. There she was close enough that the house could beam its promise to her, set memories of summer nights to humming on the porch, let the upstairs windows in the three dormers catch the sun in a wink. *Give me one more go at it,* said the house.

Chapter 7

Tess

There is a surprise in everything that the unseen moves. There are miracles at work. Tess read one poem per day. She had just read these words from the Nigerian poet Ben Okri, and the words were staying with her. Since Rocky had arrived on Peaks, Tess had learned to expect the unexpected from her. She had just gotten a call from Rocky. "Come to the old Costello house. I just bought it." Did that mean she was staying permanently? Had Hill finally courted Rocky long enough and hard enough to win her over? Were the two of them buying a house together? As Tess tossed one leg over her bike, she scraped her ankle on the pedal. If her synesthesia had been intact, she would have seen a brilliant orange line shooting up her leg. Now she only felt the colorless throb of pain.

Four months ago, the surgery that had repaired her exploding appendix and knotted-up colon had chased away nearly all her precious synesthesia. She had been tossed out of her multisensory world of synesthesia and into the drab world of the five senses firing predictably, one at a time, without intertwining, and she thought she had lost her mind, or the mind that she wanted. Now all she had left was a whisper of her coupling with numbers and shapes, which was entertaining and somewhat comforting, but nothing compared to her full Technicolor synesthesia. Before, numbers 1 to 10 had been softly molded cubes lined up like soldiers. The numbers 11 to 20 had climbed up a slope, and 21 to 30 had broadened and merged to the right. Now the way she saw the number 7, her granddaughter's age, was like a dim memory of a cube seen through a haze, indecipherable and frustrating. In her physical therapy, she no longer felt the tingling buzz of constricted muscles as the sound of bumblebees.

Tess parked her bike by the yellow truck outside the Costello house. Now that Rocky owned it, she had to stop thinking of it as the Costello house. Why did Rocky buy a house with such a painful history?

She opened the front door and yelled, "Welcome Wagon." Was Rocky too young to even know what the

Welcome Wagon was? Rocky and Cooper appeared from the kitchen and greeted her.

Walking with her young friend through the house she had bought with alarming speed, Tess felt useless: she could neither smell colors nor see the colors of Rocky's name, nor experience the colors of dust and mold as yellow and blue.

"How can you stand it?" Tess demanded. It was morning, and Rocky's deep brown hair caught a glint of sun as it poured through the living room window. Old polyester curtains, stiff with dirt, were tied primly to each side. Even from the arched doorway between the living room and dining room Tess could smell the dense scent of dust and mold.

"You cannot imagine how gorgeous my life was and how bland it all looks now," said Tess. "I'm complaining, aren't I? I'd be dead without the surgery. You have my permission to tell me to shut up."

"I don't want you to shut up," said Rocky, shining her flashlight into a closet. "I do want you to tell me that maybe, just maybe, buying this house was a good idea and that for at least an hour we won't talk about the girl who now refuses to call me back. Why do I see this house with bright pulsating light at its core while my brother and Isaiah think it's the worst piece of shit on the island? Isaiah said the beavers have invaded the property down the road, damming up a stream to make a pond."

Tess tried out the window seat and pushed open the window, letting the cool morning air rush in. It would be a lovely spot to read, to curl up with a grandchild and watch birds at the feeder on a winter afternoon.

"You've been hanging around me for too long. Maybe my synesthesia is circling around you like a cloud until I can get it back. But if you see something that no one else sees, I can only tell you this: Believe what you see. And if it is the unseen that speaks to you, believe that too."

Tess tried to loosen her neck muscles by rotating her shoulders up and down, pulling her arms behind her, then spreading her shoulder blades wide by stretching her arms in front of her.

"I should do that too," Rocky said. "I stayed awake most of the night, trying to get a feel for the house. I have a gut feeling that this house has got more life ahead of it."

Rocky ran her hand across the faded images of daisies in the wallpaper that lined the walls of the living room and the entry from the front door. What was stirring in her? Sitting on the window seat, Tess wiggled her toes under Cooper, who had sat on her feet. Tess hadn't had a dog in years, but if she ever had a dog again, she wanted it to be a clone of Cooper.

"You're going to tell me to smudge the house with dried sage, aren't you?" asked Rocky.

Tess tried unsuccessfully to picture Rocky gliding through the house, holding the burning incense of a tightly wadded hunk of dried sage. "Smudging" was a way to cleanse a house of old spirits.

"No, but I'm impressed that you know what smudging is."

Rocky cranked open another window in the kitchen, the kind that opens out like an arm welcoming the day. Moist ocean air slipped in through the screens in fish-like waves. She and Tess continued walking slowly from room to room, stopping in corners, admiring another bay window and a stair railing worn smooth by hands. As Tess let her hand run along the wainscoting and door frames, feeling the nail holes, she said, "Tell me again what happened when you slept here last night."

"I heard a shudder, or a sigh," Rocky responded. "I don't know what else to call it. You know how kids shudder when they've been crying hard? Like that. Except, it was the house." Tess stopped walking, her attention focused entirely on Rocky. "But I must have fallen asleep. I woke up at one point, or at least I think I was awake, and it looked like there was water running down the wall, just for a few seconds. Now that I say it out loud, it sounds ridiculous."

"I have to say that I am more than a little shocked. This area of things—smudging, crying houses, phantom water—is not generally in your repertoire. But it all points to a general sadness that happened at one time in this house, which we know is true about this place."

Tess wore a tank top, long cotton pants, and sandals with rubber soles. A little chill rose on her arms, and she rubbed them as if she could scrape off the offending goose bumps. Tess knew what had happened in this house; everyone did. What was surprising about Rocky was that she was not alarmed in the same way that others were.

As if she had heard Tess's thoughts, Rocky said, "I'm not freaked out. If anything, I completely get it. It's sad, but it's not like the place is haunted with vengeful energy. Even I know that's not true." Rocky turned to Tess. "How do we mend a broken house? This kind of thing is your area, not mine."

Tess had pulled her hair up in a fat knot on top of her head, and the morning chill now found her neck. "This is all speculation on my part. There are only so many things that I know how to do. I'm a semi-retired physical therapist. I'm not sure that qualifies me to fix a sad house. Have you told anyone else about this?"

"No. Isaiah would tell me to air it out and shampoo the carpets."

Tess wore light pants with enough Spandex in them that she could easily squat without popping the stitches. Now she rested in a squat, one of her favorite thinking positions, with her feet wide and her butt down. Rocky leaned into a door frame, tapping her foot with uncontainable energy.

Finally Tess stood up, arching and stretching her spine. "When my mother died, I was eight years old, and what I remember most after her death was the lack of color. She knew I had synesthesia. She had it too, even though she didn't know what to call it back then. My world was stripped of color for months after her death. That's what has happened to this place. It's been stripped of color. Even with my synesthesia MIA, I can tell you that this house has been drained of color. What you can do to help this house is to bring life back inside it."

Tess rubbed one hand along the floor.

"I think all you have to do is to love it again, like the Costellos did, back when they were young and healthy. They loved it by just living and breathing. A house carries the vibration of the people who live in it. This house wants to start over, just like you started over with Cooper."

Tess had completed her methodical examination of the entire house, running her hand over old bathroom sinks that stood on aluminum legs, over a clawfoot bathtub balanced on four bricks, over the pantry shelves that still held specks of flour in their crevices. It had taken both of them to heave open the warped door to the widow's walk, only to discover rotten boards in the decking. Finally, Tess sat on the front steps of the porch with Rocky.

"Here is what I forgot to tell you," said Tess. "I dreamed of a doctor bird last night."

"Are you waiting for me to say something?" asked Rocky.

Tess got up, and together they walked around to the back of the house. Every bit of the woods surrounding the house threatened to engulf the house with its green reach. Several animal trails opened into the dense shrubbery.

"About what?" Tess squinted her eyes against the blast of a summer day.

"About dreaming. Do you want me to formulate some hypothesis about your dream? Most people expect me to."

"I didn't say one thing about asking for your interpretation of my dream. In fact, you interrupted me.

What I was going to say was that I dreamed of a doctor bird, which is a very rare hummingbird found only in Jamaica. They have long, dramatic tails that look like the train on a black wedding dress. And the feathers are iridescent black, shot through with green. The bird in my dream got very large and sat down in a chair. He whispered something, and I desperately wanted to hear him, so I got closer. It sounded like 'reunification' or 'reunion,' or maybe the words that he said just looked like a reunion. And his words smelled like allspice," said Tess. "This is very strange that my multiple senses are firing as usual in my dreams. Heartening, really."

For the first time in months, she was truly hopeful that she could return to who she really was, not simply putting on a good-natured smile. Becoming herself was a hard-won achievement that had taken many years, and she was too old to pretend to be happy with less.

"I had never considered the multiple layers of complications available when a dreamer has synesthesia. It makes sense that you would dream as you used to be, just the way people with amputated limbs dream of being whole," said Rocky. "Is there more?"

"Yes. When I woke up, I could have sworn that I heard Cooper barking, like he was very far away. I didn't like that part. There was an urgency in his barking, an alarm," said Tess.

"I was never an expert with dreams. I left that to the other therapists. But I know the basics: treat everything in the dream like a story and let the dreamer make her own way to figure out the meaning."

Tess swatted at a mosquito. "These miserable creatures aren't supposed to be out until dusk. What's wrong with them? Maybe they're confused by the early heat." But the desire to make sense of her world was too powerful to be distracted.

Returning to the content of the dream, Tess whispered, "Rare, bird, shiny, black, message, reunion, Cooper barking, message, doctor, allspice, good dog, bird, doctor, black feathers. I've almost got it."

But she lost the links between the images as quickly as they emerged. Without the connecting fibers of her cross-firing senses, she felt hobbled. "Gone. Just when I thought I had it, gone."

"It must be like trying to see in the dark," said Rocky.

"I couldn't agree with you more," said Tess.

Rocky shoved her hands into her pockets. "What if Natalie doesn't ever call me back? What if I scared her off?" she whispered.

Tess wasn't surprised by the abrupt change in topic; she'd felt the undercurrent of the girl since she first arrived at the old house.

"Is this what the house is all about? Oh, good Lord. Are you suddenly trying to make a home based on one phone call from an unknown girl? What does our gallant Hill think about all this?"

"He's celebrating the end of the school year with a camping trip up near Canada," Rocky told her. "He'll be back in two days, and believe me, I can't wait to see him."

Tess was not surprised. The last time she had seen Hill and Rocky together she had felt a tinge of envy, then wonder, at two people so clearly on the verge of love.

"You're the only person I know who could have seen through the disaster to get to the heart of this house," said Tess, hoping this qualified as the good assessment that her friend needed. But why did she have the horrible feeling that Hill would never live in this house?

Chapter 8

Melissa

Melissa was headed directly into her senior year of high school, and she was battling with the two and a half pounds she had allowed her body to gain since January, six months ago. That was slightly less than one half-pound per month, but the pace of it still took her to the crumpling edge of terror. She felt every ounce layered on her razor-sharp body, dragging her down like a set of iron weights that had to be accommodated in every move, every twitch of her eyelids.

She brushed her hair out of her eyes. She had just completed three hundred sit-ups, down from the five hundred sit-ups that she was doing one year ago. Five hundred sit-ups kept her warrior fit and tight, skin pulling over her pelvic bones. Three hundred sit-ups took her into the great swamp of unknown land, and it sometimes meant she had to find Cooper and press her body up against his black, furry bulk before her heart would stop racing. But three hundred was the goal, and she was there.

Melissa looked in the mirror. She saw an enormous face looking back, fat and horrible. She squeezed her eyes shut and fought off the image. Melissa decided to try what Tess had suggested. Tess was old, she didn't know how old, but grandparent old, and yet not like a grandparent. Tess was white-haired and oddly gymnastic, with rubbery bones and joints.

Tess had said, "When I wake up in the morning, I look in the mirror and say, 'Good naked morning. My name is Gorgeous Goddess Babe.'"

"Good naked morning. My name is Melissa." She'd work up to the gorgeous babe part.

She sat down and gripped the sides of the chair and shook. Some days were harder than others. She had bailed out of the world of restricted eating. Now, if it would just leave her alone.

She put her camera in her pack and headed for the ferry. She had a part-time job at the YMCA for the summer, checking people in, handing out towels. But once she was done, she was free to take pictures on the streets of Portland. It was the last week in June, and the summer stretched out long and broad before her.

Chapter 9

"Have you decided if you're going out for cross-country again in the fall?" asked Rocky. Her young neighbor had just returned from a run with Cooper. She hoped that Melissa would say no, that she would allow her body to continue to soak in the food that she had denied herself during her junior-year affair with anorexia. But she knew better than to state her preference. Melissa's battle with restricting food had been nothing short of heroic, and Rocky was her staunch admirer.

"I'm not sure. There's other stuff I want to do, like with photography. Mr. Clarke has said I could be his assistant for senior year. And I might still have to go look at more colleges, like I haven't looked at enough already." Melissa put the glass in the sink.

"How are we going to break it to Cooper that you've got one more year at home and then, whoosh, you're out of here?"

"It's a good thing that a human year is seven years in dog time. Do you think that's true? Or does it just make us feel better because their lives are so much shorter than ours?" asked Melissa.

Rocky didn't want to think of Cooper getting shortchanged in any way, but it was true with dogs. No sooner did you start to really love a dog than you started counting the years that were left. Cooper was five, and already she wanted to slow down the clock.

"I don't know, but I'm pretty sure they don't fret about time the way we do. Hey, when am I going to get to see the 'Dogs of Portland' photo show by the famous photographer Melissa? Everyone except me has seen it. No fair. Your mother told me it was gorgeous."

Melissa squirmed so much that she was in danger of sliding out of her shoes. "I've got it on my laptop. I could go get it. I mean, do you have time now? Or are you too busy?"

"The only thing that might happen is that Isaiah would come over and remind me for the tenth time that the truck needs to get repaired so it can pass inspection. Other than that, my date book is free for the rest of the night. Wait, I actually have food in the fridge. Would you and your mom want to come over for dinner?"

"This is Mom's yoga night, and it's her one non-negotiable time, which is sort of adorable. She thinks she has to be totally available to me at all other times. I had to practically force her to go to this class, which she has been dying to go to for a year. She won't eat until she gets home at eight-thirty, later if they stay for meditation," said Melissa.

"Okay then, go get your laptop and I'll fire up my little grill. Tess is threatening to teach me how to make pasta prima something or other, but I'm in the mood for burgers. That okay with you?"

Melissa squeezed her face into a grimace. "Gack, red meat. Can I bring over a frozen veggie burger, or would something other than flesh contaminate your grill?"

"I can make exceptions. Go, run like the wind and bring me pictures and veggie burger abominations."

As Melissa went out and slammed the screen door, Cooper looked inquiringly after her. He did not like his pack divided and was faced with the worst decisions of his day when his humans split up.

"Okay, big guy, go with her. Do whatever you do with her that makes her smile. I'll stay here and guard your fifty-pound sack of dog food from invaders."

Cooper stood at the door and waited for Rocky to open it. He galloped after Melissa. Was this what happiness felt like? Rocky planned to see Hill later in the evening, to surprise him on his first night back from man camp. She was learning the balancing act of retaining what she felt for Bob while making room for Hill. There was no denying the exquisite longing for Hill that made her twitch unexpectedly. This would be an experiment: how did he deal with surprises?

Rocky made a dinner of broiled hamburger and Classic Coke (for herself) and veggie burger and Diet Coke (for Melissa); she fed Cooper, and then they settled in to watch Melissa's slide show on her laptop. They squeezed their chairs together at the maple dining table to peer into the screen. Melissa had added music by a band that Rocky had never heard of. A procession of dogs came into focus with the special effects that Melissa had learned in Mr. Clarke's class. Rocky oohed and aahed, exclaiming and laughing.

"You really get these dogs. There's something very loving and touching about the photos." Rocky knew she had to stop right there; Melissa would reject too much acclaim as idiotic, or she might simply call Rocky idiotic for praising something that she had created. Either way, Rocky might have already gone too far.

Melissa wiggled shyly, unable to contain a ripple of acceptance. "Yeah, I think some of these are okay." She closed down the laptop.

"I have ice cream. Mint chocolate chip. Want some?" asked Rocky.

"Stop right there—too much. My personal food borders are in danger of being violated."

Rocky did not expect this repartee from the girl, the closeness that it suggested. This was the first time Melissa had acknowledged the war that she had fought with food. She was finally emerging from that conflict; Rocky had not seen the monstrous clutches of the eating disorder in months. Still, she knew that Melissa had wrestled the beast to the ground in her own way, sans therapists, and Rocky had accepted the job of watching from a respectful distance. She chose her words carefully and made them brief.

"Invasion noted. Cooper needs one more walk for the night. Want to come with us and we'll swing by your house at the end of the loop?"

At the sound of two of his favorite words, "Cooper" and "walk," the dog arose from what had appeared to be a solid slumber beneath the table. He went to the door and then looked over his back at the two of them.

"Who can say no to this dog? Sure," said Melissa.

The network of footpaths was extensive, and Rocky chose the one that dipped to the beach at one point. It was past eight o'clock, and the light still lingered in the sky.

"Can I ask you something personal?" asked Melissa.

"Okay, as long as I can always decline to answer."

"I know you really loved your husband, and it was awful how he died and all, but now you've got a boyfriend, which I think is awesome, don't get me wrong. But does it mean that you stopped loving your husband? I was just wondering because my mother has never dated anyone since my dad left, and she told me once that she still loved my dad. Did it click right away with you and Hill?"

What was the girl asking her? Was there enough love in the world to go around? Was love finite? Did each person only have enough love for one good relationship? Rocky stopped picking her way along the boulders that sheltered the narrow strip of beach, unable to walk and think at the same time, given the weight of the questions.

"I knew Bob was different from anyone else when I met him. I was a lifeguard at a pool, and he was trying to learn how to swim, and he was awful at it. He was a weird combination of strong, vulnerable, nutty, dedicated to animals, and funny, and the sum total fascinated me. I knew he was fascinated by me because he told me every chance he had. And I loved his hands. They were big and square, man-hands, yet because he was in the medical field he had to keep his hands clean constantly, and they were just . . . beautiful. The man had beautiful hands," said Rocky. She had no idea if she was providing good information about love or only her own idiosyncratic attraction.

"That's what love is?" said Melissa. She leapt from a boulder to the sand. Cooper launched into euphoria as soon as his paws touched the sand, bounding at a group of gulls that acknowledged his sense of power by flapping out to sea.

"What I want to say is that love got bigger over time. Sometimes love got smaller. If we tried to change each other and tried to blame each other for our own miserable perception of life, then love grew smaller. But overall, the capacity for love grew bigger, and I don't think that the bucket size is gone because Bob died."

"What about Hill? He's crazy nuts about you, and I think you like him. Is that love?"

Rocky's spine undulated at the thought of Hill, of the newness of their relationship that had recently gone from archery teacher and student to something else. Cooper brought Rocky a stick, and without thinking she heaved it into the ocean. "Damn, I didn't mean for him to go swimming. He tricked me. He waits until I'm distracted, and then he gets me to throw his stick into the ocean. My entire house will smell like wet dog again."

"So, back to Hill . . . ," said Melissa with her hands on her hips.

Rocky wiped her hands on her pants. "As crazy as it sounds, I can't wait to see Hill and he's only been gone two weeks. It doesn't make my great big husband any less important. There's got to be a physics equation for love. Maybe you and I can figure it out. Please don't tell me you're asking for a class assignment."

Melissa stuffed her hands into her armpits. "Nope. I just trust you, and someday I'll have to know the rules of the game. That wind is cold. My mom is probably home and all *namaste* by now. I should head back," said Melissa.

Rocky was relieved that the girl seemed satisfied by her answers, particularly because she wasn't sure that she could offer even one more tidbit.

By the time Rocky and Cooper came home, it was nine. She looked immediately to her phone, but there was no blinking light. She called the number that Natalie had given her, the digits already engraved in her brain. This time a message machine picked up and she heard Natalie's voice over the tinny sound of music, "Leave a message."

"This is Rocky. I want to meet you. Please call me."

Chapter 10

After Melissa went home, Rocky walked to the ferry, put on a jacket for the fifteen-minute crossing, and picked up her Honda in the parking garage. There was only one place she wanted to be. Rocky wanted to be with Hill. She wanted to tell him everything about the girl who called, the odd catch in her voice, the terror of going one step further in the direction of meeting the girl. Rocky needed Hill's physicality; she wanted to hear his steady voice, the way he could equate all of life to archery. Most of all, she wanted his arms wrapped around her before she doled out the information. Hill lived in Brunswick, north of Portland, and Rocky drove as if she were swimming underwater, losing oxygen.

Hill gave off a cinnamon scent, with a background of pencil shavings mixed with something like wind and his own good sweat, which, when fresh, was nearly intoxicating. She imagined the scent of him as she drove. Rocky understood the unique function of the olfactory part of the brain, so tied to memories and emotions. This was the good dog part of the brain where scent carried all the information and all the emotions that she needed right now. She pictured a dog's brain evenly split between scent and sound, both leading directly through the heart.

How had Hill's scent wormed its way into her brain so essentially? As a couple, they were new, several months in the making. She had sniffed the majestic symmetry of Hill, and she was ready to let go, to rest in his arms. They had not yet made love together; Hill was keenly aware of the loss that she'd suffered when Bob died.

"We can go as slow as we need to," he had said. "Your husband made the terrible error of dying, and I know that you're still sad and you'll miss him for as long as you live. I am 90 percent through a divorce, so you and I aren't exactly at the starting gate. But I don't want anyone except you."

She reached his street in Brunswick, led by the scent of him on her lips, her skin, consciously skipping the part where she would have called him to say, "Hey, I'm thirty minutes away from your house. I'm coming over." No, this was the next stage in their relationship, the natural stage with unimpeded connections between them, where her arrival at his front door would be unquestioned and he would sweep her in like the welcome tide that she was. This was what her life would be like without Bob.

Hill had passed all the tests with Tess and Isaiah. "You must have the good dude radar," Tess had said. "You've found two good men, and for some women that doesn't ever happen. The same jerks keep reappearing." Rocky had thought that was an unusually harsh comment from her primarily Buddhist friend and said so.

"I'm not being harsh, just descriptive," Tess said.

Rocky was less than a block from Hill's house when she saw another car in his driveway. Something about the car, the unfamiliar angle of it and the silver glow of it nudged close to Hill's truck, said ownership. *I belong here.*

Rocky put her foot on the brake and stopped, turned off her headlights, and gripped the steering wheel as a sour note mixed with her saliva. Hill was oblivious about closing the drapes in his living room, and the kitchen curtains were perpetually open on the top half of the windows. The woman came to Hill's shoulder, petite and fair-haired, with a hand on his cheek, a tilt to her head. Rocky turned the engine off. Hill's arm rose, lifting the hand from his cheek. Exit stage left by Hill, followed by the woman, whom Rocky knew without a moment's hesitation. This was Julie, the wife who had been gone for two years.

She could hear her brother's warning. "He's separated from his wife. That doesn't mean divorced, and it shouldn't mean available. If they had grown up Catholic like us, they would know that adultery is grounds for purgatory, except purgatory has been banished from our lexicon of afterlife locations. Wait a minute—the pope did away with limbo, not purgatory." Rocky was surprised that Caleb remembered anything from their spotty Catholic education. She had been confident that Caleb's hesitation about Hill would disappear as soon as Hill divorced.

The living room window offered a panoramic view. Words were spoken, not many, it didn't take many, and she was in his arms. No, it didn't take long at all.

Rocky turned over the key, put the car in reverse, and slowly backed up, away from the cul-de-sac, without her headlights on. She inserted the back end of her car into a driveway, turned around, and clicked on her headlights only when Hill's living room window was a dot in her rearview mirror. How could she have been so deluded into imagining that Hill spent every minute thinking about her? The man had been hedging his bets. She should have paid better attention to the guidelines for purgatory.

Chapter 11

How could she have been so wrong about Hill? She had trusted him, and without warning, he was having an affair with Julie. Well, they were still married, so it couldn't be called an affair. But the toxic burn of betrayal shocked her. What did she know about dating, about starting relationships? Nothing.

A piece of buttered toast sat cooling on a plate, untouched. She had wanted to tell Hill everything about the strange girl, about the Costello house, about the pressing need to call Ray about her job. She stabbed the toast with a knife and tossed it into Cooper's bowl.

This was the drop-dead date for calling Ray Velasquez to confirm the date she was returning to her job. Everyone had been understanding when she left; she had had her own mega, grieving, mental health meltdown after Bob died, and she had not inflicted her woes on her vulnerable clients. She had created her very own vision quest off the coast of Maine while ferrying sick dogs and cats from Peaks Island over to Portland.

Rocky looked at her phone, nestled in its cradle, like it was a rattlesnake coiled and ready to strike. Rocky pictured Ray waiting for her to call. Not that the man lacked for one million other things to do with his life, but he had to know if she was coming back to her job in the fall. She pictured him in his office at the university, a remarkably quiet place during the summer. There was normally just a smattering of students taking summer classes, and they rarely made use of the counseling center.

Her house was back in western Mass along with her old life and her furniture, her finicky furnace, and her paved driveway. Her career waited for her with great sticky fingers ready to guide her back to her office. This would be so much easier if she hated her job. The truth of the matter was that she loved everything about her job. She was totally engrossed with the college students who, for the first time in their lives, sought out therapy on their own and tried to grapple with alcoholic parents, bulimic roommates, the agonies of their first broken heart, or the terrifying grip of depression. Their resilience was nothing short of dizzying at their age, and Rocky was thrilled each time a college kid came back from the brink of a personal disaster.

She took the cordless phone out of its cradle. Cooper had stationed himself in front of the screen door, catching the morning breeze, lifting his nose in celebration of a good dog day. Peterson entertained herself by pouncing on Cooper's tail whenever he moved it.

Rocky put the phone on the maple table close to the dark circular outline left by an abandoned beer can. She spoke directly to Cooper.

"You don't have to make choices like this. As much as you might disagree, I can't stay in the almighty now every single minute like you do. I know, you're a dog, and you are constantly rejoicing."

Cooper exhaled a sigh and pushed up to a sitting position, giving her his full attention. His pink tongue rested happily in his slightly open mouth, forming the perfect Lab smile. Rocky reached for his head, and her fingers found the places along his skull that pleased him. She sat down next to him, cross-legged, and looked out the screen door and allowed the morning breezes to wash over her. She draped one arm over his back and he let her.

Ray had phoned her in May. "Rocky, I fully supported your need to unscramble after Bob's death."

Rocky noted that the word "grieving" was no longer used. Now she was "unscrambling." "Now it's time to come back, because if I have another year like this one, with students backed up from here to Boston trying to get an appointment, then I'm going to need medication. Call me."

Rocky had meant to call him back in May. Then her brother, Caleb, called her. "The lease is up with your renters. You'll be glad to know that they did not burn the place down, although the fire department was called because the flue was closed when they tried to start a fire in the fireplace. Twice. Apparently English professors have a flat learning curve with all things related to fire. The house smells a little barbecued. They want to know if you'll rent to them for another year. I told them no. And let me save you from making the call where you ask me to help move you back into the house. Tell me now so that I can schedule it. I've got a life and a job. August, right?"

Rocky needed to shoot something before she made her next phone call, even if it was just the round target tacked to some hay bales. She packed her bow and arrows, slung them over one shoulder. Cooper was never invited for archery times, and when he saw her gather her equipment, the center of his brow rose up in disappointment, his black body slumped to the floor, and he sighed with a flutter of his lips. Rocky looked back at the dog. She had one hand on the door, ready to depart.

"You're right, this is the one place that I don't take you."

Cooper lifted his head. His ears cupped in Rocky's direction.

When she had first found him in November, left for dead with an arrow protruding from his chest, Rocky didn't ever want him within a mile of an archery range again. She figured one arrow lodged in his body was enough for this particular lifetime.

To Rocky's surprise, Cooper dropped his head to his front paws. What did he hear? Was it something in her tone? Did he discern worry, confirmation? Rocky was never entirely sure, but he seemed to understand the non-negotiable nature of her decision to leave him at home.

Rocky usually relished the walk to Tess's house. Now she vibrated erratically from the crush of seeing Hill with his living, breathing wife, from Natalie's unanswered phone call, from her new house purchase, from the call she had to make to Ray. Archery helped her think, and she longed for the solace of it.

She felt the warmth of the day on her bare legs; the moist air swirling around her was peppered with sea salt. She traveled the central paths across the island, taking a dirt road, then diving into the woods, emerging once in someone's driveway, then past a ball field tucked into the interior of the island. She trotted the last half of it, glad for the kinesthetic distraction.

Tess had already left on the ferry for her ritual day in Portland that culminated with dinner and darts with her ex-husband. The backyard was completely Rocky's, and she could shoot arrows until her arms turned to jelly. She tacked a new plastic-coated target to the stack of hay bales. She shifted into the archer. With her body taking the cue, her head began to clear, jettisoning everything except bow, arrow, target, body, and wind.

She found her spot where the grass was trampled from the consistent pawing of her feet, sometimes shod, but recently bare. It was the first week in July, and the warmth of the ground wrapped around her feet. She hefted the bow. Rocky had advanced to a thirty-five-pound bow, and it was like starting all over again. She turned sideways, her left shoulder toward the target, notched the arrow, and pulled back.

Her right arm quivered as she pulled back. She struggled to pull up and back, her thumb grazing her cheek. Hill's steady mantra had become her own: breathe, loosen the knees, exhale, find the center, allow the eyes to travel to the target and the arrow will follow. Release.

What if Bob had a child? Who was Bob if he had failed to mention something as life-altering as a child? She released the arrow, and it lodged solidly on the outer edge of the bale, leaving the paper target unscathed.

Rocky plucked another arrow from her quiver. She shook her body, trying to rid it of the distress that crawled over her like ants. If Bob knew there was a kid and didn't tell her, there was something elemental about her dead husband that she hadn't known. Would he have chosen to hide this, stashing the evidence in a secret compartment? She notched the next arrow. She pulled the arrow up and back, her muscles trembling less this time. Release. The arrow sailed over the top of the target. Her aim was off, but the process of breathing and releasing was having the desired effect of clearing her thoughts.

Hill had warned her: "Every time you go up in weight with the bow, you're going to be a beginner again. Accept it. Your body has to adjust everywhere: legs, spine, arms, even the way that you breathe. If you get mad and resentful about going back to beginner mode, it's only going to take you longer." But then, why should she believe Hill?

Rocky pulled out another arrow and another, shooting, adjusting, observing. What if the girl was lying? Could it be a scam? What if the kid was delusional?

And again and again, with each arrow, she wondered if it was true. More than anything, she wanted to hear from Natalie. What if something had happened to her? She couldn't think of a good reason for Natalie to take such a bold step by calling and then suddenly disappear.

Rocky imagined that she and Bob would have had children one day. They had thought that the time constraints rested with Rocky. But the punch line was that the time constraints had really been with Bob and his heart malfunction, not her maturing womb. Neither of them could have seen the twist that took them by surprise. Imagining that Natalie was part of Bob had opened a floodgate of unexpected maternal feelings in Rocky.

Would they have had children? They had not gone the route of fertility clinics, despite not using any kind of birth control for the last three years; they had just assumed that one day a baby would crash-land in their lives. "Let's just see what happens. Things always work out for us," Bob had said. He was proof positive that things don't always work out. Sometimes there is a disaster of such proportions that you don't ever get over it. The disaster tosses you into a blender, shreds whatever was known before as true, then spits out all the parts and says, *Now pull yourself back together.* The resulting creation is unrecognizable.

Anyone in the same room with Bob for more than ten minutes would have said that he'd make the best father because that was how Bob was with animals and kids. Rocky had never been as sure about her potential for mothering. She was uncomfortable with kids until they turned fifteen and sullen; she understood sullen, moody, sarcastic adolescents. Toddlers, babies, and eight-year-olds with huge new front teeth all looked somewhat alien to her, but Bob would have been perfect with a small child, showing her the way.

When Natalie appeared, she presented the perfect fully grown child who had in fact crash-landed in Rocky's life. The idea of ever having her own child had grown malformed and hazy after Bob died, but the nugget of the dream was ignited again with the cold call from Natalie. "I've been looking for my father." The feeling had started, much to Rocky's amazement, in her nipples—or rather, around her nipples, as if she had collided with a full migration of monarch butterflies as they flapped their way to Mexico, giving her areolae a tremor unlike any she had felt before. Yet she recognized it instantly, the instinct to suckle, absurdly late in this case if Bob really had been the father, if Natalie really was an instant stepdaughter. The faucet of mothering had been turned on, blurring Rocky's brain.

She retrieved the arrows, some of which had pierced the outer edge of the target, and then she walked back to her worn spot of grass and did it all over again, thwacking arrows with her beginner's mind. After two hours, she slumped on the ground, her right arm and shoulder screaming.

She dreaded calling Ray because she had waited so long. She knew what Caleb would say. *Man up, take care of your mess.* Rocky longed for someone else to do some of the heavy lifting. She hadn't realized there were so many hard things waiting for her until Bob died. When he was alive, the jobs of daily living were divided—maybe not evenly, but a division of shared burdens in any equation looked attractive now.

Rocky had picked up the phone a dozen times and had not been able to call Ray to tell him that she had decided to resign. If she wasn't a psychologist, who was she? She had worked like a demon to get through grad school: four years of course work after her bachelor's degree, plus a grueling dissertation and one additional year of clinical training. What was she thinking? Did she really want to throw away a perfectly good job?

She was no longer the wife of Bob; now she was Bob's widow, a job title that made her cringe. She was thirty-nine, too young to be called a widow. And now she had been betrayed by Hill. Would she have gone back to her old life if she had never heard Natalie's voice? The catch in the girl's voice had taken hold and carved out a clearing, like chain saws chewing through a forest.

Back at the cottage, Rocky turned the tap on and filled her coffee mug with water. Her mouth had gone suddenly dry. She drank the water down in three gulps. She carefully placed the mug in the uneven sink, the bottom worn into pocked erosion. She looked over her left shoulder to the phone. The cat had settled in next to Cooper along his backside. Now was the time, with everything in its place: the mug, the dog, the cat, and her parched throat.

Her watch glowed 1:23 P.M. Ray would be at the office, either on the computer or on the phone with his youngest son, who had just graduated from high school. No matter what he was doing, she was about to ruin his day.

"Hi, Ray. It's Rocky."

There was a pause, as if they were already staring each other down.

"So the phone lines do work out in Casco Bay. Good to hear your voice," he said.

Rocky heard the hope mixed with irritation.

"I'm not coming back to work," she said as quickly as she could, before the words grew fat in her throat and choked her.

Ray exhaled deeply. A door slammed. "That was not what I wanted to hear. You are leaving me high and dry. I don't want to lose you."

"I am so sorry. . . ."

"Is there anything I can say to change your mind? You know I don't have much wiggle room with salary. Are you okay?"

"It's not the salary. Every time I think about going back to my house, it's filled with the essence of who I used to be. I was a wife, and our house fit us perfectly, but that's not who I am now. Too much has happened. . . ." Rocky stopped to catch her breath, realizing that she hadn't offered one meaningful, concrete reason for quitting her job.

"I suppose your career change from psychologist to dogcatcher figures into this equation in some way that I can't fathom. Do you want to sleep on this for a few days and get back to me?"

She heard the hurt in his voice. "No. If I think about this any longer, my head is going to blow apart. This must look a little crazy from the outside, but the bottom line is that I'm staying here," said Rocky. "I just bought a house, and I'm going to remodel it."

"You bought a house?" His voice climbed an octave. "You should have told me. You had to be thinking about this for months. I needed to know long ago, not now when I've got to start a new job search. You know how this will affect all of us here. Thanks for the consideration. I am not going to say anything else because I'm too mad at you," he said, followed by a click and a dial tone.

Rocky was expecting everything he'd said, only worse. He was right: she had been selfish not to tell him when she truly knew that she wasn't returning. Ray had been generous and kind, and Rocky was a terrible human being.

Peterson suddenly decided to wash her chest, a difficult access point for a cat. She stuck her tongue out as far as possible and then dipped her head forward, hoping to make contact with her multicolored chest. Cooper lifted an ear to assess a noise, a rustle of leaves and dried grass. Rocky had at least two creatures who agreed with her choice to stay on the island.

After the shame of her procrastination was exposed, she felt a wave of relief wash over her, not unlike the time when she was five years old and her father made her take a stolen pencil back to the Cumberland Farms store. After she had confessed to the clerk, she had not been sent to live out her childhood in a prison cell; she had sucked in the sweetest breath of air. Just like she did after telling Ray that she had resigned.

Chapter 12

It had been five days since the abrupt call from Natalie. Rocky left two more messages, trying not to sound too urgent, trying to sound welcoming. She slept at the rental house just in case Natalie called.

As she surfaced from sleep, she heard the crows waking, calling each other. She pictured the crows as a pack of teenagers, texting each other constantly, from the moment they woke until night when they tucked their beaks under one wing and slept.

Rocky had taken to feeding the crows at Tess's house when she practiced archery. She spread dried bread and stale crackers and experimented with feeding them bits of meat, which they had liked quite a bit. The crows had clear preferences: they would not eat pineapple or oranges, and their enthusiasm for vegetables seemed to change from day to day. One day she left some carrot peelings, and they were the food delight of the day. The next time she brought carrot peelings the crows ignored them, leaving them to the jays, who were clearly lower in the avian hierarchy and willing to take the castoffs from the crows.

She had been going to Tess's house three times a week to practice. She preferred to go in the morning before the wind came up. She fed the crows only after the last arrow had pierced the paper target attached to her stack of hay bales. She practiced with her longbow for an hour, then she collected her arrows, took down the paper target with its concentric rings, and placed the arrow, bow, and target on Tess's deck. Finally, she went inside to get the food for the crows. Once she noticed the crows' interest, she did not vary her sequence of behaviors. This was classical conditioning at work, and she was glad that her least favorite part of graduate training finally had a palatable use.

After months of this regime, the crows arrived precisely when Rocky sent her last arrow slicing through the air. A call had gone out moments before from a scout stationed in the tree branches. Rocky could only assume that the call meant that she was nearing the end of the cycle that preceded the dispersal of food. It was not a large island, and the robust bark of a call could have been heard over most of the land—not all of it, but most of it.

Rocky knew that crows were capable of counting— or more to the point, she knew that humans had been able to discern the counting capabilities of crows. Thus, it was entirely possible that the scout was calling out a number to the entire murder of crows. *She has two more arrows left. Come and get it.* She heard odd quacking sounds from the crows, and she didn't yet know what those meant, but she had identified the general sound of *come and get it.*

Rocky had recently added one more element to the routine: changing the sequence of events slightly as an experiment. The experiment was so narcissistic that she was glad the crows couldn't tell anyone except the other crows. She had routinely said, "Hello, crows," when she arrived, and "Good-bye, crows," when she left. Did they have a name for her? Surely there was a special call for humans, although she had yet to decipher it. She wanted them to know her name. It seemed fair at this point in the relationship. In fact, she might have a better shot at a relationship with crows than with, say, a man. A man like Hill, who had said he was single, if separated. And then *bam,* his wife returns. The crows wouldn't ever do anything like that. Did they mate for life like mallards, swans, and voles?

Maybe the most she could hope for was that after consistently feeding them, the crows would learn her name.

Rocky had long known that food is the strongest way to reinforce an action or a sound, and that food must be solidly associated with the desired behavior to form a well-traveled route in the brain. As she put out the bread, she said, "Rocky, Rocky." This was a good two-syllable sound for the crows to learn. Who knows? And who knows when and how she would tell Hill about seeing Julie? How would she do it? Would he call her? Would he tell her instantly when he came to her house tonight for their previously planned dinner? Would he reach for her hand, looking glum and guilty, or awkward and pained, and spill it out?

Rocky and Bob had been married for eight years, and they had been together for a few years before that. She honestly couldn't remember how people break up. She wanted to hate Hill, but there was nothing similar to hate percolating through her. She was filled with wanting and desire, longing for his skin and breath. She wanted to tell him about Natalie, she wanted to be wrapped in his arms while she told him about the sound of Natalie's voice.

Everything Rocky knew and believed said that she needed to tell Hill exactly what she'd seen and talk it out before her feelings turned into a gangrenous wound. In a fit of passive pouting, she wanted him to bring it up. The image of Hill and Julie from the night before was intruding into her thoughts, her body, and a huge glob of rejection had taken over her heart.

As if nothing had happened, he called and left her a message: "I'm back and I can't wait to see you. We're on for dinner? See you after work. I'll stop at the fish market. Let me know if you want cod or monkfish. Or do you want me to choose?"

The terror of rejection had been as unpredictable as a lightning strike. There is no way to know how lightning will burn through the cognitive circuitry, leaving one victim with a lifelong limp, while another will never be able to smell onions again. Rocky had suddenly lost her senses, her belief in love after Bob, and her ability to say what she was thinking and feeling. Hill was going to leave her, and in the hierarchy of breakups he was going to take the high road—no phone breakup, but a face-to-face, which ranked much higher than a text message or e-mail.

She knew which ferry he'd take and exactly how long it would take him to walk from the dock to her house. When he was within a mile of the house, Cooper stood and went to the door, looking over his shoulder at her.

"I'd love to know how you do that. Is it sound or smell or canine radar?" Rocky asked the dog. "Does the man have a vibrational frequency that you can hear?"

Hill appeared along the dirt road, swinging a white plastic bag. Rocky desperately did not want to let on that her heart had smashed into the windshield as she sat in pulverized awareness in her car, watching Hill and Julie in the house. She hugged him, hands on his shoulders, keeping one iota of control.

"I brought a loaf of French bread from the bakery near the Casco Bay Line. I know you like their stuff. Can I tell you how great it is that school is out and I don't have a mountain of papers to grade?" His summer job was teaching English as a second language to recently immigrated Somalis, and there was absolutely no grading. He pulled the baguette out of the white plastic bag, which also held his selection of fish. How did he keep that strange rosiness to his cheeks? A mere thirty-two years old, he was younger than her by seven years. If she was trying to accumulate reasons to hate him, being younger didn't count. Was this the last time she'd ever see him? She took the bread and the plastic bag and tossed them on the counter.

"Come and sit," she said. All nine hundred square feet of the cottage pressed in on her as if she was out of alignment. She sat on the couch. If she had had an idea of how the night would go, it vanished when Hill arrived. Why wasn't she using every blasted communication skill that she promoted? Tell the man what she saw, ask for clarification, use "I," and tell him how she felt. Settle in for an adult conversation. Rocky grabbed the bottom edge of her T-shirt and pulled it over her head.

"Rocky?"

Good. She had startled him, and as if she watched from a distance, she had startled herself. Her sense of equilibrium had come unhinged. She reached in back and unhooked her bra, shrugging it off in front of her. She slipped next to him on the couch and closed her eyes when his hands found her breasts. The air around them softened her throat and the connective tissues that held her together. This was how her house would smell forever with Hill tucked into it: feral, fresh, full of want. She wanted to grab one morsel of how her life with him might be.

Rocky had not counted on loving a hunter, a man trained to mute his intentions as he waited for the inattentive moment with a deer or a pheasant. She had been inattentive, and he had deceived her. This was the last time she'd touch him, and the secret knowledge gave her a drunken edge.

"Are you sure?" he asked, sliding his hands over her ribs, articulating each one.

Her back arched like a sea serpent cresting. "Are *you* sure?" she asked. This was where he would tell her, his essential honesty coming through.

Hill's hand cupped her breast, and a sweet gust of breath escaped from his lips. "I have been sure since the first day I met you," he breathed into her ear.

An unclear and avoidant answer. Rocky slipped out of his arms and curled away from him, wishing that he would be the one to say it, to tell her about Julie. If he would do that, they might have the one-second window of opportunity to save themselves. But she had ambushed both of them with her preemptive strike.

"Weren't you going to tell me? I saw you with Julie," she said, her voice still thick and liquid. "You're going back, aren't you?" she asked, pushing damp hair from her face. She made a feeble attempt to claw her way out of the pit of vengeful blaming that now threatened to trap her indefinitely. The night air surrounded her, and she felt suddenly naked and unprotected. Foolish.

Hill, far from the land of words, his lips already full and languid, tried to surface with a strong swimmer's kick. His dark eyes remained dilated, and he froze in the assault of her accusation.

"No. Wait, how did you see Julie? Where? Jesus, what just happened? Rocky, this is not a black-and-white situation. We're neck deep into divorcing each other, but . . ." He paused, his entire body pulling toward her. He reached a hand out to her cheek and touched the wet that streamed down her face.

"Are you okay? This is not what I wanted to happen, not like this," he said, his words still heavy and thick.

"I drove to your house and saw you with her. You should have told me she was coming back. I trusted you," she said, scooping up her bra and shirt, wiping the moisture from her cheeks, wishing she hadn't cried, wishing she hadn't already done something that she'd regret. Rocky leapt up with her clothes and ran for the bathroom. She slammed the door.

She wadded her clothes into a ball and hugged them to her chest. Hill tapped on the door. "Go away!" she yelled.

Silence. Hill was not a persuader or a cajoler. He would not beg. If she told him to go away, he would. He mumbled something to Cooper as he passed through the kitchen. He let the screen door slam on the way out. She pressed her forehead against the bathroom door until Cooper whined in protest and she opened the door. The black dog looked at her, then toward the screen door, then back at her. This was a language she could understand. "Oh, shit," she said to the dog.

Rocky struggled back into her shirt, abandoning her bra, and ran out of the cottage, with Cooper at her heels. The gravel dug into her feet, slowing her usual long stride. She passed Melissa's house and saw Hill just ahead, near Bracken Road. "Hill, stop," she called to him. He must have been stunned, she thought, or he would have heard her wincing along. The man could hear a leaf fall from a tree. She caught up with him.

"I want to know why. Why weren't you going to tell me?" she said.

Hill's eyes were red, but it was his anger that made her stop. Every protective mechanism in her system told her to back up, danger. He looked like he had been struck with a sharp stick: fists clenched, muscles tight, eyes dark and steady, lips fixed over his immobile jaw. She had never seen him like this.

"I thought you were leaving me, that you were coming here to tell me that it was over, you were going back to Julie. I should have said something. . . ." She extended one hand toward him and then pulled back.

"This is not at all like me," she said. "I'm in unknown territory. Bob never, I mean, neither of us ever wandered." Wandered? "I didn't know I would feel this horrible, it never occurred to me that you would lie." Her teeth had begun to chatter, and not from cold, even though a breeze foretold rain. She looked over his shoulder and saw a bank of dark clouds advancing on the island.

Hill closed his eyes for a few seconds and his breathing changed; he was struggling for control, fighting against a force that clawed at him.

She knew she was supposed to say how she felt without accusing, labeling, or attacking. She knew everything she was supposed to say—she was the freaking expert at teaching this to young couples when they fell from grace into the first dark pit of fighting. So why was it so hard to say?

"I was afraid," she said finally. "And now I'm so embarrassed, no, mortified, that it is taking every bit of strength to stand here instead of running away."

Hill exhaled a long slow breath. She caught a new scent from him, hormone fueled, with an underlay of adrenaline.

"Why didn't you just say something, ask me? Isn't this what psychologists do, they communicate?" he said, flexing his fingers, releasing tension. A dim flash of lightning illumined a deep section of the incoming blanket of clouds. The long delay before the rumble of thunder meant the storm was still far off.

"Bob and I went from point A to point B, and we just kept going, we never veered from each other. I never thought of leaving him and never imagined that he'd leave me," said Rocky.

"And yet he did leave you."

Rocky nodded dumbly as the words hit her from a new angle, slicing in with discomfort, revealing the core of her fear.

"You're the widow, I know, the sad one, but have you noticed that I'm going through a divorce and it's the hardest thing I've ever done?"

She started to answer until Hill put up his hand. "I know that Bob can never come back. . . ."

"And Julie *can* come back," Rocky said.

Cooper, who had been pressed into Rocky's legs the entire time, turned and trotted off. She heard the quick, young footsteps a moment later.

"Hey," said Melissa, looking at both of them. "Whoops, looks like I'm interrupting something."

"No," said Hill, with a deep weariness in his voice. "I was just leaving."

"Are we having a fight, or are you leaving for good?" asked Rocky.

"We are having a fight, and I'm leaving to go home and shoot about one hundred arrows into a hay bale."

Chapter 13

Hill

When he was a child, he assumed that everyone knew about the way to catch anger and pain, that if caught quickly it was nothing more than an ugly thing that lived on the outside of the body, like a crumpled Kevlar shield. He had learned to meet anger and pain head-on, like the rip-roaring dragons that they were, and when he held his ground they changed into whatever lived underneath. His grandmother had taught him this, the very same grandmother who had taught him to hunt for deer and, if they were very lucky, pheasants.

She had warned him about testosterone long before the full effect of it kicked in. They had been up near Canada when he was ten. His grandmother was one of the best archers he ever met. She used a longbow her whole life and would never consider a compound bow, not even when she hit eighty and her arm muscles grew smaller and softer. They had settled in a high tree blind on the first day of bow season.

"I've been coming back to this blind for thirty-seven years," said his grandmother. "Since before your father was born. I've repaired it so many times that the birds must think I'm a neighbor." She sat on a piece of wood five inches off the platform, enough to let her rise with ease if she heard a deer, notch an arrow, pull back, and take aim. She rarely talked.

"If your grandfather was here, he might tell you something different about testosterone. Men like to brag about it, and I've never heard a man say one sensible, helpful thing about something so powerful, frightening, and wonderful. But I want you to listen to me. In a few years your thinking is going to get disturbed. You'll get angry quicker, you'll want to punch a hole in the wall, other boys will want to pull you into a fight, and if your heart gets broken, you could lose your mind," she said.

In the distance, they saw a doe and a yearling. His grandmother wasn't interested in them.

"How do you know I'll do all those things? I might not," he said. His feet had gone to sleep, so he shifted and endured the hot prickles as his feet woke up again.

"Because of testosterone. It will feel like someone opened up your skull and poured a drug into your brain, and at first it will be very hard to control. When it feels like someone has hurt you and you get good and mad, there's something I want you to do to make your brain work again. I want you to get your bow and as many arrows as I hope you'll always have. You'll need to steady your breathing first, soften your knees like I keep telling you to do, and let all your focus go to the center of the target. That's what will work off the anger and pain so you can get underneath it. It could take hours at first. But if you let anger and pain lead you around by the nose, that testosterone will be like throwing gasoline on a fire."

He heard a crow in the distance. He didn't think they were going to get a deer today. Grandma was talking too much.

She shifted her weight and opened her plaid wool jacket at the neck.

"You're going to get nice muscles too, which will help in archery. Testosterone can make you fast. You'll like that part. I'd buy some testosterone if I could get my hands on some, just for the upper body strength. Have you been paying attention to anything that I've said?"

"Grandma, will you still love me when the testosterone comes?" He was suddenly afraid of the future, of smelling like the eight-point buck that they hunted, of losing his mind.

"Oh, we're in this forever," she had said, rubbing his hair.

When Hill returned from Rocky's house, he opened the creaky gate to his backyard, where he kept his target range set up year-round and still taught a few students. He went into the garage and got out his longbow and every arrow that he had. He set up with the bow, steadied his breath, softened his knees, and let his focus stay on the target. He shot again and again, for the longest time that he could remember. When his upper body muscles cried for mercy, he sat down on top of his picnic table and saw what was beneath the anger. He still wanted her. He wanted to be in this forever with Rocky.

Chapter 14

The phone hung heavy in her hand like a gun. Rocky had traced each digit of Natalie's phone number on a pad of yellow Post-it notes until the number was etched through five layers. The desire to call the girl was unrelenting. Rocky had no choice but to call her again, yet she fought against it, digging in with her full weight, as if by doing so she could stop the force of the girl coming toward her. Natalie had probably regretted calling her in the first place and was long gone. Rocky punched in the numbers.

This time Natalie answered on the first ring.

"This is Rocky. I'd like to meet you and help you figure out if Bob was your father," she blurted out before the girl could bolt like a wild horse.

"I got your messages. I was afraid of what you'd say. Are you sure? I mean, I know I came out of nowhere and kind of surprised you," said Natalie.

"I have to transport a dog tomorrow. I'll be in Portland. I can meet you at the Casco Bay ferry on Commercial Street. I'll have on a baseball cap that says PEAKS ISLAND. There are benches right along the street. Three o'clock. Can you be there? Is that too far for you to come?" Rocky said, her speech jerky and abbreviated.

"I'll be there," Natalie said.

Rocky had to deliver the first canine calamity of the season: a basset hound who had been found howling along Island Avenue. He was only a minor calamity; this was a dog that someone would ultimately claim—if not the owners, then the first people who went window-shopping through the shelter. The dog was huge for a basset hound, shaped more like a walrus, and he was a gentle talker, a smooth baritone with imploring eyes who promised loyalty.

"Good luck," she said as the hound bayed at her. All hounds sounded like they spoke the same few sentences. *I've found something right here, I can smell it! Let's go, times a-wasting.* Rocky admired their singular nature and their fresh joy at each discovery. What would she discover on the park bench by the ferry?

She spotted the girl immediately. Natalie looked like one of the lost children out of a Dickens novel. The day was warm, and yet she had on a wool cap, beneath which her shoulder-length hair stuck out in a soft cloud of blond. She looked like the kids in the magazine articles who were tossed out by their families or who ran away and lived on the streets selling whatever they had—sex or drugs—to live. Her socks came up to her knees, and her shoes were silver wedge sandals. Her shorts were rolled up too high, and tender flesh expanded at the edge of the denim roll. Her sweater was impossibly tight. If Rocky had to guess— and she tried very hard not to—she would have said that Natalie's body language alerted every male from Portland to the Canadian border. Nearly every generation of kids exhibits highly sexualized clothing or behavior in order to notify others of their ilk that they are available for mating. They are members of a tribe, and the tribe calls for a sexual drumbeat, whether the kids are in Ohio or Borneo.

The girl wore a ragged green hoodie over the thin sweater, zipped just shy of her breasts. This was Rocky's last chance to observe her before Natalie knew she was being watched. Rocky searched for signs of Bob in the girl's bone structure, her shoulders, the shape of her knees. Rocky gulped in a breath of air. This could be anything: a bad hoax, a desperate kid trying hard to believe that she had a tendril of connection. Or Bob's daughter.

Her hands gripped the steering wheel. More than anything, she realized, she wanted this girl to be Bob's child. More than air, water, food, blood. Please, she prayed, be his child, and I will take you in, and I will tuck you safely into a house in the center of the island. Just in case Bob was listening over her shoulder, as she felt that he did from time to time, she didn't want to entirely let him off the hook.

"Bob, I'm going to kill you if this is your kid. Except you're already dead. Thanks a lot."

She wrapped her damp palm around the door handle, ready to press down, when a soft buzz vibrated near her ear. Rocky swatted at her head, ducking a bit. The cab of the truck was a small space, and she couldn't find a bee or any other insect to account for the noise. Had Bob turned into this, a wisp of air with a strange hum in a language she couldn't decode? Would she have told Hill about the odd moment when her hand hovered on the door handle? Or had she still kept Bob hermetically sealed from Hill? She felt just as alone as she'd been when she'd arrived on the island eight months earlier, when she had been fresh from a summer of gut-twisting grief. She opened the door.

Rocky stepped out of the truck and realigned her body, the way Hill had instructed her to do during archery practice. She kept her knees soft and let her weight fall downward, extending through the earth.

"Natalie?" Rocky sat down next to her with space enough for another person between them. She was sure the girl could see the pounding of her heart, the way she had to swallow several times before speaking.

The girl held a bag on her lap, stained canvas, one strap hooked around her shoulder. She didn't look surprised. Where had Rocky seen this look before?

Since she had begun practicing psychotherapy, she'd cataloged the first expressions of therapy clients when she encountered them. When she met them in the waiting room of the counseling center, she took in two things: the handshake and the expression. Either their faces were pulled into the hyperalertness of anxiety, muscles tight and hands damp with the sweat of dread, or they were on the other end of the spectrum, their entire corporeal form pulled downward by the weight of depression, facial muscles sagging, eyes daring the world to say one positive thing. She knew that she was meeting people on one of their worst days—why else would they be looking for a therapist?—but still they fell consistently into the two main camps. The handshakes had more delicate permutations, ranging from the constant state of withdrawal of those who dreaded touching another human to the studied firmness of those who were determined to mark their status. The handshake was the only time when Rocky touched a client, and she tried to make the most of it diagnostically. Graduate training had been unequivocal about maintaining physical boundaries between therapists and clients. Rocky relished first contact and envied the massage therapists, reflexologists, and other body therapists who had the entire body from which to understand clients.

A soft breeze lifted off the bay and found the bench. A nearby food cart sold organic, freshly squeezed lemonade and hot dogs. What two things could be farther apart on the nutritional scale? She stuck out her hand to Natalie, who had still not spoken a word.

"I'm glad you could make it," said Rocky, wrapping her fingers around Natalie's hand. She detected an effort on the girl's part, right after a pause. She could almost hear a voice in the girl's head that said, *Give a firm handshake.*

"Now it's your turn to say something," said Rocky, smiling with encouragement.

The girl pulled her hand back to the canvas bag. "Thanks for coming. This is so important to me. It's weird, like I missed my one chance to find out who my father is and I was too late. He was really out here, I had a father, and I missed him. That kind of fits my life, you know what I'm saying?"

"Hold on, let's back up. What makes you think Bob was your father?" Rocky looked longingly at the lemonade, but she didn't want to break the spell of the moment.

"I grew up in foster care. When you turn eighteen, you can get your own records. I was legally emancipated when I was seventeen. No, that's not right. My caseworker said it wasn't really emancipation, but it felt like it to me. Do you know what that is?"

"I do. It's not easy to go through the court process. I know you had to have a way of proving that you could support yourself financially, which is incredibly hard. Was it worth it? You would have been on your own at age eighteen anyhow."

"I guess you've never gone through foster care. Yeah, it was worth it."

The sting of Natalie's words found a tender, unprotected spot in Rocky's chest.

"So again, what makes you think my husband was your father?"

Natalie bit down on her lower lip, as if she was hesitating. "I have two different copies of my birth certificate. One went with my records and didn't list a father. My mother must have refused to list a father. And that's the one that has traveled with me. But then there's this birth certificate. Look at this one."

Natalie pulled the satchel close to her body and dug into it, extracting a manila envelope. She opened it and slid out a folder. She opened the folder on her lap and peeled off the first page, handing it to Rocky.

The horn on a ferry sounded a departure blast. A man pushed a shopping cart filled with a sleeping bag and a small backpack surrounded by bottles and cans; he rolled to a stop under the shade of a small tree. Two boys jumped their skateboards down the wide, low steps of the park, and the hard wheels smacked the concrete. Rocky took the paper from the girl and pulled it toward her as if the air had turned thick and resistant to movement.

She forced herself to start at the top. "Birth Certificate." "Live Birth. Eight pounds, three ounces. Female." She saw that Natalie had just turned eighteen a few months ago. Mother: Paulette Davis, age twenty-one. Father: Robert Tilbe, age twenty-four. Ames, Iowa.

Robert Tilbe. The sight of his name in print, on something official, disoriented her. Rocky took a sharp breath in through her nose and felt the muscles along her neck tighten. He would have been enrolled at the University in Ames when he was twenty-four.

"Why do you have two birth certificates? Can I see the other one?" said Rocky. She gripped the birth certificate with Bob's name on it. She rubbed her pointer finger along his name.

"Here," said Natalie. "You can look at the original, because that's the one that I thought was right for a long time. Like, my whole life. But when I asked for my records, because I just wanted to see everything that had happened to me and what Protective Services had done and said, and you can't believe how ginormous my file was, that's when I found the one with Robert Tilbe's name on it."

Natalie slid another document out of the folder and handed it to Rocky. The fingers holding the paper were small and delicate, the fingernails bitten low and jagged. Not like Bob, nothing about him was delicate. Natalie's eyes were wide open and brown.

The other document listed the father as unknown. The girl could have shown her the first document and never let this other one surface. That would have been more convincing. The kid was either scrupulously honest or she was several steps ahead of Rocky.

"Why now?" said Rocky, glancing down at Natalie's hands, the chipped nail polish and the macramé friend- ship bracelet.

Natalie looked down, suddenly overtaken by a shy wind. When she looked up, her eyes overflowed, and she quickly wiped her cheeks with the back of her hand.

"Because I wanted to know if I had anybody. You know, everyone kind of belongs somewhere, and I wanted to find out if I belonged."

If he had left her with a daughter, she'd . . . what? What would Rocky do? Would she suddenly belong somewhere too? Would she have somebody?

"Where are you living now? I know you said Worcester, but what are you doing there?" said Rocky.

"I'm kind of in between jobs. And I've rented a room in a guy's house in Portland. I found it on Craigslist. I was going to come to Portland anyhow, so don't think I'm stalking you or anything. It could just be for the summer. He's okay, a little loud when he gets drunk, but he's okay. I know how to take care of myself."

Rocky pictured the girl living with a guy who got a little loud when he was drunk and all the things that could go wrong. Natalie hadn't said that she was living in Portland when she first called.

"Have you found a job yet? Please tell me you have a job."

Natalie stuck her chin out in a way that looked new, like she was trying it out. "I'm applying. I have fast-food experience."

Rocky crossed one sandaled foot over a knee. "You don't have any income, and you're renting from a guy who gets drunk. This is a bit worrisome. Can you get help from any of the foster families you lived with?"

Natalie gathered her papers together, mashing them into her canvas bag. "You have no idea about foster care, do you? When the families are done with you, they are really done. And I didn't exactly leave on the best terms with the last family."

Natalie got up. If the girl had been a golden retriever, or a cocker spaniel, or a mutt, Rocky would have scooped her up, made sure that she had food to eat and a safe place to sleep. She'd have scratched behind her ears and tried very hard to let her know that not all humans were weirdos who dumped dogs in scary places like an interstate highway. She might have fostered her until a home could be found. She didn't like the idea of Natalie crashing with a guy who drank too much. At age eighteen, the girl would think that she could handle the situation; she wouldn't know about the way things could go sideways.

"Wait a minute," said Rocky. "There are already about twenty permutations of how this thing could go. We have to find out things that are important to you and to me. If Bob was your father, we have to consider that he didn't know about you. If Bob truly was your biological father, then all of this is new to me. But it might mean something good to you. Or not, I don't know. Maybe it will be worse for you if you find out he was your father. But in the midst of it, I don't think I can stand the thought of you living in a skeezy apartment with a guy who gets loud and drunk." Rocky took a breath, as if she were going to dive to the bottom of a pool. "I have a spare bedroom that you could use for a very limited amount of time until we get this figured out. If you get a job, you should pay me something for rent." She did not want the girl to walk away, to live with a drunk guy she found on Craigslist.

Natalie was in line with the sun, and Rocky had to shade her eyes to keep looking at the girl. "Until we figure this out, you're welcome to stay there. It's summer. There might be a little work in Portland or Peaks."

"I didn't come here asking for a place to live. I don't need someone taking care of me," said Natalie.

"I can hardly take care of myself," Rocky responded. "But this is important. Bob's name is on that birth certificate, and I want to know why. Or some Robert Tilbe is on it. I guess you're desperate to find out or you wouldn't be here. It's like a business offer," said Rocky, trying to sound official so she wouldn't scare the girl off. She leaned back on the bench, feeling exhausted but suddenly less alone.

"Maybe," said Natalie, "Maybe for a few days. But I can leave anytime that I want to. And I'm not a kid. I'm eighteen."

"Deal. You can leave anytime you want to. Me too."

Chapter 15

Natalie had been at Rocky's for three days, taking the ferry to Portland each day to look for a job, returning each day on the six o'clock to say that she had put in job applications, looking discouraged. What would have been different for Natalie if Bob had been able to read her stories at night, slather peanut butter on crackers for her, and watch proudly as she kicked a soccer ball with the other kids? Rocky played the scenario a hundred times in her head. Would Natalie be a first-year college student by now? Would her biggest worry in life be who to sit with at the dining commons? And would Rocky have been the complicated stepmother—never enough, never right?

Rocky wanted to refuel Natalie, go back to the beginning and drain off the foster care of fourteen years. If Bob were here, his big mountain-sized steadiness might brace her up, even at this late date.

What did Rocky have to offer a kid who wasn't a client at the local college? Was she anything at all like a parent? Should she inquire about the job search as she might with a friend or a roommate? Should she bolster the girl up with the bottomless well of support that a parent can provide? Or should she just help Natalie figure out the truth of her background?

Natalie walked into the house and held out her hand to Cooper. The dog dropped his tail and smelled her pant legs and her feet, as if he were vacuuming her.

Natalie backed up with the core of her body, arching away from the dog.

"You're bringing Cooper all the good smells of Portland. He's just curious," said Rocky. The girl looked unaccustomed to dogs.

"Good dog," said Natalie, sliding her hand into her pants pocket, moving away from him.

Rocky knelt by Cooper, ruffling the fur around his neck to demonstrate his koala bear nature. "He's a big hunk of burning love. Everybody loves this guy, but take your time with him if you're not used to dogs."

The next day Rocky had been up since sunrise, and she and Cooper had already walked the beaches and trails for an hour. She'd had coffee, fed the dog, and looked over her sketches for the house remodel yet again. Natalie began to rustle in the bedroom.

The corroded hinges of the bedroom door announced the girl. Natalie wore a tank top covered by a faux Western shirt. Rocky admired the aim at personal distinction: the shirt came complete with snaps at the cuffs and two pointed triangle tips over each breast.

"Help yourself to cereal. I've got the boring kind, but I see you bought cereal also. Let me know if you need anything," said Rocky, looking up from her drawings on newsprint.

"So it's okay if I open the fridge?" said Natalie, looking every bit like a dog that has been kicked on a regular schedule.

Natalie had asked the same question each day, and each time it left a dark bruise on Rocky as she wondered about places where the fridge was off limits. "It's okay to open the fridge, and before you ask about the one inch of milk left in the bottle, yes, it's okay to finish the last of the milk. In fact, I beg you to finish the last of the milk." Was Natalie too brittle for the slightest bit of joking?

The first time Rocky met a college student who had lived nearly her entire life in foster homes, the landscape in her counseling office had curdled. The student had come from a state that declared eighteen-year-olds adults and no longer in need of support. Her foster family said good-bye and good luck. The student showed up at the counseling center dazed and terrified before Thanksgiving vacation, wondering where she was supposed to go when the dorms closed. Rocky had hooked her up with a group of foreign exchange students who were in the same boat, but for a different reason.

Ray, her now former boss at the counseling center, had told her, "A lot of college kids go through struggles with their parents, and maybe they've got a parent who's a little crazy or demanding or even a son of a bitch. But when the kids call home, someone answers the phone. That's the true dividing line with students who were foster kids: there's no one at the other end of the line."

Natalie took out the carton of milk and poured the last of it over a cereal that she had picked out at the grocery store yesterday. The little bits of cereal were multicolored in vivid Crayola style.

"Wow. It's hard to know if you should eat that or use it to paint the house," said Rocky.

Natalie pulled the bowl toward her on the counter, hemming it in protectively with her hands. Rocky cringed, hearing how her words could have sounded like criticism instead of friendliness in Natalie's world. "This is my favorite cereal," the girl said. "It's been my favorite since I was in first grade, except I couldn't ever have it with one of my first foster families. I was with them until I was five. They kept me in the basement when I wasn't in school, and it wasn't like a really great finished basement with rugs and stuff. This was a bed-next-to-an-oil-burner kind of basement. And they wouldn't let me eat with them. I only remember eating meals at school."

Rocky's jaw tightened. She wanted to reach back in time and pull the child to safety.

"I've just always wondered why they wouldn't want a five-year-old girl to eat. I'd kind of like to go back and ask them, you know what I'm saying?"

Rocky crumpled when the girl spoke. It was the crystalline purity of the question, without revenge or malice, the open honesty that unhinged her.

"There's no good answer to your question. They were either ignorant beyond belief, damaged at the core, or malicious as all get out. They were wrong to mistreat a small child," said Rocky. She wanted to leave the land of hungry kids in basements behind them. "Do you want to go look at a house with me? I bought it, and almost everyone but me thinks it's a disaster."

Natalie pulled a chair out from the maple table and sat down. Rocky scooted the drawings closer to her side of the table, eager to make room for the girl.

"But you told me that you already have a house back in Massachusetts. Why would you need two? Who needs two houses? It wasn't like you and my father had kids or anything."

You and my father. Hearing the words felt like a pin inserted under Rocky's eyelid. Natalie said it so definitively. Why did she get the sense that she had done something wrong, that she had stolen Bob from the girl?

"What matters now is that you're here," said Rocky. "We'll figure out the rest later. Finish your paint-chip cereal and we'll take a walk to the other house."

She wanted to see Natalie's reaction to the house, not that she expected any expertise from the girl. Did she want to use the house as a Rorschach test, a place onto which this tormented kid could project her dreams and fears?

Rocky had forgotten how long it takes girls to get ready. What could Natalie be doing in the bathroom? Restructuring each hair follicle?

After half an hour, Rocky began to remember exactly how long it takes girls to primp for public appearances.

"Natalie, I'm leaving. You said you wanted to see the house."

Cooper sensed a departure and was already at the door, looking back at Rocky. The bathroom door opened, blowing out a heavily scented cloud of skin lotions, hair products, even a deodorant layered with chemicals meant to mimic flowers, musk, something lemony, all brewed in a mixture that made Rocky's eyes water.

"I'm ready," said Natalie, adjusting her hair with the slightest touch, moving it a fraction of an inch closer to her face, not away.

Natalie and Rocky walked through the empty rooms of the old place, opening windows, letting accumulated moisture escape. The living room had a fireplace, the face of which was brick painted white but darkened by smoke to an uneven gray. The remnants of nuts, left by opportunistic rodents, lay scattered around the grate. The fireplace pulled at Rocky, wanting more, wanting the gurgle of voices gathered around a warm fire, not the damp ash of neglect.

Rocky ran a hand along the brick mantel. "I hope this thing works. I love a fireplace. I mean, they're not the most energy-efficient, but they make up for it in atmosphere."

Natalie put a hesitant foot on the hearth. "We had one of these in one foster family. The dad said it smoked up the house." She withdrew from the hearth as if it were too hot for her feet.

Natalie walked lightly, making only a faint connection with the floor, as if she were weightless. The girl was the very image of ripeness common among girls in the hard years of late teens to early twenties. Ray had called them "the simian years." But she lacked something that kept her attached. What elemental substance had been omitted from Natalie's development as she advanced from foster home to foster home?

"So you could just buy this place?" asked the girl.

Rocky heard the subtext about money, about having enough money to see something that she wanted and the power to buy it.

"I'm making a giant, scary shift in my life," said Rocky. "I don't know what the full picture is yet, but yes, I was able to buy this house. There's something about it that I can imagine. I want it to be a warm and happy place again."

Natalie ran a hand over the kitchen counter. "And so, you're the dog warden on the island? You've gone from psychologist to dog warden. Isn't that like a weird career move? You're not going back to your house in Massachusetts?"

Rocky pushed up the sleeves of her shirt. "I've been on a strange career trajectory for some time."

Natalie turned her back to the counter and hoisted her butt onto the ledge of Formica.

"Is this okay? Can I sit here? I had one foster mother who would have had a fit if I even came into the kitchen, never mind sat on the counter. Except it was okay for her kids. She had two boys."

Rocky looked around at the wreck of the empty house. "This is essentially a work zone. The counter is earmarked for the Dumpster within days. You don't need to be careful." Had Natalie felt at home anywhere? "How long did you live with your birth mother? What happened?"

Rocky hadn't meant to ask so abruptly. She sounded as subtle as a meteorite falling from the sky, but it was what she had been thinking about since the moment she woke up.

Natalie looked at a place where the wall met the ceiling. "I sort of remember her, I think I do. But my old caseworker said it's not possible. I was two years old when I was first taken away because she was arrested for drugs. She took some big dive into crack that middle-class white girls aren't supposed to do, especially not the ones from Iowa. She was ahead of the curve. When she got arrested, she was so high that she forgot to tell them that she had a kid and that the kid was alone in the apartment. When someone finally found me, I'd been there for three days. There wasn't any food in the apartment. It's good not to remember things from when you're little. My old caseworker said some part of me might remember, but I don't know what part."

Cooper settled in near Rocky's feet, sliding to the floor with his rump against her shoes.

"My mother spent eighteen months in Ludlow prison, and when she came out she didn't pause to let any dust settle on her. She went back to crack and disappeared. Gone. I guess there are a lot of places where someone can disappear."

"Ludlow? That's in Massachusetts. I thought you were born in Iowa."

"I was. But my mother didn't stay there. Something happened, I don't know what, and she moved to Massachusetts, so that's where I entered the system. That's what they call it, 'entering the system.'"

Rocky reached down and stroked Cooper's head. "Did you ever see her again?"

Natalie rubbed the back of her neck and rolled her head from side to side as if she was adjusting her muscles.

"I was four the last time I saw her. It was a supervised visit at the caseworker's office. I remember sitting on a woman's lap. We were both kind of skinny, our bones rubbed together. She told me that I was her little girl and that was the last time that anyone ever said that to me. She died right after that, out west somewhere.

Do you know how many times I've recited this to shrinks? I don't want to talk about it anymore," she said.

"Me either," said Rocky. And she really meant it. If she heard one more word about four-year-old Natalie, she wasn't sure that she could stand it.

"Let me show you the upstairs and maybe you can give me some ideas," said Rocky, running her fingers through her dark curly hair. "The thing with a remodel is that you can get a fresh start and make a house however you want it to be. Tell me how you'd like a house if you could start over." Was she telling Natalie that she could start over, or was she telling herself? They gingerly walked up the narrow staircase, each step creaking in response. The banister was burnished from over eighty years of hands.

Cooper, who didn't like stairways, waited at the bottom of the steps, ears up.

Four bedrooms upstairs held a powdered scent, mixed with damp sea air. Rocky had discovered oak floors under the wall-to-wall carpet; she could already picture the sanded gleam of the wood with sunlight streaming across them. They walked into the smallest bedroom.

"Most old houses have very little closet space. These two bedrooms actually share one closet," said Rocky, opening a door. "Look, if you go through this closet, you come through into the other bedroom. Kids must have loved this. Take a look."

As Natalie poked her head into the closet, Cooper barked. The dog rarely barked, so Rocky immediately left the room and trotted downstairs to see if anyone had come to the house. No sooner had she gotten to the bottom of the stairs than she heard a pounding sound from upstairs.

"Hey, this is not funny. Let me out of here!" It was Natalie, but it sounded like she was in a box.

Rocky flew back up the stairs, taking the steps two at a time. The closet door was shut, and Natalie was pounding so hard on the door that it vibrated. With a tug, Rocky pulled it open, and Natalie exploded from the closet as if it was devoid of oxygen.

"What did you do that for?" asked Natalie, dusting off her clothes.

"I didn't do anything. We've got all the windows open downstairs, and the wind probably just slammed the door shut. Are you okay?" The girl had been in the closet for little more than a minute, yet she was clearly shaken. If Rocky could have reprimanded the house for bad behavior, she would have.

"I'm fine," said Natalie, mustering up an unconvincing level of bravado. "Let's see the rest of your house."

Natalie had little to offer in remodeling ideas other than putting in a larger bathroom. "This is disgusting," she said when she saw the tiny upstairs bath with the green sink on pitted aluminum legs.

"I know it's hard to see the potential of a house, especially when it's been abandoned for years," said Rocky. She wanted the house to reach out and inject hope into the girl, to draw her in, not slam her in a closet. She'd give Natalie more time to get used to the house.

Cooper was in exactly the same spot when they came back down.

"I think it's unanimous: the house needs a lot of help," said Rocky. "Let's head back to the cottage. I know you said that laundry was on your list, and I've got to drive around the island to check on our feral cat population."

She had almost said "home," *let's go home,* and she wondered if Natalie had heard the unsaid words brimming up in her throat. They walked back in silence, with Cooper peeing on critical canine communiqué outposts every twenty feet. Compared to the old Costello house, the rental cottage looked simple and uncomplicated, like a plain burger, no pickles, no lettuce. Cooper drank deeply from his water dish and then stretched out long on his favorite spot by the slid-ing glass door.

"What's up with this statue?" asked Natalie. She nodded her head toward the one piece of artwork in Rocky's house, poised on an end table by the couch.

The two-foot-tall sculpture, lovingly carved, was of a woman playing the saxophone, eyes closed in ecstasy, dress blowing, knees splayed slightly as she leaned back into the music.

"That's from my brother, Caleb. It was a prototype for his musical sculptures. He's got a waiting list now, people are crazy about them. I'm sort of his business contact for Portland, where he sells them. His newest one is a fiddle player standing on one toe."

Natalie had gathered a bag of dirty clothes and was headed to the one Laundromat on Peaks, but some-thing stopped her.

"What's it like to have a brother? I mean, it sounds like you like him or understand him."

Rocky turned the saxophone woman about a quarter-turn to the sun, as if it was a philodendron.

"When we were growing up, he had a learning disabil-ity. He was two years younger, so I looked after him. He describes it as me beating the daylights out of the bullies who picked on him. Then at some point it all switched around, and he became my friend, my go-to guy."

Rocky was going to say more and tell the girl how her brother propped her up after Bob died, how he was the only person who was willing to tell her that she looked like shit after grief threatened to drown her. But talking about Bob with Natalie was filled with land mines. Natalie had never once said, *Sorry about your husband collapsing on your bathroom floor and dying.* Even with a teenager's neophyte system of empathy, this felt like a harsh oversight. Had life been that hard for Natalie?

"I don't have a brother or a sister. Not that I know of. Sometimes the foster parents said that all of us were like brothers and sisters in their house, but we weren't ever going to be family. We don't do lunch, send birthday cards, or call at Christmas," said Natalie.

Cooper picked up his head from where it had rested on his front paws. He tilted his head, listening to a sound beyond the narrow band available to humans.

"Who were you close to? Of all the families you lived with, who could you talk to about important stuff?" asked Rocky.

Natalie bent over to pick up the white plastic bag of laundry. "It wasn't any of the families. It was one of the caseworkers. Not that she was so special, but she was there for a lot of the switches from one home to another. Then she left. She had a baby of her own. I guess her baby was more important."

Natalie lifted the bag and held it in front of her in a peculiar way, not hoisted over one shoulder, as Rocky would have done.

"But who did you talk with about emotional things, about dating, or dreams of what you wanted, you know?" asked Rocky, following the girl to the door.

Natalie turned to face Rocky, keeping the plastic bag between them. "You still don't get it. I didn't have a brother who grew up to become my go-to guy. I didn't have anybody, and if I had dreams, I kept them close to me so that no one could steal them in the middle of the night."

Rocky placed a hand on the door frame. "You're right. I don't know what it was like for you. If you want to tell me more, I'd like to listen."

Natalie's chin shook minutely. "Why would you want to listen? I mean, why would you care?"

Rocky bit her lip and did not attempt to crack through the rhetorical question. But as Natalie walked away with her bag of dirty clothes, the question settled around her shoulders.

Chapter 16

Cooper

He shut his eyes in order to see. A trumpet of scents opened up a stellar universe, larger than anything his eyes would ever see.

His kind was different from wolves in a fundamental way that had to do with what the long snout searched for in the world of smells. When it came to sniffing out humans, wolves scanned for the acrid scent of humans in order to survive by avoidance; they determined if humans were near, and if so, how close they were and what threat they carried? The canines who had long since come in from the wild had unearthed endless ripples of meaning about humans: they had dissected their chemistry and understood their clang of fears, the splash of anger and the tremble of devotion that drove them like thunder. There was nuance to the rush of scents, and it helped if he closed his eyes. If anything, the canines who had bonded with humans long ago were now more complex than the wolves.

The black dog discerned the small and large agonies of his pack. The girl, Melissa, circled food with the bold flash of a warrior, and he helped her as much as he could, sighing bravery into her hands as she ran her fingers through his fur. He accepted her skirmishes with food, her need to hide from the very substance of life as if it were the enemy. It was not his battle, but he understood the depth of her courage when he smelled it on her, and for that he loved her as he would love a pup with large awkward paws.

His companion, Rocky, grew stronger each day, filling up with the tender buds of beach, water, sticks and leaving the land of grief and the search for the dead. He had tried to lead her with his breath, with his eyes, with the endless permutations of tail wagging, his ears turned this way and that, his spine curling in ecstasy, but her comprehension, as with all humans, was unreliable. Still, he had seen the look in her eyes that canines do not find with all humans, and he was grateful to have found her. She was his, and he would never be taken from her.

But the new one, the visitor, clouded her intent, twisted the flow of chemicals that pulsed out of her skin in puddles, and caused the black dog to swallow light, to curl his tongue, to make ready his long bones. She was without a pack, a perilous state for dogs and humans. She was young, not much more than a pup in human terms. Even so, a tiny cloaked molecule coursed through her, so well hidden that a lesser dog might have missed it, and even he was not entirely sure of its meaning. Now that Cooper had sensed it, he would wait. He closed his eyes to see.

Chapter 17

Tess

Tess's granddaughter had just celebrated her seventh birthday, and as her birthday gift, Tess had invited her to Peaks Island for a sleepover all by herself. Usually Danielle came with her little brother, Sam, and they slept together in their grandmother's loft, or all three of them slept on the new screened porch. Coming alone was special, and the news of it had made Danielle squeal with joy.

They ate pizza on the deck near the ferry. In the summer, the restaurant near the dock pumped out its loudest selection of music. Tess wore earplugs. Danielle vibrated with excitement.

Tess saw the child's lips moving and said, "What did you say, sweetie?"

Danielle pointed to her ears and shouted, "You can't hear me with earplugs. Take them out." Danielle plucked imaginary plugs out of her ears.

Tess got the main gist of what the girl said. She pointed a finger in the air in the wait position. In between songs, Tess removed the spongy earplugs. "Let's start walking home before the next song starts. We can stop for an ice cream cone."

Tess selected one scoop of coffee ice cream, and Danielle picked fudge ripple. They sat on a bench near the grocery store and ate their cones, watching the comings and goings of the customers emerging with multiple plastic bags.

They tossed their napkins in the trash barrel on the sidewalk. It was Saturday evening, and the accumulation of plastic water bottles, paper, and Styrofoam had simmered to the top of the fifty-gallon container.

Danielle reached up and easily placed her small hand in her grandmother's. Tess squeezed softly, and a lovely buzz of violets swirled around her nose. This was the slightest improvement in the rewiring of her senses. Or she was making it up.

"Are there some mothers who don't love their babies? Did your mother love you?" asked the girl.

What a strange departure from ice cream and summer evenings. Tess looked down at the top of the girl's head. Several barrettes held her long bangs off her face. Danielle wanted her hair to be one length. As it was now, her thick red hair was chopped into a cascade of layers, making it look like ocean waves. Why was the child asking about mother love?

"I'll tell you, but I'd like to know why you're asking."

Danielle hopped over a bump in the sidewalk where a tree root had burst through. Her plastic sandals slapped down with a suctioning noise. "I heard you on the phone with Mr. Isaiah. You said Natalie is sort of like Rocky's new daughter. I saw Natalie in Portland when Dad and I were looking for new shoes for me. Natalie told me that her mother couldn't love her and that she had to live in foster homes. I asked her what foster homes were, and she said that they're for kids who get born to parents who don't love them and they are given away to people who are paid to take care of them but not to love them."

Danielle took a breath and launched in again. "My mother loves me, and so does Daddy. You loved my daddy when he was a little boy. Did your mother love you?"

Something like used engine oil had seeped into the world of her granddaughter, and drops of it cascaded along her ears and down her neck. Did Natalie have to use the very words that would cause Danielle to worry?

"I was wonderfully loved by my mother. I just didn't have her very long because she died when I was young.

And my father loved me the best way he knew how. He was rather stern."

They were nearing the driveway to the house. Tess let her hand rest along Danielle's shoulder. "I'm glad that you're asking about this. I think you're a scientist. You've just spotted something unusual, and now you're examining the world to see if you can find any more of these unusual sightings."

The child put her hand in Tess's pants pocket and held on, something she hadn't done in months. Tess felt a thread of fear coming off the girl for the first time. The sensation was faint, but the urgency of fear coming from her granddaughter added texture to the emotion.

"We don't know what went wrong with Natalie's mother, but it had to be something terrible and big. Huge. And her mother must have had no one else to help her with her child. This is not like it is for you at all. This would never happen to you. You have family who love you and would do anything to take care of you. I would never let anything bad happen to you."

Was it bad luck to make such absolute promises? Tess knelt down to eye level. "What happened to Natalie is terrible and it's sad, but now she has to figure out how to make the best of her life. Now she can choose who will be in her life and who won't. She doesn't have to let people in her life who don't care about her."

Danielle patted her grandmother's cheek in a sudden gesture that Tess hadn't seen from the child before. They stood up and continued along the gravel road. Danielle twirled in a mixture of skipping and turning.

"If Rocky knew about Natalie when she was little like me, Rocky would have driven to her house right away and told the foster home people that she would take care of her. Wouldn't she?" asked Danielle between twirls.

"Yes," said Tess. "You are probably right about that." Is that what was driving Rocky now, trying to rescue a child from the past? Rocky wasn't even sure the child was Bob's. Only DNA testing would give a definitive answer.

Tess and her granddaughter shared a common tweak in their DNA: they each had synesthesia. Tess wondered what it would have been like if someone had explained this simple and amazing fact to her when she was Danielle's age. As far as Tess could determine, the child had a synesthetic response to sound and smell. Wind chimes made her feet itch. A ripe banana looked like a green mist. Tess tried not to overwhelm the child, but she was fascinated by the inner world of her granddaughter.

Tess tucked the child into bed. She had a spare bed-room as well as the loft, but sometimes Danielle ended up in bed with her grandmother.

"I want you to know right now that we are not eating popcorn in my bed," said Tess. "It felt like I was sleeping in a gravel pit the last time you slept in my bed."

Danielle giggled at her grandmother's attempt to be stern. "It was popcorn, not gravel!" Danielle spread her arms and legs under the sheets as if she was making a snow angel.

"Gramma, do you remember what tomorrow night is?"

Tess never got tired of hearing the name that applied to so many but sounded so sweet from her own granddaughter: Gramma. "Yes, tomorrow Rocky is coming to play cards with us. It's practice for our big island poker tournament right here. We'll have to practice tomorrow afternoon after we get back from checking on the rental houses. Do you remember Texas Hold'em?"

"Yes."

Tess grabbed a brush and pulled it through the girl's hair and began to braid it into two short braids.

"Do you remember what a straight is?"

"Oh yes, I like straights. They taste like chocolate."

Tess logged another cross-firing of the senses.

"That will prove to be a helpful advantage that is best kept to yourself. What's a better hand, two pairs or three of a kind?" Tess fastened the two braids with a hair tie.

"I can't remember that one," said the girl. She squeezed her face together as if doing so would help her remember.

"Well, that's why we have our little study cards. We'll look at them at breakfast and then we'll practice in the afternoon. Rocky can't remember things the way you and I can. Her straights don't taste like chocolate. I'm willing to guess that, for her, even a royal flush doesn't have the carbonated fizz it had for me. We are going to beat the pants off Rocky."

"How does Rocky remember the cards?" Danielle sounded concerned as she leaned back on her side of the bed, her head sinking into a down-filled pillow.

"She has to remember the numbers and the faces that she has in her hand and make an educated guess about the cards that we have, but she can't smell them or feel them or taste them like you can. Poor Rocky." Tess was determined to make Danielle's synesthesia an asset. Her son claimed that she took the matter too far, but even he was charmed by Danielle's whimsical frankness about her perceptions of the world.

"Did you pick out three books to read tonight?" asked Tess.

"Yes, they're right here," said Danielle, patting the small pile beside her. It often took the girl a good long time to slow down enough to sleep. Her feet still tap-danced under the covers. The three stories would help. Tess put several pillows behind her head and settled in to read. Had someone read stories to Natalie? Or was there a large blank spot where the reservoir of stories, warm blankets, and children fresh from the bath was meant to be?

"There's one special thing that I wanted for my birthday, but I'm afraid you won't let me have it," said Danielle, opening up a large book called *B Is for Blue Planet*.

Oh no. Was the child going to blackmail her dear old grandmother into getting her ears pierced? "What is it?" said Tess.

"I want to learn archery. I know I'm too little, but Rocky could let me watch until I get bigger. Did you know that you learn a lot just by watching and practicing something in your mind? It's called visualization," said Danielle, who was becoming more energized by the minute. She might still be awake at midnight.

Visualization? When Tess had been in second grade, education consisted of repetition and little else. But archery with Rocky? The woman could be a blundering disaster with young children.

"I'll ask her and see, but I can't promise. It will be entirely up to Rocky," said Tess. "She's not really used to young children," she added hesitantly.

"I know that. Rocky is jumpy yellow with little kids. I can explain visualization to her," said the girl.

Tess smiled. Perhaps there would be a mutual benefit.

Chapter 18

Rocky and Danielle were in Tess's backyard. Previously, archery had been a completely solitary activity, which was how Rocky had liked it. But Tess had been persuasive. "She wanted this for her birthday," Tess had emphasized. Rocky had given Danielle the rules for watching her practice archery.

1. No talking, singing, or humming while Rocky was shooting.

2. Danielle had to sit behind Rocky at all times, not on the side, and definitely not anywhere near the target.

3. When—and only when—Rocky had shot every arrow from her quiver and said, "All clear,"

could Danielle get up, dash to the paper target, and help her retrieve the arrows.

Rocky paced off the distance from the target. She set up her equipment: the longbow and the arrows made from osage orange by a traditionalist in Nebraska. Tess had a small wrought-iron table that held the quiver.

Danielle was a froth of electrical movement; her energy level, if properly captured, could have lit up most of Peaks Island. Rocky remained clueless about young children. She only knew academically what a seven-year-old kid could comprehend.

"Let's review a few of the rules. What is the first rule about watching archery?" asked Rocky. Since the archery practice had not officially started, Danielle was free to cavort around her grandmother's backyard in nonstop kinetic abandon.

Danielle stood very straight and brought her right hand over her eye in a salute. "No talking, no making noise, Rocky, sir." Danielle looked like a mini-version of Tess, whip smart and agile, with the same wayward hair, thick as a sunburst. Was the little girl mocking her? No. Well, yes.

"Very funny. But this is important. And don't do that 'sir' thing. What's rule number two?"

"I have to stay behind you so you don't shoot me by mistake like you did Hill. Gramma says it was because you thought he was a bad man, but Hill was really a good man, and then he was your boyfriend. She said it was very sad that your husband died before you moved here," said Danielle, pirouetting around and around as she spoke. She had on yellow shorts; her matching yellow flip-flops had been tossed aside. Her toes looked like little flower blossoms.

The image of the child's tender legs, arms, or God forbid any other part of her pierced with an arrow sent a shudder up Rocky's neck. How many people could say that they had shot someone? It was true, Rocky had made a terrible mistake last winter and shot Hill in the leg when she thought he was a stalker. He was not. He had said that being wounded in love had given him extraordinary credit with his high school students. For that reason alone she had decided never to enter archery competitions, afraid that she'd be called some catchy nickname like "Special Forces." Rocky put down the longbow and sat down on the garden stone wall where Danielle would have to sit as a spectator. The girl joined her.

"That's why I made the rules. The only way possible that I could concentrate would be if I knew you were completely safe. The longbow is a weapon, a very serious weapon," said Rocky.

Danielle stopped her girations, which she could do even while seated. She squeezed in next to Rocky and patted her thigh. Rocky felt the benediction of the girl, the sweetness that she never got from all her angst-driven teenagers and college students.

"It will help you think better about your bow and arrows if I sit still," said Danielle with a solemnness that startled Rocky. What do people do with young children? Should she tousle her hair, put an arm around her? She felt the pull to do so; her hand even jerked into action, but she pulled back, afraid to touch the child.

"Thank you. I need all the help I can get. Each bow has a certain draw weight. This bow takes thirty-five pounds of effort to pull back, and I've been stuck here for months," said Rocky. With the midmorning breeze, soft and sweet off the ocean, and the crows cawing back and forth in the trees, she began to relax a little. "If this looks like something that you'd want to try, we can get you a bow to practice on next time."

Danielle kicked her feet, and as she did she leaned slightly into Rocky to get a bit more traction. "I'm on a soccer team, and I can sort of kick with my left foot, but I have to tell my left foot to remember to kick the ball even when I'm not playing soccer. I tell myself when I'm in bed, when I'm in school, and when I ride the ferry."

The child smelled like fresh air and salt water. All her bones were tiny, like bird bones. How did people talk to children without talking down to them? Was there a frequency, a certain bandwidth that one had to find?

Rocky stood up. "I'm going to try your technique. When I'm other places, like out walking Cooper on the beach, or in the shower, I'm going to remind my right arm to pull back as if I really am shooting my bow. You just gave me a very good idea. Now, let's see if I can shoot some arrows. Are you ready to keep your butt glued to that stone wall?"

"Yes, I am," Danielle said with a squeal.

"And what are the magic words that mean you can dash around like a comet again?"

"All clear!" shouted Danielle.

"Very good. And after you have retrieved all the arrows, we can feed the crows. They'll be waiting," said Rocky.

Danielle did exactly as she had promised, and while Rocky was impressed with her ability to be quiet and almost motionless on the stone wall, there was something distracting about being watched. The gains that she had been making with the thirty-five-pound bow evaporated; she consistently hit the outer ring, no matter how much she tried to quiet her breathing. She had two more arrows to go. From her peripheral vision, she saw the black swoop of the crow who would soon announce the end of archery and the beginning of crow treats.

Rocky kept her left side to the target, pulled up and back with her right hand, and let her eyes rest on the center ring.

"Natalie!" screeched Danielle with such a piercing cry that Rocky spun around in alarm, and as she did she released the arrow as the little girl burst from her seat to reach Natalie. For one split second, the arrow and Danielle raced to Natalie. Before the arrow even struck, Rocky knew the world could end right then and there. Her beautiful arrow struck the ground three feet in front of Natalie. Everyone stopped moving as if they had been flash-frozen.

Danielle and Natalie began to speak simultaneously. "I got up and I shouldn't have." "I shouldn't have come back here, I'm sorry." "I made a noise, I'm sorry, I'm sorry."

Rocky fell to her knees and dropped the bow. The microsecond of a miracle that saved them all from disaster descended on her, and she put her hands over her face to hide an onslaught of tears. She could have hit one or both of the girls. She could have killed them. She was not an archery teacher.

Rocky felt two tiny hands gently patting her back. She threw her arms around Danielle in a crushing hug. When she looked up, Natalie stood exactly where she had stopped, three feet from the arrow, watching Rocky and the child with a dark, penetrating gaze, head slightly down, eyes focused sharply. Had she been afraid or angry? Was it the sight of Rocky hugging the child?

"I was looking for Tess. Sorry to screw things up here," said Natalie. She turned and bounded from the backyard.

Despite the near calamity, one crow made his heralding call when she had shot the last arrow, which she forced herself to do for fear she'd never shoot again. She yelled, "All clear," to help Danielle remember the rules. With the announcement of the end of archery, the murder of crows soared in. Rocky pulled out a bag of dried bread and showed Danielle where to put the food for the black birds. As they stood back and watched the crows swoop and dive at the bread, Danielle said, "It sounds like they say, 'Rocky, Rocky.' Wouldn't it be funny if they knew your name?"

Rocky blushed. No one had noticed before, and she had not been entirely sure that the conditioning had worked. But yes, one crow had clearly said her name.

Chapter 19

Tess cajoled Rocky into the special Italian grocery store in Portland. "You need to get aired out," said Tess. "If you're going to live here and take in stray youngsters, you need to know where to buy delicious food, since you're going to be cooking. I don't think I've ever seen you cook. Do you cook?"

Bob had been the one to hover over a savory tomato sauce, reduced down to its regal essence, the one who chopped vegetables with joyful abandon and who even made multiple dishes with eggplants. He'd had the flare and passion for food.

Rocky's parents had had a contentious relationship with food. Her father came from a direct line of Italians for whom food was a daily sacrament, a way of anointing oneself with love and olive oil, washed down with Tuscan red wine. Rocky's mother was a hopeless Irish cook who was an astonishing disappointment to her Italian in-laws.

When Rocky married Bob, her mother had said, "Thank God he cooks. Take my advice: hand over the kitchen to him entirely."

Rocky pushed open the store's heavy glass door, then followed Tess through the store, carrying a wire basket and feeling like a child who was only there for portage.

"You were rather skeletal when I first met you last year. Skeletal and an unpleasant shade of yellow," said Tess. She examined two varieties of extra-virgin olive oil.

"What was yellow? My skin? My name? Are we in synesthesia land?"

Tess selected one bottle and put it in Rocky's basket. "Not just your skin. It was all of you. You looked like a houseplant that had been kept in a closet without benefit of photosynthesis, deprived of nutrients. You had stopped absorbing life. Understandable, completely understandable, considering the death."

For the first few months of living on the island, she had created a flimsy and entirely false identity. She had specifically omitted that her husband had died in a flourish of cardiac disaster. It had been six months since Rocky came clean with her reasons for coming to Peaks Island and confessed that she had been in a desperate escape from the stranglehold of grief. Rocky still flinched if someone said the word "widow."

"What color is the word 'widow'?" asked Rocky. "I mean, what color *was* it?" She knew that, to the synesthetic, all letters come in particular colors and that the colors of some words are unique. She was sure that Tess would say "black," because that was what the word felt like to her.

"Green, a dense forest green like the kind you see in old boatyards. *W*'s are always green, but it's not just that. Green is the most absorbent color. It sucks the most light out of the spectrum. It fits the word, don't you think?"

Rocky picked up some yellow onions with papery skins and pretended to compare them. "I don't want to be the widow. I hate it. I'm too young. Bob was too young. And now I'll always be a widow. Bob did that."

Tess took the onions away from her. "It's a powerful word, and it's meant to be. You can't dodge it. And you don't know how to pick out onions." Tess moved on to the pasta aisle, her back straight and her joints loose. She turned back to Rocky and said, "And personally, I think you've been too rash about Hill."

The mention of his name gave Rocky an unexpected ache. Was it true that memories and consciousness lurk everywhere—in the palms of our hands, the cells along our necks, the tips of our ears? Does a breast have a memory, an awareness of its own? Her body, wise and primal, had already recorded the warm scent of Hill and made room for him in her blood-stream, the capillaries carrying images of his arm bones and nose cartilage straight to her brain stem. That was where all the trouble was brewing—in her brain stem. Rocky was about to split in half, with her bodily desires seeming to have a spectacular advantage.

Why couldn't the girl be Bob's daughter? She wanted to surge ahead and sweep Natalie into her life. It was as if Bob had sent her, with all her war wounds, right to Rocky's door, and suddenly Hill didn't fit as cozily as he had before. She wanted to marshal all her efforts to scoop up this girl and make a family. Why else would she suddenly buy a house badly in need of renovation? The two events had come together like interlocking gears. How could Hill understand?

As if Tess had been listening to Rocky's thoughts, she said, "He's the best choice for an archery teacher for Danielle. I fully agree with that."

Tess shook her head and grabbed a bag of penne.

They brought their Italian booty home to Rocky's cottage, and under Tess's tutelage they made a vegetarian pasta dish with a mountain of mushrooms. It was done by midafternoon. They sipped a red wine that the grocery store owner had suggested and finished off the meal with blueberries in cream.

"If Natalie comes back from job hunting, she could join us," said Rocky. Aside from the brief respite in the grocery store, she had thought of nothing but Natalie all day.

Tess tilted her head back and slid a spoonful of blueberries into her mouth. She hummed with pleasure.

"I saw Melissa the other day, and she looked a little bereft. Don't forget the rest of us. You're some sort of role model for Melissa, although I can't tell you why. It would help her if she saw that you savor food, that you have a passion for it." Tess rubbed her bare toes along Cooper's spine. He had just eaten the heel of a baguette and lay near Rocky. "I was meant to live in Italy, I'm sure of it," sighed Tess.

The first week with Natalie left Rocky itching and as vigilant as she'd been taking in Cooper when he was an unknown to her, just a dog recovering from surgery. At night she heard every noise from the other bedroom. She woke suddenly if there was a suspicious absence of noise. Was the girl still breathing? Had she come here to die? If she was truly Bob's daughter, then that would be just like him, landing in Rocky's life and expiring. There, she heard the symphonic creaking of the bed; the girl must still be breathing because she'd rolled over.

Cooper stationed himself close to Rocky's bedroom door, as he always did, but something was different about him: a zing of electricity traveled beneath his loose skin, sort of a yellow alert on the domestic terrorism scale. Either the dog had picked up on her anxiety or he was also having trouble adjusting to a houseguest. Cooper seemed a bit edgy. Once, when Rocky peeked at the digital clock, the numbers glowed 2:31. Cooper picked up his head and looked at her, his eyes catching the green of the clock.

"What?" whispered Rocky. "Just because I can't sleep doesn't mean you have to stay awake too." The dog sighed and rolled completely to one side, stretching out his body to catch whatever coolness he could from the floor. She caught a glimmer of night shine from Peterson's eyes from her perch on the dresser. Apparently no one was sleeping. It was the first week in July, and the nights were filled with a symphony of sound: nocturnal creatures rustled and searched for food, insects heralded each other with mating calls, and even the plant life grew with such abundance that Rocky feared it would shake the cottage.

During the days, Natalie went into Portland to look for jobs and had even looked into the local college just in case Portland turned out to be the place she wanted to live. Rocky understood the permeable, inexact nature of someone her age. Natalie could move anywhere because nothing held her.

"July is a hard time to find a job," said Rocky when the girl came back empty-handed each day. "Most of the summer jobs were taken back in May."

They had agreed that Natalie could as easily stay at Rocky's until they found out for sure about her parentage—or more precisely, her paternal genesis. But time had begun to morph and flip over; there was something redemptive about having the girl sleep in the next room, and Rocky didn't want new information, either confirming or denying the paternal line, to disturb the balance.

She had finally stopped listening for every tiny creak in the house and fallen back to sleep, the night sounds having turned into a drowsy comfort. The snap of crickets, the ping of bats, and Cooper's breathing were sounds of well-being wrapped around her. She was suddenly yanked from the depth of sleep by Cooper's wet nose pressed into her face. He had given a high sound to reach her.

"What?" she said, reluctantly reaching up out of her slumber.

The bathroom was between the two bedrooms. When Rocky first arrived on the island, she had been soothed by the plain linear construction of the cottage: rectangular, small, with each bedroom barely large enough to contain the beds and dressers. Rocky heard a sound unlike the crickets or the bats or anything from *Peterson's Guide to Mammals of North America*. Natalie was in the bathroom, and a strange sound slipped under the door, carried by the night.

Rocky sat up and looked at Cooper, who was at full alert—not intruder alert, but standing, ears up, tail in a very slow wag.

"Okay," she said, getting up to go stand outside the bathroom door, afraid to knock, afraid not to, stuck in a dry, hollow fear of the eighteen-year-old girl huddled in the bathroom. Cooper nudged her hand with his snout. She tapped with one knuckle on the thin door.

"Natalie, we've got lousy acoustics in this house. You sound like something's wrong. Can I come in?"

The crying sound stopped, and Rocky heard only her own heartbeat.

"I guess," said Natalie. "I guess you can."

Rocky turned the dented metal doorknob and pushed open the door, gently, as if a baby were in the house and she didn't want to wake it. Natalie sat on the toilet lid, one knee pulled up, her arm crooked around the knee.

The tender skin around her eyes was scorched raw and red, scratched up by the salt of crying. Her head rested sideways on the point of her knee.

With her clients, who sometimes cried during therapy, Rocky had learned a steady approach. She handed them a box of tissues and then waited. When she first began her clinical internship, a crying client had instantly ignited tears in Rocky's eyes. She confessed this problem to her supervisor, who said, "You're responding like a friend. They have friends. What they need is a therapist. Don't try to stop the tears and don't hug them. Give them a box of tissues and a space to cry. This may be their only place to cry."

Natalie was not a client. She was a girl in Rocky's bathroom who might be Bob's daughter. The girl had fallen from the sky, crashed through the roof, and here she was, lighting up a maternal subset of Rocky's organs that had never been tapped before. Rocky had no idea what to do. Tissues were not needed; Natalie had used half of the roll of toilet paper and filled the small rattan wastebasket.

Rocky stepped into the tiny room and sat on the rim of the white fiberglass bathtub. Cooper lay down in the doorway, blocking any last-minute decision to bail out. There had to be something that she could say. The wall clock in the kitchen echoed in sharp clacks.

"Life is . . . ," started Rocky, searching for a soothing word, a verbal ointment to apply to the girl. Whatever she said was going to be wrong, she already knew that.

Natalie reached out with her right hand and took Rocky's unassuming fist and held on. They sat together in the bathroom holding hands, saying nothing, not looking at each other, while the space inside Rocky where children were conjured long before they were conceived lit up with a soft phosphorescent glow.

Chapter 20

"You've been walking in the garden of the dead again," said Isaiah.

This was the first time Isaiah had been in Rocky's newly purchased house since she'd signed the papers. She had asked for his advice about local contractors.

"That completely does not sound like an old Maine proverb," said Rocky.

Isaiah's face and arms turned darker in the summer, the sun painting his skin somewhere between a rich mahogany and walnut. The white hairs along his brow stood out in amplified contrast.

"When my mother's people came from the Dominican Republic, they brought a saying for every occasion, but most of the sayings had to do with birth, sex, or death. I'm going to spare you the fables about sex. But am I right about the garden of death?" he asked.

Rocky had been pulling back old brown lineoleum in the kitchen, only to reveal more old lineolum. She knew exactly what he meant by the garden of death.

"How did you know?" she asked.

Isaiah bent down, took out his pocketknife, and cut through a loose flap of dried-out flooring. He held it up to the light and examined it. Rocky felt the house twitch under such close inspection, the way dogs do when they first meet each other.

"Isn't it odd how things have their own time in glory when everyone wants them and we can't see beyond them? Like this god-awful kitchen flooring that a woman thought was beautiful at one time," Isaiah said. "Asbestos house siding, there's another example. These were once grand and admired, and people were proud to have them in their homes. Now they're dreaded by homeowners who can't wait to rip them out. They had a beginning and an end, a life span," he said as he tossed a section of the lineoleum out the kitchen door. He turned his head slightly to look at her, and one bushy eyebrow rose.

"You don't exactly have a poker face when it comes to emotions. No wonder Tess and her little granddaughter can beat the daylights out of you at poker," said Isaiah.

Rocky paused and leaned into the long handle. "How did you hear that I lost at poker? That was only two days ago."

"Two days ago? In island time, that's old news. Now everyone wants to play poker with you. Don't accept any poker invitations where they play with real money," he said. "You're as easy to read as a seven-year-old kid. Oh, that's right—you got beat by a seven-year-old," he added, letting a laugh ruffle up through the deep registers of his chest and echo off the walls of the empty house.

Rocky shoved the scraper along the floor with renewed energy. "I think they cheat. That would be just like Tess. She's probably teaching Danielle a slick move with synesthesia."

"Poker is a game of skill and good fortune, combined with the ability to refrain from telegraphing every thought. But you, Madam Dogcatcher, are not good at masking your feelings. You either got very little sleep or distressed sleep. You've just made one of the most anxiety-provoking decisions of your life. Buying a house is right up there with the holy trinity of death, divorce, and public speaking. The dead often visit us when we make huge decisions. They also visit us when we take in wayward children."

Rocky had a red-and-white cooler near the door to the basement filled with Coke and beer. She pulled open the lid, put her hand on two Cokes, and offered an inquiring look toward Isaiah. She had hoped that they would skip the conversation about wayward children.

"Sure, I'll have one too, although Charlotte says the only safe thing for me to drink is water. We've got diabetes in our family, and all this sugar is tempting fate," he said, reaching for the cold can.

Rocky popped the lid on her can. "I know why I've been thinking so much about Bob again. This is the first time I've had to make this kind of decision without him. I'm not just ticking off time while a job waits for me back in Massachusetts. I've bought a house, such as it is, and there is no job waiting for me, since I let go of a perfectly good position that I actually loved, complete with health insurance, dental, an eventual pension, and all the accoutrements that American workers long for," said Rocky.

"What would Bob think? That's the question. I need to get you a bumper sticker that says WHAT WOULD BOB THINK?"

"I don't need the bumper sticker because it's already stamped on my brain and I wish it wasn't. It shouldn't matter so much what he thinks. This is my life without him," she said.

Even as she talked with Isaiah, some of the nocturnal dread poured off her. Her lungs expanded and she exhaled deeply.

"You're a full-service friend, not to mention former Methodist minister, boss, and public works director. I'm skipping some of your professions. What I really wanted to know was, who would you recommend to do a remodel on this place? You know everyone. Let's take a break outside while you pontificate."

The two friends walked out the kitchen door and stood in the driveway, looking at the white exterior of the old house as if information could be read from the clapboards. The side entrance to the house opened on the kitchen, and Rocky knew that everyone except company came in through the kitchen, not the larger entrance from the front porch. She wondered if Isaiah could feel the house pulse with expectation. Rocky wanted to make sure she found a carpenter who understood the old house and took time to work with it respectfully.

Without a pause, Isaiah said, "Russell Barry. Good, solid carpenter, as long as you're not in a hurry. And he writes poetry that I can understand. I'll call you with his phone number tonight." The older man surveyed the house, looking at it from top to bottom. "The skeleton of the house looks solid. I'm guessing it was built early in the twentieth century. Those were good building years. They used good wood and they didn't skimp.

"Remodeling this house might be a good way for you to focus your energy," he remarked. "You've got a lot going on, and I can't figure out how you keep everything sorted out. Where's your handsome archery instructor these days? I haven't seen him lately. Hill is a teacher, and he's levelheaded. I like him. He works with all kinds of teenagers and could offer advice about teenagers appearing on your doorstep looking for a biological father."

Isaiah shaded his eyes with his hand, his skin glistening with the fog, soon to be followed by brilliant sun. "By my reckoning, school is out, unless Brunswick goes by a different calendar." He glanced at Rocky, and a sting of tears erupted in her eyes.

Rocky wanted to say that Hill was teaching a summer course, or that he had never come back from the camping trip, but too many beats had already passed. Isaiah picked up the crowbar and sledgehammer that he had just brought Rocky to use on the house. Even without a contractor's advice, Rocky had said she wanted the old wallboard taken out.

Rocky kicked a white plastic bucket, and it skittered along the gravel drive.

"That's only a partial answer," said her friend. "Now use your big girl words. No more kicking defenseless buckets aside."

Rocky set the bucket upright. She wore shorts, a tank top covered by a thick blue workshirt, and hiking boots.

"Since you already knew that I lost at poker, I thought you knew about Hill." Rocky noted new admiration for Melissa: she had not spread juicy romantic gossip when she had the chance. "He's back in touch with his supposedly soon-to-be-ex-wife, Julie. I would never have gotten involved with him if I'd thought there was even a tiny chance of them getting back together," said Rocky.

Isaiah tilted his head and looked up at the treetops, as if absorbed in the process of divination. He picked up a bag from the building supply store and nodded toward the house. They went back inside.

"It was too soon after Bob's death for me to start up with someone new. I made a mistake, thinking that I could skate through the labyrinth of grief and fall in love. I know that was against the rules of inevitable agony." She turned away from her friend, pulled up her shirt, and wiped her eyes.

"Okay, the real thing is, I didn't see it coming," she admitted. "I mean, she'd been gone for so long, and I thought I could tell if the chemistry was good and solid. Now I have to factor in that my relationship radar is shot," Rocky said, going straight for the long crowbar, drawn to it like a moth to a porch light.

"You knew he was married right from the start, even if they hadn't lived together for nearly three years. Those were the facts, and he didn't hide them. I brought you some protective eye goggles. If you're going to do demolition work, which is not the best idea you've ever had, then you need to wear them. You're mad and hurt, and now you're going to swing a crowbar around at the walls. Did Hill tell you he was going back to his wife? I thought they both had lawyers."

Rocky dug into a paper sack from the building supply store and extracted a new pair of goggles. She pulled them over her head and let them rest temporarily on her brow.

"He didn't have to tell me. I saw them," she said. She snapped the glasses into place. The plastic was not 100 percent clear, and she tripped over a stack of wood. Isaiah followed behind her with the sledgehammer.

"Let's think about your demolition approach for a minute. I'll take a pop at this wall. This is one of the walls coming down, right? Just to get it started, mind you, then you can tear at it. Get the sections off in big chunks if you can. It saves time. You saw Hill and Julie doing what exactly?"

Rocky twirled her dark, thick hair and tucked it into the stretch band of the eye gear. Her hair was a difficult length—long enough to be a nuisance, but not long enough to tie up on top of her head.

"I drove up to his house unannounced and saw them. She was inside the house, and he had his arms around her." Even as she said it, the words sounded less substantial than the gut-twisting slam she had felt when she saw Hill framed in the light of his kitchen.

Isaiah said, "Stand back." He tapped the wall, listening for the location of the studs, then swung the sledgehammer and cracked a hole between two of the studs. He made several more holes above and below it.

"Take it away, crowbar queen. Go at it, but avoid the studs. I know you want to destroy something. But what did Hill say? And as far as the hugging goes, there are national leaders who hate each other and they hug and kiss every time they meet. They have missiles aimed at each other and they still hug when they meet, regardless of politics or religion. So tell me, what exactly did Hill say? I assume that you talked this into the ground with him."

Rocky inserted the sharp curved end of the crowbar under the edge of the plaster wall. Every few inches a piece of lathe had been nailed to a stud, and she experimented with the best way to pop off the maximum number of slats at one time.

Yes, one would think that they would have had a good long conversation about hurts and betrayals. "I didn't exactly give him a chance. I didn't want to hear it, and I didn't know that I'd be taking such a chance with Hill," said Rocky. Her feet spread wide, knees slightly bent, she yanked hard and a three-foot section of the plaster board popped off. "It's possible I acted like a three-year-old."

Dust filled her nose, harsh and smothering, depositing decades of remembrances from the former occupants into her lungs. She closed her eyes and tasted Hill, the creamy insides of his arms, the scent of pencil shavings that seeped off him, the way she had tasted the slick presence of guacamole along his tongue when she had once kissed him.

"Didn't they teach you anything in graduate school? Sit down and talk to the man, for God's sake. You didn't know that love was a high-risk business? It surely is. But not taking the risk is terrible," said her friend. Isaiah put his soda can on a windowsill. "Stay away from poker. Good fortune doesn't seem to be on your side right now. I'm sorry about Hill. I didn't see that one coming either."

Rocky called Russell Barry that evening and set up a time for him to look at her place so that he could give her an estimate. When she told Isaiah the next day, he said, "I'll come over and introduce you two, in the time-honored tradition of Maine carpenters."

Rocky had resisted the idea, but Isaiah had insisted. By noon on Tuesday they were both at the house waiting for Russell. She felt the house changing already, filled with expectancy and longing, the ragged curtains fluttering by some internal wind, unaided by any breeze from the windows.

"You'll be glad that you've got the cottage while the house is being remodeled. I can't think of much worse than living in a construction zone. Charlotte and I nearly had a double homicide on our hands when we had our kitchen remodeled," said Isaiah.

"It's not like I need you to broker this deal for me. I can figure out how to talk to a carpenter. I mean, I have before," she said. That was a lie. She had left carpentry negotiations to Bob, who had loved to speak man-talk even though he couldn't have hammered two pieces of wood together.

Bob had explained to her, "I get my manly needs met by talking the talk with the tool belt crowd. I accept my actual limitations in carpentry, car mechanics, and plumbing, but I love the talk. Indulge me." If Bob ran into trouble with carpentry, he always consulted with Caleb. When Bob the veterinarian sought advice from

Caleb the housepainter/sculptor, Caleb glowed for days. Rocky had marveled at the transmission of male ranking.

Now that she had purchased a house on her own, Bob was dead, and Caleb was three hours away, she was secretly relieved that Isaiah wanted to hang around and establish some ground rules with the builder.

The two friends took another tour of the house while they waited for Russell to show up. They started in the basement. The floor was dirt and the walls were fieldstone. Old canning jars remained on the shelving, waiting to be filled with sugary syrup and fruit. The rich smell of earth filled her nostrils, a mixture of over-ripe mushrooms and decaying leaves.

"It's not beautiful in the cellar, but the good news is that back here in the center of the island you've got some elevation, so water might not collect. It would be easy enough to pour a cement floor if you wanted one," Isaiah commented. "We'll ask Russell about that. I mean, you'll ask him. I'm here as the official island greeter." He had just run into a cobweb, and it stuck to his dark face, snagging on his stubble.

She understood that in the animal kingdom two male elk "greet" each other by pawing the ground, sniffing, tossing back their heads, bellowing, and then somehow conveying their agreement that they come from the same herd and no harm is intended. In humans the encounter is similar: two men say hello, shake hands, slap each other on the upper arms, and lower the register of their voices ever so slightly.

As Rocky and Isaiah climbed the narrow stairs from the earthen cellar, she heard the crunch of tires along the driveway and was suddenly gripped with anxiety. Here was a guy who could help the house or create havoc. What if the house didn't like him? What if she paid him and he never did the work? A truck door slammed before she was able to spiral out further with what-if thoughts. She'd establish her place with Russell later.

Isaiah cleared his throat as he walked across the driveway to greet the carpenter.

"Russell," he said, nodding his head as if he balanced powerful antlers. His voice had lowered a notch.

The carpenter stepped down from his black diesel truck and closed the door with a solid clunk. He approached the older man, arm outstretched, they shook hands and then solidly clapped each other on the upper arms. Rocky was sure that she heard the primal sound of antlers rubbing against each other in agreement.

Chapter 21

The House

The house was built the same year soldiers came home from a war, in 1918. Some people mailed away for house kits from Sears, a sturdy enough product, but the house in the center of Peaks Island had been built by a shipbuilder. The beams were thick and solid, and the molding around the doorways was abundant but not lavish; unlike the large homes on the hillside of Portland, this house was not showy but was graced with just enough carved wood to announce its longevity as a place where people could stay for generations.

The widow's walk on the third story was a folly among the island people. Even on the third story of this house, one couldn't really see the ships coming in for all the trees, but the shipbuilder said it was bad luck to build a house without one. Although no woman would ever worry the widow's walk with her pacing, children would be drawn to it, and the house would brighten with their hours of play, snug in the small space.

By midcentury, the shipbuilder, his wife, his children, and his grandchildren had all died or moved on; the next family stayed a decade or so until life on the mainland drew them away, taking four children and a wife whose heart broke when she closed the front door for the last time. The last family was a fisherman and his wife, lured into the house by all the embedded whispers of the sea, the shipbuilder's stories that had lingered in the floorboards and the horsehair plaster of the walls. Late at night the new family sometimes heard the creaking of wooden ships, the wind grabbing hold of the sails, impossible as it all seemed by daylight. Over the course of their decades-long tenure, the couple had had a total of two children, one who was killed in the final days of the war in Vietnam and one who moved to Buenos Aires as soon as she got the chance, four dogs (two Airedales, one dachshund, and a mixed breed called Buckeye), and a steady supply of cats who kept the house free of rodents.

The house soaked up the habits of the people who inhabited it: the way they slept, snored, and exhaled, the way they ate breakfast with the radio on and an aluminum pot of coffee percolating on the stove. The wood, plaster, glass, wiring, and old copper pipes that brought in fresh water and took away the soiled water did not add up to a whole that was in itself a sustainable building. The insides, the guts of the house, had to be pumped up by the trials, agonies, and delicate moments of joy coiling through the lives of its inhabitants. The house was a balloon that stayed firm and inflated by the ruckus of the people who lived there.

The house had been without inhabitants for three years, and now, for the first time ever, it was under renovation. The woman with the dog arrived and tore out wallboard and gasped at the lack of insulation. She was dreaming of a family as she brought in carpenters who assessed the house with appreciative eyes, who knew a good strong banister when they touched one.

The house longed to be filled, to be adorned with fresh paint, to have screens replaced and floors sanded, to start anew, to wrap its arms around a bustling con- glomerate of people who would want nothing more in the world than to come home to it each night.

Chapter 22

"How does paternity testing work?" said Rocky. After pacing the fifteen feet between her bedroom and kitchen for an hour, she had finally dialed the 800 number for the DNA Diagnostic Center.

"If you're pregnant and have had more than one partner, getting a paternity test is the wise thing to do," said a practiced female voice.

"Back up," said Rocky. "I'm not pregnant. And this isn't about a baby. My husband died more than a year ago. A girl just contacted me and said she's his biological daughter. Can we still test for paternity?"

"If the alleged father is deceased, then DNA from another family member can be used."

"His parents are dead, and he didn't have siblings. He had one uncle."

"They are generally not considered a close enough genetic link for something as important as paternity issues. If this is a paternity case, it may not hold up in court. There are other sources . . ." The woman paused. "We can use hair follicles. And any material left from the coroner's office that can be used as well."

Bob had died at a hospital; Rocky had never heard anything about a coroner's office. His body had been taken directly to the funeral home before being sent to the crematorium.

"I can check with the hospital, but if you can determine paternity from a hair follicle, I might be able to come up with that." She had kept one sweater and two shirts, but when Bob had died it was late spring and they had just been cleaned; no telltale strands of hair clung to them.

"And we would need a cheek swab from the girl."

"Yes, of course. How long would it take to find out the results?"

"Under normal circumstances, five to seven days."

"And how much does this cost?"

"Seven hundred dollars, roughly. The price has dropped considerably over the last few years."

"I know this is a ridiculous question, but is there any chance the test might be covered by insurance?"

"Not unless you have the same insurance as the senators from your state. I shouldn't have said that. I've just had a request denied for my son's second appeal for his bone marrow transplant. But in answer to your question, there is not a chance in hell that insurance will pay for this."

"I'm sorry. You just put this into perspective for me. You're right, no one is sick here, just lost and searching."

Rocky would put out the $700 for the test. There was no question about not doing the test. She couldn't wait to tell Natalie.

What did she have left from Bob that could be used for paternity testing? He'd been cremated. She had finally washed the pillowcase that had held his scent for months; by then it was so badly yellowed that Rocky tossed bleach into the washing load in hopes of saving it. The result was disaster for the pillowcase: it emerged from its bleaching with a lacework of holes. Rocky had thrown it away.

DNA testing for paternity was more complicated with a dead father. A sibling of Bob's would be the next best thing, if he'd had a sibling. His parents had died before Rocky appeared on the scene. But there was a paternal uncle in Eugene, Oregon, a man who had never attended a wedding or birthday celebration and had never appeared in any family photo that Rocky had seen. When she and Bob had married, Bob said that his uncle was not the kind of man he wanted at his wedding. "Just believe me on this one," he had said to Rocky. In fact, she wasn't sure the uncle still lived in Eugene. She had tried to call him when Bob died, but there had been no response to the call she made to the number she found in the white pages online.

In the TV dramas, DNA testing is the magic elixir, like a test for mono or strep throat. Men are cleared of false accusations and sprung from their death row prison cells, all because of DNA testing. That was how Rocky wished this could go. If they couldn't locate the strangely elusive uncle, then something of Bob himself would have to be located: a hair follicle, an old razor, a toothbrush. Everything like that had gone symbolically into the trash on day 365 after his death. Still, there must be something. Perhaps someone else had kept something of Bob's.

Rocky was generally straightforward with people. Friends and family had sometimes made the erroneous assumption that because she was a therapist she would act like a therapist all the time and be thoughtful and introspective in every situation. "Do you think a podiatrist wants to examine feet at a party? Or that an accountant is just dying to balance your checkbook?" offered Rocky, time after time. When she was working as a therapist, she brought all of her skills to the task and served her clients in the best way she knew how. But when she was off duty, she felt free to be a fully flawed human. She saw few advantages in soft-pedaling information. But she was oddly cautious with Natalie. She was afraid that if she said the wrong thing the skittish girl would disappear.

The sliding glass door was open, and the prolific smells of animals, birds, and plants mingled with the ocean air drifting into the cottage. She waited until Natalie was finished with her pizza to give her the DNA news. They had eaten with their chairs facing out, as if the vista of tangled bittersweet was a large-screen TV. It was Thursday night, the one night Hannigan's Grocery Store offered pizza. Theirs had been basic pepperoni with not one vegetable in sight. Between the two of them, they had polished off the best part of a liter of Coke. Rocky had finally found someone who shared her food tastes, even if it was an eighteen-year-old girl. They each used a section of paper towel to wipe their mouths.

"I found out some information about paternity testing today," said Rocky, balling up a used paper towel.

Natalie's eyes widened. She looked down and folded the paper towel in half, then again, and again, until it was the size of a credit card. Her cuticles were newly darkened with blood on both hands, and her nails were bitten to the quick.

"What do I have to do?" asked the girl. She clutched the wad of paper in one palm as if she was trying to compress it into an even smaller size.

Rocky stood up and took both plates to the sink. Then she threw her wadded-up paper towel into the cardboard pizza box. She pointed to Natalie's hand for her to toss hers in also.

"Oh. I didn't know I still had it."

Rocky closed the pizza box and tossed it into the plastic recycling tub.

"It's not so much what you have to do. You're the easy part. One cheek swab from you is all we need. But it's finding something from Bob that has me baffled. I need to find something of his for testing."

"Do you have anything yet?"

"Not yet."

Natalie rubbed her cheek with the back of her fist, the way a toddler might wipe away tears. But she was only pushing wisps of hair from her face.

"It's only a matter of time before we find something of Bob's that we can use. He had an elusive uncle, and I'm trying to track him down. Eventually, we'll have a clear answer about who your father is, or who your father is not. We should talk about what this will all mean. What will it mean if we find out that Bob was your father?" asked Rocky. She turned her chair slightly to face Natalie and then sat down.

Natalie slid to the floor and sat cross-legged, looking oddly younger. "I want to know where I came from, how I started. I want to know if I have any family. What if I have kids of my own someday and I need to know medical history?" Her fingers twitched; she brought one hand halfway to her mouth and then, catching herself, placed it with a controlled steadiness under her thigh. Rocky wanted to ask, *What will it mean about me?* But she did not.

"I get the need to know if you have family. And what if you find out that Bob isn't your father? What then?"

Natalie's mouth drew tighter, pulled in a way that Rocky hadn't seen before.

"You don't want to believe me, do you?" said Natalie, with a wounded gash in her voice. "Why is his name on my birth certificate? Isn't that enough?"

"The big question is, why wasn't his name on the first birth certificate? Why didn't your mother leave some information about him, or any indication of his identity? We need to be sure—100 percent sure—for your sake," said Rocky, keeping her voice soft.

"You mean we've got to be 100 percent sure for your sake. You don't want me to complicate your life. Like part of him is still around in me. That's too weird for you, isn't it?"

Cooper stood up and moved to Rocky's chair. He planted his considerable back end on her foot. He faced out, looking at the girl. Rocky automatically reached down and stroked him from head to body, ending in a resounding thump on his side.

"It would change a lot of things. I don't want you to get your hopes up and then get hurt. I think you've been hurt too much by things outside your control. Let's get as much information as we can." Rocky paused, stumbling over words that wanted to come out as she tried to utter only the words that she would allow out. "It's been nice to have you here. So don't worry about staying too long. I could use some help around here. It's going to be crazy while the other house gets remodeled."

Natalie had on her shortest shorts, and detritus from the floor stuck to her thighs when she suddenly stood up. "Do you want to know how many times I heard that? *It's been nice to have you here.* That's what people say right before they get rid of me."

Natalie didn't wait for an answer. She leapt up, pushed open the door, and marched down the driveway.

Cooper stood up but did not indicate that he wanted to go out with the girl. "Is this what parenting is like? What did I say wrong?" said Rocky.

The enormity of the girl's injury snaked into Rocky. This was not the way it would have been with her clients. Rocky always urged her clients to develop resilience, expand their support systems, and work on new responses to hardships, but Natalie had gaping wounds that seeped into Rocky as if she was the cause. Parental guilt was new to Rocky, and the weight of it pressed hard fingers into her skull.

Chapter 23

This was not about Rocky being afraid she'd be alone forever. This was about the dark horse that staggered through her chest at night when she reached across the bed for her husband. This was about forgetting for even one second that he was dead and having to remember all over again. This was about thinking that Hill could fill the dark space that had hollowed out in her, that she could stuff him in like insulation. If only Bob would come back for one minute, she'd do anything for one minute. What would she ask him? *Is this child yours? And would you mind so very much if I loved again?*

She could love this child. Already the stirrings were in the same ballpark as the love for a romantic partner, the same but different. The way a house is a house, yet

Rocky's house back in western Massachusetts was different from the creaky little house that she rented from Isaiah, and different again from the house she'd bought in the center of the island that needed reconstructive surgery.

Rocky wasn't blind to the damaged infrastructure with the girl. All kinds of things might have happened to her once her mother's attention went to drugs rather than a toddler. Hearing the story from Natalie felt like a spray of gunfire, but she got the main gist of it, and she understood the usual pathways that parental disintegration takes with kids.

Ideally, babies and toddlers should develop like marsupials: the healthiest development happens if a kid, or a joey, knows that it's always okay to hop back into the maternal pouch. Little ones grow best when they know that someone has their back. If scary bad guys arrive on the scene, if a monster under the bed or a fever of 102 degrees appears, the kid has someone to count on. The parent doesn't have to be perfect; the parent just has to promise to be there.

Natalie didn't have access to the marsupial pouch once her mother got swept along the current of drugs. Small children without protection will find ways to survive that either drive them toward people or drive them away from people; they develop a ramped-up neediness or a fine-tuned distrust. Natalie didn't seem like the kind of person who trusted many people, but here she was, camped out in Rocky's spare bedroom.

Natalie had left for the day—another day of looking for a job or going to the library, that's what she said. Rocky had received no phone calls so far asking for her help as animal control warden.

"Come on, Cooper. Let's do some demolition work."

Cooper scuttled to a stand. If Rocky was leaving the cottage, so was he. They loaded into the yellow truck, with Cooper filling every inch of the passenger seat, and drove the two miles to the recent acquisition of real estate.

Russell the carpenter wasn't due until ten or so; this was his late day. But there was a wonderful blue Dumpster sitting next to the house, ready to receive the damp curtains, the walls thick with mildew, the faux paneling, the cracked linoleum. The idea of reclaiming the true nature of the house was exhilarating to Rocky, as if the house had called to her. While Rocky waited for Russell to show up, she grabbed a crowbar and began pulling down old Sheetrock in the pantry. The rest of the house had plaster walls, so the pantry had to be a more recent renovation. The curative properties of distraction were a balm to her agitated state. She had recently discovered that she was damn good at demolition; she liked tearing things apart, ripping entire walls off in huge slabs.

Had Hill forgotten her? Rocky didn't want to veer in that direction; truly she had enough to think about with Natalie. She didn't want to be the ex-girlfriend who kept calling, or driving by his house, or stalking him by text or e-mail. Rocky had worked with hundreds of clients who had been dragged through the emotional barbed-wire terrain of brokenheartedness. They wanted answers to the unanswerable questions. *Why did he stop loving me? . . . How does someone simply stop loving someone else? . . . If I could just talk to him, get him to listen, we could fix this. . . . If she could tell me what went wrong, I could change, I know I could.*

There were no acceptable answers to any of these questions, and Rocky knew it. But still, something didn't add up about Hill, about the ferocity of his affection, the steady zeal of his attention, the way he had stroked her neck down to her collarbone and the way it had ignited an essential ember in her, sending heat spiraling up her spine. No, that all could have been the lust of new love and she simply hadn't recognized it. Those chemicals last six to nine months and can be mistaken for deep and abiding love. She didn't want to get confused between lusty chemicals and love.

Rocky headed for the second floor with her crowbar. One bedroom was water-damaged beyond repair. The roof had leaked for years. Both Isaiah and Russell had said that trying to bring the plaster back to its pristine past value would result in heartache and a huge expense.

"I can just smash it to bits?" Rocky had asked yesterday.

"That's right," said Russell. "I'm amazed at the number of women who love demolition work."

Rocky didn't hesitate. She tossed the crowbar onto the floor, slid a paper mask over her mouth and nose, and secured the front of her hair with two large clips. Isaiah had told her to wear a mask when she was tearing the house apart or she'd coat her lungs with molded plaster and who knew what else. What was in plaster anyhow? She put on safety goggles and picked up Russell's sledgehammer with the six-pound head. She aimed directly at the wall. Once, twice. She kept her knees soft, the way she did with archery. The plaster broke up in webs of chalky granules. The lathes underneath responded to her direct hits. The thin slats popped off with satisfying cracks.

If she got lucky, large hunks of plaster came off, like layers of sunburned skin, revealing the ribs of lathe beneath, rows and rows of horizontal strips that offered little resistance to either the crowbar or the sledgehammer. Working away at it, Rocky thought only of smash, dust, rip, pop, toss it out the window into the Dumpster below. She looked down the stairs once at Cooper, who lay at the bottom with a smear of dust on his black fur. She wished that she had left him home and hoped that he wasn't breathing in too much of the detritus from the house. He would have clearly earned a swim in the ocean after this.

By midmorning she had stripped two walls down to the studs. The white paper mask and the protective eye gear had become unbearably hot. Her sweat had been absorbed by the white powder, forming a sort of goo on her arms and legs. The bedroom was on its way to starting over; Russell would add new wiring, insulation, and clean, uncomplicated drywall. The nearly hopeless house was on its way to being reborn.

Rocky heard the gurgle of Russell's diesel truck. Two doors slammed shut. Good. He had a worker with him today. She needed to consult with him about something, but she couldn't remember what because all she'd been thinking about was Hill and how he might have forgotten her even though it was Rocky who had shoved him out the door in a rage. That didn't mean Hill should forget her.

Russell wore a blue-and-white kerchief around his head, knee-length canvas pants with an impressive amount of shred, and work boots.

"I see you've been busy here this morning," he said after letting his gaze swivel around the war zone of her labors. He shook his head. "Women and demolition."

Chapter 24

Melissa

"When we're developing photos in the lab and something shows up that we hadn't seen before, focus on that which was previously unseen," said Mr. Clarke. Melissa was taking his special photography course that he offered during the summer. He sounded suddenly formal and mysterious, as if the answer to a massive secret would come into focus in the developing trays. Melissa decided to pay attention; it was her new approach, since she was going to be a senior in high school. She would pay attention. She could always forget what a teacher said later, that part was easy. Strands of growing up had braided together for her at the end of the school year, and she felt older.

Was all this leading somewhere final, like a recipe for a cake, and then she'd stay the same ever after?

Was everything a destination, like graduation from high school, the beacon of light toward which she was crawling on her bloody knees? Yes, graduation was a destination. Or like the day she would pack up to leave the island for college—now there was a huge destination point in time. Would she get to that destination and then be the same forever? She hadn't asked these questions out loud because she knew what her parents would say. *Oh no, you'll never stop changing. Life is a constant state of evolution.*

For two people who got divorced because of irreconcilable differences when Melissa was six years old, her parents consistently gave the same answers to most questions. Melissa didn't want to hear their predictable answer. The idea of change exhausted her, and if she had to think about constantly changing throughout her entire life, a mindless gargoyle might grab her by the throat and choke the life out of her.

The gap between her and Mr. Clarke, the photography teacher, was as wide as the ocean. He was old, older than her mother or her father, but despite that he was teaching her to see, and for that she was grateful. Clearly, he was still a separate species, and for the time being she'd wait to find out if he could be trusted with her most important thoughts. She had tested Rocky, an unlikely adult, and she had proven trustworthy, until now. Why would Rocky take that foster girl in? Couldn't she see?

Something showed up in the photo of Cooper and Natalie. When Natalie had first arrived, Melissa stopped in, returning Cooper from one of their photo shoots in Portland. Melissa had automatically taken a picture, first of Rocky and the girl, and then Natalie with Cooper, the king of the island. That's what her mother called him. Everyone knew him. When she took him on a run, people stopped her to pat him and talk with him. *How are you today, Cooper? Is this girl running you too hard?* And he was the last male dog complete with testicles that she'd ever seen. He wasn't much of a role model for the spay and neuter movement. The other one in the photo was Natalie, the ultimate in helplessness, the foundling who had crept into Rocky's life like a virus, slipping under the skin of their lives.

Melissa had photographed them with her digital camera, not the old Pentax K1000 that Mr. Clarke insisted on for the first part of the course. She downloaded the photos to her computer. Right there, she noticed the look in Cooper's eyes. Not in his eyes really, but in his body. Natalie had her hand on his head, as if she was a natural part of Rocky and the dog, but some part of Cooper was pulling away, the muscles along his scalp or maybe on his neck. Even along his front paws there was a slight tilt away from Natalie. Couldn't anyone else besides Melissa and the camera see this?

Now that Rocky was wrapped up with Natalie, Melissa felt change looming toward her with a large and bottomless pull. Rocky had just bought that old house, and who but Rocky would have picked something so decrepit? The house was two miles from Melissa's house. Once the renovation was finished and Rocky had moved in, Melissa would no longer be able to see her as she bumped along in the yellow truck with Cooper's black head hanging out the passenger window. Melissa had gotten used to Rocky living just down the road from her. Why did Rocky have to change things?

Who cared if Rocky was going to move to another part of the island? Not Melissa. She would not care. It wouldn't change her job of walking Cooper and taking him along with her to Portland when she took photos of other dogs. Rocky had taken the ferry into the building supply place to pick out toilets or something and left Cooper at home. Melissa didn't know how long it would take to remodel the house so that Rocky and Cooper could move in. At least several months, maybe longer if the job wasn't completed by winter.

Melissa's job was to take him for an easy run at a good dog-friendly pace. That was the deal: when Rocky went off-island, which she needed to do several times a week, it was Melissa's job to look after Cooper, take him to the beach, and throw unlimited slimy sticks or tennis balls into the ocean for him.

Cooper was a majestic swimmer, a true dog Olympian. It was Melissa who had discovered that Cooper could shake on command after emerging from the ocean with salt water glistening in his black fur.

"Cooper! Stay. Shake," she had said one day after being drenched for the third time. To her amazement, he stopped where he was, a good ten feet from her, and agreeably shook the water from his body, starting at his massive shoulders and chest, letting the loose skin roll from side to side, his entire spine vibrating as water shimmered off him in an arc of salty spray.

She tried it again after he returned from retrieving another ball from the ocean. The next time he galloped out of the Atlantic, he held a sodden tennis ball in his soft mouth, delicately balanced on the tips of his formidable fangs.

"Stop. Shake," said Melissa. Cooper stopped, dropped the ball, and shook again without getting a drop on her.

Melissa had not been able to contain her excitement when she first discovered this. She had charged back to Rocky's house with the dog to show off his new trick. She and Cooper ran down the dirt road, and Melissa picked up speed when she saw Rocky's truck.

She called to her as she bounded up the steps of the deck.

"Rocky! You're not going to believe what Cooper can do. This guy is so smart, they should put him in the AP classes. I can't believe it."

It had been delicious to show Rocky something new about the dog, something only Melissa herself had discovered. When they walked down to the beach with Cooper, Rocky responded with a big openmouthed laugh when she saw Cooper's on-command water shake.

"I never would have thought to ask him," said Rocky. "I never would have imagined that he understood. Who knows what else this guy knows?"

Melissa had glowed.

Rocky spent hours every day at the weird house doing demolition work. Who cared if Natalie was there some of the time? At first, it was all about Natalie finding a summer job in Portland, and now look what had happened. She was following Rocky around like some wounded animal. Who cared if Rocky believed everything that weird chick said, the oh-so-poor foster kid? The five-star wacko, that's who she was. Melissa still had Cooper. He was waiting for her at the cottage.

She trotted down the familiar gravel driveway, lined on either side by thick tangles of rhododendron and bittersweet. She walked the last bit to cool down. Perfect—Rocky wasn't back yet, so she and Cooper would get in a good beach run. She loved the way Cooper greeted her. She tilted up the planter on the deck to get the key. Nothing. While she considered what this meant, the door opened and there was Natalie, her light hair wispy and jagged, eyes wide, set in determined helplessness.

"Hi. I've already walked Cooper. Rocky doesn't need you anymore. I mean, she doesn't need you to walk Cooper anymore. That's my job now."

Natalie stood in front of the door, closing it partially so that the dog couldn't get out. Melissa stumbled as she backed off the step, hit by the force field beaming from Natalie. She heard Cooper's claws on the floor. Then he barked, and the hair rose on the back of her skull.

"I don't believe you. Open the door and let him out," said Melissa. She'd already decided that Cooper was more important than saying the right thing.

Melissa was far smaller than Natalie in weight, and there was an undefined quality about the other girl's body, like she'd never played any sports so she didn't look like a high school girl. But she had done something, and it just might have included fighting. Melissa had never fought with anyone, never hit anyone, and she wasn't sure that she knew how. She was willing to find out. Melissa stepped onto the broad step in front of the door and flexed her fists. Her eyes never wavered from Natalie's face.

"If it's that important to you, go for it. He's just a dog," said Natalie, stepping aside just enough so that Melissa could open the door, just enough so that they had to breathe in each other's scent, bristling as they came within inches of each other. When Melissa opened the door, Cooper burst out, giving her a high-pitched whine of a greeting, wrapping around and around her thighs and bumping into her. Then he walked a polite twenty feet from the house and let out a long overdue pee.

"Tell Rocky I'll bring Cooper back when she gets home. No, tell her to come to my house to get him."

Melissa and the dog trotted along the dirt driveway without looking back. Natalie had lied about walking Cooper. That dog hadn't peed in hours.

Chapter 25

Natalie had been staying with Rocky for ten days when finally she had seen the girl's arms uncovered. Rocky had walked into the house at the end of a particularly hot midsummer day and found the girl uncharacteristically poised on the counter, in a tank top. Rocky saw the scars from across the room. She stopped, despite the urgent request from the dog for his dinner, his ungainly dancing steps that he performed for his food, his black claws tapping on the linoleum as he moved from the plastic tub of food in the pantry to his bowl on the floor. Back and forth, as if Rocky would never get the hint.

Natalie jumped off the counter and lunged for her denim shirt hanging on a chair and put it on.

"Don't look at me," she said. The double meaning in her panicked voice was unmistakable: *Look at me, don't look at me. See me, don't see me.*

Part of Rocky sagged, the part of her that knew how hard something had been for Natalie, how much Bob would have moved heaven and earth if he had known this child existed. Rocky would have to do it for him now. She knew what Bob would do. She had watched him soothe broken animals at his clinic, the ones who'd suffered at the hands of the worst end of humanity.

"Let's feed the dog first."

Cooper supervised every step of his food preparation. He peered into the fifty-gallon plastic garbage can as Rocky dunked a coffee mug into it and it came out brimming with kibbles. He escorted her back to the food dishes, staying five feet away, and watched as she poured the kibbles into his bowl. He looked up at her and waited for the touch, the reassuring rub of Rocky's hand on his flanks. Only then did he lie down to eat.

"Bon appétit, big guy," said Rocky.

She popped open a can of cat food, and Peterson appeared at the screen door within five seconds. She placed the cat's dish on the other side of the joint water dish. Peterson glanced at the dog and arched her calico spine upward in warning.

"Play nice, Peterson. Cooper thinks your cat food is creepy, and he doesn't want it, so relax." Rocky was killing time, letting the girl recover from whatever agony gripped her.

Rocky pulled a package of lasagna noodles out of the cabinet, pointing it at the girl. "I'm going to dazzle you with my budding cooking talents. You can help if you want. Bob was the real cook at our house."

Natalie hadn't moved after pulling her shirt around her. The girl stood in the center of the kitchen, her back hunched as if she was trying to hide the center of her body, trying to hide everything about her, her arms wrapped tight.

"I've learned a lot about cutting while I worked on college campuses. I don't know if this helps, but I've heard just about everything you can imagine from people who cut."

Rocky also learned a surprising amount from Bob's canine patients. Abused dogs that showed up at Bob's clinic either cowered pathetically, shivering and whining as they crouched on the floor, often urinating uncontrollably, or were overly aggressive, willing to survive at all costs by attacking, but visibly terrified at the same time. Bob's job was to attend to their wounds and assess the damage done by starvation in cases of neglect, but before he could do that he had to establish the examination room as a safe place, and he had to become a safe guy.

Bob had responded in the same way to the abused dogs whether they were overly submissive or overtly aggressive. He talked, often ignoring the dog completely, but he kept up a steady flow of words, with heavy doses of *good dog* tossed in. In the midst of his monologue, he would pull out dog treats from a cookie jar and set them between him and the dog, allowing the dog a respectful distance. Bob would move slowly, and eventually either the dog would nod off in exhaustion or Bob would be able to hold out his hand, palm up, for the dog to sniff.

"It doesn't always work," he had told Rocky back when she assisted him at the beginning of his career. "There is a tipping point with animals where they are unable to see safety when it's right in front of them. All they can see is danger and potential threats because that is precisely all they've known, and that makes them very dangerous pets. Some animals can come back from the tipping point, and some can't."

Rocky didn't have a huge repertoire of language about food preparation, but she talked steadily while Natalie stood frozen, keeping Rocky in her sight constantly, rotating her head like an owl. Rocky talked about boiling the noodles, about popping open the jar of sauce, the miracle of having mozzarella cheese in the fridge, her regret about not having other ingredients that would no doubt improve the lasagna, even if she didn't know what those ingredients were.

"What do think, is 350 degrees the best setting? The last time I looked, everything that went into an oven was cooked at 350 degrees. Do you like Parmesan cheese?" asked Rocky.

She was a terrible cook, but Natalie couldn't possibly know the full extent of her disastrous cooking. She might even get the girl to eat the stratified layers of thick noodles that looked like seaweed, smothered in bottled sauce.

Natalie unclenched her body. "Sure, 350 degrees sounds right."

The thing with lasagna is the timing. Rocky wanted to ingest something profoundly high in carbohydrates, something that would stem the tide of what Natalie was sure to tell her as soon as she asked about the scars. Asking questions is all about timing and being ready to listen. More than anything, Rocky was filled with a desire to feed the girl the way Bob would have gone about it, step-by-step. Maybe if she cooked like he did, then Natalie would vicariously get some of the feel-goodness that Rocky had always gotten from her husband's cooking.

She mimicked Bob's foodie body language. At each step of the process, she placed a finger in the bowl of thick sauce or shredded mozzarella and licked the essence, touching her lips lightly, uttering a pleased "ahhh." She let the noodles swell in a bath of boiling water, watching them expand. Then she laid them out in the nine-by-thirteen pan she had bought in Portland. The first layers of noodles hovered over a thin layer of the sauce. She spread the cheese layer with her fingers, topped it with more sauce, then more limp noodles, until she had filled the pan. When three layers were squeezed together in a pattern of compatibility, she slipped the pan through the throat of the oven and patted the door shut with her oven mitt. As the lasagna began to heat up and expand, the entire thing heaved and moaned. The topping of freshly grated Parmesan sweated into a glistening coating until it darkened and formed a burnished layer. Rocky and Natalie both jumped when the timer went off.

Bob had never made lasagna in July. What was she thinking? The house was blazing hot from the boiled noodles, the 350 degree oven. Sliding the lasagna to the center of the table, she sat across from Natalie and wiped her face with a blue dish towel.

"I'm sweating and wiped out. The truth is, I'm not a cook, and we don't have to eat this if it's terrible. If we're going to test it, we better eat it outside before we both pass out from the heat."

On the deck, the lasagna sat midway between Natalie and Rocky. Natalie pulled the cuff of her shirt down over her hand and used it to protect her hand as she grabbed the edge of the hot dish.

"Can I scoop it out on our plates?" asked Natalie.

Rocky nodded, handing her a thick white plate that looked like it came from a restaurant. They both loaded up and gingerly balanced the plates on their legs. Cooper's pink tongue tipped over the edge of his bottom teeth as he panted; he soon headed to the cooler grass and rolled on his back to rub in the full essence of the sweet green stubble.

"You can take your shirt off if you want to," said Rocky. "I've already seen your scars, and you've got to be roasting in that shirt. Your choice."

Natalie slowly dipped her fork in a three-inch section of noodle, and a glob of cheese slid off it. She put her plate down on the weather-beaten cedar table that was no bigger than an end table. She unbuttoned her shirt, revealing her tank top, pulled her arms out of the sleeves, and placed the shirt on the back of her chair. The scars along her arms varied from webs of fine white lines to thick raised welts. Some of the injuries looked brighter, as if she had cut her arms within the past few months. Natalie held her arms out for Rocky to see. She turned them over to reveal more scarring on the flesh of her inner arms, some old and firm, some more recent with a telltale red shimmer.

Rocky put her fork down with deliberate slowness. She did not want to picture the girl slicing her body. She swallowed hard. "It looks like you had a lot of feelings that needed an outlet at one time. Did cutting help?"

"It was the only thing that helped when I was thirteen and living with family number seven. I learned not to do it so that I needed stitches. But the family saw them anyhow and thought I was a danger to the little kids in the house, like I'd really hurt them, you know? If I cut, I knew I was real and I had real feelings, and I didn't want them to take that away from me. So they put me in a special group home, as if that would make things better." Natalie rubbed her forefinger along her inner arm. "I sort of went back to cutting, just a little, when I started to look for my father."

They both pushed their plates away. As the meal cooled, flies took the opportunity to land in the red sauce. Natalie had a bottomless reservoir of horrors to tell her. Rocky would have to listen, it was the least she could do. No, more than that. She owed it to Natalie. It wasn't just because Natalie was an adolescent in need; it was because someone should have been there to protect her. If that someone was Bob, Rocky wanted to make up for lost time.

Chapter 26

Natalie

N atalie had shifted from the foster care system to her own apartment to Franklin's apartment. Her moves had been ordained by the Subway restaurant where they worked in Worcester. If Natalie hadn't been drawn to the vegetarian sub sandwich and Franklin hadn't already been working there, helping the manager with her Facebook page in his spare time, they wouldn't have met. The fast-food franchise was at the heart of it. Franklin had a future; Natalie could see that as clear as anything, and she wanted to be a part of his future, at least for a while.

Franklin traveled nightly over the Internet, scouring the links that he sought, reading them like tarot cards and divining their destiny. Most nights they stripped off their clothing as soon as they returned to his apartment on the second floor, leaving behind the gases of bread yeast and processed meats, mayo, and the sharp tang of pickles. She liked to pull on one of Franklin's T-shirts that stopped at the top of her thighs. She liked to be naked beneath the T-shirt so that she was draped in Franklin.

Natalie had a litter of scars, high on the inside of her thighs and on the tight muscles of her forearms. Franklin was pulled into the red raised ridges. The first time he saw them he ran his thumb along the ridges and examined them as if he was in an art museum.

"Did someone else do them, or did you?" he asked.

"It was an inside job," she said, suddenly trying to pull the T-shirt down to cover the slats of scars. "It was me, and me."

"What did you use?"

"Hey, it was a long time ago, back when I was thirteen, which is why they look so stupid. I don't do it anymore. Especially since I get like keloid scars, which are worse than regular scars. They get bigger. One thing about being a floater is that caseworkers and therapists come with the territory. One of them actually helped me figure out another way to take care of feeling bad."

But Franklin was drawn to the scars, touched them daily, and watched them from across the room as if reading them, assessing their value.

"You and me, we're a gold mine," he said every night as he slipped in next to her on the mattress on the floor.

They were two months into the living arrangement, and one month after Natalie had given up her room in a rental house, when he asked her, "Can you do a couple more of those?" He ran his tongue along the raised scars on her arms.

"Get out of here," she said, pushing him away.

He placed his hand on her wrist and encircled it. "I'm working day and night on this project. And I want to bring you along with me, but, babe, you've got to bring something more to the table. You know what I mean?"

"How does cutting bring something to the table? Even saying that I'd do it, which I won't."

He slowly pulled one arm over her head and pressed closer to her. His knee opened her thighs. The pillow hadn't had a pillowcase on it all week, and a stale scent of hair oil rose up.

" 'Cause you're a fallen angel. You're the sweet meat that's going to draw in our players when we find them. And I know they're out there. Who can resist a sweet angel who hurts herself? They'll be standing in line to save you."

With his other hand, he started at her collarbone and ran his fingers along the central line of her torso, stopping briefly at her belly button and then going to the scars on her inner thighs.

"I'm the mastermind, but you're the honey in the trap."

"I could do a few more. It's no big deal," she said.

When she was positive that Franklin was too busy admiring the scars on her thighs and working up to the inevitable destination between her legs, she tilted her head back and let out a sigh that Franklin would think was desire.

Once she moved in with Rocky in July, it was important for Natalie to pursue work. She applied for two waitressing jobs in Portland. These were real waitressing jobs, not like her job at Subway, where she had been counter help. She was more like a sandwich construction worker at Subway, asking the customers if they wanted peppers, lettuce, tomato, chopped olives, or onions as she dipped her spoon into the plastic tubs of sandwich extras. And sauce, did they want sauce? Ranch, southwestern, blue cheese, all of which were mayo-flavored from prepackaged mixes. Each sandwich was wrapped in tissue paper with the Subway logo and tossed into a plastic bag that Natalie spun in the air to twist it closed before she handed it to the customer across the great divide of the counter.

She had applied at the Portland Hotel; predictably, they didn't want her. They didn't say as much, but not being wanted was a language that Natalie understood immediately. She had learned the language of inference from the procession of foster parents. Everything depended on what was meant and very little on the words that were actually spoken.

At age six, Natalie had braced herself to learn inference from the body language of the Graftons, the family she lived with for all of her first-grade year. She was the only foster kid there, and the parents had two sons who were fourteen and sixteen. The brothers looked like grown-ups, yet they weren't. They had tricked her the first time and then the second time, pulling down her pants, using their fingers on her with their ragged boy fingernails, telling her what would happen if she told their mother or father. Their parents would bury her in the depths of the murky backyard pond, they had insisted. It hadn't mattered when she cried, so she no longer cried. But at six, she studied the large boy who waited for her and learned what preceded his want of her. Because she was a floater, not a real kid, not a biological child, she had to reckon her days and nights differently. In the Grafton house she was fed, which she liked very much, and she even ate at the same place as the mother, the father, and the two large boys. This was so much better than her previous family, who hadn't allowed her to eat with them. She was clever at six, and food was something that she needed to live. The boys could hurt her with their fingers, but it was a fair balance in order for her to have food. Then they promised to do more than that, and one of them had unzipped his khaki shorts and showed her his penis, and said that was what he'd use on her the next time. Natalie knew that this could split her apart and she might die from it. The boys showed her a picture of exactly how on the computer.

Natalie had to keep strict attention on both boys when she was home. She learned that if the boys stayed in the computer room with the door closed and they were uncharacteristically quiet for too long, they might be looking at pictures of people doing naked things and then they would wait for her in the laundry room or the two-car garage. The older boy drummed his fingers on the table when he planned to surprise her. She couldn't believe that he didn't know that this gave him away. At first she thought he was sending her secret messages, but then she realized that his body acted without a big hunk of his brain. The younger boy stared at her when she watched TV, glaring like he was both mad at her and wanted her. This was his giveaway. And most of the time these twitches and glares gave her a way to avoid them, but not always. They were very big and strong, and she was only a first-grader. Natalie discovered that even though she thought the penis would split her in half, it had not, not like she imagined.

"**We don't** have anything available now," said the headwaiter in the hotel, "but if something comes up, we'll give you a call."

He was twenty-three or twenty-four, and Natalie knew that his parents had spent a fortune sending him to college, an easy $35,000 a year. Here was their $140,000 investment, curling his lip up on one side, and he couldn't lie better than that? If every single waitress called in sick with dengue fever, he still wouldn't call her. Natalie had known that when she walked into the lobby with its richly carved front desk and the press of money filling the air.

She walked downhill to Commercial Street and picked a more likely place. The Lobster Shack. No second-guessing was required to figure out what they served. She pushed open the door to a battalion of tables all covered with red-checked plastic tablecloths. Two waitresses carried large round trays, and they wore street clothes, shorts and T-shirts with the LOBSTER SHACK logo on the back. The woman working the bar was fast, filling pitchers of water and pints of beer from a tap, shoveling ice into glasses for tea. She was a machine. She had worked hard all her life, and she liked to work. Natalie knew that this woman— hair pulled back into an almost ponytail assisted by hair clips—liked to work because work was better than home. The giveaway was the shape of her arms, the way her arms had become long, hard, and sinewy, as if no one had ever lifted a bag for her, opened a door when she was loaded down with four grocery bags, or helped her carry a child. Natalie would need to be careful with her. She approached the bar.

"Are you hiring any waitstaff?' asked Natalie. She wished she hadn't picked this place, and she glanced back at the door to the street to gauge her exit strategy.

The woman behind the bar looked up and locked her eyes on Natalie in a metallic click, as if to say, *I've got you.*

"I'm hiring help who don't whine, don't call in sick ten minutes before their shift starts, or give food away to friends. I'm hiring waitresses who have a memory that can hold five orders for five minutes and who don't ever spit in anyone's food. I know it's a tall order, but that's the way it is. We have standards."

Natalie knew that bullshit would be useless; she might as well stand there in her underwear because this woman could see everything. She slammed down the beer tap again, and Natalie flinched. Sam Adams gushed into a tall glass.

"Well, do you want to apply or not? My lunch crowd is coming in."

This woman was a floater just like Natalie. She'd bet $100 on it. What was it about her that screamed *foster kid*? The way she scanned the room for trouble when each customer entered, the way the bar was her command post? Was this what Natalie would look like when she reached the unimaginable age of thirty? Not if she could help it. Not if things worked out.

"Yes, I'd like to apply. Yeah, thanks."

The woman reached under the bar and pulled out an application and pushed it toward Natalie in one efficient movement in between two orders of iced tea and another beer. Natalie filled out the application using Rocky's address on Peaks Island, noted her GED education, and listed her job at Subway as her past job experience. She gave the number for her pay-as-you-go cell phone as her contact number. She prayed this woman wouldn't call her. Natalie pushed the application across the bar, then melted off the stool and headed for the door.

"Hey," said the woman with a bark that echoed off the wall. "You live on Peaks? Since when? I know everyone out there."

How could she make this woman shut up? Natalie would never in one million years work for her, not the way she saw straight through her.

"I'm just there for the summer," said Natalie as she pulled open the door, letting heat and daylight stream into the dark bar. She ran down Commercial Street until her lungs burned like a woodstove. She needed to look out for people like that bartender. She couldn't afford to be seen.

Chapter 27

Melissa

Melissa knew the truth when she saw it, and Natalie was not the real thing. That girl was not hopeless and helpless like everyone thought. And that cutting on her arms? Oh please. Melissa lived in the unending daily drama of high school, and she saw plenty of girls and a few boys who took a razor or something sharp to their arms and made desperate but surface scratches, bubbling up in lines of dotted blood. And why the arms? Because they wanted everyone to see. Why did this make adults go completely stupid?

Melissa knew a thing or two about deception, real deception. She was a master at it, and a true master never, ever lets anyone know about the lie. Last year she had fooled her mother, her father, and her track coach into thinking she was a lean, muscled runner, which she was, but she had also been a starving runner, restricting her food to a squeaky three hundred calories a day at the peak of it. Now she was up to nine hundred calories a day, some days even more, and she needed every ounce of courage she had to keep from screaming as flesh began to soften her angular shape.

Rocky had known about the anorexia, but she had never spoken the words out loud, and for that, Melissa was grateful. It was like they made an unspoken agreement. Rocky was a psychologist, but she didn't play that card. It was an honor thing; Rocky had given Melissa the impression that she knew how to wrestle anorexia to the ground. Even now, Rocky would sometimes get near the topic, but then back off, as if to say, "Okay, kid, you handled it and you're getting better, but I'm here if you need me."

It had been Cooper who had truly seen her and dragged her back, with his big soft mouth, the way he relished his food and burped at her like he was giving her a lover's kiss. The way he kept her feet warm when Rocky let him stay overnight at Melissa's house was almost more than she could bear back then, back when she was being crushed by her fear of food. She could almost hear the dog say, *Come here, girl. I know who you truly are, and I still want you.*

It seemed so long ago, and in high school time it was long ago. She was on the verge of being a senior, light-years from the quandary of junior year. Even now she could walk into a room filled with fifty high school girls and tell within thirty seconds which ones had anorexia and which ones were throwing up. She didn't know how she could do it, because she never could have known before the bad year of not eating, but now she could. If she had to describe the dominant features, other than the skin pulled too tight across their faces and a slightly chilled look to that skin, she had to say it was the way they assessed each other, each one looking for the thinnest, then hating and loving the thinnest one like she was a doomed princess. Sometimes there was a dark haze around the eyes, but the whole thing happened so quickly, it was hard to pick apart.

This new girl on the island, Natalie, was working something, but it wasn't the truth. Melissa saw it in her the first day when Rocky let her stay at her house, the way Natalie acted all careful and sad. She was spreading out like an oil spill, getting into the creases of everyone's skin before they knew it, and when that happened they all went blind and couldn't see Natalie, not the way she really was.

It had been wrong to follow Natalie, but there were so many things that Melissa had done wrong in the past that this was just one more. Melissa was still on the cross-country team, and she was four pounds heavier than she had been last year. The old Melissa felt it was wrong about the four pounds, and the new Melissa had to use every ounce of her strength not to give in to old Melissa. She'd kept waiting for her coach to say something, or her other teammates to call her fat, but so far no one did.

She worked out at the YMCA after her job checking people in at the front desk two days a week before taking the ferry home. She'd been walking along the sidewalk in Portland, still steaming from her workout, when she saw Natalie through the window of the Abernathy Silver shop. What the hell was she doing in there? Nobody in high school would hang out in a silver shop, unless they were with their parents. Natalie wasn't technically in high school, having escaped with her GED, but she was one of them. Melissa stood at the corner of the display window, looking sideways to be sure Natalie hadn't seen her. That's when she saw Natalie's hand slip like water from the jewelry that hung on the wall to her skirt pocket. She was perfectly situated: Natalie's body blocked the salesclerk from seeing her hand, and besides, the clerk was conveniently busy with two women who looked like they could afford to buy a ton of silver. Wait, was this right?

Was the so precious Natalie shoplifting? Then she did it again. Shit and shit again.

So this is Rocky's special girl, the long-lost love child from her dead husband, the foster kid. She's a thief.

Melissa walked quickly down the street and stepped into the entryway to the bookstore. She didn't want Natalie to know she'd seen her.

Something lifted off Melissa; the metallic weight that sat on her thin bones dissipated as she rustled in her backpack for her camera. No, the camera was too big. She'd use her cell phone instead. She wanted to photograph the golden child, the oh-so-helpless girl who had dropped into their lives like a flesh-eating virus.

Natalie came out of Abernathy's, walked across the street, and approached a white van that was parked diagonally across from the bookstore. Natalie pushed the hair out of her eyes and dashed across the busy street, plunged her hand into her pockets, and tossed the jewelry into the driver's side window. Melissa cupped her hand around the cell phone. *Click, click, click.* The guy had on a hat and sunglasses and a long-sleeved shirt. *Click, click, click.* The van must have been sideswiped by a red car; a jagged red line remained along the driver's side. She tried to see the license plate, but a car from New Hampshire obstructed her view. The van made a right turn and was gone. Then Melissa pocketed her cell phone and stepped inside the bookstore. She gulped in a breath of air.

She had not actually gotten a photo of Natalie stealing, nor of her tossing the merchandise, but she did have a photo of Natalie with the profile of the man. Melissa couldn't bear the thought that Rocky might not believe her; she was all gooey-eyed about the girl. She didn't have anything real to show Rocky, and it would have to be fantastic before Rocky would believe her. What would this photo prove? Nothing.

From inside the bookstore, Melissa looked to see where Natalie was going next. Natalie was getting careless because she thought she had everyone fooled. Melissa would follow her and then hop back to the island before Natalie and go get Cooper. He was her damn dog, not Natalie's, and she wasn't giving up now that she had some ammunition.

Melissa followed Natalie for a few streets and then gave up when she entered the Portland Public Library. Natalie would just be using the library computers. Who cared about that? Melissa ran all the way down the hill to Commercial Street and nearly skipped to the ferry.

Chapter 28

Natalie

Returning to Rocky's cottage day after day was harder than Natalie anticipated. She'd been on the island for two weeks. Her storehouse of rancid resentment toward Rocky sometimes softened, and this worried her. Rocky tried so hard to cook food for her, baking lasagna in the summer when they could have had cottage cheese or peanut butter sandwiches. Natalie was annoyed by the sweat that ran along Rocky's face, the way she stuck her tongue out of the side of her mouth when she burned her hand while baking, and the way Rocky talked to the dog as if he understood her. Feeling as if something foreign had seeped into her pores when she was asleep, Natalie shook her body to get rid of it.

Something had to give, and Natalie waited for opportunities. When she opened the door to the cottage, she felt her bones itch. Rocky was just like that statue on her table, the one with the chick playing the sax, clueless to the world around her, all giddy with music. Didn't Rocky know that people lie?

The cat bolted for freedom the minute Natalie entered, not even pausing to ask for food. Did the cat know something? She had watched the Animal Channel during one of several stints at a group home and knew that animals can sense fear and they know if someone doesn't like them. But that had been about horses. Maybe cats were different. The cat couldn't know that Franklin lived in an apartment in Portland, feeding Natalie all the help she needed from his computer-filled brain. The cat couldn't know any of that, but the cat didn't want to be around her, and she hoped Rocky wouldn't notice the way the cat was repelled by her. Natalie wanted the cat to go away. It shouldn't be hard to make a cat disappear if she had to. The dog was a different matter.

He sat by the door as if waiting for Rocky, looking occasionally over his shoulder at Natalie. The black dog reminded her of someone back in one of the six grade schools she'd attended. One of the schools had this grandparent program, and there was an old man who came in and read to the kids; that's all he did. But he had a loose smile like this dog, and all the kids wanted to be near him. Natalie hadn't sat near the old man but stood beyond reach, listening to him read.

Rocky had easily let Natalie move into the spare bedroom. "Temporarily," Rocky had said. Until what? How much time did she have? Until DNA tests could be pulled together. Franklin reveled in the challenge that the DNA registry had produced.

"Clever," Franklin had said. "They think this is a big whoop-de-doo, but I should be able to chisel through this in two days. One week, tops. Tell me what you need because I want to be in and out before they have time to blink. Secure database, my ass."

Who says stuff like *big whoop-de-doo*? Computer geeks, that's who, with their pasty skin and poor hygiene. Franklin didn't know that it would be unnecessary to break through to the DNA tests, but the guy needed something to do and Natalie needed him. It was better if Franklin didn't know everything.

Rocky's cordless phone blinked a tiny red light. Messages. It would be a good idea to stay on top of those. She pressed the button to play. The first message was a man's voice.

"I got your message. Let's do a rewind. I miss you. Julie is filing for divorce, and neither of us are contesting, which I would have been happy to tell you, but . . . Nothing is entirely simple, and I didn't want the outcome of my marriage to be simple. It meant something. I want to talk to you. Call me back."

Natalie tilted her head to one side and then hit the Delete button. A boyfriend for the grieving widow sounded like trouble. Best to eliminate him immediately. She wanted Rocky's full attention, and a boyfriend would dilute the impact. Time to send the boyfriend packing. The dog looked at her. "None of your business!" she said to him.

The second message was about a rabies clinic the following week. Some vet guy who wanted Rocky to help him advertise the clinic and then help him vaccinate a colony of cats over on Island Avenue. Having access to Rocky's phone was helpful. But Rocky also had a cell phone. How far did Franklin's freaky brain go? Could he tap into Rocky's cell phone too? That would be gold.

She heard Rocky drive up, slam the door of the truck, and walk up the steps. She'd been practicing at her personal archery range for several hours.

Natalie leapt to the couch and curled into a tight ball, grabbed the want ads of the Portland paper, and put her head on the throw pillow. She lifted her head sleepily when Rocky came in.

"Did you know that Cooper can tell when you're coming home about five minutes before you drive up?" said Natalie.

Rocky had just received a welcoming dance from the dog, his full-body gyration all spine-curling, tail-spinning joy.

"This is a small island. He must know I'm coming home before I do," said Rocky, smiling. "What did you do today, besides being led around by Cooper? Were you sleeping? Are you feeling okay?" said Rocky, depositing a bag of groceries on the counter.

"I'm okay," Natalie said softly, adding a half-smile. "I was waiting for one of the restaurants to call me back about a job. They said they'd call me this afternoon. That's why I was waiting here. I guess I did fall asleep. Um, you have a message. I saved it. I'm sorry, I know I shouldn't have played it, but I did. I thought it might be about a job, and then I remembered that I gave them my cell number. I'm sorry, I won't do it again."

"Relax. My phone messages aren't all that interesting. Did someone lose a cat or something?"

Natalie sat up. "No. A vet guy called about a rabies clinic."

"Now that is important. It's possible you've heard my one and only interesting call," said Rocky. She sniffed the air.

The smell of heavily scented cleanser filled the air.

"I've been washing down all the cabinets. Tess stopped by and showed me how to do it. And that girl stopped by, your old neighbor. I keep forgetting her name. Marisa, is that it? I don't think she likes me. She's the kind of girl in high school who wouldn't like me."

Rocky scratched Cooper at the base of his skull. "Do you mean Melissa? Why wouldn't she like you?"

"I can tell by the way she looks at me. She's jealous that I'm spending so much time with you."

Rocky ran her fingers through her dark hair and sighed. "I wonder if there's a culture somewhere where teenage girls band together to protect each other rather than eviscerating each other," she said. "It could just be about territory. Or about Cooper—Melissa is pretty tight with our big guy here. Let's call it that."

Natalie opened her eyes wide, careful not to look left or right. "I'd never stop her from being with Cooper. That would be awful."

"You're the newcomer. Just give it some time. Let's see these cabinets," said Rocky.

Rocky opened one and howled with delight. "Now that's a different story. I can actually put all four plates in there without sticking to unknown substances. Nicely done, Martha Stewart."

They polished off a dinner of mac-and-cheese out of the box and canned green beans, a special request from Natalie. They sat on the deck with a spray can of Deep Woods insect repellent between them. Natalie slapped at the mosquitoes that were undeterred by the chemicals.

"Maybe Melissa is jealous," said Natalie. "I'd understand if she was. I've never had anything before, or anyone, and now I've got you. I mean not really, I don't have you. That sounds weird. But you're like a cool person, and you're letting me stay here."

Rocky laughed. "Would you please put that last part in writing for my brother? I've always told him I was cool, but I had no backup documentation."

"I've been jealous of other kids for as long as I can remember, jealous of their mothers who drove them to school and kissed them good-bye, of their fathers who coached them in little kid soccer. I was jealous because they had clothes that weren't all skanked out. I get the jealousy part. I understand it."

It was good to see Rocky laugh, to see her relaxed. Off guard.

Chapter 29

Rocky's copy of *Peterson's Field Guide to Mammals* was looking frayed after eight months of continual use. It had been her constant reference since she became the animal control warden on Peaks Island. She often kept it in the truck so that she could study it as soon as she got a call from someone about bats, deer, skunks, or raccoons.

Isaiah had asked her to attend a community meeting about the rising population of beavers on the island.

"I know you have a lot on your plate right now, what with kids showing up at your door and suddenly buying a house, but as the animal control warden, you need to be aware of the dilemma. Not that I'm expecting you to do anything about the beaver problem. They're not in your job description," explained Isaiah.

Rocky had seen evidence of the beavers on the back shore of the island, around the marshy land behind Battery Steele and on the land next to her new property. Maybe the beaver appreciated wild wisteria as much as she did. Smaller trees had been meticulously nibbled by the animals, leaving telltale stumps with sharp, pointy heads. She wondered if all beavers used exactly the same tree demolition techniques. Did young beavers observe as their parents selected trees for their home building? Did they sit and watch as their elders gnawed chunks of the tree, first girdling it, then working into the depth of the trunk?

"Who's running the meeting?" asked Rocky. She had stopped at Isaiah's office in the public works building to drop off her report on animals transported to the mainland.

"The City of Portland Public Works along with the Forestry Department. The beavers have chosen public land as well as private land, so it's not just a community problem," he said, sliding Rocky's two-page report into a well-worn manila folder. "This would be a good opportunity for you to observe. By that I mean listen and don't say anything. Emotions can run very high about what to do when wild animals and human real estate collide. You'll be in attendance to show your broad depth of concern over animal-human coexistence."

"Got it. Sit on my hands and zip the lips," said Rocky.

"Yes. Being silent will give you a wise and benevolent look. You could use some of that."

When Rocky went home, she consulted her *Peterson's Guide* for background information about beavers. Her calico cat, named after the guidebook, leapt down from her perch on top of the fridge to sit on the very page Rocky was reading. She tipped the book toward the floor, and Peterson slid off, landing with insult on the rug.

"Sorry, Peterson, this is work. Go annoy Cooper." With her back to Rocky, the cat tried to maintain dignity by immediately licking a paw and cleaning her face, as if she had truly intended to be in that very spot at that very moment.

"You aren't fooling anyone," said Rocky as she ran her big toe along the cat's spine.

Beaver: Castoridae. She flipped through the book and noticed that Peterson had remarkably little to say about beavers. Squirrels got seven pages, mice got twelve, but beavers merited only two, according to the tome on mammals. Beavers, despite their prowess in dam building and aquatic house construction, are really large rodents. She read the usual physical descriptions: thirty to sixty pounds in weight, rich brown in color, tail shaped like a paddle about six inches wide and ten inches long, and huge front teeth that can slowly but persistently buzz-saw through trees. Beavers are chiefly nocturnal. Rocky wondered if animals would still be nocturnal if humans weren't around. Did they take the graveyard shift so that humans wouldn't bother them?

She continued reading. Beavers prefer to eat and build with hardwoods, especially birch and maple. They live in family groups in their lodges consisting of parents, yearlings, and kits. Family groups may form colonies, and one colony may defend itself against another encroaching colony. But there's one bottom line: beaver colonies unite to share in repairing a dam. They are essentially water and forestry management specialists. Sort of like the guys coming to run the meeting on Peaks.

On impulse, she picked up the phone and called Hill. He hadn't returned her call two days earlier, but she was determined to pull herself out of the morass of reactionary rejection.

He picked up quickly. "I got the feeling you weren't going to call me back," he said.

"What do you mean? I never got a call from you," she said. They were already disagreeing. How had they drifted so far from sweet expectation and yearning?

"I left you a message. I'm not making this up. Why would I do that?"

"I have someone staying with me, she could have botched up a phone message," said Rocky.

"Who's staying with you?" asked Hill.

"Natalie, a girl who thinks that Bob was her biological father. A lot has happened, and I want to talk to you instead of acting out. I have to go to a meeting tomorrow night with the Forestry Department, and I could use your help with the whole wildlife management angle on this meeting. This is about a beaver population, and my wildlife encounters have been confined to cats, dogs, skunks, and raccoons. Will you come out?"

"Your deceased husband has paternity issues?"

"Yes. Maybe. It's not entirely clear yet. Seven o'clock tomorrow evening at the library."

"I wouldn't miss it."

Rocky and Cooper walked to the meeting in the community room of the library. She sat near the back of the room to keep Cooper out from underfoot as people arrived. Hill pulled a metal folding chair next to hers and sat down. He dipped his head down slightly, a gesture that in a young girl might have meant shyness, but with Hill it had to mean something else. She hated the way his cheeks flushed red, as if he had just come in from the cold, and the way the dark hair of his eyebrows and his brown eyes revealed a seriousness that his loose body camouflaged. She hated the way his wrist bones slanted out and sloped back to the long bones of his forearms. She especially hated that he had assessed the entire room of people the way a hunter would and that he had probably noted that her heart was beating double time. Her heart skittered and stuck in her throat.

"Both groups are here," he said quietly, turning his head and leaning into Rocky's ear.

Her bones felt disconnected, floating outside the sockets. "What do you mean?" she whispered.

"The same thing happened in Brunswick a few years ago," said Hill, keeping his voice low. "We have the save-the-beaver people on the window side of the room and the kill-the-beaver people on the bathroom side of the room. This always happens."

Somewhere on the island the beaver colonies had banded together in a meeting to decide what to do about the human encroachment. But their meeting was simple: they all agreed that when the dam was broken, they should fix it. There were no other options to consider when aquatic home designs depended on a particular water level.

Several options were offered by the kill-the-beaver group. Beaver pelts could be sold to Russia and the profits funneled into the school fund. The opposing side shot out of their seats in protest. "There's no market for beaver pelts in Russia. Maybe eighty years ago, but not today!" said a woman who taught at the school. She added that the schoolchildren would not want money gleaned from beaver cadavers.

"Cadavers are bodies, and we were only suggesting that their skins could be sold. But now that you mention it, the meat could be donated to either the homeless shelter or some very high-end restaurants in Boston," said one man whom Rocky vaguely recognized as a patient she had seen exiting Tess's physical therapy office.

The save-the-beaver people had only one viable suggestion, which was to acquire the land as a trust and just let the beaver live there.

Hill leaned over to Rocky again. "Great idea. And maybe they can speak beaver and get them to stop flooding the back roads and personal property. But it's hard not to vote for the furry guys with the fat tails."

"This isn't going well, is it?" asked Rocky. She wanted to soothe this thing between them. She moved her foot next to his and nudged him.

"Do you mean the meeting or us? If you were back at your university job, you wouldn't be having half as much fun. Does the girl have evidence that Bob is her biological father?"

"Not as such. We're looking into DNA. I haven't figured out a way to get DNA material from Bob. Right now I'm tracking down a long-lost uncle in Oregon and also trying to dig up something of Bob's that would yield, you know, cellular matter. And I'm not going back to my job. I resigned. I bought a house," Rocky whispered.

"When did all this happen? Never mind. Did you buy a house on the island?" Hill's voice had risen to a level that could project to the back of a classroom.

The entire row of people in front of them turned around to look at them.

"Yes. Can we talk about this after the meeting?"

The meeting yielded a standoff. The last of the summer sun glinted on the ocean as they exited the library. Hill automatically placed a hand on the small of her back as they walked and then, suddenly self-aware, he shoved his hands into his pockets.

"Before you say anything else, I need to tell you something. I should have said something about Julie, and if I had, this is what it would have been. She did nothing wrong in the marriage. I screwed up, but she was the one who left, and I didn't want her to leave. She was the one who bolted out of the marriage, took the dog, took the microwave, tossed everything into a trailer hitched behind her father's big silver diesel pickup. I did not see her for the next two and a half years. Until she showed up at the house and, as luck would have it, until you happened to show up as well," said Hill.

"You should have told me. I thought we were . . . ," said Rocky, suddenly feeling incoherent.

"Should I have called you the second she walked into the house? Should I have told you that she came to deliver the divorce papers and she broke down and cried? I hurt her, and as everyone involved agrees, I was a giant asshole. I spent one stupid night in a motel with a woman after an archery competition, and no matter what I said after that, there was no reaching Julie. She reacted like a chemistry experiment bubbling over, corroding everything in her path. So, yes, when she showed up I tried to comfort her, and I'm glad that I was able to."

Rocky's backlog of righteous rage searched desperately for an outlet.

"Julie and I crashed and burned before you ever moved to Peaks. I don't come with the best relationship credentials. The easiest part of my day is teaching

130 students in my English classes, and I can promise you that no other teacher at the high school would say the same. And grading papers at night and on weekends was less complicated than my personal life." He slapped a mosquito on his arm, and a small dot of blood rose up.

"I was afraid that you were going back to Julie. And then I went straight to crazy angry," Rocky said. They stood toe to toe. Cooper had walked ahead of them, and now he stopped and turned around, as if waiting for a response.

"If we have a chance, you can't just throw me out the first time you get scared. I mean, what was that at your house?"

"That was a de-evolved version of me." She put her hand on his forearm and slid it over his wrist, tucking into his fingers, knitting them together.

"I can't stop thinking about you," he said. "But you jumped to a terrible conclusion and never asked me anything, never talked to me, and you decided I was guilty. While I may be guilty of many things, one of them is not that I would lie to you. I will tell you every awful truth," he promised. "I will not lie to you, at least not about big things. If you ask about hairstyles, butt size, or shoes, then I might resort to creative answers." His hands moved toward her face, hesitated, and touched her so lightly that it might have been a breeze. "I want to hear more about the girl who says Bob was her father." He squeezed her hand.

"I want you to meet Natalie. Come on, she's home by now." Rocky pictured the three of them, snug in the cottage. She thought of the beavers banding together so that they could eat and huddle together at night. She knew what she'd do if she was a rotund beaver with a flat tail and buck teeth and if a little lost beaver showed up seeking shelter.

As they approached the cottage, Rocky said, "If Natalie is Bob's daughter, then I have to do anything I can to help her."

"What if she's not family? What do you do then?" said Hill.

"Then I might still have to do anything I can to help her," said Rocky. Cooper clattered along the deck, and the front door opened, spilling light from the kitchen.

"I heard Cooper . . . ," said Natalie, stopping abruptly and staring at Hill. Her hair was wet, and she had a towel wrapped around her.

Hill turned away and stepped back. "Bad timing. Sorry about that. I'll call you," he said, retreating, waving a hand in the air.

"Good night," said Rocky, wishing she could have banded together with Hill and Natalie.

Chapter 30

Natalie

The next day Natalie walked into the cottage and saw a pile of Rocky's clothing on the couch. She'd met the boyfriend for the grieving widow. Deleting his phone message hadn't been good enough. She knew how to handle men, knew their essential weak spots. That was no longer the problem. The real problem was that Hill took far too much of Rocky's attention.

"Natalie, I'm meeting Hill in Portland tonight, and we'd like it if you would join us. Come on, it would be fun," said Rocky.

"Do you mean, do I want to go on a date with you two? No."

Rocky had washed her hair and blown it dry with the hair dryer, something Natalie hadn't seen her do in the two weeks she'd been on the island. Usually Rocky was a wash-and-go gal. She was primping too much;

she had tried on two different pairs of pants and had finally settled on a skirt. A skirt?

"Wait, I guess I can come with you," said Natalie.

Rocky paused in midstroke as she rubbed lotion on her legs. "Good. This will give you a chance to get to know him."

Oh yes. Getting to know him was just what she wanted.

They met Hill at the dock on Commercial Street in Portland, where he had parked his truck. He looked uneasily at Rocky. "The truck isn't an easy fit for three people," he said.

"I can sit in the middle, I don't mind," said Natalie, getting in before protests began. She squeezed in, letting one leg press casually against Hill as she straddled the two bucket seats. "See, this works for me," she said with a smile in her voice, a young-little-girl smile that no one could object to.

Rocky got in and leaned forward to speak to Hill. "We're only going to the park, it's not like we're going to drive forever. I think we can all manage," she said, fastening her seat belt.

Hill gave her a sideways glance and started the truck.

"Can I put my bag behind the seats?" asked Natalie. Why would they say no?

Turning slightly away from Rocky, she picked up her canvas bag with her left hand and reached up and over

Hill's shoulder. The side of her left breast grazed his arm. Contact. He flinched and moved away. Two white-and-gray gulls examined the heel from a baguette on the sidewalk. One lifted off with the bread in its beak.

"Where did you say we're going?" asked Natalie.

"A free concert in Deering Oaks Park, just on the other side of downtown. Tonight it's some fiddler."

The traffic on an early summer evening had swelled with people cruising for parking. Hill buzzed his window down and leaned his left elbow out. "I only brought two lawn chairs," he said. "If you'd told me that there would be three of us tonight, I would have thrown another chair in."

At the grassy congregation of kids, families, dogs and couples, Hill did exactly what Natalie imagined a good boyfriend would do: he offered her his chair, insisted that she take it, and then sat on the ground near Rocky, leaning back uncomfortably for half of the concert, propped up on his hands. He stood up halfway through and said, "I'll be back in a few." He picked his way over blankets and around chairs, making his way to the bathrooms.

Much later, when Rocky and Natalie had returned on the ferry and were walking along the darkened roads of Peaks to the cottage, Natalie said, "I think it's better if I don't hang around with you and Hill. I don't know how to say this, but I get a feeling from him, an uncomfortable feeling. That's all I'm going to say."

They were on the long dirt road, going past Melissa's house. "What do you mean?" asked Rocky. They crunched along in silence, distress building like a storm. They opened the door, and Cooper burst out, greeting Rocky with his high singing voice, his tail wacking everything in sight.

"It's probably nothing. But do you know that feeling you get when you're scared and there's nothing really happening that you can point to, not exactly? Like I said, it was probably nothing." Natalie walked into her bedroom. Rocky followed.

"Wait a minute. This is very serious. I don't want you to feel uncomfortable with my friends, so could you be more specific? Did Hill do or say anything tonight? The man hardly spoke eight words the whole night. He was quieter than usual, but he has a lot on his mind. Natalie, talk to me."

She sat on the bed and kicked off her sandals. "I really want to go to sleep. Is that okay? Forget that I said anything."

She heard Rocky and the dog go outside. She had already learned that the more Rocky had to think about, the longer the walk. She didn't return for an hour. After that, Natalie saw the light from her bedroom glaring beneath her door long into the night.

Chapter 31

Tess

It was the height of July, her granddaughter wanted to come more and more often, and Tess saw no reason to say no. If she had scheduled a physical therapy patient, then of course the child couldn't come. Danielle was only seven after all. But on days when Tess was doing her other job managing the houses with summer renters, then Danielle could easily come along. And since the island was only four miles around and most of the rental houses were on the perimeter, facing out to the Atlantic or the bay side, they could ride their bicycles. Tess kept a bike for Danielle at her house. "I want summer to be so long," said Danielle, slipping on her helmet. She snapped the strap under her chin and straightened up the bike from the side of the deck.

Tess grudgingly put on her helmet, aware that she could not ask the child to wear a bike helmet if she didn't wear one herself. Tess loved the feeling of salt air fluttering her hair as she rode her bike, and she regretted all the safety precautions of childhood that her granddaughter faced. Her ex-husband, Len, had chided her about riding without a helmet.

"You wouldn't forget to wear one if you'd ever treated someone with a brain injury in the ER," he had said.

His logic, honed by years in surgery, was indisputable. What Tess had not told anyone—and some days she tried not to tell herself—was that since her surgery the sound of Len's voice had found its way into her again, filling up crevices she had not felt since she was a college student meeting him for the first time.

Tess now met her ex-husband in Portland once a week for dinner and darts. This was what remained of their early years when they were married and he was a young doctor who had put his family up as collateral against his gamble with alcohol. Len was single and sober now, defrocked of his medical license long ago and humanized at last. He had woken up sober with a second wife who found his sobriety tedious and unflattering next to her own love of the drink.

It was true that Len had broken the once-a-week rule while Tess recovered from surgery. He had even slept on her couch for the first week, and she had allowed him to check the tidy stitches riding low on her abdomen. She shooed him back to Portland when she felt better, upgrading to their once-a-week visit, letting him take the Casco Bay ferry out to Peaks Island until she could resume their normal schedule. She pushed any further thoughts of Len away; that fantasy would be best left unrealized.

Now she was watching their granddaughter with relentless vigilance, making sure all protective gear was in place, as if Len had given the child a monitoring system. On summer evenings, when no grandchild was present to remind her of the rule, she loved nothing more than mounting her bike and riding without a helmet.

"Summer *is* long. We can practice extending the moment while we ride," said Tess. She pushed off with her right foot. They bumped along the dirt road, coasting down the slight hill.

"Is that a Buddhist thing? Daddy says you're a Buddhist and that's why you painted the Buddha man on your bathroom door. I look at him every time I pee," said Danielle.

"Not quite. If Buddha was riding bikes with us today, he'd be so busy feeling the way the air touched his skin as it comes off the ocean that he wouldn't think about a moment being long or short, or if the summer was going away too quickly."

They came to Island Boulevard and turned left. Tess rode on the outside, keeping the girl tucked between her and the grassy edge.

"Would Buddha wear a bike helmet? Daddy said I have to wear a bike helmet, and he said that I should remind you to wear yours. Buddha's head looks too big for a helmet," said Danielle. They passed a tangled hedge of bittersweet.

"That's a good question. Let's see. If he were here right now, on his bike, with you and me . . ." Tess paused, giving herself time to think and be honest with Danielle. Then she decided that she had no possible idea. "I think he would wear a special large helmet, and he'd tie up his silky orange robes so they wouldn't get caught in the spokes. And he'd say this was the best place ever to ride his bike."

They rode twice around the island, a first for Danielle, who was now so big that she didn't ask once to stop. When it was time for Tess to take the girl back to Portland, Danielle brought them to her favorite place to sit, on the top deck of the ferry.

"When will I be old enough to take the ferry by myself?" asked Danielle, pressing her thigh next to her grandmother's.

"Are you in a hurry? Let's take our time, little one, just like our bike ride," said Tess, kissing the top of the girl's head. The child smelled like fresh air, the way sheets do when they've been hung outside.

"I'm not in a hurry, but it's good to be ready," said Danielle with all the wisdom of a skinny Buddha.

Tess's first physical therapy client arrived at her door exactly five months after her surgery for the double whammy of appendicitis and a twisted bowel. Even though her synesthesia had failed to return as her body mended, she needed to get back to work, with or without it.

"Hello, Harold. Come on in. Sorry to keep you waiting these last few months."

Harold was a few years older than Tess, seventy-five or so, and most of his body was pulled tight. Tendons and muscles were ready to twang at the first touch. That tightness, coupled with the decreasing muscle density of advancing years, made him the perfect candidate for disaster. He wore a hat from the feed store in South Portland. Layers of sweat left demarcations along the bulb of the hat, like the walls of the Grand Canyon.

"Good to see you, Tess. Glad you're still with us." When Harold took his hat off, some of his thin gray hair stood up straight and the rest was pinched in tight from his hat band.

Tess led him past the entryway to the first door on the right, bringing them to the treatment room. Her office consisted of a massage table covered by creamy flannel sheets. Adorning one wall were charts of the body, with dots along a highway of meridians from the skull to the torso to the feet. A plastic replica of the spine dangled from a hook on the far wall.

"Before you tell me what's wrong, could you stand right here?" asked Tess.

Harold stood facing her, looking like a schoolboy.

"Thank you. Now would you turn around?" she asked.

Tess tried to keep this part of the assessment short; Harold was the kind of man who shunned attention, and being looked at so intently was nearly intolerable to him.

Tess sighed. "Dang it all. Any day now I keep thinking that it will be back. That all my multisensory facilities will return to me. I don't feel at all normal without them."

"Should I come back some other day?" said Harold, still facing the back wall of the treatment room. "I wouldn't have called, but I was at the meeting about the blasted beavers last night, and it felt like a hot poker had run up my leg."

"No, dear. I can see that it's your hamstrings that are yanking everything south of your hipbones out of whack. I can see it, but it's like watching an old black-and-white movie. The mechanics of the body don't change. The bones, nerves, and muscles will get into trouble no matter if I see them as colors or as pudding. Hop on up to the table, please."

Harold backed up to the table and placed his chapped hands on the edge. He winced as he lifted his buttocks to the edge.

"I've waited until you got better, and I wasn't sure I could wait any longer," he said.

"You old fool. Portland is rich with physical therapists. Some of them are very young and beautiful. Show me how much you can straighten your right leg."

Harold gripped the table and tried to straighten his right leg. His overvigilant hamstrings didn't allow him to extend it from the table at any more than a forty-five-degree angle.

"Very good," said Tess.

"Good for nothing."

"Show me the other leg, please."

He could raise his left leg even less.

"How long have you been hobbling around like this?" said Tess. Her alarm was mixed with tenderness for Harold. She wanted to be stern with him, but even without the advantage of synesthesia, she could see how much pain he was in.

"Oh, never mind," she said. "Don't tell me. Swing your legs over and lie on your stomach. I'm going to apply some pressure to the muscles near the sciatic nerve, and it might feel like a red-hot bolt of fire at first, but then it will get calmer and calmer. I promise."

Everything about working with the body felt new to Tess. The feedback loop was still there, the sensation flowing from a patient's body into her hands. But the feedback had been a full orchestra before, and now it was a solo flute player. Harold's flute player was out of tune. Tess placed a knuckle in his right gluteus maximus.

"Keep breathing," she said. "Now I'm going to raise this leg just slightly and move it to the outside a few inches." As soon as she felt the first flutter of resistance, she stopped. Tess released the pressure on Harold's butt and rested his leg in her hands for a minute. When she lowered his leg again, she placed a finger midway down the back of his thigh, a light touch, to alert all the energy circling around his glutes that Tess was back and she was the new traffic cop directing a river of clogged-up energy to come south. She tapped lightly at his ankle.

"I can't figure out what it is that you do. Nothing that you do feels big enough or hard enough to fix what's wrong with me," he said into the hole of the face cradle, his words muffled by the flannel.

Tess began to work on his left side, repeating the sequence. Harold's muscles gave in to her touch. At least she was getting back to something that reminded her of who she was. Inch by inch, she was returning.

Chapter 32

Melissa

Melissa had been replaced by the new girl, the oh-so-helpless foster kid, the I'm-so-damaged-touch-me-gently girl. Melissa had never been deposed before, not in all her sixteen years, and even if she had fallen from grace in some weird caste system at school, it was inconsequential high school stuff. High school was one long drama filled with friends and wannabe friends, betrayals and alliances. In the big picture, Melissa knew it was a time-limited engagement. She had precisely one more year of high school. Over the summer she had already felt herself growing older, catching subtleties and double entendres that had eluded her in her younger years.

With Rocky, it had been different. Rocky was an adult, and she had treated Melissa like she was important, not fragile or eating-disordered; she treated Melissa like she mattered. They shared Cooper the dog, or almost shared him. The black Lab knew stuff about Melissa that nobody else knew, not Rocky, not her mother, not anyone. More and more it had been the three of them, a team with their own inside jokes.

All of a sudden, this girl appeared looking for her biological father and told Rocky in her breathy little-girl voice, "It was Robert, and now I'm too late."

Well, part of that was true. If her father really was Rocky's husband, he was dead. That was why Rocky came here in the first place. Her husband died right on their bathroom floor. Rocky told her the whole story back in January. Melissa had advanced to the rank of confidante, and no adult had ever nominated her for that position before. She ingested the intoxicating elixir of her exclusive status until Rocky told Tess, and then Isaiah, and then the entire island knew she was a widow and a psychologist and all the other stuff she had hidden for months.

Why did the girl have to show up, following Rocky around like some half-feral cat? Was Melissa the only person who smelled something rotten? Rocky let her move right into the little rental cottage. Suddenly Melissa was the stranger, the one on the outside.

If Rocky was really a psychologist—and Melissa still had a hard time picturing the archery/animal control lady as a psychologist—then Melissa figured she would be quick to pick up on a big fat liar like Natalie. A kid can't fake it with another kid, not ever. Kids fake it all the time with adults. Melissa had been shocked by how easily she misled her track coach and parents and every other adult during junior year with her dive into the world of anorexia. Except for Rocky—that was one thing Rocky had not missed. And yet here was Natalie, working Rocky like the grit of sand between her toes, rubbing, changing everything. It was like Rocky had gone stupid.

She had seen Natalie walking Cooper twice. That was Melissa's job. Melissa had been on a pier one day and saw how Natalie walked Cooper along Centennial Beach. Natalie was in la-la land, and she wasn't in tune with him, not like Melissa was. Natalie was on her cell phone the whole time. Cooper brought the girl a perfectly chewed stick, dropped it right at her feet, and she never even looked up.

Melissa felt like she had ants in her brain, churning little ant trails with their pincher mouths; this wasn't such a bad turn of events once the ants in her brain began to help her see Natalie in a way that no one else could. Melissa knew that Natalie wanted her out of the way, but Melissa would not go down easy. Natalie was not going to replace her as Cooper's buddy. She wasn't sure what would happen to Rocky; she might be a lost cause, but not the dog. That skanky chick was not moving in on her dog. Well, Rocky's dog.

Mr. Clarke, her photography teacher, said that the best portraits are of people before or after their game face. Mostly after. They can give you their best side, their biggest smile, but only for so long; eventually everyone gets weary and some little true part looks out to see if it's safe. Those are the best photos, when a little bit of the real self looks out. That's what she was going to do with Natalie. She'd let her be the wounded girl for a while. But sooner or later, some little part of Natalie would part the curtains and think it was safe to peek out. When that happened, Melissa wanted to be ready. In the meantime, she had to think of a way to keep Cooper.

There were other things that burned Melissa these days: the way Natalie rode in Rocky's truck, sitting in the passenger seat as if she'd been born on the island; the way anger crested in her throat and tried to choke her; the way her skin flushed unbidden as she sat on the couch watching a movie with her mother that showed lovers clutching in high definition.

"You look embarrassed," said her mother, Elaine, turning to look at Melissa. "They're in love, sweetheart. It's okay."

What did not hurt her these days? Her camera, placing one eye against the viewfinder the way Mr. Clarke taught her to do, taking a breath, and, on the complete exhale, taking the shot. The camera steadied her, gave her a clear focus, a way to capture time, faces, a fleeting wing from a great blue heron. The images allowed her brain to slow down, to rest on one image.

The movie ended with the young lovers hand in hand, finally clothed, having overcome predictable obstacles. Melissa unfolded her legs and made ready to get up.

"I know that I've asked a few times, but I'd love to see the photos that you're working on," said her mother. In fact, this was Elaine's third request, and Melissa was prepared to feel the old impulse to hide from her mother, to make another excuse, but the feeling was oddly absent.

"Okay. Let me get my laptop," said Melissa. They sat together on the couch, with the computer on the coffee table, as Melissa narrated a slide show.

"You've seen this one. This is the one called 'The Dogs of Portland.' Are you sure you want to see it again?" asked Melissa.

Her mother smelled good, like a gingersnap. When Melissa was little, her mother had always smelled delicious. Even when Melissa had been in junior high, her mother's lingering scent in her sweaters or hats had been enough to make Melissa wiggle with pleasure. It was only last year and the year before that she had failed to notice her mother's scent of spice and sweetness.

"Are you kidding me? I can't hang your art on the refrigerator anymore, so I'm grateful for any viewing," said her mother as they reviewed Melissa's first show. Then Melissa opened up the new file.

"These are the new dogs of Portland, at least all the ones that I could find over the last two weeks. And Peaks Island too. See, here it starts with Cooper again. I'll show you later why I did it that way, starting with him."

The images of dogs blurred one into the other—big dogs, tiny spots of dogs, overindulged dogs being carried as if they had lost the ability to walk. As Melissa showed the photos to her mother, the acidic drip of Natalie's presence on the island momentarily faded. The slide show ended with Cooper sitting on the ferry, looking out over the Atlantic.

"See, Cooper will be the connecter from the last study of dogs to this one. He's a link." Melissa wasn't sure that her mother would understand this artistic term, so she let it sink in. "I'm thinking of adding some people to my work. You know, photographing people," Melissa added.

Her mother ran her fingers through her hair and tucked a piece behind one ear. "You have an artist's eye," she said. "I can't wait to see your next photos."

Melissa was so close to telling her mother all about Natalie and how something wasn't right, but she didn't want to sound like a whiny girl, she didn't want to spoil this moment on the couch with the two of them.

"I better go study now," said Melissa, closing her laptop.

Her private photos could only be downloaded with a special password. The photos of Natalie needed to stay hidden until she decided what to do with them. If anyone, especially her mother or Rocky, were to ask her why she didn't like Natalie, Melissa wouldn't have been able to explain it. There was the shoplifting, of course, but that wasn't enough, that wasn't even the worst of it. She could not have formed the words to describe the feeling that shimmered in the air when Natalie was around, looking so openmouthed, soft, and helpless.

Melissa took photos whenever she could and let the camera find the instant when the unseen revealed people in surprising ways. She'd seen it often in photography club with Mr. Clarke.

"Look here," he'd say. "When the camera caught this image, the person was just beginning to look away.

Or here—do you see the muscles around the mouth, smiling but not really smiling? If you're going to take photos of people, let them pose first and get that out of the way. I've said it before and I'll keep telling you until it becomes second nature. They will give you the same story they give everyone about themselves with their standard pose. Your job is to get beyond that. One way is to emphasize one side of the face and let the other be in shadow. No one is completely symmetrical. One side of our face is always a bit more serious, more paranoid or afraid or angry. Let that part of the person speak to the camera."

Melissa had begun to look at everyone in a different way, but the person she wanted to really see was Natalie. In the jewelry store, she'd glimpsed a Natalie that no one on Peaks had seen, the real Natalie. And there was that guy in the van. Why didn't Natalie just tell Rocky she had a boyfriend? Melissa wanted to find out more, and she could begin by waiting in the bookstore after cross-country practice, hoping to see Natalie meet the guy again. All Melissa had to do was stand in the bookstore and shoot.

"Believe what you see." Mr. Clarke had said this a hundred times, maybe more. He drilled it into them like the multiplication tables. He told them to see like the camera instead of the human brain, which has perceptual problems, like not noticing the power lines in the background of a shot, or a garbage can, or the rear fender of a car.

"With digital cameras, you can clean out a distracting background, which is good in a pinch, but train your eye to be the viewfinder and the lens. You'll be surprised at what you'll see. Then you're ready to move to digital cameras after you've trained your eyes and your brain."

One day while she was camped out in the bookstore, hoping to see Natalie meet up with the guy in the car, she saw a man in camouflage gear walk by with a dog. The man had all the trappings of someone who was homeless. He had a backpack covered in a black plastic bag to keep it dry, and he wore tough, military-looking boots in the summer, a time when there was no need for boots at all. She let him come into focus just as Mr. Clarke had taught her. Gradually, he didn't look scary at all, not like homeless men had looked to her before. His dog was short-haired, tight, and serious, not at all like the dogs in her first study. How did he feed his dog? Where did the dog stay when the man went into a store? Melissa got an idea for a fine-tuned version of "The Dogs of Portland"; she could photograph homeless people and their dogs. She couldn't wait to tell

Mr. Clarke, which she did as soon as she saw him the next day at photography lab.

"Interesting riff on your first study," he commented. "Are your parents okay with you photographing homeless people? They are not like a species to be observed. Many of them are ordinary people who have slipped through the cracks, and your job would be to tell their story," he said.

Melissa had instinctively not asked her parents. "Sure, my parents are fine with the idea. My father is a lawyer, and he volunteers one day a month at one of the homeless centers," she said, hoping that she'd never run into her father, who would in fact be furious with her for hanging around a district of Portland known for crack, alcohol, and homeless people. "I get what you're saying about the story," she added, even if she really didn't get how she would tell their story.

She wanted desperately to dive into the grittiness of her new study, to abandon the dogs who frequented the expensive shops and restaurants of Portland's tourist center—the pugs, the short-haired terriers, the Chihuahuas, the retrievers. She had clicked away at the dogs in their owners' arms; some were even pushed in strollers. It was not until she drew closer to the Chester Hill district, where runaway kids and people without permanent housing congregated, that Melissa met the dogs with a different kind of character. Her parents wouldn't find out because no one from Peaks ever went to the Chester Hill district.

After Rocky readily agreed to let Cooper go with her to Portland, Melissa and Cooper took the ferry on Saturday. Dogs couldn't ride the ferry without a ticket, especially a big dog like Cooper, who weighed in at more than ninety pounds. He took up as much space as two six-year-old kids. Dog tickets were the same price as tickets for kids, and Melissa was glad the ticket price wasn't based on weight.

In the summer heat, Cooper was one large solar collector. The sun amplified BTUs through his black fur, slowing him down to a large, panting canine. The ferry ride offered him relief, however temporary. As soon as they stepped onto the ferry, Melissa could immediately feel the temperature drop by ten degrees. The ferry was nothing more than a large metal object bobbing around in the icy Atlantic. Midway through the crossing, the ferry entered the deepest part of the channel and the temperature dropped another ten degrees. Cooper spread his body on the cool metal of the ferry and closed his eyes as the one cool breeze of the day lifted the tips of his ears away from his face.

As they approached Portland, the heat pulsing off the land reached out to meet them.

"We are back on the continent, big guy," said Melissa. This would be his first day as Melissa's backup as she shot photos in the predominantly homeless section of Portland.

Melissa and the dog walked up the hill from Commercial Street and over to Chester Hill. Cooper had to have a leash in the city, and it took about six blocks before they got the system right. Melissa was not used to responding to every stop and start from the dog. And clearly, Cooper did not appreciate the micromanagement of the leash.

"You hate this, don't you?" asked the girl as they crested the hill. Cooper's tail hung several notches lower than usual.

"It's just a formality. This is a city, and this is city gear. If you're a dog, you've got to wear a leash. You're still the king of the island, but here in Portland you've got to be stealth. I mean, you've got to act like other dogs."

They had reached the outer edge of Chester Hill. A woman wearing two sweaters and a knit hat—far too much clothing for a July day—stopped along the sidewalk. Her face, toughened by sun and wind, had a leathery look.

"I used to talk to my dog all the time, just like you. Talk, talk, and talk. If I didn't have that dog to talk to, I would have killed myself thirty times over. She was a spaniel kind of dog with big brown eyes and a sad face. Every time I felt something sad, she'd give me that look, and I'd end up telling her it wasn't that bad. And then I wouldn't feel so bad either."

Cooper walked in between the woman and Melissa and sniffed her hand. He sat down and gave the woman his best openmouthed smile.

"I had to give my dogs up, not the spaniel, but the one after that. When I was evicted, I couldn't take the dog. Her name was Dropsy. Homeless shelters wouldn't let her in. The worst day of my life was taking her to an animal rescue place."

The woman knelt down by Cooper and leaned her head against him.

"Here's the dividing line, right here. If you're homeless, and you want to sleep in a shelter, you can't have a dog, period. There's a lot we can't have, but the worst part for me is that I can't have my dog."

She put her face in Cooper's neck and breathed deeply.

"This here is a good-smelling dog. Are you taking good care of him and making sure he's got water to drink? "

"Yes, m'am, I take good care of him."

The woman pushed up and dusted off her knees. She continued on her way. If Melissa had been thinking, she would have taken a photo of Cooper with the woman as she sniffed his fur. Was this what Mr. Clarke had meant, about the camera feeling like an intrusion on something private? How did you get past that sense of invading someone? But as she and Cooper continued their walk, she knew she should have taken the shot. She'd remember the next time.

The next day, Melissa and Cooper walked for several hours in Portland, and the black dog was a magnet for every person who had grown up with a dog but more recently had been stripped of their dog. She heard the same story from people: they had had a dog once, but now they couldn't. Only the people who found alternatives to the shelters had dogs. These were the people who slept outside, tucked in the crevices of highway underpasses, rolled in sleeping bags under kind bushes, boldly in the parks on the benches, or on boats if they were able to do so without getting caught. Their dogs looked like they were bred for the hard life; short-haired, tight muscles, forty-five pounds or so of loyal canine trotting smartly beside their human. Street-smart, they were expert in crossing busy streets and not flinching around strangers, but they were not overly friendly either. They lived on the edge of possibilities with their person, and they knew it.

Melissa asked permission before she shot, and without exception, the owners were proud of their dogs.

They had the devotion of a good dog, a smart and agile creature who didn't judge them by their material acquisitions or their lack of housing. If Melissa squinted, the men looked to her like nomadic warriors, carrying their sacks of essentials with their warrior dog at their side. *Believe what you see.*

At home she downloaded her shots from the day. In one shot, a dog stood watch while a man collected food from a restaurant Dumpster. In another, a dog's eyes had darted to the side, one ear erect, as he listened to some scratch of a sound while a man sat on the sidewalk, his back against the brick wall, with a good breeze from the ocean reaching Chester Hill. Melissa had spent all day with Cooper, and that was just how she wanted it.

On Sunday her friend Chris had suggested that they take Cooper to the assisted living center in Portland where her grandmother lived. Chris thought the dog might cheer everyone up. Her grandmother lived in the special Alzheimer's unit, and both girls agreed that if anyone needed cheering up, it was this group.

Cooper had charmed the pants off the staff, and he walked right into Chris's grandmother's room, sat next to her chair, and pushed his big black head into her alabaster hand.

"Smoky," she said, her eyes clearing. "Where have you been? You haven't been chasing the neighbor's chickens again, have you? Oh, you rascal."

Melissa pulled out her camera, knelt down, and began to shoot. *Click.* Chris's grandmother didn't notice the camera. Cooper gave his soft, dark gaze to the old woman and pressed his body close to her polyester-clad legs. Then he sank to the floor and lay at her feet. Chris slid her grandmother's shoes off and gently placed her feet on Cooper's broad back.

"Smoky, you're as warm as a furnace." She leaned her head against the plastic upholstered padded chair and smiled.

Later, Melissa related the story to Rocky and Tess. "It was like he knew how sick she was and he had something to give her. We were there forever, close to an hour."

"I think Cooper would be a natural as a therapy dog," said Tess. "There's a woman in Portland who has classes for dogs. She teaches them to be therapy dogs for hospitals, rehab centers, even at libraries for kids who have reading difficulties."

The three of them were at Rocky's cottage, and for the first time in weeks Natalie was gone and it was just them again. Melissa stretched out on the weathered deck, and the tiny muscles around her ribs softened. Cooper thumped her with his paw.

"He's either ready for another photo shoot or he wants me to throw his stick," said Melissa. She rolled her head to one side and looked at Rocky. "I could take him to dog therapy school. But, I mean, he is your dog. You'd have to get him enrolled. What do you think?"

Rocky looked up from her building supply catalog. "Does anyone here see the irony in this? I've just quit my job as a therapist, and you two think my dog should become a therapist! But I'll look into it."

Chapter 33

Cooper

As each day ended, the new girl returned to their home and Rocky welcomed her. As he did with all of his people, he studied her behaviors, their predictable sequencing: which hand reached for the white food door, the time of day her bathing took place, what signaled her leaving the house. Nothing alarmed him about the girl's actions. It was her scent that troubled him. A mist hovered over the girl, a cancerous glow draped in a man's scent.

The scent flooded Cooper, lighting up his brain like a sky jammed with stars. The girl had mated; the scent was only thinly covered. It was possible to sort out the intentions of humans, but they were a changeable lot, often confused by their own longings. He sorted out the intentions of the man from his actual deeds.

This was what made living with humans so fragile and so rich.

With other mammals, it was simple to sort out the prey from the predators, even when one mammal played both roles, as they mostly did—prey to some, predators to others. Some creatures, like deer, were purely prey with almost no predator in their nature. They had a clear destiny. Rabbits were the same unless one counted the bloody mating battles between males.

The scent of a predator was unmistakable. Foxes, coyotes, fisher cats, the elusive wild cat—their destiny demanded that, in order to live, they had to kill and kill fast, strike hard, snap a neck, slit an abdomen open. They were built for battle with fangs and claws to rip flesh. The girl's scent, mingled with the man's, pumped out the sureness of a predator.

The layers of scent within a predator were complex. Cooper smelled fear on Natalie. Her pure expression of fear was carried by the sweat and hormones that she left everywhere in the house. Mixed in with her fear was another, the man's fear, but his came from the drive of the predator. What predators fear is that they will miss their kill and go hungry. What the girl feared was unclear, but a fearful creature was a dangerous one, no matter what the source.

Cooper understood predators. His body was built to bring down food if he had to, with his speed and fangs, the bulk and power of his muscles, the rip of his claws. His own power lay coiled, ready beneath his soft mouth, tamed for the most part by the thousands of years his kind had slept near humans. Joining with humans so long ago carried with it the comfort of safe havens when dogs were fortunate enough to find them. But every dog carried the thread of genetic material that could be instantly tapped if the home was in danger. There was a responsibility for everything, and he willingly paid the price to protect his pack. The scent hovering around Natalie made Cooper stand up. He would have to listen more intently, sniff more carefully. Something was coming closer.

Chapter 34

Rocky had reluctantly agreed to call the woman who trained therapy dogs to visit hospital patients, those under hospice care, and even little kids in library reading programs. Tess had urged her to include Melissa.

"This would be something that Melissa could do that would help others and keep her connected to you and Cooper. I know you wouldn't notice right now, but she is feeling tossed aside by you, just when the two of you had become friends. She looks up to you. Cooper is perfect for the job. Once they meet him, they'll say that he's already 90 percent on his way to being a therapy dog. They'll let him skip five levels. He'll be like the genius kids who go to Yale when they're thirteen. You could be his best case study. Tell them that he almost has you up and running as a fully functioning human."

Rocky had considered a pithy comeback, but everything that Tess had said about Cooper was true. She wasn't at all sure what she would have done if she hadn't found him. Rocky had called on Monday morning and agreed to meet Caroline, the dog therapy trainer, at the parking lot of the Casco Bay ferry in Portland.

"I have two main questions before we go any further," said Caroline. She was tall, in her fifties, and wore a T-shirt with ducks on it.

Rocky was prepared for Cooper to wow Caroline, and he did not disappoint. He sat peacefully by Rocky's side and sniffed Caroline's hand with a level of decorum befitting British royalty.

"First question. Is your dog predictable?"

Rocky swallowed. Jesus. Predictable? "Yes, most of the time he's predictable. He's very good at predicting me. Psychic almost. Although unusual circumstances can prompt unusual responses. Or new circumstances require an equal response, just like in physics. It's a law of physics." Rocky was stalling, waiting for the purpose of the question to be clarified.

Caroline's mouth straightened. "What would you call unusual, on either side of your physics formula?"

"There was a stalker on the island a few months back. So, for example, when Cooper was in my car and he recognized the stalker before any of us could, he, well, he showed agitation," said Rocky, hoping that she had aptly described Cooper exploding like a bomb in her car, sputtering and barking.

"I see."

Rocky sensed a change in Caroline's personal tides.

"What's the other question?"

"Has he ever shown aggression?" asked Caroline, looking at Rocky without giving her an inch of room to manufacture a coded answer.

"What exactly do you mean by aggression?" said Rocky.

"This isn't a hard question, and you must admit, it's an important one. We have to screen out dogs that have suddenly shown an aggressive side to their character. Has Cooper ever gone for someone? Has he ever lunged at someone? Bitten anyone?"

Rocky ran the episode of the stalker's apprehension quickly through her head. Had Cooper bitten anyone? No. But he gave chase to the stalker with a ferocity that had shocked her, and she had no doubt that Cooper would have gladly sunk his fangs into the man's leg. He might have done just that if the guy hadn't knocked Cooper to the ground with a tranquilizer dart.

"No, I'm sure of it. He's never bitten anyone," said Rocky. Why did this feel like such a fat lie? "I'm his second owner. The first owner died, but I can give you the name of the vet who has taken care of him since he was a puppy. She's over in Orono."

"Let me put the question to you in another way. If Cooper thought anyone was threatening you, what would he do? Would you have voice control of him? This is important."

The day Rocky found Cooper, she had changed. Not all at once, one doesn't in matters of love, and both of them had approached the new relationship with differing levels of caution. The day she found him, feverish and filled with infection from his wound, she knew he would not have lasted much longer. But how much longer would she have lasted if he had not come into her life in his full-throttle style?

Somewhere along the line the deal was finalized: this dog was signed up to be with her for the rest of his life. He slept by her bed, near the doorway, his black fur catching occasional glints from the moon. His breath carried hints of kibble, chewed sticks, and God only knew what else. His breath carried absolution for her impenetrable sadness. His tongue was without gile or irony, incapable of twisting itself into sarcasm.

The day she found him, she had been in a dank cave of regret and hideous self-blame. The love of her life had died, and she could not resuscitate him, bring him back to the land of the living. She had had no intention of committing to a ninety-pound canine; she simply wanted to get him on the ferry to the mainland and let a vet save him. Love arrives like that sometimes, on a blue tarp in the back of a battered pickup truck, oozing infection, giving in to the warm hand of a lost woman.

He had loved her like there was no tomorrow. In fact, the dog had insisted that there was no tomorrow; there was only now. Every minute of the day was ripe for eating, drinking, eye gazing, scratching, being petted, being the pettee, running, pushing into as much body contact as possible, retreiving, coming home, listening for her steps. The first time she was overcome with laughter at his Cirque de Soleil tennis ball catches, the dog rewarded her with a gentle lick.

Rocky had at first bristled at the wet-dog smell that filled the rental cottage. Eight months after she found him, however, he had come to smell of ocean, sand, muscle, sheer joy, contentment, his huge black Lab smile, his fangs that glistened with happy dog saliva; it all mixed to fill the house with the breath of love.

She blessed the day she found him. She could have missed him. She could have missed this life with him.

Caroline waited for an answer.

"If push came to shove, he would protect me. He knows the difference between a real threat and a three-year-old with a plastic shovel. Dogs like this don't come around often, and I'm lucky for every day that he's with me. I've got a young friend who wants to train him to work with Alzheimer's patients. Please give him a chance," said Rocky.

Caroline knelt down in front of the dog for one last evaluative look. He tilted his head slightly to the right, lifted one eyebrow, and opened his chest toward her in his best openhearted pose, and Rocky swore she saw it, just for an instant, that thing Cooper did—his direct energy burst of good juju. For a second, the dog was the ancient wise one and Caroline the young acolyte kneeling before him. He accepted the woman completely, for all her past grudges and mistakes, for her future jealousies and sorrows.

Caroline stood up, brushing off her pants. "We'll give him a try, a probationary try."

Chapter 35

Melissa

"The woman said Cooper was an unlikely candidate for dog therapy school," said Rocky. She had stopped by Melissa's house and stood in the doorway. "She had two major questions for Cooper, and I have to say, he did not fare well."

Melissa braced for disappointment. She didn't say what was most obvious to her and what she'd like to tell the therapy dog lady, which was that Cooper had nudged her back into food when food had become her enemy. He had done it with his soft black Lab smile, his oily scent, and the scratch of his black claws on the floor. But that was all between Melissa and Cooper.

Now Rocky said Cooper was an unlikely candidate to be a therapy dog.

Melissa backed up and gave Rocky room to enter. She mimicked her mother's gestures of hospitality for guests and hoped that she got it right. Rocky was not entirely a guest, but it was less confusing to avoid exceptions. "What were the questions that he flunked?" asked Melissa.

Rocky walked into the kitchen and helped herself to a glass of water from the tap. "First she asked if he has ever been violent, aggressive. She wanted to know if he's ever bitten someone."

Melissa jumped to his defense. "He only *wanted* to bite someone. He never actually bit the guy. And he protected you—that's different. What was he supposed to do?"

Rocky noticed a tray of brownies on the butcher block. She lifted her eyebrows at Melissa and turned her palm up at the moist chocolate squares.

"Help yourself. I made them," said Melissa.

Rocky slid a butter knife under the backside of one of the brownies and bit half of it. "The second question was even harder. She asked if he's predictable. Cooper has done some very weird shit, and I could never in a million years say that he is predictable." Rocky inserted the remaining hunk of brownie into her mouth and rolled her eyes in ecstasy.

Melissa frowned. "Who is totally predictable? That's an unfair question. He's a dog, not a machine. You're not predictable. I'm not predictable."

"Slow down, cowgirl. Cooper gave her the look—you know, his irresistible look—and I was as honest as I could be with her. She said that he'll be on probation, but that she'd try him out in therapy dog training. I wonder if we should really think about this. She may be after some über-calm dog that wouldn't blink if a tree fell on the house."

Rocky lifted another brownie square from the pan and ate it in two bites. A crumb lingered on her bottom lip. "Would you happen to have any milk to wash down these brownies?"

Melissa opened the dish cabinet and pulled out a sturdy glass. She filled it with milk and set it on the counter in front of Rocky. She marveled at the way Rocky had churned through food since the moment she had stepped into the house.

"I guess you didn't hear what I just said. You and Cooper are signed up for therapy dog classes in Portland. It's all set. The first class is this Wednesday, day after tomorrow. Do you think you can fit it into your schedule?" Rocky drank the glass of milk in a series of gulps that left her small Adam's apple bobbing.

"What? We're in? That is so great!"

After Rocky left, Melissa's entire body filled with the juice of something sweet, like pears or tangerines. Rocky really did care about her. And for the first time in weeks, Rocky hadn't mentioned Natalie's name, not even once.

Tess had been asking Melissa for weeks to photograph her granddaughter Danielle, so of course when a day finally worked for Melissa and she arrived with the ancient Pentax K1000 that Mr. Clarke insisted she use, Natalie was there, slinking her way into every crevice on Peaks Island. If this kept up, Melissa was going to go live with her father in Portland.

Just yesterday, Natalie had whispered to Melissa, leaning in close as she passed her on the street to the ferry, "Off to see your lesbian friend?" She had hissed it, licking the words off her tongue like a snake. Sure, Melissa's friend Chris was gay, but that wasn't what Natalie meant and she knew it. It was only a matter of time before Natalie dropped an innocent comment to Rocky like, "I know this couldn't be true, but do you think Melissa is gay and she just doesn't know it?" And then it would go viral in an instant. Those kinds of things always went viral. Melissa didn't know what she was, but she wanted to find out in her own time.

Tess had asked and asked. "Come on, Melissa. You're on your way to becoming a top photographer. I don't have a good picture of Danielle, and before you know it, she'll be in college. This is a good summer for us. I want it documented."

She had finally agreed to 7:00 P.M. on the back shore. The light would be good in that time and place for the special golden tones that Mr. Clarke told them all to grab. Melissa stiffened as soon as she arrived. Why was Natalie here? She had already taken Rocky—did she have to steal Tess too?

"Over here," shouted Danielle. "I have on a princess dress." Danielle stood on tiptoe, twirling on a rock, in one hand a garden stick transformed into a magic wand. Tess held a sheer scarf aloft, the cheap kind sold in the tourist shops, splashed with maroon and yellow. The wind grabbed the scarf and splashed it over the child's red hair.

Melissa began shooting, bracing the camera, releasing a breath. Natalie stood in the background like the misery that she was, which apparently only Melissa could see.

"I am the wind, Princess Razzle-dazzle," intoned Tess, her long white hair rising, prancing like a filly. Once these two got going, Melissa knew, they could be out on the rocks for hours. What would it be like to have a grandmother like Tess?

Melissa heard a laugh slit through Natalie's veneer, and it made Melissa turn a few degrees, enough to get Natalie, the forlorn foundling, into the viewfinder; she clicked and clicked before turning back to Tess in her fluttering scarf and the child in her princess costume. The two of them danced to inner songs grooved into their weird genetic pool.

With the old SLR camera, Melissa had to either develop the film herself in the high school lab or send it out to be developed, making sure to check the box requesting a CD version, which was just what Melissa did with the roll of Tess and Danielle. As she scrolled through the photos several days later, the photos of Natalie emerged on her screen. Melissa had forgotten that she had even taken them. The shots quickly etched a scar in what she knew about the girl: bitch, skank, liar.

"This can't be true," said Melissa, clicking on an image on her laptop. She didn't care what Mr. Clarke said about the camera's unbiased eye. He didn't know Natalie.

How could there have been such longing on Natalie's face as she watched the old woman and the girl dancing over the rocks? No, it couldn't be true. She didn't want to see one cell of Natalie that was anything but despicable. But there it was, the same look that people have when they see a puppy, the way a dog can bring out the sweetness in a person. She'd seen the same look in the nursing home with Chris's grandmother, the way the old woman's face and eyes went clear and soft when Cooper was there. And here it was with Natalie, a secret part of her that lasted as long as it took to shoot three pictures. *Believe what you see.* Even if she believed it, which she did not, she'd never show these pictures to Rocky.

Chapter 36

Rocky had already been to Home Depot outside Portland three times since Monday, and the guys in the plumbing department greeted her by name. There were two bathrooms in the house, one on the main floor and one upstairs. They were each the size of a Mini Cooper. Rocky could have started anywhere with the remodel, but for the sake of comfort, she wanted a bigger bathroom upstairs and new fixtures for both rooms. She also wanted toilets that were reliable and didn't require plunging.

When she had first hired Russell to work on the house, he explained that he had a long list of clients on the island and refused to work anywhere besides Peaks.

"I can fit you in between other clients as long as you can be patient. We can do it bit by bit. That's how I work," said Russell after going through the house with Rocky. "I like the feel of this old place. If doing the bathroom remodels will make you happy for now, let's do that. And I suggest that you get all the outside work done in the summer. Like a roof—you are in desperate need of a new roof. Despite what Isaiah says, you've got basement troubles. Order a new sump pump right now, because you're going to need it."

Russell wore a navy blue and white bandana tied around his head. He had a wife who worked at Whole Foods in Portland and two teenage kids. On Thursday nights, Russell went to his writing group, and so he had to stop working by three (since Thursday was also his night to cook dinner) and could start no earlier than ten on Friday mornings.

"We sometimes go pretty late if everyone shows up," he said in explanation. "I do primarily poetry. Narrative poetry."

Russell had instructed Rocky to go to Home Depot to look at toilets the week before, which she had done. When she had first stepped into the cavernous building supply store, she realized that she knew nothing about toilets. Signs hung from the ceiling dividing the store into areas: plumbing, electrical, lumber, gardening. Rocky had headed for the land of plumbing.

"Can I help?" asked a man in an orange vest with white lettering.

"I'm interested in toilets," said Rocky.

The plumbing expert had led her to a row of toilets suspended from shelves seven feet tall, with each one tilted forward so that the customer had a full view of the shape and best profile of the toilet. This was the essence of being a widow: picking out a toilet at Home Depot without the benefit of one's husband and his opinion. Bob would have loved this.

"I have an old house that I'm remodeling, and I need two reliable, vigorous toilets," said Rocky.

"All of these toilets are tested to take down twelve golf balls in one fast evacuation. Nowadays, all the water is released into the bowl instantly, as opposed to the ones installed in the nineties or earlier."

"Twelve golf balls should do it," said Rocky, amazed at the new euphemism for poop. She had spent a little more time there, selecting the size of each toilet and the height of each seat; eventually she picked out mid-range models. After the store clerk promised to have the toilets delivered by the Casco Bay ferry, she had walked out into the sunshine of an early summer evening, having picked out the first toilets of her life.

Now, one week later, she was back to return one of the toilets: it was the wrong color.

"Hi, Rocky."

Rocky studied the jumbo nametag for what she hoped was an imperceptible moment and said, "Hi, Mark."

"How's the remodel going out on Peaks?" he asked. Mark was an early-thirty-something guy with a tattoo of a scorpion on his forearm. The wattage of his enthusiasm was far dimmer today.

"It's going okay. Consuming. Terrifying. But I got your phone message about the replacement toilet that I ordered and the new shutoff valve. Do you remember? You guys sent me two toilets and one was a blue toilet instead of white by mistake? Why did you add a $50 permit fee to the installation price? I'm just replacing old toilets with new toilets. No permit needed, right? My builder says we don't need it."

Mark looked perplexed. His eyes went unfocused, and Rocky imagined him accessing all the data in his brain about permits and toilets. As a last resort, he clicked on the computer at the plumbing counter.

"You're right. I'm sorry. It's been a bad week," he said.

Mark tapped away, deleting the $50 charge for a permit she didn't need.

"My girlfriend of three years broke up with me. It's been hard."

Like a doll with two faces, one in front and one in back, Rocky's therapist head swiveled around and snapped into place. Mark looked different, softer, less like a potential plumbing adversary who might or might not help her get all the right stuff she needed. He was no longer a hurdle to jump over as she remodeled her house. A pilot light went on in Rocky's long-dormant psychology world.

The tail of the black arachnid rose ominously at the beefiest part of Mark's forearm as he typed.

"Have you ever traveled to Mexico or Central America?" she asked.

Mark pulled a sales receipt from the printer. "No. Why do you ask?" he peered over the top of the screen.

"Because of the scorpion on your arm. I've seen them in Mexico. But they're not as dangerous as their reputation would lead you to believe. Their bite is more like a wasp bite. They look dangerous, and yet they're really a lot of bluster."

He looked down at his forearm as if he'd forgotten that the tattoo was there. "No. It's my sign," he said, not hiding his sadness. Being a scorpion, astrologically speaking, might even have led to the demise of his relationship. If he was like most people after being dumped, he was looking everywhere for an explanation.

"Okay, I've fixed it. So now, with the installation and the valve replacement, it's $329, not $379," Mark said.

He loaded the boxed toilet onto a flatbed push-cart and rolled it through the arena-sized store, with Rocky walking alongside him. She happened to have the truck, so she could easily take her new acquisitions back on the ferry. As they walked, Rocky felt something important shifting with each step through the big-box store. Their promenade was about more than a purchase. She hadn't felt this clear about who she was in a long time. She was remembering what it felt like to be a psychologist. It felt good—not the same as before Bob died, but good.

"What I want you to remember is that I'm a therapist," she said. "No, I didn't mean to say that. I just wanted to let you know that I'm a therapist. I am." She hadn't referred to herself in this way in well over a year. Not in fifteen months, according to the Dead Bob Calendar. She'd been the animal control warden. Was she a new amalgam of psychologist/animal control officer?

Mark turned to look at her as they glided past the storm door section. Rocky took a breath as they passed the long aisle of exterior lights.

"I've got two things for you, and they're important. Number one: don't listen to any sad songs. The minute that you hear a sad song, turn it off, leave the building, or put your thumbs in your ears. Number two: join a gym, a volleyball team, a bicycle club—anyplace where you can run your heart out. Aerobic exercise is as good as a mild antidepressant without the side effects. And you wouldn't like the side effects of most antidepressants unless you want to forgo erections."

Rocky stopped there because she didn't want Mark to cry in the middle of Home Depot and she knew that if she said much more that was exactly what would happen and then he'd hate her later and maybe sell her the wrong kitchen faucet when it came time for the kitchen remodel.

If possible, his shoulders slumped even lower. "I'm doing okay. I've got a dog, and she and I go hiking a lot," he said. He pushed the cart to a cash register and stepped around to become the cashier. Rocky knew he could have sent her to another cashier, but he wanted to talk a little longer.

"That's good," she said. "What kind of dog?" She was relieved to hear that he had a dog, the best kind of therapist at times of loss and grief.

"She's an Australian Labradoodle. I would have gotten a dog from the shelter, but my girlfriend wanted a fancy dog, plus she's allergic to dog fur, and these dogs are strong on the poodle end of hair. When she left, she didn't want the dog. Or me."

Rocky slid her debit card through the machine. "I have one more thing for you: do whatever that dog tells you to do. If she wants to go for a run, then go for a run. If she wants to retrieve sticks until your arm falls off, do it. Before you know it, she will have saved you."

Mark pushed the cart out to Rocky's yellow truck and loaded it up. He closed the back gate with an affectionate pat.

Rocky got in the truck, leaned out the window, and said, "Mark, your Labradoodle will be pure chick bait. When you're ready, that is."

Mark gave a shy smile. Rocky felt like a psychologist again, but new, still transforming, one who was trying to figure out her relationship with her own highlighted flaws. A psychologist who gave canine advice.

Chapter 37

The next day, Rocky and Natalie waited in Rocky's yellow truck. The truck was really part of Isaiah's small fleet of public works vehicles, but Rocky had been the sole driver since last October. The ferry from Portland made its wide swing and slid into the dock. The cargo department of the Casco Bay ferry had called Rocky to let her know that a shipment from Home Depot was arriving.

Natalie drummed her fingers on the edge of the open window.

"Why doesn't your carpenter guy do this? I mean, you're paying him to do the work," said Natalie.

Cars came off the ferry first, then cargo, and lastly passengers. The ferry workers unloaded the cargo and forklifted crates to the side of the landing. The procedure was reversed after all the passengers were unloaded: first the cars departing the island drove on, and then the passengers bound for the mainland walked aboard. Rarely did cargo leave the island. As the ferry pulled out for its fifteen-minute voyage, Rocky drove the truck to the landing and backed the truck up to the Home Depot shipment. She set the emergency brake.

"Russell has a very long list of people who want him to remodel, build decks, tear out windows, put in windows, and I don't know what else. Right now he's back at the house with an electrician replacing wiring. If he had to sit here and wait for sinks and bathroom vanities to arrive from Portland, it would be a big waste of time. Since no one is demanding my animal control warden skills at the moment, it made more sense for me to do this part."

She hopped out of the truck. "Come on. Let's get this stuff loaded into the truck."

Natalie moved so much slower than Rocky, as if an opposing force had a harness around her, pulling her back. Was it wariness? Or was it just the result of a bad-luck life? Rocky had not seen Hill since the night of the concert, not since the unholy seed had been planted by Natalie. Rocky understood the effects of early abuse; she had seen the ragged imprints of it in therapy, glazing over the hearts of people who were long past the clutches of perpetrators but reliving the experience daily. What was it about Hill that had unsettled Natalie? Rocky had scheduled a meeting with the director of Southern Maine Foster Services in Portland on Monday. Today was Friday. She had thought about telling Nat, but each time a bolt of misgiving had stopped her. Was she betraying the girl?

They lifted the bathroom vanities into the back of the truck, each of them lifting one side.

"Sinks come in boxes?" said Natalie. The flesh around the top of her hips puffed at the top edge of her low-riding jeans.

"I know, I said the same thing. Who would have thought you could squish bathroom vanities into boxes?" said Rocky.

They loaded the boxes and a large plastic bag of PVC piping into the back of the truck.

"Let's stop at Hannigan's and get some cold drinks. I know the guys at the house could use something cold," said Rocky. She had one foot resting on the bottom rim of the door, hesitating. "Look, you don't seem to be able to find a job in Portland. And for the moment, I can't come up with a source of DNA from Bob, so we are at a temporary standstill on the paternity issue. Why don't I hire you to help with the house remodel? You might find demolition work quite satisfying. I do."

Natalie's eyelids fluttered for a few seconds as if her electrical charge were temporarily interrupted. Rocky had thrown the girl a surprise pitch. Natalie got into the passenger seat and looked down at her hands. Rocky and Natalie had opened the DNA kit just yesterday, and Natalie had willingly rubbed a swab along the inside of her mouth, then handed it to Rocky. She had looked at the swab, half-expecting Bob to appear, to hear his voice.

Rocky started the truck, driving up the steep road to the main street. The truck responded with an acknowledgment of the extra load.

"I'll pay you cash, $10 an hour to start. You can work with me, where you'll learn practically nothing about carpentry, or you can work with Russell, where you'll learn important things that will actually be marketable skills."

No answer. Natalie examined her blunt fingernails as if they held a message.

"Is this a terrible job offer?" asked Rocky. She parked across the street from Hannigan's.

Natalie slowly licked her lips. "I could try it for a few days. I've never done anything like this. But I still need to go to Portland one day a week to look for a real job."

Maybe Natalie was just a moody teenager and everything was going to be okay. Given her childhood trauma history, one had to expect that Natalie would have delays in emotional maturity and in her ability to form attachments. Rocky wanted a future for Natalie, college or carpentry or who knew what, but a future nonetheless, and she was elated that she might be able to help Natalie. Rocky ran into the small grocery store, dipped around to the bread shelves, and pulled out her cell phone.

"Russell? This is Rocky. Do you need any teenage-type helpers this summer? No? Well, I've got an offer for you. I want you to hire this kid that I'm going to bring over. I'll pay her, but she can be your apprentice. Thanks."

They arrived at the job site loaded down with cold bottled water, one liter of Coke, and a sack of sandwiches. Russell and the electrician looked up. They were outside measuring electrical wire as if they were wrapping yarn into a ball.

"Hey, Russell," said Rocky. "I'd like you meet Natalie, your new apprentice."

Russell and the electrician put the wire down and appraised the girl with a practiced male glance that took two seconds. Russell stood straighter. The electrician spread his feet a little wider and attempted to suck in his belly. But Rocky saw none of the strange reaction that had erupted around Hill. She gulped down an unwelcome thought about Hill, schoolteacher, archery instructor, a man who cheated once on his wife.

"Russell, I expect you to take good care of her while she's working, and if you see any wolves closing in, your job is to shoo them away. She's my guest."

"I could use some extra help. Why don't you start on Monday? I start early and end early," said Russell. He turned back to the electrician, and the spiked pulse of heat from the two men quieted back down. Rocky wanted this to be a good thing for Natalie.

Natalie nodded her agreement, even though Russell had moved on, his tool belt clanking.

Rocky pictured Natalie walking to work each day, bringing her lunch with her, learning the intricacies of house renovation. She pictured the girl coming home each night tired with the sweet satisfaction of hard work.

Chapter 38

Natalie

F ranklin spun between the three laptops like a tap
dancer; smooth and agile at one moment, sharp as
crocodile teeth the next moment, clattering and snap-
ping. They had found a discarded office chair in back
of the building, and he used it to roll from one screen to
another on the makeshift table of cinder blocks topped
by an old door.

"You gotta love firewalls," he said without looking
up at Natalie. His face and upper torso were illumined
by the triptych of computer screens, giving him an
icy blue tinge. Natalie didn't know the last time he'd
actually been outside. He had explained the difference
between an albino and someone like him with his very
blond hair, light, almost translucent skin, and pale blue
eyes. "The main difference is that I've got a drop of

melanin in my system. I can tan, or freckle, if I do it very gradually, not like albinos. But what's the point?"

This was one of the things that Natalie had found intriguing about Franklin when they met working behind the counter at Subway back in Worcester. Franklin had stood out, glowing in the fluorescent light that beamed from his torso. Her interest had hit a critical peak when she heard about his crazy computer skills from one of the other workers. She didn't know how he did it, but Franklin could plug his brain into the hard drive.

Their efficiency apartment in the Chester Hill district was perfectly situated amid drug dealers and drug users; she'd never run into the adorables from Peaks Island in this neighborhood. Natalie had especially wanted the third-floor location—it rang an old bell with her.

"Look at this," he said. "They must have three-year-olds install their firewalls. No. Three-year-olds could do a better job. We're all going to hell on a fast train if this is the best protection that the state health department can offer us."

Natalie had left the island in the middle of the afternoon. She looked at an array of documents from the Department of Children and Families on one screen, all crimped with state seals.

"They've scanned in existing documents," said Natalie. "Even I know you can't change that."

Franklin smacked his forehead with his palm. "You're right. I guess I'll have to give up." His voice had risen in a strained soprano. "Oh please, do you actually think that I can't work around this, dislodge it from its alleged protection? You've forgotten my artistic genius with your birth certificate already? Watch the master at work."

He turned to screen number two. "This is the one that's putting up some resistance, which makes my day more interesting. Get me a beer, babe."

No one had ever called her "babe" before, and she liked it, really liked it, as if this man calling her babe was going to dig a moat around her and she'd never have to live in another foster home again. Well, she'd never have to live in another foster home anyhow, but she could still feel the clutches of the worst of them—like the one with five foster kids and only one hairbrush for all of them and the little kids in kindergarten brought home lice.

She walked into the nook of the kitchen and retrieved a beer for Franklin. He called to her from his computers, "Now this one is putting up a fight. The DNA testing companies have got some balls. Can you imagine how many people are trying to phish into this puppy? This one thinks it's smarter than me, but they are so wrong. They've got as many layers as their IT team can dream up. But guess what, babe? They'll never see me coming, and they'll never know I was there."

Natalie twisted the cap off the brown bottle and put it within reach of Franklin's porcelain white hands. It had taken her a long time to find Franklin, and she'd do anything to keep him, for as long as she needed him.

Not long after she moved into his Worcester apartment, she had said, "Let's go look up death notices and probate stuff," making it sound as good as watching *American Idol*. She wore a baseball cap at the time, and nothing else.

"You've got to be kidding me," Franklin had said. "Are you nuts about dead people? Don't go all perv on me."

He was one to talk. She had tracked his history with porn sites. Natalie stroked his thigh. "No really, I saw this program where people die and nobody claims their great big estates." She shrugged, handing him the idea to run with. It didn't take Franklin long to get started and for him to believe it had been his idea.

"There is money out there, *chérie*, waiting for us, like fruit off the tree." He ran his hand along her butt and cupped her ass like it was a free cantaloupe. "We're going to follow the money. I've got a plan."

It had taken them close to a year, and she'd just about given up, when all the pieces fit together. Probate stuff takes forever to work its way through a system, but with Franklin at the keyboard, it had only been a matter of time and faith.

Franklin and Natalie had moved to Portland in May, fueled by her belief that with Franklin by her side, she had a plan that was solid. When she first contacted Rocky in June, she had left Rocky's return messages unanswered for days, letting Rocky be the one to seek her out. Franklin sold her stolen merchandise on eBay, and they had enough money for the apartment. Today she had brought him earrings and watches, the things that sold easily. They had big dreams—different dreams, but equally big.

"I need to get back by early tonight. Something about a card game," said Natalie. She left the topic open, knowing that if Franklin wanted sex, this would be the time. But his head bobbed back and forth from one computer to another. For guys like Franklin, sex was less enticing than a formidable computer challenge.

Chapter 39

Melissa

It was Friday night, and the second class with Cooper in Portland. There were five other dogs in the class for therapy dogs. One was a blond cocker spaniel with appealing sad eyes who acted like he was on tranquilizers. The remaining dogs included two young golden retrievers who could concentrate for exactly ten seconds before they spun out of control, one Shih Tzu, and one beige standard poodle for whom Cooper had developed quite an amorous liking. Each time Cooper came within ten feet of the large poodle, he expanded his chest and held his head higher.

Cooper did everything that Caroline, the instructor, said. *Sit, stay, heel.* Melissa had had no idea that Cooper knew how to heel. No one on the island had ever asked him to heel. Cooper was going to be the valedictorian of the therapy dog class. He might turn out to be the best dog that Caroline had ever trained.

The goldens flung themselves around and would nearly have levitated had it not been for their leashes. While the golden retrievers flubbed all three of the first essential commands, Cooper sat regally on Melissa's left side.

"Make eye contact with your dog! Make sure that you've established eye contact," recited Caroline over and over.

Melissa wanted to tell everyone in class that Cooper could also shake on command when he emerged from the ocean, glistening with seawater, a treasured stick in his mouth. But she didn't. That would be bragging. After class, the guy with the cocker spaniel said, "How did you learn to train dogs?"

"I didn't. I swear. This is just a naturally smart dog," said Melissa.

Melissa and Cooper walked down the hill to Commercial Street and stopped at an ice cream shop. Melissa went in and ordered a vanilla cone with an extra cup. She spooned half of the ice cream into the cup and set it on the sidewalk as she and the dog waited for the ferry back to Peaks. Cooper flattened out on the sidewalk and braced the cup between his front paws. He used his considerable pink tongue to slurp out the contents. Melissa ate her cone, turning it, catching the milky drops that tried to escape from the tip.

Being with Cooper made her feel different—a little like a grown-up, more like she had substance and solidity. The flow of who she truly was had started to crystallize and form a coherent picture. She was the girl with the brilliant dog. Rocky's brilliant dog.

The smaller ferry ran at this time of day, and almost everyone on it was a regular. She and Cooper walked on, the dog snug at her side. Two little boys ran up and said, "Hi, Cooper!" One of the boys looked up at Melissa and asked, "Can I pet your dog?" She knelt down by Cooper and let the boy pet Cooper's head.

The woman with the British accent who clerked at the grocery store nodded to her. "Did you two have a nice visit in Portland?"

Melissa stood up and then found a seat. "We're going to dog therapy school. Cooper is learning to be a therapy dog," said Melissa.

"I expect he's got a bit of a head start in the school of therapeutics," said the woman with an appreciative nod to the dog.

When she was with Cooper, people looked at her with a smile, then a tinge of envy. People didn't hesitate to talk with her, even strangers, and Melissa could suddenly make conversation, a skill that had eluded her until recently. Life before Cooper seemed far away and layered with self-loathing. Life since Cooper's arrival made her cheeks rise up.

The ferry approached Peaks Island, made a large swing around, and slid into the mouth of the dock. She could not contain her euphoria for one more second—she had to tell Rocky about Cooper's brilliant performance in class. As soon as her feet hit the cement loading area of the dock, she sprang into a run, patting her thigh to let the dog know that he could run alongside her. They darted up the hill, her long thin legs stretched out, his broad chest pulling him forward in canine bursts.

They headed straight to Rocky's house. Rocky had to be home by now. They ran along Island Avenue, then sprinted along a maze of streets and dirt roads, past her own house on their dirt road, laughing and gasping. Rocky's yellow truck was there. Rocky was going to flip out when she heard about Cooper. Melissa bounded up the steps to the deck as she had done hundreds of times, heading straight to the front door. She could feel Cooper's delight; he loved coming home where Rocky and his food barrel lived.

Melissa pushed open the door, too excited to knock. The kitchen was empty, but she heard voices and felt the bulging hum of people in the house. She entered in five steps, which was all it took to make her way past the bathroom to see into the living room. There was Rocky, Tess, the little grandkid Danielle, and Natalie. They sat around a card table, each with a splayed group of cards in their hands.

"Hey! Join us. I'm getting solidly beaten at poker again," said Rocky.

Little Danielle squealed and said, "Natalie is teaching me card games like Crazy Eights."

Natalie looked weirdly demure, with a downward tilt to her head, eyes cast up, like an old picture of Princess Diana. A slip of a smile escaped from Natalie, one that any girl from high school understood. *You're not wanted here. There's no place for you here,* the silent smile said.

"Oh crap! I don't have another chair," said Rocky. "You can sit in for me next hand. It will give me a chance to recover from the beating I've been taking."

There was no way that Melissa was going to sit across a wobbly cardboard table and play games with Natalie.

"No thanks. I'll just give Cooper some water and a treat," said Melissa. A chemical that Natalie emitted had transformed Melissa's euphoria into sludge, clogging her eyes and her heart.

Natalie stood up and spoke to Rocky. "Can I feed Cooper? You've done so much for me, and I would feel better if I could help."

Melissa had squatted down to pick up Cooper's water dish. She looked at Rocky, waiting for her to tell the girl to back off, waiting for her to say that Melissa had taken care of Cooper since November when he was still recovering from surgery and that no one knew him better than Melissa and Rocky and if the girl wanted to help she could go sweep off the deck. Everything stopped in the room, all the air was sucked out, along with all the card-playing fun.

"What's wrong?" said Danielle, breaking the spell.

Rocky looked from Melissa to Natalie. "Maybe next time, Nat. These two just got back from Portland and—hey, that's right. How was the second night at doggie therapy school?"

Now the girl was Nat, not Natalie. She had wormed in closer. Melissa bit her bottom lip as she filled the dog's dish at the faucet. She was not going to cry in front of this chick. She dropped a dog biscuit near the bowl. "It was fine. No big deal."

Without saying good-bye, because if she said one more word she was going to cry, Melissa turned and walked out of the house. She was almost back on the dirt road when Rocky caught up with her and grabbed her shoulder.

"Wait a minute. What the hell just happened? Would it kill you to be civil to her? You have no idea what her life has been like," said Rocky.

Melissa spun around. "You don't get it. Why can't you see? You don't get anything!" shouted Melissa. She wasn't grown-up anymore; all of her substance had evaporated. She turned and ran the rest of way to her house.

Chapter 40

"You did *not* drag me over here to go to junk sales," said Rocky. It was Saturday morning, and she and Isaiah were in his truck, idling at the curbside where a hand-lettered sign said ESTATE SALE 9–2.

"No, we are here to see if we can squeeze another year out of the dog warden's truck," said Isaiah. "And Tess told me that you have teenage girl trouble times two, not to mention the quandary about paternity. You've got troubles with the first man you dated after Bob's death, you quit your job back at the university, and you bought a fixer-upper house. You need what we refer to as an off-island respite. We all do at times. It cleanses the spirit." He unsnapped his seat belt.

"Correction. Animal control warden. So I've got too much going on. Your solution is to bring me to an estate sale?" said Rocky. While irritated, she was relieved to be off the island, with the weight of Natalie temporarily lifted.

She had driven the yellow truck on the ferry and taken it to a garage. The truck had not passed inspection for as long as Rocky had been on the island. Isaiah had followed in his truck.

"There are treasures to be found at these sales. Come on, let me scratch this old itch. Besides, you're not going to find another black man who likes tag sales. It goes against our stereotype," he said.

"There's a stereotype? I'm not in the loop on estate sales, tag sales, whatever you call them. I wouldn't know what's a stereotype and what isn't."

Rocky sighed, pressed the release button on her seat belt, and opened the door. The house was small, one story, with a gaping garage spilling possessions. Rocky wanted to turn away. Isaiah caught her arm and led her up the cracked sidewalk.

"You'll love it, and we have four hours to kill before the truck is brought up to minimal standards. You might find something interesting for your new house. That's how island people shop: we find stuff over here in Portland that nobody wants anymore, and we drag it back over on the ferry. Charlotte calls it island chic."

"Wait, what's the stereotype?" she said, dragging her feet as they neared the driveway.

"I had to take some refresher courses about ten years ago before I could start teaching shop at the high school. 'Teaching Across the Cultures: A Multi-Ethnic Approach to Teaching.' It was taught by a skinny blond gal from Indiana. She informed us that black people don't buy used clothing. Just like that. She said it had to do with poverty and overidentification with the middle class and rejection of the lower classes. I raised my hand and asked if she thought that it might also be genetic."

"You did not," said Rocky.

"I did. Unfortunately, she tried to answer me. Just for laughs these days, I try to fracture any remnants of the myth. If I see anything good for Charlotte, I'll pick it up for her. Your young houseguest has a peculiar fashion sense that I can't put my finger on. But this could be the mother lode of clothing for her if she likes the vintage look," he said.

"Buying clothing for an eighteen-year-old isn't safe territory. I've already said the wrong thing to her five times over."

They approached a long table piled high with men's jackets and sweaters.

"Here's a great selection for you," said Rocky. She held up a sweater with an LL BEAN tag on the back of the neck.

"Are you kidding? I'd never wear used clothing," he said.

Rocky whipped the sweater at him and lashed him on the arm.

"You are one crazy old man," she said.

"I resent that. I'm not old. Go away and don't bother me. Go look through the house and appear interested."

Rocky was left in the driveway between rows of tables stacked with record albums, mismatched plates, salt and pepper shakers, and a huge selection of dented aluminum pots and pans. Two men in overalls wore nail belts that jangled with coins; they were obviously the ones in charge. One man dipped his hand into the nail belt and made change for a customer who held a box of canning jars. The crowd was thin, not more than ten people in all. The two men had gray hair, with a matching two days' worth of beard along their jawlines.

"Ninety-two when she died. Listened to her records right up to the last minute. Stayed here in her house," said one of the men.

With a suffocating tug to her throat, Rocky realized that this was their mother's house. They were selling off every single thing from their mother's life: her Tupperware, bath mats, her walker, and, in several boxes, a selection of hand-painted ceramics of birds and mammals that looked suspiciously Disney-like. Rocky looked too long at the box of creatures.

"That there is good stuff, very good stuff from the seventies. You don't see it anymore. My mother took a class and painted every one of them herself in a ceramics class."

The genuine pride in his voice stopped Rocky. She squatted down and picked up a ceramic bunny.

"She had them for all the holidays. It's a complete set, right through the calendar," he said, fiddling with his nail belt.

Rocky gently placed the bunny back into the box. "I wouldn't want to break up the set." She backed away from the box as if it held cadavers.

"I can talk to my brother about a deal for the whole set. In the meantime, the whole house is open," he said. Rocky looked up and saw that his eyes, a watery blue, held the tinge of grief that is impossible to miss once you've seen it in the mirror.

"Thank you," she said. She entered the house through the garage reluctantly, like stepping into a mausoleum. It was worse on the inside; neatly ironed dish towels, threadbare and patched, sat on the kitchen counter, beckoning someone to touch them. No one else would ever wash and iron them with such care again; this was their last moment of dignity, carrying all the love and tenderness of the woman who had died.

By the time Isaiah returned to his truck, Rocky was buckled into the front seat with a box of dish towels and embroidered pillowcases on her lap. A ceramic bunny sat on top of the pile of cloth. Isaiah was empty-handed. He quickly scanned her haul while he started the truck. She stared straight ahead.

"Nice rabbit," he said.

"They made me take it."

"Of course they did. Those two looked like pretty tough negotiators."

"Can we please see if my truck is fixed yet? And no more tag sales. Estate sales, call them what you will. This is too raw and primitive, pawing through the belongings of the dead."

He drove slowly away. "The dead don't need or— one can only imagine—want this stuff. What did you do with Bob's personal belongings?"

Rocky put her hand on the ceramic bunny. "Don't you remember? I told you that I put all of his clothing into black plastic bags and drove them to a Salvation Army store far enough away from our town that I wouldn't see men walking around in Bob's clothes. I threw away things like his combs, shaving equipment, and toiletry bag. I could never have done what these two guys did and let strangers paw through Bob's belongings. The weird thing is, I suddenly need something of Bob's for the DNA test, something mundane like a comb, just a piece of hair, a toothbrush."

The day was hot, and a thick haze had settled, filled with pollen, carbon monoxide, and all the molecular castoffs from human activity.

"I just thought of something. After his veterinary business was sold to his partner, I never went back there again. He had a closet where he kept gym clothes and who knows what else. What if they haven't cleaned that out yet?"

Isaiah turned his head and frowned. "That was well over a year ago. Surely they would have cleaned out Bob's gym shorts by now."

"But what if they haven't? This could be our best lead for the DNA test. I'll call tonight."

Rocky shared almost everything with Isaiah. She would certainly share the result of the phone call to Bob's old partner. But she wasn't ready to tell anyone about the next phone call she had to make. The call to the foster care system felt deceptive and awful, and she wished that someone would stop her.

Chapter 41

Rocky didn't tell Natalie that she was going to the foster care office. If she had, the girl would have thought Rocky was checking into her background, which she was. She hadn't needed the prompting from Isaiah, and she wasn't sure that it was prompting.

"We've got people right here on the island who are foster parents, and they are solid and good in all the important ways that I can think of," said Isaiah. "I don't think I could put in the labor-intensive parenting that they give to children." He didn't say one word about doubting Natalie, but he knew the perfect way to let an unspoken sentence dance in the air.

The Southern Maine Foster Care office was within walking distance of the dock in Portland, less than a mile, and Rocky welcomed the walk. She had called ahead and requested an appointment with the director regarding a child who had been damaged by the foster care system. She hadn't known that her tone carried the steel brush of accusation. She had pulled out her best pair of black pants and uncomfortably tried on her best PhD credentials. Clearly, she had not endeared herself to the director with her phone message.

"I don't know where you get your information about foster parents, but your tone is insulting," said the man behind the desk. His nameplate said IRA LEVINE, MSW, DIRECTOR. He notably had not risen when Rocky walked in. She truly hadn't intended to start the meeting off with an ignorant insult of his life's work. She had said, "I'm here to find out about a kid who was abused in the foster care system. One of many, I presume."

I presume? When did she ever use that phrase? Just that one word could have tipped Ira Levine over the edge. It would have had that effect on her.

"My apologies. I've been out of the psychological world for over a year, and even then I wasn't the most tactful person. My only experience with the foster care system was with college students who had been belched out of that system."

Ira winced at her use of the word *belched.* He took a breath to quell what must have been a temptation to throw Rocky out.

"Let me start over. I have a kid who showed up on my doorstep. She thinks she might be the biological daughter of my husband, who died over a year ago. She looks damaged in eight different ways, and she has some horrific stories to tell about foster care, where she was . . ."

Rocky paused and deleted words like *dumped, thrown, composted.*

" . . . where she was placed from age three or so until age seventeen."

"I'm sorry about your husband. I assume that she was not just in one home. How many homes was she in?"

"She said about twelve or more. She said she might not remember all of them."

"And you want to know what exactly from us, the perpetrators of her horrible existence?"

"I'm making a concerted effort to officially drop my offensive misconceptions about foster care, based on bad TV specials. I am dropping my weapons. My sarcasm has been checked at the door. Honest. I'm here to get suggestions from you about the best way to help her."

Ira Levine rose with glacial slowness, walked around to the front of his desk, and extended his hand. "Dr. Pellegrino, please sit down. I'm very protective of the parents who open their homes to children and who do work that is so hard you cannot imagine. We have fifteen hundred children in foster care in Maine, all of whom were in crisis and needed a safe place to live. We try to provide that. We provide extensive screening of foster parents, mandatory classes, and ongoing support for the child and the foster parents. We struggle against a perception that parents take in kids for the money. Believe me, there is little financial gain to be had."

If they both took off their shoes, Rocky knew she'd be taller than Levine. He wore the thickest soles possible, one step before something more contrived. But still, she'd never seen Vibram soles quite that thick. He had the slightly protruding belly that arrives so quickly for men in their forties, practically overnight, even if they've indulged in doughnuts and cinnamon rolls only as special weekend treats.

"She wasn't in the system in Maine. Natalie lived in Massachusetts. I know the system might be different in each state, but I wanted to ask you, or someone, what happens to a kid if, by consistently terrible luck, they did live in twelve abusive homes."

"You should start with the Commonwealth of Massachusetts. I can give you a contact number for Boston. You might consider softening your approach before you call them," said Levine. He wrote a number on a sticky note, tore it off, and handed it to her.

Rocky folded the yellow piece of paper in half and slid it into her pocket. The director had just lobbed her to the state of Massachusetts with amazing speed. And he hadn't answered her question.

"Thanks," she said.

She turned to leave. To the right of the door, Levine had a bookcase crammed beyond capacity with books, newspapers, journals, photos of a boy and a girl in dated school pictures, and a small photo frame that held two words in the center, written in calligraphy: TZADIKIM NISTARIM. She picked up the framed words.

"Not enough vowels for me," she said, holding it out to him with a shrug.

"Nor for most people," said Levine as his eyes softened a bit and the muscles around his mouth relaxed.

"What does it mean?" asked Rocky.

"The full answer would take several decades of Hasidic study. But the short answer is 'concealed righteous ones who protect others from dark and mysterious forces.'"

"Sounds like *Star Wars*. Sorry, I don't mean to be disrespectful, but dark and mysterious forces are the bread and butter of George Lucas," said Rocky. She placed the framed calligraphy back in its nook on the shelf.

"Who knows? Maybe our Mr. Lucas makes all his movies with *tzadikim nistarim* in mind. It is from Hasidic Jewish lore, and the belief has all the makings of the fantastical. But then, most religions lean in that direction, with seas parting, water turning to wine, and lions sleeping with lambs, metaphorically or not."

"But what does it mean beyond that?" Rocky had her hand on the door handle.

Levine turned a level gaze on her and smiled. "That at any given time there are a specific number of people who support the world, or maybe it's just a village. Their caring and righteousness are what keeps the village alive. Without them, we would perish. But here's the thing: they don't know that they are *tzadikim nistarim* because of their extraordinary humility and goodness. In fact, if people think that they might be members of the club, then that alone is proof that they are not. The world keeps turning because of them, we keep falling in love, we keep having sweet babies, and we write books and make sculptures because of them. And they go unheralded."

"Who do you think they are in your village?" But Rocky already knew what he would say, and now something was wrong and the sting of it settled into her.

"In my village? They are the foster parents who take in damaged, snarling children who have been through hell. They willingly love our throwaway children. They protect children who are ready to throw themselves headlong into the first disastrous pit they stumble into—drugs, sexual abuse, or worse. The foster parents think they are just average schmucks, doing what anyone would do to help a kid. They don't know that they are holding up the world."

Rocky dropped her hand from the door handle. "Can I call you again? I know that I came here with an attitude, wanting you to help me fix this kid from what she said happened to her in fourteen years of foster care, but I've been ignoring an obvious alternative reality with her."

"Do you mean the possibility that what she's told you isn't true? It may be true or not true, but I'm almost positive that all her years of foster care were not abusive. Call me if you think I can help." Levine paused, realigned his posture, and said, "Leave me her name, and I'll see if I can help, although I'm not sure that we can offer anything. I have an old friend in the Massachusetts system."

Rocky scribbled the girl's name on a scrap of paper from the bookcase. "Mr. Levine, did you grow up in foster care?"

"Yes, and then I was adopted by my foster family. They literally pulled me out of the ashes." Levine rolled up his right sleeve and revealed a weave of burn scars that started at his wrist and ran up his arm, beneath his shirt, to a stopping place that Rocky did not want to imagine. "Fire and skin are unequal competitors."

"Shit," said Rocky.

"Exactly," said Levine. "Your girl is eighteen now. She can access her own records. Perhaps she can show them to you. That might clear up a lot."

Chapter 42

Tess

Tess had invited Natalie to come for lunch after her first few days as Russell's apprentice. The girl had just run her eyes across a bookcase. She stepped carefully in the older woman's house, touching the dried branches that hung suspended from the ceiling beams, with bits of beach glass wrapped in copper wire, spiraling around, aroused by the breeze that blew through her windows. Natalie opened a slender volume of poetry from a stack on the coffee table.

"I read one poem per day, and each one is like your story, or mine. Tell me a story that did not begin with love or the want of love," said Tess. "There isn't one. Even the moment we are conceived, love is the main topic. Even if love wasn't there, someone was reaching for it."

Natalie stretched her arm out and touched a dead moth that rested in a desiccated exoskeleton on a windowsill.

"I won't ever know," said Natalie. "I don't remember my mother. I've seen pictures of her. My caseworker gave me a photo of her when I was about ten. There were three girls in the picture: my mother and two other girls with big 1980s hairdos. This was before she ever had me. She looked like one of the shy kids begging to be liked. Her two friends were bigger than her and all puffed out with attitude. I think my mother wanted to be like them but she wasn't. Maybe you can't tell that much from a photo, but she looked like the one on the outside. I lost the picture in one of the foster homes."

Tess put her hand on the fridge door and paused there, like a gull held steady by an offshore wind, suspended above the earth and sea.

"It's hard to grow up without your mother. Mine died when I was very young, which is not the same as your situation, not at all. But it does create a longing, a dreaming for something that keeps dancing away, out of reach."

"Did you have a father?" asked the girl.

"Yes, dear, I had a father. And therein lies the difference. I had one parent, and you had none, and having one is a world away from having none."

Something flashed through Natalie, a smoldering fire that ignited along her neck and her fists tightened. "You don't know. Believe me, you don't know."

The girl had a wound as big as a canyon, and the effort it took to keep it in stasis hit Tess hard. "Of course. That is one of the most ridiculous things that I could have said. You are right. I don't know what it was like for you."

Natalie's fists began to unfurl, but Tess knew it would be hours before the jets of fighting-ready hormones retreated from her system. She pulled open the fridge. "I have ginger tea with chamomile. I understand that your preference may be Coke or Pepsi, neither of which I have. But you can dump a bunch of sugar in the iced tea. I know most teenagers have a strong desire for sugar. Do you?"

Natalie let a paper-thin edge slip into her voice. "Do I what?"

"Do you want sugar in your iced tea?"

The girl had edges. She was not amorphous. That's good, thought Tess.

Natalie rearranged her face, softening it. "Oh, sorry. I'll take iced tea and sugar."

Tess poured them both a glass of tea and set a sugar bowl in the center of the kitchen table. No wonder Rocky wanted to help this girl. The child was in a constant state of unraveling and knitting back together. She must be exhausted. What could Tess do that would help Natalie sink into who she was and let her rest, if even for a moment?

"Did Rocky tell you that I'm a physical therapist? Semi-retired, special patients only. You look like your shoulders are carrying too much tension for someone your age. I've just signed up for a training course in craniosacral therapy, and I'll need some victims to practice on. It's a light touch, the patient stays fully clothed. Um, something like this."

Tess reached out to place several fingers along the back of Natalie's neck.

"Get your hands off me!" said Natalie, spitting the words. Her hand swung around and connected with Tess, knocking her hand away as if Tess were a wasp, with stinger in launch position.

Tess instantly understood her mistake, and it was one that she rarely ever made. Don't ever surprise someone by touching them; always ask permission. What was she thinking? She was rusty, or worse. Her skill as a physical therapist might have been more deeply embedded within her synesthesia than she at first imagined.

"I'm sorry," said Tess. "I don't know what I was thinking. I just broke the cardinal rule of my profession. We never touch someone without asking."

Tess stepped away from the girl, turning her palms up, keeping them in sight and close to her body. Natalie's face crumpled; the skin was tight around her eyes, and her lips were pulled back. The girl was unrecognizable for a moment, her tender helplessness tossed aside. She quickly realigned, darting her eyes toward Tess, looking exactly like someone who was embarrassed that she'd been seen without her clothes.

"Sorry about that. I don't like to be touched," said Natalie, stepping back into her body again.

"Can we start again, dear? Let's have our drinks. If you stay long enough, you'll get to be adored by Danielle," said Tess. "She's coming for a few days. I'm suddenly her favorite person, and I'm making the most of it before she notices that I'm an old lady with funny hair."

Natalie scooped sugar into her glass, taking exaggerated care, as if someone was going to charge her for any dropped crystals.

"Why don't you come with us tomorrow? We're going to take flashlights and explore Battery Steele on the north shore. Danielle would love it, and so would I. We can all scare the daylights out of each other."

"What's Battery Steele?"

"It's what's left from World War II when the Navy was sure the Germans were going to invade America.

It's a huge cement building, a bunker really, covered with ten feet of dirt on top, where the biggest guns of the day were kept at the ready."

"Sounds scary."

World War II had been terrible, but it had also been only three years long. Considering for a moment how long current wars lasted, Tess cringed bit before replying, "Oh yes, deliciously so. If I want to get distracting thoughts out of my head, I either meditate or go to Battery Steele and scare myself silly."

If ever Tess needed her synesthesia, it was now. Would it grow back and mend the way skin does, knitting itself with blood? She wanted to mend the way Cooper had mended; his limp was barely detectable now.

She seemed to be missing something elemental about people, as though she'd forgotten something she knew about them before she lost her synesthesia. Without her full force of tangled neurology, people appeared to her more like shells. She no longer lived in a world of vivid color associated with tactile sensations. She didn't like it. She wanted her brain back the way it had been, buzzing and cross-firing.

Tess had to figure out how to get it back. There had been the physiological shock of surgery, like being in a train wreck, or any kind of car accident. Amnesia often surrounds an accident, or at least the time prior to the event. Clearly something had altered her brain, perhaps something chemical, since it wasn't something physical like a brain tumor. All of her training told her to start with the simplest and most obvious explanation. A flood of adrenaline had washed over her brain during the surgery, her pain centers had been dulled, and all her resources had been redirected to her large muscle groups. Even if she could figure out how her brain got disabled, would it matter? Could she get it jump-started again?

"What time tomorrow?" asked Natalie.

"I'll give you a call at Rocky's to let you know what time. I have an extra bike for you. That way we can all ride over together," said Tess. "I'd like to take an official tour of the place with one of the local historians," she added. "I could never remember all the information they have in their heads."

The next day Tess and the two girls bicycled along the back shore to Battery Steele and waited outside while the pitch-dark entrance belched dank air at them. Several other people, tourists, showed up at ten before the hour.

"When do they turn on the lights?" said Natalie. Tess heard the tremble in her voice, masked by irritation.

"I packed flashlights for all of us," said Tess. "Here, take yours." She pulled three small flashlights out of her bike basket. "And the history tour guide brings big flashlights. Don't worry. I've been in here lots of times."

Edging closer to her grandmother, Danielle slid her hand into Tess's.

"I told you it was a little creepy, and that's the fun of it, but it's scary in the way that roller coasters are scary. You know everything's really going to be okay, but one part of your brain doesn't believe that and it gets scared. The other part of your brain knows that roller coasters stay on the track."

Danielle looked up at her grandmother. "Is that what happens when we get scared? Our brain splits in half?"

Before Tess could answer, a car crunched along the gravel road and came to a stop. The island was home to a team of amateur historians, and today's guide would be one of them, Wilbur Kerns. He got out of his car, carrying a clipboard. Wilbur's khaki pants were neatly pressed, and his Peaks Island Historical Society T-shirt was tucked tightly into his waistband.

"Good morning, everyone. Looks like the whole gang is here. Are we ready to go into Battery Steele and see what it was like to live in the bunker?"

Natalie's knuckles turned white as her grip turned viselike on her flashlight. Tess feared that she'd crush it.

"Wilbur, before we go in, would you please mention that people are free to leave at any point? I see you have extra flashlights with you. Can you spare one for a guest of mine? Natalie, please carry one of the large flashlights. There, now you're a double-fisted light-bearer."

Natalie accepted the large, heavy-duty flashlight, and the group followed Wilbur into the concrete bunker. A tangle of vines hung over the exposed side of the concrete. Natalie stayed outside the clutch of tourists and glanced back at the light streaming through the entrance.

"Okay, I'm ready," said Natalie quietly.

Wilbur said, "Could you please close the door, young lady? None of you are old enough to remember the rules of blackouts, but in order to prevent planes from seeing targets at night, everyone had to use black shades on their windows and military facilities had to be extra careful. As we walk further along the corridor of the bunker, we will experience the full impact of total darkness."

Hanging on to Danielle's little fist, Tess turned to see where Natalie stood on the outer edge of the group. With only illumination from flashlights, it was difficult to get a read on Natalie's face. Tess didn't want to make another mistake with the girl.

She leaned down to Danielle and whispered. "Let's stand by Natalie. That way we can all huddle together when Wilbur turns out the light." They slid to the back edge of the group and sidled up to Natalie.

"On the count of three, we'll all switch off our flashlights for a moment. Ready? One, two, three."

Tess did not remember this as a part of previous tours. As soon as all the lights were out, the group gasped. Tess felt an immediate dizziness with no anchor for her vision. She was afraid to take a step for fear of falling. Danielle squealed with delighted terror.

Suddenly, a light came on. Natalie had turned on both her flashlights. Tess knew it was partly the distortion of the downward cast of the lights, but the girl's face looked contorted in anguish, her lips pulled back.

"I can switch on the lights whenever I want to," she whispered.

"Yes, of course you can. Wilbur, this doesn't make sense. The soldiers didn't stumble around here in the dark. That's why they had the concrete bunker. What's the point in making us stand around in the pitch dark?" said Tess.

"No historical point. It just adds an amusement park fright to the tour. It wakes people up. Lights on, everyone, we'll keep walking the length of Battery Steele," said Wilbur. "There are storage rooms on either side of the walkway, mostly empty except for some wayward beer cans."

The group followed Wilbur, but Natalie remained frozen in place.

This was not what Tess had planned. She could see that the girl had been blindsided by something, an old haunt from the past, a primal fear of the dark. She wanted to salvage the outing.

"Natalie, it's too lovely today to skulk around in Battery Steele. Let's go outside and take a walk along the ocean road," said Tess.

"No," said the girl sharply. "You go ahead. Do not change plans for me. Do not! Here, take your flashlight and take the big one too. Just light up the doorway until I'm out of here."

Her voice was high and tight. Tess wanted to let her save whatever face was left to save. "This is a good day for a ride. Take your time and enjoy the day. We'll give you all the highlights the next time we see you," said Tess.

Natalie bolted for the door and heaved against it until daylight streamed in. The girl did not pause.

"Where is Natalie going?" asked Danielle.

"To gather herself together. Something frightened her, and she's embarrassed that we saw her so undone. Come on, let's catch up with Wilbur before he does something ridiculous again."

Chapter 43

Natalie

N atalie grabbed the bike and began pedaling as fast as she could away from the stupid bunker. How could she still be afraid of the dark? She wasn't a kid anymore. She wanted to take back everything that had been stolen from her, and that included getting so scared of the dark that she could throw up. That old guy had just surprised her when he turned off the lights; she hadn't been ready, that was the problem.

She rode across the center of the island, not entirely sure where she was, but doubting very much that she could get lost. Surely cutting through the center was a quicker way to get back to Rocky's house. The path grew suddenly narrow and presented her with the option of going left or right. She got off her bike and walked it. There were no houses in sight.

A crow shot down from the tree branch. Natalie felt the sliver of air brush her cheek. The crow landed ten feet in front of her, directly in the middle of the footpath. The black bird turned his head sideways, looking at her with one eye.

She wanted to stamp her foot, flap her arms, or shout to make the bird go away. The muscles along the back of her neck tightened, then both muscles on either side of her spine contracted, arching her back, the way it did at the dentist's office when he aimed the drill into her mouth.

The bird was too large. Birds shouldn't be this big, but it was just a bird, and birds couldn't hurt you. It was a crow; everyone knew crows. What was wrong with her? If she just kept going, she'd find her way. She must have missed a turnoff on one of the trails. The crow took an awkward step toward her.

She had hurt a bird once—a robin that had flown into a sliding glass door and dropped to the ground in stunned silence. She had picked it up, placed her small finger on the chest, and felt the strum of the heart. There had been other foster kids in the home, just two, but they had been younger than her eleven years and bothersome. She had taken the bird indoors and pushed it into the little boy's face, just to scare him a little, to make him go away from her. She didn't remember what happened after that, but later the foster parents were mad, really mad, and they didn't want her after the bird incident.

The crow toddled a few more steps toward her. She moved one foot slowly backwards, so that the crow might not notice. Were crows like horses or dogs? Could they smell fear? The thought that the crow could sense her fear made her more afraid. She was too far from the road or any houses to be heard, even if she was willing to scream, which she was not. If she allowed someone to rescue her, then they would call Rocky, and maybe Rocky would look worried and tell her to take a rest on the couch and bring her a cold drink. Maybe, but not now.

The crow hopped toward her. Sweat scalded the sides of her torso. Her hands were limp, as useless as if they had been detached from her arms. What would the crow do if she turned her back and ran? The large muscles of her thighs were thick and sluggish. The black feathers caught the slanted sun through the trees. The crow was electric, glistening with light. Now that he had found her, now that he had seen her like this, groveling and terrified, he would always look for her.

The crow made a strange quaking sound, and another crow floated to its side. And another. Why weren't they moving? It was like they knew her, and knew she didn't belong here. She bent down slowly and picked up a stick, a good solid one.

"Get out of here," she said, her voice thin and cracked. She threw the stick, and the trio of crows rose into the air, easily avoiding her wild throw. She pushed the bike, looking constantly over her shoulder, waiting for the flock to descend on her. The crows called and followed her, soaring from tree to tree until she emerged on a dirt road again. She swung a leg over the bike and jumped on, pedaling hard, cursing the crows, the stupid history tour guy in Battery Steele, and mostly Tess and Danielle because they saw her when she was afraid and she didn't want anyone ever again to see her afraid. She had to get to Franklin. They needed to work faster.

Chapter 44

Tess

"I like Natalie," said Danielle the morning after the Battery Steele debacle. Could this child be going into second grade in just a few months? Time was passing too quickly. Just yesterday they had talked about Danielle riding the ferry by herself, with her babysitter stationed at the Portland pier and Tess at the island pier.

Tess felt the soft ghost of time crawl up her sleeve, brushing the fine hairs of her arm. Must the child grow older? The sweetness of this age grabbed at Tess and made her want to fall to her knees with gratitude.

Tess had startled awake several times during the night, aware of her granddaughter tucked in close, giving off the smell of peach. Was it the color peach, as she had always known it, not the fruit? Could it be coming back? Her magnificently braided sensory neurons might be traveling back to her at this very moment. The child smelled like the color peach because the letter *D* in her name was peach-colored, and it had been for as long as Tess could remember.

She was encouraged by this passing smell of peach to hope that her synesthesia was returning. Tess had snuggled as close to the child as she dared without waking her, to breathe in her scented color. Now the girl wiggled awake, alert instantly.

"Will Natalie come today?" said Danielle.

Tess was startled by the instant question about Natalie. She got up and pulled a sweatshirt over her cotton pajamas. The mornings were chilly on Peaks, even in the summer. "Tell me something that you especially like about Natalie," said Tess. Danielle was still in bed, with the white comforter tucked deliberately under her arms and all the pillows behind her.

"I like that she's not grown-up all the way. She's afraid of stuff like the dark the way I am. My dad says that I shouldn't be afraid of the dark because everything is the same at night. Only it isn't, and Natalie knows it."

Tess sat cross-legged at the end of the bed. "And that's what you like most about Natalie, that she's afraid of the dark like you?"

Danielle placed both hands behind her head, looked at the ceiling, and pondered this. "Yes," she said with a confirming nod of her head.

Tess saw no reason to beat the child's logic into the ground. "So be it. Let's make skinny French pancakes and eat them outside. Your job will be to cut up the strawberries. Can you do that?"

Danielle shot up out of her languid mound of covers. "We can eat outside?"

"Yes," said Tess.

"They're called crepes. I'm seven. You don't have to keep calling them skinny French pancakes."

"Of course I don't. Now let's get to it before Rocky arrives with her weaponry and begins shooting arrows in the backyard. Then we'd have to eat our crepes with flak jackets on. You can take the strawberries and milk and eggs out of the fridge while I shower."

Tess thought about Natalie as the hot water streamed down her. How quickly the strange girl had woven herself into Rocky's life, and to some extent her own. Natalie had been the first person Danielle thought about this morning. Should she be wary about her granddaughter being so rapidly attached to Natalie? Tess was keenly aware of how devastating a rejection can be for a young child. Natalie could blow out of their lives as quickly as she had blown in.

She shut off the water and toweled dry as the Buddha on her blue bathroom door looked at her, offering his shaded gaze.

"I know," she said to the image. "And may you have a peaceful day too. But it's much easier for you here in the bathroom than it is for the rest of us."

Danielle hollered from the kitchen. "What's the other thing that we need to make the crepes?"

Tess yanked open the door. "Wait for me, little chef."

As she hopped around the bedroom, diving into her fresh cotton pants and her favorite hoodie, she heard another voice.

Tess paused, hand on her hair, ready to tie back the flow of white hair into a fat clip. It was Natalie. How odd, how serendipitous that she and Danielle had been thinking of Natalie and now she had dropped in. She felt the morning coolness of the floor as she padded to the kitchen.

"Natalie! We're having skinny pancakes, I mean crepes. Mine has jam on it, but you can have yours any way that you want," said Danielle, nearly vibrating off the stool she stood on. "I know how to mix everything that goes in them, like eggs and flour."

Natalie gave Tess an inquiring look, asking permission.

"Yes, yes, sit down and watch our master chef at work," said Tess.

"I just stopped by to say hi and that I'm sorry about running off yesterday at Battery Steele." She tipped her head off to an angle and shrugged her shoulders together. "Rocky is gone, and Melissa took Cooper over to Portland, so I got a little lonely. Are you sure it's okay if I join you?" asked Natalie.

With anyone else, Tess would have hugged her, or rubbed her arm, or fussed with her hair. But Natalie's personal space extended far beyond the national average of three feet.

"It's more than fine. We have an exciting morning planned, but first we eat," said Tess.

"Come on, Natalie, I'll give you the spoon to lick. Gramma thinks it's gross, but I like it." The child beamed at Natalie, looking up at her with little sister love.

Natalie walked tentatively into the kitchen, as if she had landed in a strange land where walking had different rules.

"This is a wild and wacky place this morning. Please stay. I am famous for my crepes," said Tess.

Natalie pressed into the corner between the sink and the counter. "I just wanted to return your bike. But okay, breakfast sounds good."

The three of them devoured the crepes in a blur of jam, juice, and glasses of milk. Tess cooked all of the batter, remembering mornings when her children were small and Len would arrive at the Sunday morning breakfast hungover and stinking of alcohol. She was still sad that he had missed so much. What had Natalie missed? Whatever it was, the missing part was elemental. Tess could see that much.

Tess was intrigued that an eighteen-year-old girl who'd ricocheted between a dozen foster homes before the system shot her out of the exit tube would choose to hang out with an old physical therapist and a seven-year-old child. Tess wanted something for all three of them to do.

"Have you ever been on the golf-cart history tour?" asked Tess.

"No," said Natalie. "Is it anything like the dank cave of that bunker place?"

"I want to go!" said Danielle, jumping straight into the air like a terrier. She had said yesterday that doing anything with her grandmother was the equivalent of a day at Disneyland. Not that Danielle had ever been to Disneyland, but this was what Tess's son had said on the phone the previous evening.

"It is nothing like yesterday's unfortunate event. We need a do-over. That wasn't one bit of fun. The golf-cart tours are a more dignified thing to do, and that's what we are this morning, dignified," said Tess, putting one hand on her hip and the other arm overhead in a dancer's pose.

Tess phoned in the reservation for the three of them. The golf-cart tours started at the dock parking lot. The three of them walked the mile into town, already filled with Saturday day-trippers who rented bikes and bought ice cream before heading for the bay shore, where they could get close to the water and build sculptures of stacked rocks that dotted the shore like art installations.

Golf carts were the limousines of the island. A golf cart with three rows of seats was the equivalent of a stretch limo. Six people settled into the golf cart, and Rosemary Steward, tour guide and librarian, got into the driver's seat of the electric cart and started it up. Danielle squeezed in between Tess and Natalie, squirming with happiness at her good fortune.

Rosemary said, "The tour lasts for an hour. We're headed first to the Back Bay area of the island, which was taken by eminent domain during World War II to create a naval base."

Tess was glad that Rosemary was the guide today; the woman had a lively sense of history and made the past personal, as if it had just happened two minutes ago. Still, Tess wondered if Rosemary could hold the attention of a traumatized teenager and a seven-year-old girl.

Rosemary drove the cart past the small downtown, past the neighborhood of tiny houses that had been built for workers in a long-departed fish factory, and finally to the long stretch of open road that faced east to the wide expanse of the Atlantic.

"The naval base was here," she pointed out. "Most of it was an underground bunker called Battery Steele. . . ."

"We know that part," shouted Danielle.

Tess shushed her.

"But we do know that part. We were just there, inside," said Danielle, attempting to use a quieter voice.

Undaunted, Rosemary continued, shouting over her right shoulder as she drove. "The part that you may not know is that the Navy built a few small houses facing the ocean, just in case the Germans flew over. Or in case German spies somehow came ashore in disguise. The houses were fakes, designed to camouflage the naval base. No one lived in them, but they kept children's tricycles and a swing set out front. Every day they moved the tricycle to a different spot so that it looked like someone lived there, just in case the Germans were watching."

Tess suddenly paid attention. Something like that was happening again on Peaks—like the fake house and the tricycle being relocated, something was being carefully moved every day. But what was it? There was nothing like that at her house or Rocky's house. Tess could almost taste it, feel the rub of it on her cheek. She pictured a young sailor in 1944, moving a tricycle each day as part of his duty, diligently keeping track of where he put it, perhaps even laying it on its side one day to mimic a child's haphazard dismount.

As the tour continued, Tess rubbed her temples.

Chapter 45

The day was already set in motion. Rocky had to drive to Massachusetts in the afternoon to sign more papers at the lawyer's office related to Bob's estate. Natalie left a note that she'd taken Cooper for a walk to the beach. Rocky had the morning off, free of interruption for at least a few hours.

The rental cottage had been a sanctuary; she was surprised at the rush of anticipatory grief she felt about leaving it for the remodeled house. Her daily routines there had taken on a reassuring shape that fit Rocky and her two animals perfectly. Whenever Rocky came home, Cooper would greet her with an exuberance normally reserved for celebrities—his large tail cleared anything in its path, his body gyrated, and his lips pulled back with impossible joy. The racket would alert

Peterson in whatever shrubbery she was dozing under, and she would appear at the screen door, ready to add her unfathomable cat greeting to the ruckus.

This morning Rocky prepared their food, the lubricant of all animals, human or quadruped. Rocky was mid-dip into Cooper's fifty-gallon drum of kibble when the phone rang.

"Dr. Pellegrino, I'm sorry to bother you at home. This is Ira Levine at the foster care agency."

It took Rocky a moment to switch from the pandemonium of furred creatures to the male seriousness of his voice. She'd been in his office only two days earlier.

"Sorry about the delayed response, but I have a hungry gang of animals and their list of demands is clear. What's up?" said Rocky. "Oh, and thanks for suggesting that we look at Natalie's files. She's going to get those tomorrow."

"That's why I'm calling you," Levine said. "Something bothered me about her file, and I couldn't put my finger on it. Something about the language didn't ring true. So I called my friend in the system in Worcester. She put me in touch with one of Natalie's old caseworkers, and I asked her to double-check something in the file."

Rocky had managed to deposit a cup of food in Cooper's bowl, so the general cacophony had shrunk down to the sound of kibble being delicately crunched as the dog lay in front of his bowl.

"Hold on a minute," Rocky said.

She covered the receiver with her hand and yelled, "Natalie? Are you here?"

She opened Natalie's bedroom and scanned the small room for the girl. She opened the bathroom door with her foot. Nobody home—she wanted to be sure.

"Okay, go ahead," Rocky said. Her skin had cooled in odd blotches. The large muscles of her back felt damp and cold. The barely covered bones of her clavicle soaked up a chill.

Levine continued. "I asked my friend if Natalie's file seemed unusual. I asked her to pull it up on the computer. That was two days ago. She has seventy kids in her caseload, and I'm amazed that she got back to me in this decade. But when she called back she said that someone had changed her original notes. Caseworkers are not supposed to keep private records aside from the official records, but let's be thankful that she did. Something is wrong with the official record on this kid. You need to hear the highlights from the caseworker's notes."

Rocky put her hand on a sweating glass of iced tea. Tess had insisted that she switch out one Coke for one glass of iced tea in an effort to drain off the deluge of sugar and caffeine.

"What's wrong?" she said.

"I would rather that you come to my office. You'll understand when you get here."

When Rocky had arrived full of accusatory rage on her first visit, Ira Levine's office had looked like the camp of the enemy. The two framed prints of coastal Maine had looked faded and impersonal. His desk had had the sanctimonious air of an administrator, a man strapped to his desk by paper and technology, out of touch with the war wounds of foster kids, the ones he shuffled from place to place. Like Natalie.

But Rocky's magnetic north had skipped a jog after meeting the director. He stood up immediately when she came in, abandoning the boundary land of his desk.

"Please sit over here," he said, pointing toward two lightly padded chairs, the kind that filled waiting rooms. They had just enough padding to keep sitting bones from rubbing on cold metal, and they were immobile enough to keep the sitter at attention.

"These are your relaxing chairs?" asked Rocky. She wore long pants, having anticipated the chill of his air conditioner. Levine wore a long-sleeved shirt, perhaps to hide his burn scars, a choice that Rocky would have understood. He had a folder in his hands.

"All the relaxing chairs are prioritized for the case-workers and the families. I put myself last on the list for the feel-good furniture."

The prints behind Levine now looked hopeful to her, inspiring. *So this is what he wants to think about while he's running the agency—he wants to feel the breeze off Casco Bay.* Rocky liked him for it.

"I have to apologize, but I have a meeting with my attorney in Massachusetts. I'll have to leave Portland in an hour. What did you find out about Natalie?" said Rocky. She placed one ankle over the opposite knee.

"Caseworkers aren't supposed to keep private notes. These copies were delivered to my office by FedEx from a caseworker in Massachusetts on the condition that I destroy them after I share them with you."

Rocky swallowed hard and nodded. Levine kept a tight hold on the manila folder.

"All case notes about kids in their system went digital about ten years ago. Records are centralized so that any caseworker can pull up a kid's record. To protect the confidentiality of the kids and families, the agency put up multiple firewalls."

Levine sank back into his chair as much as the unforgiving stainless steel allowed. He sighed and looked briefly at the ceiling. The stubble on his neck was dark and coarse.

"What you saw of Natalie's record had been altered. There is evidence from two sources that the firewall was breached. The first source is this file from a veteran caseworker who took an interest in a little girl fourteen years ago. The second source is an initial indication that an unauthorized trail has been detected in the system. As near as I can tell, any computer message leaves a trail, something like the dust left by meteorites. Their IT guys swear that a breach has never happened before. They're all over this at the moment."

"Why would someone alter a kid's case file, if that's what happened?" asked Rocky.

"Good question," he said. "What I've got here are the personal records of a caseworker who had a habit of keeping her own records so that she was free to write down what was clinically important about a kid, but without the claustrophobic fear that the details might get subpoenaed in court documents."

Rocky understood. Her mentor had instructed her in the unwritten code for writing case notes. "Imagine that everything in the case file will be subjected to a courtroom of judges and lawyers," Rocky's mentor had told her. "If you think that a client might have a personality disorder, such as borderline personality disorder, you need to be absolutely certain by means of psychological testing, by collaboration with psychiatrists, and by clearly eliminating other possible diagnoses. Otherwise, don't give someone a label that will follow them for years. And if a client tells you that his wife is sleeping with his best friend, be sure to write, client *reports* that his wife is sleeping with a friend. We aren't lawyers or private investigators," she had said.

"I get it. Do you want me to read the notes?" Rocky asked in a small voice, the remnant of her casual tone having slipped away. She already dreaded what she was about to hear.

"It's better if I give you the highlights. Massachusetts sent me the official record. I've picked out the discrepancies." He opened the folder and looked down. He took a large breath. "Natalie first came into contact with protective services when she was two. Her mother was put on probation for buying and selling crack. It was noted that the little girl was undernourished, and the mother was assigned a caseworker who arranged for parenting classes, including appropriate nutrition. The major condition of probation was attendance at an addictions clinic. The mother attended for five months. Then we have no more mention of the mother and child until eighteen months later, when the mother was found dead from stab wounds and an overdose in an apartment in Ludlow. The final report said that she had enough drugs in her system to kill her, but that the official cause of death was multiple stab wounds. She had been dead for approximately five days when the body was found."

Levine stopped, shifted his feet, and ran his tongue around his dry mouth. Rocky did not want to picture a woman's body in a state of decomposition after five days.

"Where was Natalie?" she asked.

"The two of them were only found by accident. The landlord came through the building to show another apartment and was hit by the smell. He called the police. The police found the little girl sitting on the kitchen floor next to the mother. Natalie was big enough to open the fridge, but she was unable to open cans of soda, which was the only liquid. She had eaten margarine, reportedly the only food in the fridge. She drank the water out of the toilet, or it was assumed that she had done so, since the toilet bowl was empty. She was too small to turn on the tightly shut bathtub faucet and unable to get to the kitchen sink. But she had covered her mother's body with two stuffed animals and a scarf. The level of decomposition was significant. And the electricity had been turned off, so the child had also been in the dark each night."

Rocky put her face into her hands and shuddered. When she lifted her head, she said, "Natalie said her mother spent several years in prison and then disappeared when she was released."

"I've cross-checked this with police records, and the police record confirms this caseworker's notes. Apparently the hacker didn't think to corroborate other sources," said Levine. "There's a bit more that matters in terms of this girl showing up in your life."

Rocky stood up. "Do you have any water? I'd prefer a beer, but you probably don't have one of those."

"There are many days when I've wished for a drink of something that would scorch out the details of what I hear about kids, what they've gone through. But no, I can't offer you a beer. Portland water is pretty good. Do you want to take a break and get a drink from the office bubbler?"

Rocky did not want to leave the room. She sat down again. "No, let's keep going."

Levine's finger was stuck on the page where he had stopped. He opened the folder again. "Natalie was hospitalized for shock, dehydration, and general malnutrition. She was placed immediately into a crisis placement for a few months until a more long-term foster family was located. If she had ever spoken, she had stopped by then and did not speak until she was five years old. No family could be located. There was evidence that her mother received monetary support, however. There were shreds of several checks found from an account in Iowa. She never cashed them."

Rocky had a sense of things stirring, the way molten lava pushes to the surface, igniting everything in its path. The ground beneath her began to shake.

"Was there a name on the check?" she whispered.

"No. It came directly from a bank. Believe me, even a busy caseworker would have tried to pursue this link," said Levine.

She ran the situation through a mental database of options, trying to understand.

"My husband would have been in veterinary school in Iowa at about that time. But I can see that there's more. Please keep going."

"There is general corroboration about the first two families. But you've got to remember that the child was mute for the first year, which must have made it doubly hard to find out how the first family neglected her. The caseworker removed her immediately when she discovered the neglect and placed her with a family where she lived for two years. The family requested that she be placed elsewhere. It was only when another child was placed in the same home that the molestation by the older boys was detected. After that, Natalie was placed in the best families they could find."

A sour drip started in Rocky's throat. "Kids that age frequently don't tell others about abuse. . . ."

Levine held up a finger to stop her. "You don't have to tell me that."

Rocky slunk down lower in her chair. "I know. This is horrible and getting worse."

Levine ran his hand through his hair. "I want to skip ahead to the parts that were nearly absent in the central file. At some point, children become available for adoption. But Natalie was never adopted. It was like she made a point of being impossible to adopt. She went on preliminary visits with prospective parents on three different occasions," said Levine. "Did you know that?"

"No," said Rocky. "Natalie didn't mention that."

There was something uncomfortable about listening to Levine read Natalie's file. Betrayal, that's what it was, dark and slick. She was betraying the girl, whispering behind her back. Rocky could almost catch the wisp of what seeped over her, the clutch of fog, not so different from the day itself, the drench of last night's summer rain leaving the streets steaming. Everything was damp. The white pages in Levine's hands drooped as if exhausted, wearied by the life of one girl. He tried to prop the pages up. His window air conditioner groaned under the weight of the atmosphere.

"Her first potential adoptive family was interested in her when she was eight. Natalie stayed with them for a weekend, and from the report of the family, she started a fire on the deck."

Levine frowned and looked over the papers at Rocky. "That's odd, don't you think? She started a fire, which sets off all the red flags about blossoming into an antisocial personality disorder, but she started the fire on the deck, where the least amount of damage would be done. This sounds more like a statement, but a statement of what is unclear. The caseworker speculated that Natalie did not want to be adopted."

A small end table separated their two chairs, and he placed the pages face down on the scratched wood.

"Was anyone hurt?"

"No, but the parents were clearly alarmed, and with a four-year-old child of their own, they said they couldn't take the risk," he said.

"What else?" asked Rocky, cataloging all the information that Natalie had omitted.

"There's a gap in time with her notes because the caseworker was gone on maternity leave for a year. Keep in mind that these are not the official centralized notes, but her private notes. Natalie was moved to a therapeutic group home at age thirteen. She was also medicated for a mood disorder, then ADD. It looks like she was on a cocktail of antipsychotics and antidepressants," he said.

Rocky cringed. The entire population of the United States was overmedicated, obligingly gulping down drugs and feeding the wallets of the pharmaceutical companies. "How does a kid go from being in foster care, to potential adoptive parents, to being in a therapeutic group home?"

Levine closed the file. "In essence, her behavior had become too disruptive for foster homes. This must have happened during the yearlong absence of her caseworker."

"What happened to the caseworker after she came back? You make it sound like she didn't work with Natalie again."

"She tried to work with Natalie again. But the girl made clear and specific threats against the caseworker and her baby. She had to transfer the case to someone else."

"What?" Rocky twisted in her chair. "Are you sure?"

"The caseworker was shattered. She had cared deeply about the girl. Yes, I'm sure."

Rocky tried to picture Natalie threatening her caseworker with bodily harm. Had it been an adolescent throwaway comment, like *I wish you were dead?* Even as she wondered, a dark sense of dread crept up her torso.

Levine cleared his throat. "The files have been tampered with. It is likely that there has been a breach of the firewalls within the agency, and she has either been lying to you or she believes what she has told you. She came looking for your deceased husband, or she came looking for you. Do you have any idea what she wants?"

Rocky looked over Levine's shoulder at the wall clock. It was already 11:00 A.M. She pushed out of the chair. "No. Maybe. I have three hours to think about this nonstop while I drive to Amherst, and three more hours while I drive back again. I only know what I wanted. If Bob was her father, we could've been a family. I know this sounds naive or delusional, but Bob wouldn't really be gone."

Chapter 46

Tess

Tess would never have told anyone, but when she heard his voice in her dreams, she knew immediately: Len was her beloved. The voice came from the steady place within her ex-husband that resurfaced when he spent considerable time nursing her back to health, not the part of him that destroyed their marriage and his career. The sharp thrill of summer had opened up wide, and this evening Tess would resume her weekly trips to Portland, as soon as she finished overseeing the change in renters at three of the houses she managed.

What were they now, Tess and Len? Old, that was one thing. Tess was at the doorway of seventy, Len was seventy-one, and despite the fact that Tess was freakishly agile (as Melissa liked to say), she knew that age was sneaking up on her like a wet dog on a living room couch—sinking down and not smelling so good. Was she ready for the next part of life? Without the comfort of her multisensory wiring, her sweet synesthesia, her ability to see the unique color of every letter and the cinematic blaze of numbers? It was returning in tiny bits, but Tess was not hopeful. When she had sniffed her granddaughter's hair the day before and been enveloped in the visual display of a peach, that might have been as good as it was going to get.

Tess still had a resoundingly spritely body, despite encroaching age. She would have been horrified if anyone ever detected the pride she took in her bodily freedom, her ability to dance without self-consciousness, to strip down naked and slide into the Jacuzzi at one of the rental houses without fear of how she looked from the back. Ego was a bad thing in any department; the blue Buddha on her bathroom door reminded her of that every morning. Still, if she could, she would endow everyone with the physical freedom she felt. So far, the only one who seemed to dance to Tess's drummer was her granddaughter. She was already planning their berry-picking adventure for tomorrow.

The windows were open, and the night air was still sweet in her house. Breezes carried from the Atlantic wrapped around Peaks Island, cooling it, spritzing it with salt water. She still had a few physical therapy patients who had waited loyally for her to return to work. Harold had another appointment next week. She was back to maximum capacity.

But the dream voice, clear and kind, what part of her ex-husband did this come from? Not the tall, blue-eyed man who attended AA meetings three times a week in Portland. Not the young, hopeful man she had married, who seemed to drink only as much as the rest of their college friends. Not the successful physician who drank from the minute he arrived home until he collapsed on the couch, growling in his sleep, or the man who arrived home with blood smeared over his face and shirt, having run his silver BMW directly into the neighbor's new fence, an event that he was unable to recall. It was his elemental self, the small boy with corn-silk hair, or the still-straight-spined man who had long since given up his medical practice and instead worked three days a week at the Portland Chamber of Commerce, helping tourists take in the history of the seaport town and locate B and Bs.

It had been twenty-five years since they divorced, and most of the hard things had already happened and gone by. She had thought of telling him how much she longed for him, yet something stopped her. She would never tell Len that she loved his arthritic hands, the way his knuckles had expanded and twisted in the direction that fingers were never meant to go. As a surgeon, his lithe young hands, his strong, confident, testosterone-fueled hands, were prized above all else. Surgeons bathed their hands like precious lovers, allowed them to grace a table for all to see, with the nails squarely trimmed, the palms devoid of calluses; surgeon hands could be placed in a museum, the prototype of the perfect hands. She had been jealous of those perfect hands when they were married, when they were young. He had loved his hands more than Tess and more than their two children, though not as much as alcohol; he had loved alcohol even more than his hands.

The sober version of Len—the Len she would have killed for in her twenties and thirties—was ever more enticing. All of him shone through his gargoyle knuckles, his swollen fingers, and even his ridged and brittle fingernails. She wanted to press her lips to the tender edges of him that had finally crept out, erupting like a slow earthquake through his hands, forcing bones and cartilage to change, creating a new sculpture of Len.

Tess had a full day of rental management and one physical therapy patient. She didn't have time to dwell on what could have been. She poured milk over two squares of Weetabix cereal and mashed up the mixture for breakfast. She had three houses to over-see today, and she hoped that the two teenage girls she'd hired were up to the demands of cleaning. One of the houses on the north side had a hot tub the size of a minivan, and Tess planned to soak in it before heading to Portland.

Tess stepped off the six-thirty ferry, her skin tingling, aware that the summer air carried expectations. She met the eyes of every person coming toward her on the sidewalk, looking to see who among them was awake with love. She opened the door to the pub, beyond the summer commotion of the Old Port, and searched the inner perimeter for Len. He sat watching the door, his back to the wall, a seltzer with lemon in front of him. Tess felt the ping in the center of her abdomen. Was this a tug in the stitches, a sign of dreaded adhesions? From the core of the ping she saw a spreading circle of white, then red, spreading out the way a ripple does in a pond. Tess stopped halfway across the room, staggering with recognition, and gripped the back of a chair while she took a deep breath.

How had it found her? How did desire for the formerly disastrous, drunken husband show up now? Had he seen it in her face? Was she pumping out some kind of adolescent hormone from her body? They had made love hundreds of times in that other life when their bodies had been moist and fresh, filled with blood and sorrow.

She slid into the booth across from him and held out her small hands like cups, waiting for him. "Here. Give me your hands. They are so lovely," she said.

Len leveled his gaze, and his clear blue eyes came forward, emerging from the way station where he had parked his heart for years. "I've been waiting," he said. He placed his hands in the small cup of her palms and overflowed them. Tess had not touched Len like this since they were young and living in the erupting volcano of their marriage.

She knew his nature, his arrogance as a young man, his rise into the rarefied world of surgery, where drugged patients lay in naked sacrifice to the surgery theater, with all the other doctors and nurses there to assist him. She understood as much as anyone the fire of alcoholism and the way it had burned every layer of self-respect from his bones until nothing was left except sobriety and the few ounces of his true nature that had survived.

"You're still there, aren't you?" she whispered.

She did not want to cry, and yet there was nothing that could stop it. She was nearly as stripped of her glories as he was. If all that she could recover of her synesthesia was the color and scent of her granddaughter's hair and a few squeaks of cross fire here and there, then she would have to live with that. Len had lived with far less. Here was the former surgeon working at the Portland Chamber of Commerce.

"It's me, as best I know me. I've been waiting for you. We could stay here for dinner and play our 307th game of darts, or we could get up and leave. My car is outside. This glaringly sober man could drive this formerly synesthetic woman to his house and they could watch the sunset from his dock." Len's house was located in South Portland on an inlet that faced south.

Len's chin trembled once. He was still a proud man, despite the loss of his profession, his family, things that some men wear like medals. They had long ago said all the hard and horrible things to each other. His drunken anger had lashed her with hurricane force. And now here he was—all that remained of him.

What is faith if not the act of love, of stepping into midair? The sounds of the pub hummed all around them: generators for the walk-in cooler, the clash of ice hitting stainless steel behind the bar, the soft clunk of a glass set on the polished dark wood, the *whoosh* of the door opening, the chemical whiff of air freshener from the bathroom, the customer at the bar asking, *Can you turn on ESPN?*

Tess pulled her hands out from under Len's. She pushed down on the table and stood up. Why now? How did love happen? She had thought she knew everything there was to know about love in her life. She held out one hand to him, timid, like a girl, crazy with expectation. Len smiled and took her hand, slid out of the booth. They walked out of the pub, the sounds and smells parting on either side of them in waves. Len leaned his right shoulder into the door and pushed, creating a space for Tess to exit. The pub had a front step of thick granite. Holding hands, they stepped off, into the night.

She hadn't meant to fall asleep at Len's, but then she hadn't meant to slip off her clothes and slide into bed with him either. "There have been others," she had whispered to him.

"I know," he had said. "You do recall that I married again after you?" He ran his arthritic hands along her thin torso. She heard a tingling of bells that started in her toes.

She had curled around his body, like seaweed, wrapped around the sinew of his legs. It was morning, and a dam had opened in her brain with the brilliant colors of letters flooding in. The days of the week cascaded in with the soft triangles and cubes. It was a bit much all at once, even for Tess.

"Len, it's back!"

"What's back?" He still quivered, like a machine with electrical currents flaring up in random sectors, sending charges through his thighs and chest.

"My synesthesia! I had noticed tiny sparks all last week, but I thought that was all I was going to get. Now it's back."

Len reached over and cupped his hand over her small breast. "Let's give it a test. Here, when I touch here, what happens?"

"Oh that," said Tess, laughing. "That is cool and tangy sherbet. Mango sherbet."

"It is going to be very hard not to take credit for jump-starting your multiple wiring and I'm fighting a truckload of egotistical urges. But since I do not want to miss one minute of multimedia future sex with you, I'm going to resist the temptation to say that my geriatric studliness was the catalyst," said Len.

"And yet you managed to say it anyhow," said Tess, rubbing her lips across the white stubble on his face.

"If only I'd been sober back then. I regret missing one second with you. I regret so many things," he said.

Len's words rolled like honey over her. She fell asleep again, curled around him. Later, as the sun rose higher with the east light gliding across his bedroom wall, Len's years of loneliness unfurled and his bones softened around her.

Something strummed her brain, a scratching sound like a squirrel trapped in the wall. Her eyes flew open.

"Wake up! Danielle is on the ferry alone. Today is the first time that she is taking the ferry alone. We had planned this in such detail. Her babysitter is driving her to the ferry for the eleven-fifteen. I assured her that I'd be at the dock in Peaks waiting for her. She had begged for weeks," said Tess. She catapulted from the bed, flush with the unabridged return of her synesthesia.

"Where are my clothes? What time is it? Never mind, I know exactly what time it is, I always do. It's eleven-twenty, Len, for God's sake, where is your phone? Our granddaughter is about to experience her first horrible disillusionment, not to mention fear . . . ," said Tess, in rapid, uncompromising fire.

Len sat up and swung his legs over the side of his bed. Former surgeons could still come to attention in seconds from a deep sleep; the training never left them. His pants were on the floor, discarded with abandon last night. He pulled out his cell phone.

"We'll call the Casco Bay ferry and tell them that Danielle is expecting you, but you'll be late. We can ask someone to stay with Danielle until you get there. Tess, please slow down. Children are safer on Peaks than anywhere I can think of."

Tess pulled a T-shirt over her head and stuffed her bra into her pants pocket. "Wait. I'll call Rocky. She can meet Danielle there."

Len handed her the phone. Tess paused, took a breath. Rocky's phone number flooded into her in a cascade of colors and shapes: a red cube, a blue oval, a rough yellow two.

"Oh, please be home," said Tess.

The answering machine picked up after four rings. Tess said, "Rocky, are you there? Pick up the damn phone, this instant . . . ," when she heard a voice. It was Natalie.

"What's wrong, Tess?" asked the girl. "Rocky's not here. She had to go to Massachusetts. Something with her brother, that's all she said. She'll be back late tonight."

Tess sat on the bed. "Please run down to the ferry, and I do mean run. Danielle is taking her first solo voyage, and I was supposed to be there. I was delayed. I spent the night in Portland, well, South Portland. I'll be there as soon as I can. Will you go to the ferry? Oh thanks. You're an angel. And please call me when she gets there," said Tess. Surely Natalie could manage meeting Danielle.

Tess collapsed back on the bed. "I feel like I'm sixteen, had sex for the first time in the backseat of a car, and my father just discovered me. He'll have to shoot you, and he won't let me go to college," said Tess, running her fingers through her discombobulated white hair.

Len leaned back on the bed as well. "Now you and I are far older than our parents were when we were sixteen. Your father is long dead, so I'm safe from assassination. And the last time I checked, you were a partially retired physical therapist. I do agree on one count: I feel like I've had sex for the first time. The quality of completely sober sex should be incentive enough for AA."

He brushed her forehead with his lips. She smelled the night on his breath.

"Let's get to the ferry and redeem ourselves," said Tess. If they left instantly, which was impossible, but if they could, they'd get to the ferry in thirty-eight minutes. Len had timed it, and all of Len's measurements were precise.

Chapter 47

Natalie

S he hung up Rocky's landline. Then she grabbed her cell and thumbed in a number. "Franklin. Change of plans. Get to the ferry, park as close as you can. Yes, close to the cargo loading area. Have the van running. I'll be on the next ferry with the kid and the dog. I know, this is sooner than we'd planned. Yes. Okay. You can tell me about computer stuff later." She hung up.

Natalie took a minute to do a slow turn in the kitchen. What did she need? The dog, who had been asleep on the kitchen floor, raised his head and looked at her. She grabbed a plastic bag and scooped kibble into it and placed a few in her pockets. Everything was falling into place with a kind of perfection that she could not have anticipated. The dog would ride trustingly in Rocky's truck, and Rocky always left the keys under the driver's seat.

What else? The statue, the one piece of art in the whole crappy cottage, was right there on the end table. That was what she needed—the saxophone player, the one that Rocky patted on the head, sculpted by her brother. Natalie picked it up. She hefted it in her hands as if measuring for accuracy. Most important, Rocky loved it, just like she loved Danielle and her dog and her whole made-up family.

Natalie opened the sliding glass door to the deck, keeping the dog inside. She held the statue over her head and walked to the edge of the deck, turned, and threw the statue at a large outcropping of rock ledge near the side of the house. It didn't shatter as completely as she had pictured, but it was damaged enough to leave a clear message. The arms broke off, along with the saxophone and one leg. Definitely not as satisfying as shattering it, but she had more important things to do.

Turning to go back in the house, she heard the crows, first one, then two, then, as if an alarm had gone out, she heard more crows in the distance. What was wrong with them?

Cooper was at full alert. Surely a dog wouldn't care about a statue. She picked up her canvas bag in the bedroom. On the way out the door she stopped and considered the cat, Peterson. A pity the cat was already out. Well, there was no need to exaggerate. The point would already be made, loud and clear.

"Let's go, Cooper. You'll have to miss your last class with Melissa today." Natalie pictured Melissa's outrage when she arrived at Rocky's house to pick up Cooper for his final class that afternoon.

He tilted his head, one ear lifting higher. She stuck her hand into her pocket and extracted a kibble. "Come on, boy, let's go for a ride." Cooper stood at the door and looked fully at Natalie, his dark eyes reading her. She felt an uncomfortable sense of nakedness. "Don't look at me like that," she said, trying to keep her voice light.

The door to the truck groaned, the metal hinges abraded by years of salt air. When Rocky drove, Cooper always rode in the passenger seat, looking like her bodyguard.

"Come on, Cooper, that's it, hop in," she said, holding the door open for him.

She had wanted to derail Rocky completely, and Cooper had been a part of the plan. She wasn't even going to hurt him, just drive him far away to Virginia or so, drop him off along the Blue Ridge Mountains, and wave bye-bye. That would destroy Rocky, unhinge her bone by bone.

Natalie pulled the truck into the line that formed for transport on the ferry. Perfect timing. There was little Danielle waiting at the front of the line to get off the ferry. Could she chance taking Cooper out of the truck right here? What if he ran off? No, the dog would help relax the kid; they were buddies.

"Come on, boy. Let's go get Danielle," she said, letting her voice rise in the way she had heard trainers do on the Animal Channel. She and the dog walked to the end of the street, where islanders greeted passengers from the ferry. Natalie smiled and waved enthusiastically. "Hey, Danielle!"

She flipped open her cell and called Tess. "Danielle is jumping up and down waiting to run up the ramp to the ice cream shop. Take your time. No worries. Can we meet you at your house? See you then. No, go ahead, you have plenty of time to go grocery shopping. Bye." The little girl bobbed up and down like a cork at sea, and the second all the cars and cargo were off she sprang forward and ran to Natalie.

Danielle reached her with a miniature body slam, throwing her arms around Natalie's waist. "I did it, all by myself! You brought Cooper! Where's Gramma?" asked Danielle as she released Natalie and transferred her hug to the dog.

"She forgot that she had something to do in Portland. She wants us to meet her. So you know what? We have to turn around and go right back on the ferry. How do you like that? Rocky said we could take her truck so that Cooper could ride with us," said Natalie.

Danielle frowned. "Where's Rocky?"

"Rocky is working on the mainland," said Natalie.

The girl pressed her lips together. "Where's Melissa?"

They walked up the incline to the truck. The child got in the passenger seat, and Cooper hopped into the back. "Melissa will meet us in Portland to take him to his therapy training classes. Today is his final class. Graduation and all that," said Natalie.

Danielle had on her bright orange backpack, and she shifted it from one side to the other. "Where are we going to meet Gramma?"

"Do you know that big park in Portland? We're going to meet her there. She said something about a puppet show. Where's your favorite place to sit on the ferry?" Natalie drove the truck across the ramp, following the directions of the bored-looking boy who pointed her to a slot.

"On the very top, but we should stay on the lower deck for Cooper. He doesn't like the stairs," said Danielle. "Are you sad today? You sound different. Aren't you supposed to be working on building Rocky's new house?"

Natalie had worked three days on the house with Russell and was glad to jettison the job. "You're much more important than the job."

They sat on the lower deck, getting bits of sun, and even then, Danielle had to pull a jacket out of her pack. Natalie crossed her arms over her chest to warm her core.

If Tess was already at the dock in Portland, then everything was off. She would have gone too far to fake it, and she'd just get in the van with Franklin and they'd drive away. The deal would be off. Sometimes you had to take chances. As they slid into the dock in Portland, Natalie scanned the area for Tess. Nothing, no old lady with white hair. She saw Franklin, glowing white like a creature of the night, hunched over the steering wheel of the van. She patted Danielle's hand. "Oh great! My friend Franklin is here. He can drive us to the park. Let's park Rocky's truck, and we can all go together," said Natalie.

Natalie pulled the truck off the ferry and swung by Franklin. She hung her head out the window. "I'll park this and we can all go together. Follow me." Franklin swept his eyes over the young passenger. Natalie pulled the truck into the parking lot of a grocery store four blocks away. She unfastened Danielle's seat belt. Danielle looked small in Rocky's truck, smaller than Natalie had imagined.

"Everybody out," said Natalie, feigning a kind of cheerfulness.

She opened the back of the truck, and Cooper jumped down. Danielle stood by him and draped her arm over his back. The dog stood angled between the child and the couple. He leaned his head toward Franklin and fluffed his nostrils. The fur on his back rose up.

Franklin took one step back. "He's big. I'm allergic to dogs."

Natalie opened the side door of the van. "He can ride in the back. Danielle can ride in the front with us."

As Natalie walked by a trash barrel, she stooped down to pick up a piece of the Portland newspaper, wadded it around the truck keys, and dropped the bundle into the barrel. That was minor mayhem. The major mayhem was yet to come.

Chapter 48

Melissa

Melissa woke in the hot pink darkness that preceded dawn. She had left the window fan on, and the honeybee drone of it had seeped into her dreams and into the entire night. Her upstairs bedroom was the hottest place in the house. Could the fan have given her nightmares? Shrouded in rejection from Rocky's world, she had a feeling of dread that refused to leave. Once the sun was up, she hoped that the last tendrils of the feeling would be burned to ashes, like a vampire.

Melissa pulled on a pair of shorts, a tank top, and her running shoes. She timed her run around the island so that she'd finish on the east side of the island when the sun pushed up, puncturing the line between sea and sky. Did anyone else feel this fractured and crazy?

After her run, she decided to work on the photos from Chester Hill. The people in the decrepit Portland neighborhood already knew Cooper, and she'd only been there four times. That was four times that her parents didn't know about. Every homeless person she met told her a story about the dog they used to have, back before the accumulating disasters in their life landed them in the club no one wants to be in: the displaced people. Several days ago, she had discovered a new subgroup among the homeless—the guys who still had dogs. They lived in strategically located tents on public land that was scrubby with dense under-growth and generally unused. Several lived on private land, a few acres behind a diner on the way to South Portland. The owner, a vet from Desert Storm, said that he had every right to let the guys set up their tents behind his diner, or at least that was the word on the street. Rumor was that all the guys back there were vets too.

Melissa knew more about the dogs than the men. There was one boxer and two very mixed-up breeds, as well as a dog that looked like a retriever mix. Not as big as a Lab, she was yellow and short-haired, and her name was Rosie. Cooper couldn't get enough of her. He held his tail high, ears alert, and stuck out his considerable chest. Rosie had dropped immediately to play position: rump up and head down. Rosie's man, still wearing desert combat boots, finally broke into a Cadillac-sized smile as the two dogs dashed around each other. He assessed Melissa, determining if she was friend or enemy. "Be careful around here, kid. You don't want to come up against crackheads. And I don't want to see you up here at night, not even with your dog."

"Yes, sir. Cooper and I only come here during the day. It's for my photography class. I take pictures of the dogs of Portland. I've got some good ones of Rosie," said Melissa.

"As long as Rosie and I are around, we've got your back," he said. "Ryan," he added, in reference to himself, not offering to shake hands, not offering to do anything more than nod.

"Melissa," she said, attempting the same nodding formality. "Can I take your picture with Rosie?"

He knelt on one knee next to his dog. Dog and human looked straight at Melissa. He didn't smile, but Rosie did. Melissa took a quick round of shots.

After Cooper graduated from his therapy training class today, she might ask the homeless shelter if she could bring him in for visits after people were allowed back inside for the evening. They had to be out of the shelter from 8:00 A.M. until 5:00 P.M.

Melissa downloaded her photos. Cooper could make people laugh, and she had lots of pictures of people who wanted to pose with him. Cooper had a stately profile. One of the best shots of the day was a portrait of Cooper seated next to a man who had smelled pretty horrible and was missing several front teeth, but when he offered his profile next to the black Lab, the camera caught his essential dignity. Why hadn't she seen this when she talked with the man yesterday?

She highlighted the photo and enlarged it. The man's face was filled with creases and crinkles, surrounded by soft places, sadness and hope, a sense of humor. In one of his eyes, she imagined the part of him that had been a five-year-old boy, sweet and sticky. She'd seen none of this in him yesterday. He was like a painting. She couldn't wait to show Mr. Clarke this photo. She saved one version and began to Photoshop another version, cutting out distracting images in the background, like the old white van on the corner, paused at a stop sign.

It looked like the van that Natalie's guy friend drove. Melissa didn't yet have her driver's license, and her knowledge of the styles and years of cars was still vague. There were lots of vans in Portland: delivery vans, plumber's vans, florist vans. But how many vans were there with a fat red scratch on the driver's side?

How did Natalie manage to infect everything that belonged to Melissa? Chester Hill and the dogs and the people and the streets were hers, not stupid Natalie's.

Could that really be the van that Natalie's friend drove? There in Chester Hill? Natalie was shoving Melissa out of every place she loved. If she could just hang on until it was time to take Cooper to the therapy training class, she might make it through the day.

Chapter 49

Rocky turned the Honda's air-conditioning on high, and the small car quickly cooled down. The image of Natalie sitting with her dead mother had etched a horror show on the backs of her eyelids. Each time she blinked, she saw the toddler sitting with her dead mother for five days. She hadn't asked Ira Levine if it was summer when the mother died, if the apartment had been hot. She had to think that it was any season but summer, when sweltering temperatures would have escalated the decomposition. Would the child have adjusted so slowly to the smell that she would not have been sickened?

The troops of the Department of Children and Family Services would have pulled the child into the agency's flow, searching first for blood relatives because surely there was someone. There's always at least one person out there, a distant aunt, a cousin. Had Paulette Davis truly been a woman completely alone? Was this possible? Humans live in packs, like wolves. Addictions can be intractable; her connections to others must have been incinerated. Crack was one of the most addictive drugs on the planet, making even heroin look sunny. Had the woman been self-medicating a mental health disorder? Peel back addiction and an array of painful disorders pops up in a heart-stopping panorama. Heart-stopping indeed. Rocky would have given anything for just a five-minute phone conversation with Bob and she'd never ask again. *Bob, is this your child?* If Bob was the father, and if he sent Paulette money for rent, then Rocky wanted a divorce from her dead husband.

The girl would have been taken by ambulance to a hospital. She would have looked like a jaundiced gumdrop, propped up in a bed with saline drips in her dehydrated arms. Her hair, still baby fine, would have been filthy; the pediatric nurses would have cut away what they couldn't comb out. The girl would have followed the nurses with her huge eyes as they asked her questions, brought her stuffed toys, and smiled their best smiles, anything to wipe off the horror that stuck to the girl. Levine had reported that the girl would not speak until she was five. His report also noted that her ability to attach to others normally was severely impaired. Attachment disorder—never a good starting place.

The nurses and doctors would have woken up in the middle of the night in their own safe beds, thinking of the girl, crushed by her stubborn silence and by the image they all had of her in the apartment. If they had children themselves, they would have gotten up in the middle of the night to sit by their children's cribs and beds, watching them breathe, afraid to look away.

Why was Natalie searching for her biological father when she had been unable to form an attachment to anyone? Why would it even matter? Natalie had told Rocky an odd version of this story; little truths had appeared, but the girl had deliberately left out the part that showed the true train wreck. She had deliberately orchestrated the tale for a purpose.

Rocky hadn't expected to be sideswiped by Levine's information, which drew a portrait of how to turn a kid into a whack job by age eighteen. First, give a baby a crack addict mother, an unknown and absentee father, and chaos and malnutrition when she should have been eating snacks in preschool surrounded by primary colors splashed on the walls and teachers reading to her. Throw in witnessing a murder, sitting next to a dead body for five days, and then grinding through foster care.

Rocky suddenly pulled back. She didn't know what was true and what was not true about Natalie's foster placements. Levine had said that the first two families were no longer used as child placements after Natalie was taken from them, but that the rest of the placements had ranged from adequate to excellent. Except that Natalie didn't stick with any of them.

She could make the drive to Amherst in three hours. If the Honda had a memory for directions in one of its computer chips, it could have recalled each toll and turn on the road: the exit to 95 South, to 495 South into Massachusetts, then west on Route 2, the rolling Mohawk Trail, the exit 16 turnoff at Athol, then skirting the Quabbin Reservoir, the source of Boston's drinking water. The roads got smaller until she pulled into the lawyer's parking lot. This had better be important.

Rocky waited in the car for her brother, Caleb. She jumped when he tapped the side of her car. If Cooper had been with her, no one would have walked up to the car unannounced. Why hadn't she brought him? She longed for his steady comfort right now. Oh yes, Melissa had to take him to his last class.

Caleb was midseason in house painting. His arms were golden, the hairs bleached by solar exposure from 7:00 A.M. to three in the afternoon, his official stopping time. It was two o'clock, which meant he'd left a job early to meet her at the lawyer's office. Rocky pictured him driving full tilt from Leeds to Amherst, a good thirty-minute drive if traffic cooperated. From the look of his hair, swept into a horizontal arrangement, he'd had the window open with the breeze pounding on his head from the left. He was not an air-conditioning kind of man.

"Thanks for coming," said Rocky as she slammed her car door.

The siblings fell easily into step with each other.

"Takes a lot to get you back to Massachusetts," he said.. "I'll have to tell this lawyer to give you a call more often." Caleb smelled like family, a combination of salt and paint.

Attorney David Prescott's office was in a nineteenth-century house in Amherst that had been converted to offices. David's office dominated both signage and size, followed by a more modest certified public accountant on the second floor and a driving school in the back of the house. It was a full-service house.

Amherst was an academic town; dominated by the thirty thousand students at the university, the town had an over-educated, dressed-down air. Rocky was positive that the faculty could not possibly dress down any further. Full professors routinely arrived in class wearing ragged shorts and Tevas. David might have been the last man in town to wear a suit. Describing the lawyer, Bob had told Rocky, with a sense of incredulity, that some men actually like to wear suits, ties, and tight lace-up shoes shined to a blinking brilliance.

Rocky's foot caught on the threshold, and she stumbled into the lawyer's office, chilled to several degrees cooler than a day in November. She seemed doomed to sit in offices as cold as meat lockers. She cleared her throat once, then again, trying to dislodge the clot of trouble she had swallowed. Rocky hadn't seen David since the final settlement of Bob's estate.

"Good to see you, David," she said, lying. It was not good to see him, which was why she had called Caleb, to somehow share the unpleasant sensation of sitting in the dark-paneled, freezing cold office that reminded her of the months after Bob's death.

Caleb sat facing David across the expanse of desk, kept tastefully clear of anything except his computer monitor and one file folder, which in this case was the Dead Husband File Folder. The lawyer patted the file folder with his fingers spread wide.

"Assets have recently been directed to Bob's estate that went undetected until very recently. They are considerable."

This was not what Rocky was expecting, and she tilted her head hard to one side. "Say again, please."

He slowly opened the file. "I was surprised too. Your husband was a pretty straightforward investor. He had basic life insurance, a basic pension plan, and a very basic will. His parents, whose estates I handled as well, were the same way. When this turned up, I have to admit I was stunned."

Caleb sat forward in his chair. "Why didn't we know about this sooner? Bob died over a year ago. Fifteen months to be exact. What was this, his backup life insurance?" Caleb's voice shook.

This was the first time Rocky fully considered that Caleb marked time by Bob's death, just as she did. It had never occurred to her that anyone else worked off the Dead Bob Calendar. Bob had been Caleb's big brother, friend, Celtic music buddy. Rocky readjusted the band that held her stub of a ponytail together. She had cut off her long dark hair when Bob died, and only now could she finally coax all of it into one fat circle of coated elastic.

Rocky's chest felt hollow. "Wait a minute. We're leaping too quickly into financial and lawyer talk. I miss Bob so much that there are days when I still think that I won't make it without him. Caleb misses him. Please proceed with tender awareness that given a choice of whatever assets you are about to divulge and the chance to have my big, flea dip–smelling husband back right now, I'd choose him every time. We are still missing him."

Caleb's eyes went bloodshot for a moment, not long enough for tears to make it over the bottom edge, but long enough to make him turn his face away. Rocky was flooded by the thought of all the ways Caleb had cared for her since Bob died. He had become the landlord for her house and nursed along renters who couldn't figure out what a fireplace flue was for; he called her at all the right times; he yelled at her when she took a job that made him worry that rabid raccoons might bite her; and he had left work early to sit in a lawyer's refrigerated office in his sweat-stained shirt. If she said a kind thing to him right now, he might kill her, so she waited until he was ready to be back in the game again. He uncrossed his legs and spread them wide, his work boots dropping clods of dirt on the polished floors. There, ready.

Rocky crossed her arms in front of her chest and watched the skin on her forearms pucker into gooseflesh. "We settled Bob's estate issues, including the insurance policy, his 401(k), the sale of his practice, and everything that was jointly held," said Rocky. She had not mentioned the arrival of Natalie. She dreaded embarrassing Caleb by dropping the bomb in front of the lawyer. Rocky turned her head one notch to catch Caleb's attention. As brother and sister, they were an evolving unit. She was the big sister by two years, and she had been his roughneck protector throughout their grade school years. The siblings had drifted apart when Rocky was in high school, a time when the two-year difference took its biggest toll. Now that they were both in their thirties, Caleb had stepped in like an armed guard to protect his newly widowed sister, as much as Rocky would allow.

The lawyer continued. "I apologize. My wife tells me that I have terrible people skills, and she can't understand why anyone hires me at all. Let me start again. I called you because I was contacted by the attorney of Richard Tilbe. He recently died and left a considerable amount of money to your husband."

Rocky was sure that David kept talking and even said an amount after this. She put one elbow on an arm of the chair and set her chin in it. She did not want her mouth to hang open. She primarily wanted support, and she wanted it to be physical.

Rocky and Caleb did not speak, but if the lawyer had held up a thermometer to the pair, their joint temperature would have sent the mercury shooting skyward. Nothing that the lawyer had just said could find a connection in the brain of either the widow or the widow's dazed brother. Rocky's brain sputtered and churned, searching for similarities, past events that could account for the lawyer's stunning news.

Rocky pulled one knee up and placed the heel of her foot on the chair. "Tell me the figure again," she said, reaching for a glass of water.

"Two point three million," said David. "I know, believe me. I was shocked when I first read the document."

"And tell me again where the check came from," said Rocky. "No, start from the beginning. I don't remember anything that you said except Richard Tilbe."

David bracketed the folder with his hands like ten fingered guards. "Bob had a paternal uncle in the Dalles of Oregon. Richard Tilbe, who was eight years younger than Bob's father. Richard had a falling-out with Bob's parents when Bob was in college and moved to points unknown until he finally settled in Oregon fifteen years ago. According to the attorney I contacted, Richard Tilbe was an alcoholic as well as being on a first-name basis with a great many street drugs. He had no contact with his family after a cataclysmic breech eighteen years ago."

Caleb still had not moved in his chair. He rotated his head in Rocky's direction. "Do you have any idea what he's talking about? I am so lost here," said Caleb.

Something about her brother's uncharacteristic shock comforted Rocky. He was a gauge for her reality. If Caleb was nearly speechless and immobile, then she had a mile marker.

"Bob's parents were dead by the time Bob and I met in grad school. I only heard Bob mention an uncle once or twice, and I think all he said was 'asshole.' No. Bob used his favorite Irish expression, 'a fecking asshole.' I figured every family has one," she said.

David flicked his eyes from Rocky to Caleb. "Mr. Richard Tilbe died three months ago at the age of sixty-two. Bob is—was—the heir, which makes you the heir in this case. The will was specific: 'to Robert Tilbe, his wife, and/or their children,'" he said, reading from a page in the folder.

"So I'm the only person left in this Tilbe family disaster, the nonblood relative?" asked Rocky.

David flipped to another page. "Richard suspected that he had a child. Through a miracle of addiction counseling, Mr. Tilbe gained sobriety ten years ago, dusted off his electrical engineering degree, and worked at the Department of Defense of all places. And he invested with genius."

If it were possible for a brain to explode, Rocky's would have splattered. She rubbed her temples. "Before you go any further, I think you should know something.

A kid, a girl, came searching for her biological father." She looked at Caleb and said, "Yell at me later for not telling you."

Caleb opened his mouth to say something and stopped.

"She's convinced that Bob was her father. We've been trying to do DNA testing, but it's been impossible to find genetic material from Bob. We have a DNA swab from the girl."

Every muscle in the lawyer's face froze. On a good day, he was not a hugely expressive man, but now he looked like he had been flash-frozen, dropped in liquid nitrogen. He blinked once and started his engine again.

"The DNA testing may be unnecessary. You should have told me about the appearance of this girl," he said, drumming his fingers on his desk. "But why would she even assume that Bob was her father?" David closed his eyes, shutting out all the extraneous stimuli so that he could race through legal implications.

He opened his eyes and looked at Caleb. "Did you know about the paternity question?"

Caleb sweat buckets all day, and now his thick hair was stiff. He looked like a blond Rastafarian. "I am completely out of this loop."

"David, keep going. Before I told you about the girl reaching out to me, what were you going to tell me about this money from Bob's uncle? The uncle that Bob never contacted once while we were together?"

Rocky could see more court cases fluttering through David's brain as he tried to call up the relevant case law. "There is a very good chance that Bob's uncle is the father of this girl. He donated DNA to his lawyer ten years ago, after his fourth and ultimately successful rehab treatment. There's a reason why this guy was banished from the Tilbe family," said David.

Another clump of orange dirt fell off Caleb's shoe, smashing on the gleaming polyurethane finish of the old flooring. Caleb nudged the clump toward a corner of the desk.

"What did the other lawyer tell you?" asked Rocky. The file in front of David vibrated with trouble.

"Richard Tilbe was solidly addicted to cocaine when he could still afford it. He taught electrical engineering at a community college in Des Moines. His descent was disastrous, leading the charge of the crack epidemic that worked its way through an unsuspecting Midwest in the nineties. He unfortunately took others with him, including a young woman whom Bob had briefly dated and introduced to his uncle at a family picnic. Richard suspected that there was a child, but the woman refused to have contact with him. He claimed to have sent money once through a bank, but the check was never cashed. He simply gave up and assumed the worst. There is no mention of a child in his will."

Rocky's mouth was dry, and her tongue felt large and clumsy. "Natalie showed me a birth certificate that listed Robert Tilbe, not Richard. . . ."

Caleb looked at Rocky. "Who is Natalie? Am I correct in assuming that this is a shit storm?"

David sat up straighter and lobbed questions at Rocky.

"When did Natalie contact you?"

"Three weeks ago."

"Did she show you any identification? Like a driver's license?"

"No."

"What exactly did Natalie say when she first contacted you?"

"I already told you."

"Did she request money?"

"Not once."

"Do you have a copy of the two birth certificates in question?"

"No."

"How exactly did Natalie locate you?"

"In case you haven't noticed, you can now use the Internet to locate your classmate from kindergarten who moved away to New Zealand."

Caleb spoke up. "And now may I ask a question? What were you thinking? Why did you let this girl move into your house? Is your brain shrinking?"

Rocky put her hands over her ears. "Stop it, both of you. She is just a girl. I thought she was just a girl looking for her father and that there was the tiniest chance that Bob might have fathered a child that he didn't know about or that he did know and never told me. . . ."

Caleb stomped both feet on the floor, dislodging every remaining bit of clay from his boots. "Not Bob. Not that he couldn't have screwed around eighteen years ago, but he wouldn't have left a kid to fend for herself. I saw this man fix the broken leg of a duck, for God's sake. A duck!"

Rocky remembered the duck that had been hit by a car, the way Bob had held the bird to his chest after setting the leg, the way he had talked to the unfortunate creature. "You'll be as good as new. I hope your lifetime mate will wait for you. She'd be so sad without you." He'd only been talking to soothe the bird, but the truth of it ground through her. Rocky had been so sad without Bob that she had overlooked a world of coincidences with Natalie.

Rocky's voice was quiet. "I thought if there was a chance that she was his daughter, I'd still have a part of him. We had talked about children, and we had still imagined that one day we'd have a baby. And if Natalie was his, he would have wanted me to help her."

David turned to his computer monitor and began to tap away with the pointer finger of each hand. "I'm sending an e-mail to Mr. Tilbe's lawyer. I've requested that he secure the inheritance money in another bank with an alert for potential online intruders. I will follow up with a phone call right after you leave."

Rocky had a sense of things rearranging, like molecules shifting around to form a new chemical. "Are you worried this has all been a scam?" asked Rocky.

David tilted his head slightly. "I am more than worried. I am alarmed. Did you say that you have a DNA sample from Natalie? I want you to send it by overnight mail to this address." David wrote down the name and address of the attorney on the West Coast. He handed the sheet of paper across his desk to Rocky. His handwriting was small and tight.

"My wife complains that my job makes me paranoid about human nature. But it's not paranoia. It's my training and experience that allows me to sniff out the opportunistic tendencies driven by greed and revenge. This new asset is safe with all the red flags that should go on it, but your own assets are another matter. I suggest that you have a very frank discussion with your young friend."

Rocky and Caleb left the office, both dazed and squinting into the afternoon sun. They headed to their respective vehicles. Her cell phone blinked at her from the seat of the truck. The only time it ever rang was when she left it somewhere. Caleb pulled his truck parallel to her car, matching driver's sides to each other, except he was three feet higher up. He had one elbow on the open window and scowled down at Rocky. "I am so unbelievably pissed that you didn't tell me about the kid, whoever she is. I promise to extract payment for this later, but right now you've got bigger problems than me. I smell something rotten. Do you know what Bob would say?"

The death of a spouse starts with terrifying and bottomless misery that seeps into the bones and saliva. Enough time had passed that her saliva no longer tasted of desperation. Instead, she was overwhelmed with rage at Bob for dying, for not telling her about the drug-addled uncle, for inheriting an obscene amount of money, and finally for being Caleb's icon of sensibility in the midst of chaos.

Rocky leaned into the back of the headrest and looked skyward. "What could Bob possibly say at a time like this?"

Caleb gave her a hint of a smile. "He always said that you were the smartest mare in the meadow."

"I never could train him to stop making large mammal references about me," said Rocky, feeling the ease of Bob's humor through the conduit of her brother. "You're right, I'm not a complete idiot. I know that this has probably left the realm of coincidence. I've got three hours to think about this on the ride home. Will you be home tonight?"

"I'll wait for your call. And how's your archery boyfriend? He's not Bob, but I kind of like him."

She hadn't told Caleb anything, not about Hill, not about the status of the remodel, not about Natalie. Since Natalie arrived, Rocky had only thought about Natalie. How had she cut Caleb out of the loop?

"Since this girl showed up, I haven't thought about anything else. I want to catch you up on everything, but right now I've got to get back home."

Rocky watched in the side mirror as he pulled out of the parking lot. She flipped her phone open. Four messages, an unheard-of number for her. Was there a dog and cat mutiny on Peaks? Melissa had programmed Rocky's phone to caw like a crow. Each message jolted her with the bird's call.

"Rocky, this is Tess. Have you heard from Natalie? I was supposed to meet her and Danielle at my house around twelve-thirty. It's one now. Where are you? Call me."

She looked at her watch. It was 3:05 P.M.

Next message. "This is Melissa. Where's Cooper? I went to your house, and he's not there. Today is our final class, or did you completely forget?"

Third message, from Tess. "Rocky. Your truck is gone, and the ferry boys just told me that Natalie drove it on the ferry to Portland. Danielle and Cooper were with her. Her cell is no longer in service. Call us immediately."

The last message. "It's Isaiah. Tess and her family are in a panic. They can't find her granddaughter. I just called the Portland police. Call me."

Fear dropped in and coursed through her like a base metal. She tapped in Natalie's cell phone. "The number you have called is no longer in service at this time."

She called Tess. If she hadn't been afraid before, she was when she heard her friend's voice. "Natalie, is that you? Where are you? Let me speak to Danielle," said Tess, her voice suddenly older and vulnerable.

"It's me, Tess. We'll find them. Is someone there with you?"

"Yes. Len is here. I never should have let Danielle ride on the ferry alone. This is all my fault."

"The best thing you can do is stay by the phone. Will you do that? I'm in Amherst. I'll be there in three hours, maybe more with traffic on 495. Call Isaiah and let him know that I'm on my way."

She made sure that her phone was turned on. The tops of her shoulders clenched in heavy fear; the hard constriction moved down her arms, and she gripped the steering wheel of the car, willing the space between Amherst and Portland to shrink, yet feeling it expand instead with the ever-thickening traffic.

Chapter 50

Natalie

"Cooper is out in the van," said Danielle. "You have to let him out. He needs air. Rocky would never leave him in a van. She's going to be mad."

Danielle sat stiffly on a green plastic chair, the kind that everyone keeps outside. Except this one was in the kitchen. Franklin had found it on the sidewalk on garbage day.

Natalie wanted to hurt Rocky, and destroying people Rocky loved was part one of her plan. This would let Rocky know what it was like for Natalie to have a shit life while Rocky had a perfect life with Bob Tilbe. Rocky got all the good parts: the loving husband, the happy-go-lucky veterinarian who cooked lasagna. She knew that Rocky had been lying the whole time, that Bob had really told her that a child of his was out there in the world, helpless and looking for him. Rocky had kept him from looking for her. She wasn't fooled by Rocky.

If her father had come looking for her, he would have loved her. She had pictured him a million times, striding up to the door of each foster family, knocking firmly. He always said, "I'm here for my daughter." And she had run into his arms, again and again.

Rocky would have to pay to get Danielle back. That was part two of the plan. Rocky had money, and Natalie wanted it. Franklin had found life insurance money. She had suffered enough. She checked the time on one of Franklin's laptops. Pretty soon there was going to be a screamfest on Peaks Island when they figured out that Natalie had taken the girl and the dog. She might have another thirty minutes or so before they started connecting the dots. She pulled the battery out of her cell phone and tossed it in the garbage can.

"Where's the other cell phone?" asked Natalie.

"Right on the mattress," said Franklin. He wiped his hand across his mouth, nodding toward the bedroom with his head.

Natalie walked into the alcove where their mattress and clothes were. Franklin was such a toad. Had he ever washed his clothes since they had been here?

She hadn't counted on Danielle looking so small in their apartment. The kid was on the petite side, like her grandmother, that was all.

Danielle still had on her backpack. "I want to go find Gramma now," she said, glancing at Franklin, who had not stopped staring at her since they came in. He pulled off his shirt. His skin was so white that lines of blue veins were visible along his temple, across his forearms, and up his neck.

"Well, here's the thing, little girl, we're not meeting your grandmother. If you're a good girl, I'll let you play on one of my computers," said Franklin.

Natalie heard the slick of predator in his voice, the same way she'd heard it from the two brothers in her second foster family. She could still control Franklin, she was sure of it, but she hadn't factored in that he'd be a perv with little kids. She had never seen him around children.

"Put your shirt on and go outside to make sure that the van windows are open a few inches. If that dog starts barking, he's going to attract attention," said Natalie.

Franklin's pupils had dilated to receive Danielle. He stepped closer to the little girl while he pulled his shirt over his head, worming his arms into it. The hair under his arms was as white as the hair on his head.

Natalie stared him down. "Go on, just a couple of inches. He's in the back. You won't have to touch him or anything."

Franklin hesitated, as if deciding. She saw it instantly—life had trained her to see potential dangers in a tone of voice, a turn of the head. She could spot sexual desire in an instant, and she knew when someone wanted to get rid of her before they did. Her hold on Franklin was evaporating, spiraling out into the atmosphere. He glanced sidelong at Danielle as he left the apartment.

When the door was closed, Danielle leapt off the chair. "I don't like him. He smells like raw potato skins. Are you mad at me, Natalie? Did I do something wrong? I want to call my house now. I want to go home."

Danielle put her arms around Natalie, reaching upward to encircle her waist. "Let's get out of here while he's gone. Come on, Natalie."

She didn't like to be touched, but Danielle's hands were tiny and soft. Why didn't this kid get it? Was this why it was so easy to hurt kids? Danielle should not trust her.

Natalie reached behind her and disengaged Danielle's hands. The little girl trembled from her head to her toes.

"I need to make a phone call to Rocky. If she does what I say, you get to go home again," said Natalie. There, that should make it plain enough. "If not, everything bad that happens will be Rocky's fault, not mine."

Chapter 51

Rocky, Isaiah, and two police officers from Portland stood on her small deck. They looked at the broken statue as if it were a body. "Has anyone touched this?" asked Officer Randy. Rocky had seen him many times on his cruise around Peaks.

"All of us, including Natalie, have touched it at one time or another. I don't think fingerprints are going to help," said Rocky. Caleb's statue had been the one physical link between her old home and here. She understood Natalie's message perfectly. *I can hurt you.*

Len and Tess were staying close to the landline at Tess's house in case Danielle tried to call.

Rocky's cell cawed.

"Excuse me. My phone generally rings if it's about animals. Don't worry. Natalie doesn't even have my cell number." She stepped away from the Portland police and Isaiah. She stepped off the deck to her gravel drive.

"Rocky? Don't say anything, just nod. This is Natalie. There is a ferry leaving Peaks in fifteen minutes. I want you to be on it. I'll call you once you get to the pier in Portland. If you tell anyone that I've called you, it will go badly for Danielle and Cooper."

Rocky nodded and then spoke loudly—not too loudly or dramatically, she hoped. "You've got a dog that I need to pick up? I understand, Sam. I can be there for the transport."

Natalie continued. "So you're not alone. Has someone called the police? It must be exciting at your house."

"That's correct," said Rocky. "No worries, we can make this work out." Rocky glanced over at Isaiah. Rocky stage-whispered to him, "Sam has a dog that needs to be transported back to the island today." She shrugged and shook her head as though to say, with the slightest exasperation, *Good Lord, what's next?*

Natalie said, "So deceptive and manipulative. Most of my therapists were exactly like you. I learned so much from them. Now finish up the call and make a convincing exit."

"You're the boss," said Rocky, feeling the ice of Natalie's pathos bounce off the cell towers. How did Natalie convince Cooper to leave with her? What would she do to him? She might hurt a dog before she'd hurt a child. Oh God, Danielle. Was Natalie re-creating the worst moment of her life?

Click. Natalie was gone.

Isaiah walked toward her. With the early evening sun low in the sky, he was surrounded by light, and his silhouette was all she could see for a moment; his dark face was inscrutable. He was not the kind of man she could lie to.

Isaiah looked drawn, saddened by the turn of events, probably edging around the bad statistics of kidnapped children. Yet he said, "The police are headed over to Battery Steele to take a good look there. Tess told us that Natalie had a panic attack of sorts when she was on a tour with them. Afraid of the dark. Tess had a hunch we should check it out."

Rocky looked at her watch. "I'll be back. Just a ferry ride over and back, thirty minutes. Who knows? I might run into Danielle on the way back. They could all be on their way home. What do you mean, afraid of the dark?" She patted her pockets for her keys. Her car was in long-term parking in Portland.

"What do you think I mean? The girl ran out of Battery Steele in a panic. She is just a child herself. We don't know if someone has abducted the two of them, or if they're delayed in Portland, or why they even went to Portland, or just what in the world is going on," said Isaiah.

"Right, you're so right. I'll be back before they're done searching Battery Steele. Should I meet you here when I get back? The kids might try to call my house."

"Yes. I'll stay here in case they try your landline. Whose dog are you bringing back?" he asked.

"What? Oh, it's an injured stray. Sam asked me if I could foster it while it recovered."

She turned and started for the ferry, unable to look into his dark eyes one more minute.

"Wait a minute!" he shouted.

Shit. Lying to him had been useless.

"Take my truck. You'll miss the ferry if you walk."

Rocky inhaled in a jagged breath. "Thanks," she said. Rocky drove the orange Department of Public Works truck to the commuter lot and parked it. She examined Isaiah's key collection, searching for a spare to the little yellow truck in case Natalie had abandoned it. Isaiah's square lettering was unmistakable: he had written a large *R* on the fat part of the key. She twisted the key off the big ring and left the remaining keys under the seat. She had eight more minutes until the ferry arrived. The universe was tipping precariously, and she vibrated with terror.

Everyone has rules, including Natalie. She just had to figure out what Natalie's rules were.

Chapter 52

Cooper

He had chosen badly, and the cost of it could mean the end of him. His first choice had not been a foolish one, nor had the one after, but it only took one bad choice to break up a pack. Guiding the dangerous girl away from Rocky's house was a good choice. It was always best to deflect danger or trick invaders by their own confusion, especially for a large dog with physical power as a backup.

He had no wish to harm the girl. Despite his strongest instincts to protect Rocky and her pack, *their pack,* Cooper had not been able to determine with absolute canine certainty where the girl belonged or her true nature. Was she a coyote, luring unsuspecting pups away to certain death? Or was she so damaged and beaten, as Cooper suspected, that her behavior was simply erratic, strumming to her shattered version of the world?

He had smelled the twist of the chemicals of fear and dread, long since bundled into a thick protective armor around the girl. She was far more wily than a chained-up junkyard dog who had been reduced in spirit to a single response set of bark and attack. He could not be sure how she would respond, so he had watched her carefully. He had felt the girl soften around Rocky, the old one, and the small pup of a girl. The softening had been followed by a quick retraction that had lasted into her sleeping, where she struggled throughout the night. He could have joined her in dreaming; he had done this before with humans to understand them. But it would have meant abandoning his post by Rocky, and he could not leave his companion.

He had been prepared to leave her at the dock, and when she left the island would be his again, with his people, his cat, the daily rhythm of his hard-earned heartbeats. He yearned to sleep with more ease, to relax his vigil, to go back to the way it had been before the dangerous girl arrived. She could not have forced him to leave. It would have been a simple thing to hop from the back of the truck and trot across the broad gangplank to the island and say good-bye to the whirl of trouble and hurt that curdled within Natalie.

How could he have guessed that, like a true coyote, she had calculated precisely to lure away the youngest human pup among them? The small girl-child was open-eyed, blind with love and fascination, as all pups are. What choice did he have except this bad choice to go with Natalie and the child, to travel across the water, to leave the most precious of island homes? He could not abandon the child—no worthy dog would.

One wrong step and then another. It is no small thing to unleash the full power of a dog. The contract with humans is clear: if a dog attacks, even to protect, humans are free to cut down the canine with a swift and fatal blow. The balance between future threat and canine attack to thwart the threat is precarious and filled with sorrow when the final decision has even one flaw.

Cooper had glanced around the landing on the mainland. Since the autumn, he had only been here with Rocky or Melissa. There had been the slightest chance that his people would suddenly appear and he could alert them to the danger. But they were not on the dock. He pointed his nose high and caught a scent of Rocky, who had passed through a few hours earlier. He longed to see her gangly shape, to bask in her comforting scent.

The truck pulled next to a man in a vehicle. When the man got out, Cooper's fur rose of its own accord. This would have been the moment to take down the man, as Cooper leapt out of the truck and onto the hot pavement. He could have easily taken the man. But the child—what then to do about the child so far from home? He had waited too long, a second too long. Before he fully understood what had happened, he was trapped in the back of an airless van, cut off from the front seat, and the child was stolen away on his watch.

The shame of it clamped around Cooper's massive neck, and he did the only thing left to him—he barked in desperate alarm, hoping that the bellow of his bark would find its way to someone.

Chapter 53

Natalie

"Where have you been?" hissed Natalie. "You've been gone two hours! I told you to open the windows on the van, not drive to Boston."

Franklin scanned the room for the child. "I took care of a problem. Where's Danielle?"

"I told her to sit in the bedroom. Maybe she'll go to sleep. All the better for her if she goes to sleep. What problem did you take care of?"

Franklin drew close to the bedroom door like a moth pushing at a screen door. "The dog. I took care of him," he said. He put his hand on the door frame. "You never told me he was so big. That dog was getting ready to turn on me, I could feel it."

Natalie froze. This was not part of the plan. Franklin was making choices of his own, and her plan did not allow for initiatives by the almost-albino. "What did you do with him?" She kept her voice even.

"I drove out to Sebago Lake. I rigged up a line with some string to the outside of the door so that I could pull it open without being right in front of that monster when he got out. Then I drove off. He's almost thirty miles out of town, and he'd have to cross several highways to get back here. I don't think we'll be seeing him again."

Danielle came to the doorway and edged around Franklin. She clutched her backpack to her chest. "I heard you," she said, glaring at Franklin. Her chin was even with his belt buckle. "I want Cooper. Natalie, he doesn't know how to cross the big roads. Come *on*, Natalie." The child's voice thinned at the end, veering toward a sob. Danielle's face began to collapse bit by bit.

Franklin put his hand on the child's head. "Don't cry. Where'd you get your pretty red hair?"

Natalie's ribs contracted, sucking inward and up. She'd known Franklin since the dark hard months of winter. Never once had she heard this voice from him, slippery and artificially sweetened. She'd been able to handle him easily, leading him effortlessly from behind, letting him think that he was in charge. She needed to pull his attention back to the prize.

"What did you want to tell me about the computer stuff, babe? I know you've been hard at work while

I was on Peaks," she said. Natalie touched her hair, wrapping one thin strand of her blond hair around her pointer finger. She took off her outer shirt, leaving just her tank top, and ran her hand along the inner soft flesh of her arm, near the old razor scars.

Franklin's lip twitched with the faintest sign of disgust. Natalie was too late to stop the tide of his change. He ran his hand over his mouth, his eyes slipped to the side. "The computer stuff? More of the same. It's not important," he said.

He had found something else. Why did people think they could lie to her?

"Is everything set with our travel documents?"

"We've got more travel docs than we'll ever use," he said. Now irritation worked into his voice. "We don't have any food in this place. Why don't you run out and get us something?" said Franklin. "I can stay with the kid."

She couldn't leave Franklin with Danielle. And she couldn't take Franklin with her and leave Danielle alone. Who knew that he'd be the one to completely fuck up this plan? She needed to call Rocky again, and she didn't want Franklin around for the call.

"I'm the recognizable one, and by now they'll be looking for me. No one knows anything about you. I'm sorry, babe, but you'll have to go for food this time.

Once we get out of the area, things will change. One more time, okay?" said Natalie.

If he said no, she wasn't sure what she'd do. She had been solidly convinced by Franklin's nerdiness, his fascination with her. "Danielle needs some food too. Pick up a couple of yogurts. She eats them like candy. And a pizza," she said.

Danielle was oddly silent, eerily watching, edging close to Natalie.

"Yeah. I'll make the food run. Anything for our little guest here."

Franklin smiled at Danielle as he left, skipping Natalie as if she were a piece of furniture. She would need every minute that he was gone. She prayed for a long line at the pizza place.

She had thirty minutes before Franklin returned. Probably fifty, but she didn't want to be surprised. Rocky was going to have to wait for a phone call. Waiting would be good for her. Natalie pulled a thumb drive out of her canvas bag, inserted it in the first laptop, and downloaded the folder "Travel Docs." As a security measure, she forwarded it to her Gmail account, the one Franklin didn't know about; after deleting the file, she deleted it again on several additional levels. Natalie did the same thing with the other two laptops. She had been practicing everything she needed to know about hacking at the city library. Franklin had been an unsuspecting teacher.

"What are you doing?" asked Danielle. The girl followed Natalie, even now, watching her.

Had Natalie ever asked such a straightforward question at age seven? What if she had simply asked, *What are you doing?*

"This is just between us girls. I'm borrowing some things from Franklin's computers. He's not going to come with us after all."

Chapter 54

Melissa

Melissa saw Rocky get on the ferry. She had been on her way to Tess's house with the photo of the van and the earlier photos of Natalie in shoplifting mode. She was sure that, given the situation, Tess would listen, especially now. Melissa would tell her everything about Natalie, every twitch and gut reaction and shudder that she had felt since Natalie arrived, because telling Rocky would be pointless. Rocky had gone as stupid as a stone.

Case in point: why was Rocky going to Portland when everyone here was in a panic because Cooper had gone missing, little Danielle was last seen with Natalie, and even the rattletrap yellow truck was gone?

Other passengers walked on, couples leaned into each other, and a young man carried on a red and white cooler. A dark-skinned family embarked—Middle Eastern, Melissa immediately thought, or Indian. She wasn't sure. They were small and compact—two parents with three children—and they all studied their smartphones. Melissa walked closer, curious, angry, drawn along in a tide she couldn't name, clutching the rolled-up photos fresh from her printer. She stopped before the metal ramp. She looked up to the second level of the ferry, and there was Rocky, only a few steps from the stairway. Her hair was sprung from a hair tie, the bottom third of her dark hair loose and thick, while the remainder of it formed a two-inch stub of a ponytail. Rocky dropped suddenly to her knees, and the family of five nearly plowed into her, all looking up dazed from their phones. They simply walked around her. Rocky sank back on her heels, head down, and even from the lower deck Melissa could see the shudder run through her.

Melissa stepped onto the ferry. The captain announced, "There will be a short loud blast." The sound from the ferry was as familiar to Melissa as breathing. The ferry marked time, speeding up in the summer, slowing in frequency in the winter to match the semi-hibernation rate of the islanders. The sounds of the metal-on-metal closure of the gate, the acceleration of the huge engine as it powered out of the dock, the gulls loudly demanding food, the *splat* of plastic shoes on the metal floor—all these sounds blurred into the background as Melissa ascended the stairs.

Rocky stood up, leaned one hip into the railing, and wiped her eyes. She turned just as Melissa reached the top step.

"Before you say anything, you need to look at these photos, and you need to listen to me," said Melissa.

Rocky started to mold her face into a macabre smile, her bottom lip still trembling. Melissa held up a hand. "I mean it. You've got to listen to me. Natalie is not who you think she is. You think that I'm jealous of her, and I am, but I'm more freaked out because you've gone so nuts about her. She's been shoplifting in Portland. You can't quite see it in this picture, but you can see her boyfriend. This is right after she stole jewelry. She gives the stuff to him. Here's his van." Melissa gave Rocky the photos of Natalie with her hand in the van window, giving something to the driver.

Rocky's hands shook as she took the photo. "When was this?"

"A few days after she came to stay with you. I wasn't following her, I swear. I was just in Portland after going to the Y. She didn't see me. Here, I just printed this picture. I was over in Chester Hill this week taking pictures of the street people outside the homeless shelter.

I haven't told anyone that I'm going there. Well, I told Mr. Clarke, but I told him that my parents are okay with me being there and they don't actually know. And now you know. Anyhow, do you see that van in the background? It's the same van. I think her boyfriend lives right in Chester Hill. That's where Natalie might be with Danielle and Cooper."

Melissa took a breath. There was so much more she had to tell Rocky about Natalie, what high school girls know about each other that no one else knows—how Natalie didn't let Cooper outside to pee when she should have, the way Natalie wormed her way into everything that had been Melissa's.

"Where is Chester Hill? You're hanging out with street people?" Rocky looked puzzled, like Melissa was speaking French and Rocky needed a translator.

Rocky still didn't get it. Melissa had never, even as a little kid, stomped her feet in frustration, but if she was ever going to do it, this would be the time. "You don't get it! Everything about Natalie is wrong. Would you please wake up?"

A man and a woman who had been nuzzling now looked over at them. Rocky grabbed Melissa's arm and led her to the other side of the ferry. "Keep your voice down. Just give me a minute to think," said Rocky.

Melissa heard something familiar in Rocky's voice, the smarter, kick-ass part of Rocky, and she breathed in a sliver of relief. She had nearly given up, had been ready to abandon all hope for Rocky as an intelligent life form. Did she dare trust her again?

"I shouldn't do this, I shouldn't involve you . . . ," said Rocky.

With that, a door opened, and Melissa wedged her foot in before Rocky could change her mind.

"You know something! I am already involved, and I swear to you that I'll do whatever you say, but you've got to let me help you."

They were going through the middle passage where the water was deep and cold; the chill rose through the vessel and wrapped around Melissa. She closed her eyes and whispered, "We've got to get them back. Don't let them end up on the news shows in the disaster section. We could never go back to the way it was before, none of us."

Rocky put her arm around Melissa's shoulders in an awkward squeeze. "Okay, this is what we're going to do. We'll get them back. First, tell me everything you know about Natalie. I'm listening."

Chapter 55

Cooper

He had been dumped out in a parking lot. Cooper smelled the direction of the ocean and the great distance. He focused on the distant scent of the ripe sea life that washed up on the shore, factored in the powerful scent of the man, and headed toward the scent of the child. He had never walked as far as the scent led him to calculate, but it was well within his ability. If he could walk in a direct line, the distance would be nothing. If he had to maneuver roads and cars, then the trip would be more dangerous. He did not want to be apprehended by other humans; if there was any hope at all of finding the child and finding his pack again, he had to be swift. A car pulled into the paved lot. As soon as he heard the car door open, he put his nose lower to the ground and trotted off, through bushes and trees.

He smelled thick aromas of canine urine; this was where canines came with their humans. His presence would be tolerated, at least in this area. It was the roads that unsettled him. And the fences—he had never liked fences. The human propensity for fences was incomprehensible to him. He imagined that it was about humans marking their territory. All other mammals were content to mark territory with urine or musk. Birds did it with sound. No matter. He would encounter many fences and roads before he found the ocean again.

He skirted the lake, heading east and south as much as possible. He occasionally stopped at the edge of the lake, taking laps of water. Several times he spotted people sitting along the edge fishing. Each person looked up, inquiringly, and Cooper knew they were wondering where he belonged. Each time, before they could decide if they should come toward him, he moved away with deliberate speed.

Part of the agreement with humans is that canines must belong to at least one person. Cooper had no disagreement with this mandate—in fact, he longed for it. But his solitary appearance could produce impediments today.

He came to his first road crossing. The road was large enough for several cars to fit the width at one time, no larger. He suddenly felt a vibration through his pads, followed quickly by a rumbling sound. A vehicle rushed by, then another. The wind of the cars blew his ears away from his face, and he blinked as fine dust swirled. He waited. When he heard and felt nothing, he quickly crossed, diving again into the brush, orienting himself and heading east. A thread of food smells lingered from the passing cars and his belly responded, a bit of extra saliva collected in hopes of food.

He passed the same road again as it curled around in its path; each time he paused, waiting for a clear passage. He trotted around fences, the kind made of wood, barriers more than territory markers. Twice humans approached him, saying, *Here, good boy, here, fella,* calling to him with caring intentions. If this had been any other day, he would have stopped and greeted them. Dogs in fenced yards announced him, some with idiotic yammering; others simply defined their boundaries with a solid bark, acknowledging Cooper.

He crossed two more roads, and night began to descend. He had been walking for hours, and the smell of the ocean was growing stronger. A loud vibration began to strum through his body, and as he continued the vibration turned into a metallic roar. He slowed his pace as the sound grew more persistent, unending. He had come to a massive road where cars and trucks roared in a continuous torrent. Until now, it had been simple to find a pause when he could slip from one side of the road to the other. He would do no good to his people dead, and surely that was how he would end up if he misjudged the flood of vehicles. He had not accounted for their speed. His tail lowered protectively, and he made his way along a ditch by the side of the vast road, walking south, feeling pummeled by the wind from the speeding cars and trucks. There had to be a way to get across the wide expanse of road. Up ahead he saw a bridge of sorts spanning the road. To get to it he would have to cross a road coming off the giant road; he saw no other way. He could not go back the way he'd come; that would only take him farther from his pack. All that he loved and protected was on the other side of this massive road.

Without warning, cars would veer off the big road onto this smaller road, but he had no way of telling which cars would pull off. He watched the gush of cars and judged his moment, coming up from the ditch and heading across the smaller black road. He was midway across the road when a vehicle seemed to come from out of the air itself—a loud truck—and it issued a warning sound to him, sharp and urgent. The truck squealed and turned this way and that like a fish caught on a hook. Cooper stopped for an instant. Should he dive back into the ditch? Instead, he forced all of his strength into his legs and lungs. He leapt for the far side of the road, feeling the rush of metal going past him, grazing his tail. There were few things in this world that were large enough to be his predator, but all of the vehicles that screamed by on the huge road were capable of destroying him and the truck had come too close.

The rush of chemicals in his blood carried him closer to the bridge, across a large expanse of grass. He stopped to pant, to exhale the terror of the crossing. His thirst was deep and demanding. He was still close to the big road, but now he could get to the bridge crossing. He closed his eyes for a moment, imagining the last time Rocky had put her hands on him, just this morning, rubbing hard behind his ears the way he liked.

Cooper heard a man's voice. "Rosie! Hey, get back here!"

Two paws pounded into him in greeting. A voracious tongue licked his face. Who was this? A dog from the city. The sweet Rosie! He lifted his head in grateful acceptance of her licks. The man approached, Rosie's man. Cooper remembered his scent.

"What the hell are you doing out here, trying to get yourself killed? Where's your camera girl?" asked the man. He knelt down and rubbed Cooper's head. Cooper felt the man's past hurts and fears tucked tight in his middle. Rosie yipped with such happiness, inviting him to run with her. He had to decide quickly if he should trust the man.

"Let's get you some water, big guy."

Cooper heard the wounded essence of the man and understood Rosie's job: she supplied him with the purest joy of the moment, all day long, every day. Rosie had become a missing organ for the man. As companions, they were well matched, and as a unit, he could trust them.

The man poured water into a metal cup and offered it to Cooper. He lapped gratefully. He sat down and looked up at the man.

"You can come with us. You're with Rosie and me now."

Chapter 56

The yellow truck was still in the parking lot. Rocky sighed with relief when the key she had pulled off Isaiah's key ring worked. Before she and Melissa could pull out, Rocky's cell cawed, and she quickly turned off the truck. She didn't want Natalie to know that she'd found another key. Rocky turned to Melissa and put her finger to her lips in a *shhh* motion and opened the phone.

"I'm here," said Rocky. "I'm at the Casco Bay dock. Tell me how Danielle and Cooper are doing."

Rocky had given Natalie an instruction, a very slight instruction. *Tell me.* She'd used a warm and steady voice. Natalie had taken Rocky by surprise when she arrived on the island in waif-like distress, but now the contorted landscape of her psyche was visible to Rocky.

And everything was at stake. Rocky could not bear to think about Tess and what she was going through at the moment. Rocky had taken in a damaged girl who had plotted with full intent to hurt Rocky and anything and anyone she cared about. If she made a mistake, she didn't know what Natalie would do. Right now everyone still had choices, including Natalie; no final decree had been etched by physical harm. If Rocky could keep Natalie engaged, keep her talking, they all stood a chance of emerging whole, able to limp back to their lives.

There was a pause at the other end of the phone. Rocky could almost hear Natalie reshuffling her hand. "They're both fine, although Cooper isn't really with us anymore."

Rocky's heart twisted. What had Natalie done with Cooper? She had to ask about Danielle, about what Natalie ultimately wanted from her, but she could not keep breathing until she found out about Cooper.

Before Rocky could form a question, Natalie continued. "Let's just say he took a trip out of town, far out of town."

Rocky clutched the steering wheel of the truck with one hand while she collapsed from the core of her belly. "Where is he? What have you done with him?" she whispered.

"He was fine the last time I saw him, before . . . well, it was a mistake, unplanned, but we'll all have to roll with it. He might be able to find his way back, but I wouldn't count on it."

Rocky shuddered. Melissa grabbed her leg and mouthed, *What, what?* Rocky held up one hand, with her palm facing Melissa in the stop position.

"Tell me about Danielle. You have a chance to take good care of her." Do not give her anything to push against. Natalie as caretaker—this was a stretch, but one that might reach her. This could be in Natalie's book of rules, a chance to take care of a little girl taken away from her family.

"I'm going to have to go in a minute, but the kid is fine. You are not going to be so fine. I want payment from you, payment for the time that my father could have been with me. He had to know about me. Do you think that I believed you for one second that he never mentioned me? I want what he would have given me. Gotta run. Keep your phone on. And remember that this will go very badly if you contact the police. This is between us, and we can finish our work together very quickly." *Click.*

Melissa's voice exploded. "What did she say? What did she say about Cooper? What about Danielle?" Her eyes were large and intense, and she was ready to do anything. In a moment of odd clarity it occurred to Rocky that she was in a war zone with teenage girls.

"She wouldn't tell me where Cooper is, but something wasn't right, she was lying. She said there's been a change in plans and that's why Cooper is gone," said Rocky.

Melissa tapped the dashboard and bit her lower lip. "I'm the only one who knows she has a boyfriend. Well, now you do too. I just bet he did something with Cooper."

Rocky factored in everything that Melissa had downloaded in one massive rush while they were on the ferry: her suspicions, the shoplifting in Portland, the man in the van, the intentional way in which Natalie had pushed Melissa out of the picture, how persistently she had attached herself to Tess and Danielle. All of it was terrifying when put together, but most terrifying of all was the realization that there was a man helping her. Should she call the police right now? Wasn't this the point at which only stupid people persisted onward without calling the police?

As if on cue, Melissa asked, "What would happen if we called the police and just told them everything we know?"

Rocky thought about Natalie and her life so filled with vengeance and rage, her belief that a good life had been denied to her and that Rocky was somehow to blame. "I think she would do something to hurt them."

Without hesitation, Melissa said, "Then you and I have to find them." She slipped her sandals off her feet and tucked them under her. "Is Natalie really Bob's daughter?"

"No, but Natalie believes Bob was her father. The truth is far stranger than you can imagine. But I do know who her father is, and it's the one card that I can play with her."

"What do we do now?" Melissa said, suddenly pumped and eager, ready to break down doors.

"Now we wait until she calls again."

Melissa slumped back into her seat. "Did you know that today was our last therapy dog training class? Caroline left me a message that said she was very disappointed that we blew off her class. Don't you hate it when someone says, 'I'm so disappointed,' especially about Cooper."

Rocky was more than disappointed. There were other words. Like "terrified"—now, there was a good word for how she felt.

Chapter 57

Natalie

It would have been sweet if she could have seen Rocky's face when she realized how thoroughly she had been played. Would Rocky have reached up and twirled her hair, the part that always fell out of the hair tie? Or would she rush out the front door, like some kind of dog warden superhero?

Natalie had been faking it that night in the bathroom when she had made herself cry just loud enough to wake up Rocky. She no longer cried—she hadn't for years—but she could create a reaction like crying, complete with tears, that sometimes offered relief, the way coughing felt good when she cleared her throat. She hadn't counted on the way Rocky would hold her hand without speaking, or the dog lodging himself in the doorway so that nothing bad could get past him. Rocky and Cooper had formed a cocoon around her.

Was that what it felt like to be held, wrapped in the arms of a parent?

She shook her head as if shaking off a mosquito. She would have had a parent if Bob Tilbe had found her. Franklin would be back soon with food. She had asked him to pick up yogurt cups with fruit for Danielle. She had seen Tess give them to Danielle. Did all little kids eat as often as Danielle? And how did Tess know just when to feed her?

One crushed-up Valium would put the girl to sleep. Everyone had wanted to prescribe medication for Natalie, and she had ended up with a storehouse of medications she refused to take. How much did the kid weigh? She didn't want to give her too much, just enough to put her to sleep. Natalie broke the tablet in half and slid it into her pocket.

She heard Franklin's familiar footsteps; he tended to slide one foot, almost in a shuffle. He knocked on the door. "Come on," he said on the other side of the door, "I've got an armload of stuff. Open up."

Natalie reached high on the door and turned the dead bolt and unhooked the chain. Typical house for a drug neighborhood: it had enough locks to slow down the cops until evidence could be flushed away.

Franklin slid a pizza box onto the kitchen counter and dropped a white plastic bag on top of it. "You'd think it was a crime to ask for a damn plastic bag.

Do you have your own bags? Of course I don't have my own bags. You wait and see. Pretty soon we'll be paying for these bags."

Franklin had no future in the world of resource conservation. One of Natalie's foster families had recycled everything possible, composted their food scraps, and were elated when they, a family of five, created only two kitchen-sized garbage bags per week. It had been hard to make them give up on her, but stealing money and cutting her arms and legs with a razor had done the trick.

"So when do we call your lady on Peaks and tell her about the ransom?" asked Franklin.

Natalie nodded her head toward the bathroom and said, "Ssshhh."

Franklin leaned against the window frame. The window was covered by a broken blind, perpetually crooked. In the short time that Franklin had been gone on the food mission, he had disengaged even further from Natalie.

Natalie turned away from Franklin and opened one of the yogurt containers. She put the tablet on the counter and crushed it with the curved side of a spoon, then scooped the pulverized Valium into the cup and stirred.

Natalie opened the door to the bathroom, where the little girl had been stationed. "Danielle, we brought food. It's time for you to eat. If you eat all of your yogurt, you can have some of the pizza."

Danielle's hair had formed little sweaty swirls around her forehead. Her red shoulder-length hair was even curlier than usual from the heat and humidity. She twisted what used to be her bangs and clipped them back severely. "It is very hot in this bathroom, and I don't want to stay in here. I would never make you stay in a stinky old bathroom," said Danielle. She was firm and angry.

Natalie hadn't thought about the lack of ventilation in the bathroom. "You're right. I'm sorry about that. But you and I skipped lunch, and now it's time for supper, so stop being mad at me for a minute and come eat something. I'm going to eat the other yogurt," said Natalie. She had peeled back the aluminum covers from both yogurt containers and began to eat hers.

Danielle looked suspicious. Natalie ate her entire cup of yogurt and tossed the empty plastic cup into the open garbage bin near the sink. The little girl picked up the other yogurt container, dug a plastic spoon out of the bag, and stood next to Natalie as she ate, delicately placing a quarter-spoonful at a time into her mouth. The child leaned into Natalie's side. Danielle was mad at Natalie, but she still trusted her more than Franklin.

Yogurt was followed by pizza, followed by a request for a drink, followed by outrage that Natalie only had Coke in the fridge. "You're just like Rocky," said the girl in a dreamy voice.

"No, sweetie, I'm nothing like Rocky," said Natalie as she led the girl to the bedroom with the mattress on the floor. "It's okay for you to lie down and take a nap. Everything will be better when you wake up," said Natalie.

The girl sank onto the impossibly dirty sheets. "Sit with me?" mumbled the girl, reaching for Natalie's hand. Natalie slid onto the mattress, pulled by the small hand of the girl who was about to have her first Valium-induced slumber. The girl curled around Natalie so that her head nudged into her thigh. The girl's skin, light and freckled, looked illuminated next to the darkened sheets. Her clothing was spotlessly washed, and even her backpack, which Natalie slipped off her shoulders, smelled clean. *You have a chance to take good care of her.*

Franklin was back on his computers. Natalie had studied Franklin on the computer since the winter, looking over his shoulder when she brought him a beer or gave him a shoulder massage, paying far more attention to his computer monologues than he could have imagined. If he was the suspicious type, he would check to see if anyone else had been on the computers, and if he did, Natalie needed an excuse. She hadn't counted on losing her hold on Franklin. A sliver of fear cut through her.

"What did you want to tell me?" she asked him. "You said you found something new. What is it?"

Franklin looked up from the deep recesses of his Web world. He was startled; his nearly colorless eyes reflected the light of the screen. "What? Oh, I saw a different way to scramble our travel plans and a better way to make the money untraceable once we get it. I've got something I'm working on here. Nothing for you to worry about," he said, going back to the laptop.

Liar, liar, pants on fire. Why did people think they could lie to her?

"I need about an hour or so here. Don't talk to me, okay?" he said, without bothering to look up at her.

With Franklin securely back in computer world, Natalie could risk leaving the apartment long enough to call Rocky again. Computer hacks like Franklin would inject hard drives into their brains if they could.

Natalie slipped out the door and down the three flights to the front stoop. She walked to the end of the street to stand under the one streetlight that was out, grateful to be in shadow. Natalie pulled her phone out of her pocket and punched in Rocky's number. She answered immediately. "Listen to me carefully. I want all the money from my father's life insurance and the sale of his business. You need to get it by tomorrow, and don't tell me that you can't because I know you can. I know you can get it in cash. I know more about you than you can imagine."

"You're right, Natalie. I can do that because the most important thing is that you are taking good care of Danielle. I can help you take good care of her. But I need to tell you something. I know who your father is, and it's not Robert Tilbe. I don't know how you searched for your father, but you were very close. Your father is Richard Tilbe, Bob's uncle. I don't know very much about him except that he dated your mother when she was very young. He probably got her started on drugs. We have access to his DNA, so we can get proof very easily. I just wanted you to know."

Natalie tasted bile in her throat. She forced it down. "Keep your phone on," she said. She had planned on giving Rocky more instructions, but she suddenly felt sick. Rocky's voice had sounded weird, not like she had before when she tried to be pleasing and helpful to the poor foster girl. She walked around the block once, gulping in night air. The odd feeling dropped from her throat to her stomach.

Natalie opened the door to the apartment and saw the three computers unattended. In two steps, she had a clear line of sight to the bedroom. Franklin knelt by the mattress with his hand on Danielle's hip. He turned to look up at her, asking with his eyes, then smiling. Natalie froze, her feet shackled to the floor as the panorama of her past played out in front of her: the grimy apartment, the shabby mattress, the ripped window shade. Had her mother tried to protect her in their shabby apartment? Franklin turned back to Danielle.

Her legs still felt thick and cold, but she walked toward the nearest laptop, ripped the plug from the wall and carried it to the bedroom. Franklin placed his hand on the child's leg as Natalie walked into the bedroom. Franklin rolled Danielle onto her back; the child didn't wake. He turned to look up at Natalie just before she slammed the laptop into the side of his head. She swung hard at his head again, knocking him to the foot of the mattress. He rolled to one side, tried to get up; when she hit him one last time, he deflated like a balloon, suddenly empty.

She fell to the floor, unable to breathe. Blood gushed from Franklin's white scalp, seeping along his white hair and onto the floor. She had to move him away from Danielle. He wanted to hurt little girls, and she didn't want a drop of his blood to touch the child. She grabbed his legs and pulled him to the kitchen.

Her brain pounded with fear, forming craters of darkness that pulled her into the bloody apartment where her mother had been killed. The caseworkers told her she was too young to remember being there, but they were wrong. She remembered the floorboards, sticky with blood, the terrifying sound of the fridge, the unstoppable thirst, and the endless blackness that came and lasted so long as she sat with her mother who would not waken.

Natalie had to escape and run as far away as possible. She found the tiny screwdriver that she had seen Franklin use when he built the computers from parts. She flipped over one computer to screw open the back of it, but her hands shook so badly that the screwdriver clattered around the one screw, refusing to go in. She finally got the computer open and pulled out the hard drive. She did the same with the second. Franklin had told her that the only way to truly erase information was to remove the hard drive and destroy it. "The past is never gone," he had said, "it's only hiding." She picked up the third laptop, the one that she used to stop Franklin. She ran it under the faucet to get rid of the blood and pulled out the hard drive.

She tossed all three of the metal rectangles into her canvas bag.

Each inhale was jagged, as if the muscles in her throat and lungs were frozen. The smell of Franklin's blood filled her nose with black sludge, and if she had to smell it one minute more she might pass out.

Rocky had said that Bob was not her father and she sounded so sure. But Natalie had found the right trail, she was sure of it, the hint of R. Tilbe that had surfaced, inexplicably, when she exited the foster care system, a tendril that her last caseworker offered her. R. Tilbe, Ames, Iowa. Just the name and a phone number (long since disconnected) scrawled on a book found in her mother's few possessions. Her mother had kept one of her books from college, one item that had escaped her desperate need to sell everything possible for drugs. A thin book of poetry, inscribed to her: "With all my love, R. Tilbe." Weird, a very weird way to sign a book to someone you're supposed to love.

She had to be right. Rocky was still lying, refusing to give her what was really hers, a legacy from her father. She needed to wash away the taste in her throat, the smell of Franklin. She went to the fridge and pulled out a can of soda. Now her hands shook so much that she couldn't open it. The can fell from her hands, and she jumped as if a bomb had exploded. She had to get out of there. Franklin had the keys to the van in his pocket. She didn't want to touch him; he was just like the boys who had hurt her, with their hard fingers and metallic eyes.

Natalie edged closer to Franklin, who was facedown on the kitchen floor. She reached under his hip and slid her hand into his pocket. Nothing. She stepped over him, straddling him, and slid her hand into his other pocket and immediately felt the hard keys. The edge of her sandals had sunk into the sludge of his blood. She scuffed her shoe furiously against the scatter rug, trying to rub off the hideous blood, the whole hideous scene, then grabbed her canvas pack and ran from the apartment. Her shirt had blood on it. She ran down the three flights of stairs, saw the van, and gulped in fresh air in desperate bursts. She ripped off the shirt, dropping it and kicking it to the curb. Once inside the van, she locked the doors, finally alone and safe, free of the death trap of the apartment where her mother lay dead. She hadn't driven the van before, but nothing mattered other than distancing herself from the horror of the apartment.

Why did Rocky sound different? Why couldn't she make her hands stop shaking? Natalie pointed the nose of the van toward the interstate.

Chapter 58

Waiting in the parking lot of Cumberland Farms while Melissa bought water, Rocky opened her cell phone at the first sound. She held it to her ear and could hear the cracks forming in Natalie. She walked to the edge of the building, the exterior brick still warm from the day.

"I want you to drop off the cash at ten A.M. at the first rest stop on Route 25 South past Portland. There are two garbage bins in the women's bathroom. Wrap the money in a white plastic bag and put it in the garbage can nearest the door when no one is looking. Then go back to your car and drive away. I'll be there, but you'll never see me. Do you understand me?" said Natalie. She sounded panicked; Rocky could nearly hear the girl's heart racing over the phone. What was happening?

Rocky willed each word to come out right. Each word had to travel as an emissary to Natalie and reach the place inside the girl where her soul had not been upended and rubbed raw with a metal rasp.

"I understand. Tell me where I'll find Danielle. You know that I have to bring her back with me. I need to get to her quickly or she'll be frightened. Is she with you? She's very young. You know how it is with young children," said Rocky, then instantly regretted her last words. She had slipped a knife into Natalie's worst wound. Rocky heard the emotional trigger go off, a bank shot from one cell tower to another that twanged with Natalie's long-contained rage.

"Oh, she'll be afraid, but for all of a day, maybe two if you're really stupid and can't figure out where she is. It's the kind of place no three-year-old would want to be. You and Tess and everyone else will race in to rescue her. That's just fucking amazing. Pardon me if I can't get worked up over her fear. No one came for me, not my father. Afraid was just the beginning for me. . . ." Natalie's voice broke up, disintegrating into a buckshot of sound.

Blood pounded in Rocky's temples. She heard the trill of the overhead fluorescent lighting, the night insects scissoring their passionate legs together in beguiling songs. A moth smacked directly into an incandescent bulb, and Rocky felt the vibration in her spine. She moved her foot and a grain of sand exploded beneath the ball of her right foot. Natalie had said "three-year-old." She wasn't talking about Danielle—she was talking about being left with her mother's body.

"What happened to you was so terrible, and you needed someone to take care of you and keep you safe," said Rocky. Not too much, don't say too much. Hot sweat spread to her shirt, drawing it closer to her body. Rocky knew what happened when the police found Natalie when she was a toddler. She had not been alone in the apartment. She'd been with her mother's body for five days.

"Don't say that psycho shit to me," hissed Natalie.

"Every kid needs to be safe. No shit intended. It's like air or food. Being safe is as basic as air or food," said Rocky. Suddenly, as if her ears had popped after a long plane ride, Rocky heard a catch in Natalie's voice where a soft place still lived.

"Tell me where I can find Danielle. And Cooper," said Rocky, keeping her voice even and middling.

"Forget Cooper. Franklin said we couldn't keep him. And you know how it is—I had to let Franklin think he was making decisions. Just like you thought you were making decisions. Do exactly what I told you to do," said Natalie. *Click.*

Melissa came out of the store with two plastic bottles of water. "Was that Natalie? What's happening?"

Rocky slid the phone back into her pants pocket. "We've got to get to Danielle. Natalie is starting to decompensate, and I need to get to her."

Melissa handed one of the waters to Rocky. "She's starting to what?"

"Sorry. She's unraveling, falling apart. She may be re-creating a scene that happened when she was just a toddler. Her mother was murdered in an apartment, and Natalie was with the body for days. They could be anywhere, but we need to try the most obvious place first, where you saw that van."

Rocky's phone cawed again. She dropped her water bottle and pulled it out, thinking it was Natalie. "It's Isaiah. I'm not going to answer it. I can't." She walked to the truck and opened the door. The phone went off again. "Shit. It's Hill. Isaiah must have called him looking for me. I'm not answering him either." She held the phone up to her cheek for a moment and closed her eyes, as if she could draw sustenance from the two men through the unopened cell phone. Her distrust of Hill, introduced by Natalie, popped like a balloon.

Parking in downtown Portland was a problem on a good day, but tonight Rocky had to think of a place where the police would be less likely to spot the truck.

She was sure that Isaiah had called them asking about it. He would have spotted the missing truck key from the clutch of keys she left under the seat.

Rocky took a guess and figured that the patrol cops wouldn't cruise through the parking garages, at least not with any regularity. She parked the truck on the third level of the garage near the cinemas. They headed on foot for Chester Hill.

"Show me where you were when you took the picture with the white van in the background. Let's start there," said Rocky.

Chapter 59

"**A**re you sure it was the same van?" asked Rocky. After starting at the place where Melissa had seen the van, they had been walking the streets of Chester Hill for an hour. It was nearly 11:00 P.M., and most of the people who carried their belongings in black plastic garbage bags were gone, tucked in for the night only to be replaced by a younger, more hollow-eyed night shift of street people. Melissa, who had spent days wandering the area photographing people and dogs, said that she didn't recognize any of them. "Maybe Natalie and her boyfriend Franklin don't really live in Chester Hill at all. The only streets we haven't checked are the alleys."

Rocky wanted more than anything to find Danielle quickly, but one look down an alley at night slowed her nerve. She had nothing with her for protection, and she had involved her sixteen-year-old neighbor. She couldn't let anything happen to Melissa, who suddenly seemed so young and unsuited for dark alleys.

"Here's what I want you to do. See that convenience store? I want you to go inside and stay there for about thirty minutes while I check out the alleys in the neighborhood. Buy some stuff, get a paper, talk to the clerk, but don't leave. You can keep a lookout to see if the van goes by," said Rocky.

"That is totally a stupid idea," said Melissa. "I'm not some seven-year-old kid. Remember, we're trying to save a seven-year-old kid. We are much better off staying together, and you can't make me leave you to go skulk around an alley by yourself." Melissa crossed her arms over her chest and did a thing with her lips that Rocky hadn't seen before that was like seeing Melissa in the future, when she'd be running the world. Melissa was right, Rocky couldn't force her to do anything. She'd never been able to override the girl's steely will.

Rocky took out the cell phone and held it in her hand. "Okay. We're doing this together."

They crossed the street. Rocky looked up and down the street to judge who would see them entering the alley. Cars cruised by slowly. One car slowed, tinted windows lowered, and Rocky saw a man assessing the two of them. They probably looked like tourists in the wrong part of town. The car kept going.

The alley was wide enough for one car, but it would be the perfect place to tuck a van. As soon as they entered its dark mouth, the stench of urine hit Rocky. She heard a car door slam shut and a bottle smash; someone turned up the bass of their throbbing music, and a dog began to bark. Deep, thunderous barks, muffled by distance, and yet there was no mistaking the source. She could have picked out his bark from one million other dogs.

Rocky grabbed Melissa's arm and said, "That's Cooper."

"I know. Which direction?"

"I can't tell. He sounds far away," said Rocky, who more than anything wanted to run in a straight line to Cooper. She'd vault fences, cars, leering guys in black cars, she didn't care, but she had to know which way. She swiveled her head around like a satellite dish, as if she could pick up his beam.

Her cell phone went off in her hand. It was Natalie.

"You've got to go get the little girl. She's trapped in the apartment," said Natalie. Her voice was small and stretched thin. "I had to stop him. He was going to hurt her. I can't go back there."

Through one ear, she heard Cooper, far off and barking. Through the other, she heard the shards of Natalie. Rocky's veins began to constrict and freeze. Who had Natalie hurt? Franklin? In her confusion had she hurt Danielle?

"Tell me where she is and I'll go and get her."

"The apartment is up high, three stairways. There's nothing to drink, and there's blood on the floor. I have blood on my shoes. I have to throw them away."

"Natalie, I'm going to help you. Tell me the address. You know the name of the street. Take a breath. You're taking good care of Danielle. I knew you would," said Rocky, praying that Natalie could hold her disintegrating mind together.

"Walnut Street. You have to hurry." *Click.*

"No!" screamed Rocky. "You have to tell me where on Walnut!"

Melissa's eyes caught the spark of the streetlight. "Walnut? Is that where Danielle is? I know that street. I wrote down the street names when I was taking pictures," said Melissa. She spun slowly around for a few seconds, and then said, "This way."

Melissa ran with long thin legs trained for cross-country, and Rocky struggled to keep up. The girl was half a block ahead of her. Rocky sucked in as much oxygen as she could. The sound of Cooper grew louder.

They ran two blocks up and two more on the crest of the hill, and then she saw flashing lights. Melissa tore around the corner. Before Rocky could make the corner, she heard Melissa scream, "Don't hurt the dog! That's our dog!"

Rocky put on a burst of speed and was hit with a wall of multicolored lights from two police cars. She couldn't see Cooper, only the back of a small crowd that had gathered.

"Sir, control your animal. We've had a report of a vicious dog. Your dogs must be on leashes. Sir, if you can't control your dog, we will have to restrain him by force," said one of the cops. Rocky saw the glint of a mace container. Cooper barked wildly and clawed on a doorway. A man with a huge backpack stood in between Cooper and the cops.

"I've had worse done to me in Iraq. Do not fucking spray this dog."

Melissa plowed through the crowd. "Ryan? You found Cooper? It's me, Melissa."

Ryan and his dog both turned to look at Melissa. So did the police. One cop was a young woman; her eyes scanned the crowd, the dogs, the homeless man, and now Melissa.

"Is this your dog? Do you know this man?" asked the cop, who slid the canister back onto his belt.

Rocky burst through the crowd and skidded to a stop. "Cooper!" She threw herself on him, wrapped her arms around his thick neck. He stopped barking to whine in delight at her touch, wrapping his body around her legs, taking a loop around Melissa, before launching back at the door, barking and scratching.

"This is it. This has got to be the place. Walnut Street," said Rocky. She turned to the cops. "We've got to get in there. There's a small child who was taken. . . ."

"Do you mean the kid from Peaks Island?" asked the cop. The cop leaned into her shoulder and spoke into her phone. "We are entering an apartment at 435 Walnut. Possible child abduction."

The cops pried open the front door with a small crowbar. Cooper slid past them and lunged up the stairs, galloping. The two cops followed at a pace that Rocky found maddening. When they hit the second landing, she surged ahead of them, pulled on by the sound of Cooper barking at a door. "It's this one, up here," she cried. She wished she had the crowbar.

One crack of the bar, and they were in the apartment. Both cops had pulled their guns. A man lay on the kitchen floor. Rocky leapt past him to the only other room she saw. There was Danielle, curled up like a sow bug on a filthy mattress. Rocky bent down and picked up the warm girl, who mumbled dream talk. Rocky held her like a baby and rocked her, shielding her from the sight of the bloody man on the floor and the police squatting next to him, calling for an ambulance. Cooper hummed at her thighs, sniffing any part of the child that he could reach. Melissa strained to get in, held at bay by the arrival of more police.

Danielle opened one groggy eye. "All clear?" she asked as if they were back on Peaks, practicing archery, not at a scene of bloody carnage.

Rocky let out a sob of a breath. "All clear. Entirely all clear."

Chapter 60

Rocky knew a part of Natalie that no one else knew, and probably wouldn't believe if she told them: the part of the girl that had spun out of control and then still helped them find Danielle. Natalie had called her a day after Danielle and Cooper were found. She had heard the choked sound of Natalie's voice, without artifice or theatrical expertise. Not a word as such, but the sound she had heard when Natalie first contacted her, the first squeeze of the girl's throat. Before she could hang up, Rocky had told her in a rush, "We found Danielle. Cooper helped us after he made it back to Portland. And Franklin isn't dead." She heard Natalie's jagged breathing, and then the connection was severed.

Even after the state police had stopped cruising the rest area outside Portland, Rocky had gone there for three days in a row, perched at a picnic table, hoping against hope that Natalie would show up. Cooper stayed by her side, not interested in ball or stick fetching, keeping a solemn vigil.

On the third day, she heard a familiar sound, the steady and true footsteps, even before she saw him. Hill had found her. He didn't say anything at first, just sat next to her, putting one arm across her shoulders. When Rocky curved into him, choking back the dashed hopes of Natalie, he wrapped his other arm around her until he had encircled her. He kissed the side of her head and swayed with her—not so much that people stopping to stretch their legs at the rest area would notice, but enough so that Rocky never wanted him to let go again.

"How did you know I'd be here?" she asked, her face still pressed against his neck.

"Melissa. I came looking for you on the island. I saw Melissa walking with Tess and her little granddaughter. She told me that if she had to guess, she'd say that you'd be here, that you don't give up easy on someone. Is that true? Could that be true about us too? Because if it is, then we're a matched set."

As if in answer, she felt the slow, appreciative thump of Cooper's tail against her leg.

"How can a person disappear?" asked Rocky. If she could find Natalie, she'd tell her that the money didn't matter, it never did. And she'd tell her about her father, the little that she had learned about him—his drug addiction, how he had made a feeble effort to find Danielle and her mother, how years later rehab finally worked for him. She'd tell Natalie that however weird it seemed, she was genetically Bob's cousin, if that mattered for anything. She had already told Natalie about the way Bob would tuck a dog or cat under his arm and carry it from the stainless steel examining table to the back room, how the creature would melt into his side, glad to be held, tucked close to the broad trunk of his body.

Every agency she had contacted, the state police, the FBI, and one private detective, had all said the same thing. If Natalie did not want to be found, there were one million ways for her to shape-shift into a new person in a new place. And there were more ways than that for a girl like Natalie to die. The human imagination knew no limits to snuffing out a girl.

Ira Levine told her the same thing, but with one qualifier. "Somewhere along the line she made a decision—she hit the tipping point. I've seen kids flick a switch after they've been hurt. The lucky kids are the ones who decide to hold out hope. That one decision can define the rest of their life. Natalie went the other way. She thought she understood the world completely, and in order to survive she was going to cut through life like a laser. It made her unable to see good, caring families when they tried to help her. Her last four families were some of the best in the system. I've checked them eight ways to Sunday. She accused all of them of hurting her in the most heinous ways. She was hurt early, but not by these families."

Rocky had seen all of Natalie's records by then, having scoured them in Levine's office for any clue.

He continued: "If she's found, she'll be arrested on federal charges of kidnapping, and judges don't like kidnappers of young children. She's eighteen, and legally she's an adult. Natalie is motivated not to be found. And according to her accomplice, Franklin, she has enough well-drafted false identification to last a lifetime."

Franklin had a severe concussion, a cracked skull, and an impressive line of stitches across his head. Rocky had gone to the hospital where Franklin was recuperating until he could be transferred to a prison. She had thought she might learn something from him, some nugget of information about Natalie, about where she had gone. The state trooper assigned to guard Franklin let her in and stood inside the room, feet spread wide, hands at his sides.

"I'm Rocky," she said, standing at the foot of the bed. "You tried to hurt me and people I love. You dumped my dog out like he was garbage. If they don't send you to prison, I will personally track you down and beat the shit out of you for trying to hurt a little girl and a dog. I promise."

The state trooper stepped forward and put his hand on Rocky's arm. "I will have to ask you to leave now," he said, pressing his lips together to suppress a smile.

Franklin hit a button and his bed whirred him to a sitting position. "Where is the bitch?" slurred Franklin through his swollen lips. "She stole my hard drives."

"You still have no idea how smart she is. She played you from the beginning. . . ."

"Visiting hours are over for this guy. Time to go," said the trooper, leading Rocky to the door.

Some people shimmer with poison, and Franklin was one of them. If Rocky had stayed in the hospital room one more minute, she would have been in danger of breathing in his air, which was toxic enough to strip the lining of her lungs. With another gentle tug, the trooper led her from the room.

Chapter 61

October

Today was the big day. Rocky waited for dawn, but the span of darkness stretched out longer in the fall. She finally gave up and turned on the light by her bed. Cooper rose instantly. What if she had lost him? What if he hadn't miraculously trekked back nearly thirty miles to Portland? What if the homeless guy hadn't recognized him and brought him back? ("Stop calling him that," Melissa had said. "His name is Ryan, and he says that he can't live indoors anymore, not after being in Iraq.") What if Danielle had been hurt? What if Melissa hadn't been hanging around Chester Hill taking photos without telling her parents?

"Cooper?"

The dog stretched, head lowered, butt up. One stretch in the morning, and he was ready for the day.

He seemed built for diving into the ocean, leaping into the air, finding kidnapped children in a third-story walk-up. Just last week, when Hill had been on Peaks, waking up deliciously warm and easy in her bed on Sunday morning, he had told her, "You, me, and Cooper. I like the combination."

"And Peterson the cat," she had said, pulling him back under the thick muff of the comforter.

Now she pulled on stretch pants, a long-sleeved shirt, and a jacket. She'd clean up for the big events later, but for now it was just Rocky and Cooper. Soon enough, Hill would be there, along with most of the islanders. She wanted to see the two houses before everyone showed up for the dedication at eleven. It was a Saturday morning after Columbus Day on Peaks, and there were no cars on the streets. Being 6:00 A.M. sort of clinched it.

If Natalie's world hadn't gone so horribly off the rails, Rocky would have insisted that the money go directly to her. If only . . . if only she hadn't staged a kidnapping and committed a federal crime. Rocky's lawyer said it best. "If she's ever found, she'll be arrested, just for starters. And the money was not left to Natalie, it was left to you."

She had thought about it for weeks after Natalie was gone, after disaster was averted with Danielle. She had walked and walked with Cooper, throwing so many sticks into the ocean for her good dog that Tess nearly had to relocate her inflamed shoulder. She appeared in Isaiah's office in August. "Who owns the land adjacent to my new house?" she had asked him, as if they had just been talking about it moments ago instead of months ago. "The land with all the wild wisteria that I saw this spring?"

"Why do you want to know?" Isaiah had been getting ready to send out his two employees with the street sweeper for the roads down front, as they did every Thursday morning.

"Because I know what I'm going to do with the money. I'm going to build a house for foster families to use. They can come out to Peaks for a respite, and they won't have to pay. Ira Levine can help with this. I don't have to figure out the details—that can be his job."

Isaiah had put down a can of Pennzoil right next to his coffee cup. "I know this is a useless question with you, but have you thought this all the way through? Does this mean you are going to live right next to a house filled with a constant flow of families and kids? Your own house is well on its way."

Rocky sat down on one of his chairs with the cracked vinyl seats. She hadn't felt this light or this good in months, not since the days before Bob died, back in her other life.

"The old Costello house was never quite right for me. I wanted to believe that the house felt right, but it didn't. I was a caretaker and now I know why. The house was waiting for me to fix it up for families who really need it. This way, there will be two houses right next to each other that can be respite houses. That's enough for about fifty families to come out here for a week who might not have been able to afford a vacation."

Cooper slid down at her feet in the contented aftermath of stick retrieving. Rocky continued. "I'm happy right where we are. Your little rental cottage is perfect. It fits me like a favorite pair of jeans. You said you were tired of renting and that you might sell after I moved out. Why don't you sell me that little place?"

Isaiah didn't answer right away. He held Rocky in a long stare, then looked out the window and rubbed the back of his neck. "Let me talk to Charlotte first. She's wanted to sell that place for years. She doesn't have one drop of sentimental attachment to it."

The surprise bonus with the wisteria land was that it had a big chunk of soggy land that the beavers were turning into their own watery world. Rocky and Isaiah had Carlos the Realtor broker the sale of the rental cottage, and he was instrumental in acquiring the property that Rocky wanted. Once Rocky told him what she was going to do with the property, he slashed his fee down to 1 percent. "I can't go lower than that. Business is business," he said. Rocky kissed him on the cheek. He came up with the idea to make the beaver zone a land trust. Now two houses were being built for the Maine foster care system. With the last bit that she had left over, she made a down payment on Isaiah's little cottage and got a mortgage for the rest.

"I come from blue-collar stock," Rocky had told Carlos. "We like to be saddled with mortgage payments."

Today was the dedication of the two houses and the land trust for the beavers. Rocky jogged along the dirt roads, and Cooper trotted in large circles, dipping into the woods, peeing at his favorite places, always keeping Rocky in the center of his circle. Part of the sky melted into gray, then pink.

Ira Levine would be here today as the representative of the foster care system. He had sent over his framed calligraphy, the words *Tzadikim Nistarim,* and instructed Rocky to have it placed in between the studs on one of the houses, sealed like hidden treasure. He had offered Rocky a job as a psychological consultant for the Portland area, and she had accepted the position on the condition that she could keep her job on Peaks as animal control warden.

Tess insisted that a fir tree be hoisted to the top of each house for good luck, even if the second house was little more than framed. Russell Barry had to figure out how to attach a big potted fir tree to a roofless house. Tess and Danielle had strung white lights on the tree. Russell said that if he had to figure out how to attach a tree to the second story, then he should get to read one of his narrative poems for the occasion.

Rocky smelled the raw lumber as she approached the new house, just a quarter-mile from the house she'd bought back in June. Raw lumber was so full of promise, free of tortured past deeds. She stood in the center of the first floor where massive flats of bathroom fixtures had arrived the day before, an unsolicited donation from Home Depot with a note that said, "You were right about the Labradoodle. Mark." Cooper brought along a newly found stick and delivered it to her feet.

The crows began to wake up. The birds called each other with plans for the day and news of the night. She might have time to get in some archery practice this morning. There were pizza crusts that she could give to the crows. Lately they had been crazy about the pepperoni.

Cooper heard Melissa before Rocky did. He dropped his stick and looked down the dirt road. He wagged his tail and let his jaw open in a happy Lab smile. Rocky finally heard the crunch of gravel. Melissa cruised down the road on her mother's bike, her camera gear already stashed in the front basket. Cooper greeted her as if he hadn't seen her in years, rubbing his large black body around her legs.

"I figured you two would be here," said Melissa, swinging off the bike. She pulled a large manila envelope from the basket. "I wasn't ever going to give this to you, but Tess said I should."

What could be so reluctantly offered? Rocky slid open the clasp and pulled out an eight-by-ten photo of Natalie, taken before all the bad things happened. Melissa had caught the look of longing, of wanting, of falling in love for a nanosecond. A breeze had blown her sandy hair across one cheek. She could have been anyone's daughter, a girl with an expectant whispered secret. Rocky felt a jolt to her spine.

Melissa cleared her throat. "She was watching Tess and Danielle dance on the rocks. I think in this one moment she saw how much they loved each other. You know how Tess is. How can you not see it? I still think Natalie was a five-star wacko, but . . ." Melissa stopped, shrugging.

"Thanks," said Rocky. She slid the photo back into the envelope. She shuffled her feet, as if she was clearing a special space right there on the plywood subflooring. "Let's see if Isaiah is in his office yet. Maybe we can drag him out for coffee before everyone gets here."

"You go ahead. I'm going to take some pictures, a series about the houses, right from the beginning," said Melissa.

Isaiah still had a sleep wrinkle on one side of his face, but he broke into a smile when he saw them. He pulled open the bottom drawer of his desk and rustled about for something. He finally extracted a coffee cup that said, PORTLAND PUBLIC RADIO. He wiped it off with a piece of paper towel. "Perfect. Charlotte donates money to them every year. She has an entire collection. The café should just be opening up. Let's see if they made cinnamon buns."

The café opened at seven during the off-season. They walked in companionable silence as autumn leaves caught updrafts. Few people could hold a silence for long, but Isaiah was one of the masters. When they reached the café, he said, "My treat." He handed the slightly chipped cup to Francine, the owner, and said, "This is Rocky's official cup until she can come up with something better."

The smell of sticky buns was intoxicating. Cooper put his nose straight up. Rocky placed her hand on the counter, and all the ceremony of the day rushed into her, filling her past capacity.

"I was wondering what she was waiting for," said Francine. "I'll put it right next to your MUTUAL LIFE cup." She reached up and grabbed his cup from the clatter of cups that belonged to the regulars. She grabbed stainless steel tongs and pulled a bun from the pan, dripping with buttery sugar and nuts, and put it on a plate.

Rocky didn't know that it would feel like this, or that she would recognize it when it happened. The sense of being home, belonging, had been an ossified emotion since Bob died. He had been her home, wherever he was, and when he left, Rocky's home had evaporated. She had been able to get through the worst months looking almost like a normal human being. Except to those who loved her. When Francine hung her ceramic cup with the others, she finally understood that those who loved her had known all along that she had been living on the cusp of the in-between land. With her cup hanging up in the café, she had a sense of things stirring and rearranging themselves in some elemental way.

"Now it's official," said Francine, dramatically reaching for Rocky's cup as if she hadn't just put it there ten seconds ago. Isaiah's easy hand on her shoulder threw the final circuit breaker.

Cooper, sensing a sea change, did something he rarely did, and almost always in times of dire circumstances. He barked. One, two, three barks that harmonized and hung in the air long enough for Francine to stop wiping down the small counter, for the two customers seated by the window to turn their heads, and for Rocky, who needed no translation, to know a bark of celebration when she heard it.

Acknowledgments

The following people generously offered me places where I could write in undisturbed solitude: Patricia Lee Lewis and her hundred acres, Lisa Drnec Kerr and Owl Cottage, and Fred Ranaudo and his sunny dining room. Susan Stinson's Writing Room at Forbes Library in Northampton, Massachusetts, offered me the collective juice of other writers. I am sincerely thankful to Hawthornden Castle in Scotland and Jentel Arts in Wyoming for their support and good humor.

Fiction opens up new realms of research, and many people shared their time and expertise with me. They include: Cynthia Hinckley of Bright Spot Therapy Dogs, physical therapist Joann Berns, Sheila Ryan of the Department of Children and Familes in

Massachusetts, the Portland Police Department, and all the good people of Peaks Island, Maine.

The homing beacon for my writing is the Great Darkness Writing Group. They are: Marianne Banks, Jeanne Borfitz, Jennifer Jacobson, Celia Jeffries, Lisa Drnec Kerr, Alan and Edie Lipp, Patricia Lee Lewis, Patricia Riggs, and Marion VanArsdell. My Manuscript Group maintains a steady drumbeat of deadlines, without which I would write even more slowly. They are: Marianne Banks, Kris Holloway, Rita Marks, Brenda Marsian, Ellie Meeropol, Lydia Nettler, and Dori Ostermiller. Morgan Sheehan-Bubla provided essential editorial reviews.

The people are HarperCollins are brilliant. I work closely with my editor, Carrie Feron, and associate editor Tessa Woodward. And I can never say it enough times: Jenny Bent, you are the best agent ever.